13th LEGION

I'M STARTING TO feel dizzy now; the air from the mask has almost run out. I wipe a hand across the visor of the mask a few times before I realise the spots are in my eyes not on the plasticised lenses. I gasp when I try to take my next breath and I realise with panic that the tank's empty, there's just what's left in the mask itself.

More of the aliens are streaming down the tunnel and I manage to fire again, my throat tightening as I try to breathe non-existent air. The dizziness floods up into my head and my legs just collapse underneath me. I can hardly move, but I can see the darker shadow of the alien wave getting closer. I'm choking, my chest tightening, but I manage to angle the flamer in front of me and fire again, forcing the soldiers back a final time. All life goes from my fingers and I see rather than feel the weapon slipping from my grasp. I try to push myself up, to find some last reserve of strength, but there is none this time. There's just a roaring in my ears and blackness swirls around me.

A WARHAMMER 40,000 NOVEL

The Last Chancers

13th LEGION

Gav Thorpe

A BLACK LIBRARY PUBLICATION

First published in Great Britain in 2000 by
Games Workshop Publishing
Willow Road, Lenton,
Nottingham, NG7 2WS, UK

10 9 8 7 6 5 4 3 2 1

Cover illustration by Kenson Low

A CIP record for this book
is available from the British Library

ISBN 1 84154 139 7

Set in ITC Giovanni

Printed and bound in Great Britain by
Omnia Books Ltd., Glasgow, UK

See the Black Library on the Internet at
www.blacklibrary.co.uk

Find out more about Games Workshop
and the world of Warhammer 40,000 at
www.games-workshop.com

13th LEGION

THE CHAMBER HUMMED and vibrated with energy that coursed along the thick cables snaking across the low ceiling. Somewhere in the distance could be heard the steady thump-thump-thump of heavy machinery in operation. Glowglobes set at metre intervals around the metal walls of the square room illuminated the scene with a fitful, jaundiced light. With a creak the lock wheel on the door span slowly; thick metal bars to either side of the portal ground through their rusted brackets. The door swung open and a figure stepped inside, swathed in a long black greatcoat, the tall collar obscuring his face. As he paced into the light, his thin face caught the yellow glow giving him a sickly pallor. His dark eyes glanced back over his shoulder before he took another step forward, easing the door closed behind him.

Suddenly the man stopped. His eyes snapped to the artefact stored in the middle of the room. It resembled a coffin, stood on end with a rat's nest of wires springing from it to fasten to hastily rigged connectors that pierced the cabling on the ceiling. The glass front of the coffin lay in shards and splinters across the floor. Of what was contained within, there was no sign. Recovering from his initial shock, the man began to examine the sarcophagus, prodding with an inexpert finger at various dials set into its sides. He stepped back and stroked the fingers of a hand gloved in black velvet through his short goatee beard, brow furrowed in concentration, lips twisted in agitation.

'Emperor-damned stasis chamber,' he muttered to himself, looking around once more. 'I should have got it consecrated by a tech-priest.'

As he walked around to the back of the coffin his gaze was caught by a darker shadow in the top corner of the far wall. He peered closer and saw a ventilation duct. Its corroded grille had been twisted and torn, ripped to one side. Standing on tiptoe he pulled himself up to look into the opening: the faint light from the room illuminated a metre or so of a narrow shaft that swiftly sloped upwards and out of sight. Dropping back to the floor, he banged his fist against his thigh with a short frustrated gesture. He pulled the glove from his right hand and reached into a deep pocket inside his coat, pulling out a device the size of a clenched fist. As he stabbed a button on its surface, the light from the glowglobes caught on a golden ring on his index finger, inscribed with the device of an 'I' inset with a grinning skull.

Raising the device to his lips, the man spoke.

'Third day of Euphistles. I have returned to the stasis generator, which appears to have malfunctioned. The specimen has escaped. I will start immediate investigations to recover or eliminate it. I pray to the Emperor that I can recapture the monster. This mistake could cost us dearly.'

ONE
LEAVING DELIVERANCE

+++ What is the status of Operation Harvest? +++

*+++ Operation Harvest is beginning second stage
as scheduled. +++*

THE GUARDSMAN'S nose explodes with blood as my fist crashes between his eyes. Next, I hit him with a left to the chin, knocking him backwards a step. He ducks out of the next punch, spitting blood from cracked lips. My nose is filled with the smell of old sweat and fresh blood, and perspiration from the blazing sun trickles down my face and throat. All around I can hear chanting and cheering.

'Fraggin' kink his fraggin' neck!' I recognise Jorett's voice.

'Break the son of an ork apart!' Franx yells.

The guardsmen from Chorek are cheering their man on too, their flushed faces looking dark in contrast to their white and grey camouflage jackets and leggings.

He makes a lunge at me, his face swathed in blood, his dusty uniform covered in red stains. I easily side-step his bullish charge, bringing my knee up hard into his abdomen and feeling some ribs crack under the blow. He's doubled up now, his face a mask of pain, but I'm not going to stop there. I grab the back of his head with both hands and ram my knee up into his face, hearing the snap of his cheek or jaw fracturing. He collapses sideways, and as he falls, the toecap of my standard-issue boot connects with his chin, hurling his head backward into the hard soil. I'm about to lay into him again when I realise everything's gone dead quiet. I look up to see what the hell's happening, panting hard.

Pushing through the Chorek ranks is a massively muscled man, and I spot the insignia of a master sergeant on the blue sleeve of his tunic. He's got the black pelt of some shaggy creature tied as a cloak over his left shoulder and his eyes are fixed on me with murderous intent. In his hand is a sixty-centimetre metal parade baton, red jewels clustered around one end, and as he steps up to me he smashes the point of it into my guts, knocking the wind out of me and forcing me to my knees.

'Penal legion scum!' the Chorek master sergeant barks. 'I'll show you what they should have done to you!'

He pulls his arm back for a good swing at me but then stops in mid-strike. Just try it, I think to myself, I've killed harder men and creatures than you. I'm still fired up from the fight and ready to pounce on this jumped-up bully of an officer. I'll give him the same treatment I've just dealt out to his man. He glances over my head and a shadow falls over me. A prickly sensation starts at the back of my neck and turns into a slight shiver down my spine. I turn to look over my shoulder, still clutching my aching guts, and see that he's there. The Colonel. Colonel Schaeffer, commanding officer of the 13th Penal Legion, known by those unlucky enough to be counted amongst its number as the Last Chancers. The swollen dusk sun's behind him – the sun always seems to be behind him, he's always in shadow or silhouette when you first see him, like it's a talent he's got. All I can see is the icy glitter of his sharp blue eyes, looking at the master sergeant, not me. I'm glad of that because his face is set like stone, a sure sign that he is in a bad mood.

'That will be all, master sergeant,' the Colonel says calmly, just standing there with his left hand resting lightly on the hilt of his power sword.

'This man needs disciplining,' replies the Chorek, arm still raised for the blow. I think this guy is stupid enough to try it as well, and secretly hope he will, just to see what Schaeffer does to him.

'Disperse your troopers from the landing field,' the Colonel tells the master sergeant, 'and mine will then be soon out of your way.'

The Chorek officer looks like he's going to argue some more, but then I see he makes the mistake of meeting the Colonel's gaze and I smirk as I see him flinch under that cold stare. Everyone sees something different in those blue eyes, but it's always something painful and unpleasant that they're reminded of. The Colonel doesn't move or say anything while the master sergeant herds his men away, pushing them with the baton when they turn to look back. He details two of them to drag away the trooper I knocked out and he casts one murderous glance back at me. I know his kind, an unmistakable bully, and the Choreks are going to suffer for his humiliation when they reach their camp.

'On your feet, Kage!' snaps the Colonel, still not moving a muscle. I struggle up, wincing as soreness flashes across my stomach from the master sergeant's blow. I don't meet the Colonel's gaze, but already I'm tensing, expecting the sharp edge of his tongue.

'Explain yourself, lieutenant,' he says quietly, folding his arms like a cross tutor.

'That Chorek scum said we should've all died in Deliverance, sir,' I tell him. 'Said we didn't deserve to live. Well, sir, I've just been on burial detail for nearly a hundred and fifty Last Chancers, and I lost my temper.'

'You think that gutter scum like you deserve to live?' the Colonel asks quietly.

'I know that we fought as hard as any bloody Chorek guardsman, harder even,' I tell him, looking straight at him for the first time. The Colonel seems to think for a moment, before nodding sharply.

'Good,' he says, and I can't stop my jaw from dropping in surprise. 'Get these men onto the shuttle – without any more fighting, Lieutenant Kage,' the Colonel orders, turning on his heel and marching off back towards the settlement of Deliverance.

I cast an astonished look at the other Last Chancers around me, the glance met with knotted brows and shrugs. I compose myself for a moment, trying not to work out what the hell that was all about. I've learnt it's best not to try to fathom out the Colonel sometimes, it'll just tie your head in knots.

'Well, you useless bunch of fraggin' lowlifes,' I snap at the remnants of my platoon, 'you heard the Colonel. Get your sorry hides onto that shuttle at the double!'

As I JOG TOWARDS the blocky shape of our shuttle, Franx falls in on my left. I try to ignore the big sergeant, still annoyed with him from a couple of days ago, when he could have got me into deep trouble with the Colonel.

'Kage,' he begins, glancing down across his broad shoulder at me. 'Haven't had a chance to talk to you since… Well, since before the tyranids attacked.'

'You mean since before you tried to lead the platoon into the jungles on some stupid escape attempt?' I snap back, my voice purposefully harsh. He wasn't going to get off easily, even if I did consider him something of a friend. A friendship he'd pushed to the limits by trying to incite a rebellion around me.

'Can't blame me, Kage,' he says, with a slight whine to his deep voice that irritates me. 'Should've all died back then, you know it.'

'I'm still alive, and I know that if I'd let you take off I wouldn't be,' I reply, not even bothering to look at him. 'The Colonel would've killed me for letting you go, even before the 'nids had a chance.'

'Yeah, I know, I know,' Franx tells me apologetically.

'Look,' I say, finally meeting his eye, 'I can't blame you for wanting out. Emperor knows, it's what we all want. But you've got to be smarter about it. Pick your time better, and not one that's gonna leave me implicated.'

'I understand, Kage,' Franx nods before falling silent. One of the shuttle crewmen, looking hot and bothered in his crisp blue and white Navy uniform, is counting us off as we head up the loading ramp, giving us sullen looks as if he wishes they could just leave us here. It's hot inside the shuttle, which has slowly baked in the harsh sun until the air inside feels like a kiln. I see the others settling into places along the three benches, securing themselves with thick restraint belts that hang from beams that stretch at head height along the shuttle chamber's ten-metre length. As I find a place and strap myself into the restraining harnesses, Franx takes the place next to me.

'How's Kronin?' he asks, fumbling with a metal buckle as he pulls the leather straps tighter across his barrel chest.

'Haven't seen him. He went up on the first shuttle run,' I tell him, checking around to see that everybody else is secured. Seeing that the survivors of my platoon are sitting as tight as a Battle Sister's affections, I give the signal to the naval rating waiting at the end of the seating bay. He disappears through the bulkhead and the red take-off lights flash three times in warning.

'I haven't got the full story about Kronin yet,' I say to Franx, pushing my back against the hard metal of the bench to settle myself. Franx is about to reply when the rumble of thrusters reverberates through the fuselage of the shuttle. The rumbling increases in volume to a roar and I feel myself being pushed further into the bench by the shuttle's take-off. The whole craft starts to shake violently as it gathers momentum, soaring upwards into the sky above Deliverance. My booted feet judder against the mesh decking of the shuttle and my backside slides slightly across the metal bench. My stomach is still painful, and I feel slightly sick as the shuttle banks over sharply to take its new course. The twelve centimetre slash in my thigh begins to throb painfully as more blood is forced into my legs by the acceleration. I grit my teeth and ignore the pain. Through a viewport opposite I can see the ground dropping away, the seemingly haphazard scattering of shuttles and dropships sitting a kilometre beyond the walls of Deliverance. The settlement itself is receding quickly, until I can only dimly make out the line of the curtain wall and the block of the central keep. Then we're into the clouds and everything turns white.

As we break out of the atmosphere the engines turn to a dull whine and a scattering of stars replaces the blue of the sky outside the viewport. Franx leans over.

'They say Kronin is touched,' he says, tapping the side of his head to emphasise his point.

'It's bloody strange, I'll give you that,' I reply. 'Something happened to him when he was in the chapel.'

'Chapel?' Franx asks, scratching his head vigorously through a thick bush of brown curls.

'What did you hear?' I say, curious to find out what rumours had started flying around, only a day after the battle against the tyranids. Gossip is a good way of gauging morale, as well as the reactions to a recent battle. Of course, we're never happy, being stuck in a penal legion until we die, but sometimes some of the men are more depressed than usual. The fight against the alien tyranids at the missionary station was horrific, combating monsters like them always is. I wanted to know what the men were focusing their thoughts on.

'Nothing really,' Franx says, trying unsuccessfully to shrug in the tight confines of the safety harness. 'People are saying that he went over the edge.'

'The way I heard it, he and the rest of 2nd platoon had fallen back to the chapel,' I tell him. 'There were 'nids rushing about everywhere, coming over the east wall. Most of them were the big warriors, smashing at the doors of the shrine with their claws, battering their way in. They crashed through the windows and got inside. There was nowhere to run; those alien bastards just started hacking and chopping at everything inside.

They lost the whole platoon except for Kronin. They must have left him for dead, since the Colonel found him under a pile of bodies.'

'That's a sure way to crack,' Franx says sagely, a half-smile on his bulbous lips.

'Anyway,' I continue, 'Kronin is cracked, like you say. Keeps talking all this gibber, constantly jabbering away about something that no one could work out.'

'I've seen that sort of thing before,' says Poal, who's been listening from the other side of Franx. His narrow, chiselled face has a knowing air about it, like he was a sage dispensing the wisdom of the ancients or something. 'I had a sergeant once whose leg was blown off by a mine on Gaulis II. He just kept repeating his brother's name, minute after minute, day after day. He slit his own throat with a med's scalpel in the end.'

There's a moment of silence as everybody considers this, and I carry on with the story to distract them from thoughts of self-murder.

'Yeah, that's pretty grim,' I tell them, 'but Kronin's case just gets weirder. Turns out, he's not mumbling just any old thing, oh no. He's quoting scripture, right? Nathaniel, the preacher back in Deliverance, overhears him saying out lines from the Litanies of Faith. Stuff like: "And the Beast from the Abyss rose up with its multitudes and laid low the servants of the Emperor with its clawed hands". Things like that.'

'Fragged if I've ever seen Kronin with a damned prayer book, not in two fragging years of fighting under the son of an ork,' Jorett announces from the bench down the middle of the shuttle, looking around. Everybody's listening in now that we can be heard over the dimmed noise of the engines. Forty pairs of eyes look towards me in anticipation of the next twist of the tale.

'Exactly!' I declare with an emphatic nod, beginning to play to the audience a little bit. I'm enjoying having a new tale to tell for a change, and it keeps them from falling out with each other, which usually happens when we wind down from a mission.

'Nathaniel sits down with him for a couple of hours while we bury the dead,' I continue, passing my gaze over those that can see me. 'I heard him explaining his view on things to the Colonel. Seems Kronin had a visitation from the Emperor himself while he lay half-dead in the chapel. Says he has been given divine knowledge. Of course, he doesn't actually say this, he's just quoting appropriate lines from the Litanies, like: "And the Emperor appeared with a shimmering halo and spake unto His people on Gathalamor." And like you say, how in the seven hells does he know any of this stuff?'

'There is nothing mystical about that,' answers Gappo, sitting on his own towards the rear of the shuttle. Nearly everybody seems to give an inward groan, except a couple of the guys who are looking forward to this new development in the entertainment. Myself, I've kind of come to like Gappo – he's not such a meathead as most of the others.

'Oh wise preacher,' Poal says with a sarcastic sneer, 'please enlighten us with your bountiful wisdom.'

'Don't call me "preacher"!' Gappo snarls, a scowl creasing his flat, middle-aged features. 'You know I have left that falsehood behind.'

'Whatever you say, Gappo,' Poal tells him with a disdainful look.

'It's quite simple really,' Gappo begins to explain, patently ignoring Poal now. 'You've all been to Ecclesiarchal services, hundreds even thousands of them. Whether you remember them or not, you've probably heard all of the Litanies of Faith and every line from the Book of Saints twice over. Kronin's trauma has affected his mind, so that he can remember those writings and nothing else. It's the only way he's got left to communicate.'

There are a few nods, and I can see the sense of it. People's heads are half-fragged up anyway, in my experience. It doesn't take much to jog it loose, from what I've seen. Emperor alone knows how many times I've felt myself teetering on the edge of the insanity chasm. Luckily I'm as tough as grox hide and it hasn't affected me yet. Not so as anyone's told me, in any case.

'Well I guess that makes more sense than the Emperor filling him with His divine spirit,' says Mallory, a balding, scrawny malingerer sitting next to Poal. 'After all, I don't think the Emperor's best pleased with our Lieutenant Kronin, 'specially considering the fact that Kronin's in the Last Chancers for looting and burning down a shrine.'

'Of course it makes sense,' Gappo says, his voice dropping to a conspiratorial whisper. 'There might not be an Emperor at all!'

'You shut your fragging mouth, Gappo Elfinzo!' Poal spits, making the sign of the protective eagle over his chest with his right hand. 'I may have murdered women and children and I know I'm a lowlife piece of ork crap, but I still think I shouldn't have to share the same room with a fragging heretic!'

Poal starts to fumble at his straps, having trouble because his left arm ends in a hook instead of a hand. I can see things might be getting out of control.

'That's enough!' I bark. 'You all know the score. Doesn't matter what you did to wind up as one of the Colonel's doomed men, we're all Last Chancers now. Now shut the frag up until we're back on the transport.'

There are a few grumbles, but nobody says anything out loud. More than one of them here has had a cracked skull or a broken nose for answering me back. I'm not a bully, you understand, I just have a short temper and don't like it when my men start getting too disrespectful. Seeing that everybody is calming down, I close my eyes and try to get some sleep; it'll be another two hours before we dock.

THE TRAMP OF booted feet echoes around us as the Navy armsmen march us back to our cells. Left and right, along the seemingly endless corridor are the vaulted archways leading to the cargo bays, modified to carry human cargo in supposedly total security. There are twenty of the massive cells in all. Originally each held two hundred men, but after the past thirty months of near-constant war, nearly all of them stand empty now. It'll be even emptier for the rest of the trip; there's only about two hundred and fifty of us left after the defence of Deliverance. The armsmen swagger around, shotcannons grasped easily in heavily gloved hands or slung over their shoulders. Their faces are covered by the helms of their heavy-duty work suits, and their flash-protective visors conceal their features. Only the name badges stitched onto their left shoulder straps show that the same ten men have been escorting my platoon for the past two and a half years.

I see the Colonel waiting up ahead, with someone standing next to him. As we get closer, I see that it's Kronin, his small, thin body half-hunched as if weighed down by some great invisible burden. The lieutenant's narrow eyes flit and dart from side to side, constantly scanning the shadows, and he flinches as I step up to Schaeffer and salute.

'Lieutenant Kronin is the only survivor of 3rd platoon,' the Colonel tells me as he waves the armsmen to move the others inside, 'so I am putting him in with you. In fact, with so few of you left, you are going to be gathered into a single formation now. You will be in charge; Green was killed in Deliverance.'

'How, sir?' I ask, curious as to what happened to the other lieutenant, one of the hundred and fifty Last Chancers who was alive two days ago and now is food for the flesh-ants of the nameless planet below us.

'He was diced by a strangleweb,' the Colonel says coldly, no sign of any emotion on his face at all. I wince inside – being slowly cut up as you try to struggle out of a constricting mesh of barbed muscle is a nasty way to go. Come to think of it, I've never thought of a nice way to go.

'I am leaving it to you to organise the rest of the men into squads and to detail special duties,' the Colonel says before stepping past me and striding down the corridor. A Departmento flunky swathed in an oversized brown robe hurries down to the Colonel carrying a massive bundle of parchments, and then they are both lost in the distant gloom.

'Inside,' orders an armsman from behind me, his nametag showing him to be Warrant Officer Hopkinsson.

The massive cell doors clang shut behind me, leaving me locked in this room with ten score murderers, thieves, rapists, heretics, looters, desecrators, grave-robbers, necrophiles, maniacs, insubordinates, blasphemers and other assorted vermin for company. Still, it makes for interesting conversation sometimes.

'Right!' I call out, my voice rebounding off the high metal ceiling and distant bulkheads. 'All sergeants get your sorry hides over here!'

As the order is passed around the massive holding pen, I gaze over my small force. There's a couple of hundred of us left now, sitting or lying around in scattered groups on the metal decking, stretching away into the gloom of the chamber. Their voices babble quietly, making the metal walls ring slightly and I can smell their combined sweat from several days on the furnace-hot planet below. In a couple of minutes eight men are stood around me. I catch sight of an unwelcome face.

'Who made you a sergeant, Rollis?' I demand, stepping up to stand right in front of his blubbery face, staring straight into his beady black eyes.

'Lieutenant Green did,' he says defiantly, matching my stare.

'Yeah? Well you're just a trooper again now, you piece of dirt!' I snap at him, pushing him away. 'Get out of my sight, you fraggin' traitor.'

'You can't do this!' he shouts, taking a step towards me and half-raising a fist. My elbow snaps out sharply and connects with his throat, sending him gasping to the floor.

'Can't I?' I snarl at him. 'I guess I can't do this either,' I say, kicking him in the ribs. Forget about the murderers, it's the out-and-out traitors like him that make me want to heave. With a venomous glance he gets to his hands and knees and crawls away.

'Right,' I say, turning to the others, putting the fat piece of filth from my mind. 'Where were we?'

ALARM SIRENS ARE sounding everywhere, a piercing shrill that sets your teeth on edge. I'm standing with a pneu-mattock grasped in both hands, its engine chugging comfortably, wisps of oily smoke leaking from its exhaust vents.

'Hurry up, wreck the place!' someone shouts from behind me. I can hear the sound of machinery being smashed, pipelines being cut and energy coils being shattered. There's a panel of dials in front of me and I place the head of the hammer against it, thumbing up the revs on the engine to full, the air filling with flying splinters of glass and shards of torn metal. Sparks of energy splash across my heavy coveralls, leaving tiny burn marks on the thick gloves covering my hands. I turn the pneu-mattock on a huge gear-and-chain mechanism behind the trashed panel, sending toothed wheels clanging to the ground and the heavy chain whipping past my head.

'They're coming!' the earlier voice calls out over the din of twisting metal and fracturing glass. I look over my shoulder to see a bunch of security men hurrying through an archway to my left, wearing heavy carapace breastplates coloured dark red with the twisted chain and eye mark of the Harpikon Union picked out in bold yellow. They've all got vicious-looking slug guns, black enamelled pieces of metal that catch the light menacingly. People hurrying past jostle me, but it's hard to see their faces, like they're in a mist or something. I get a glimpse of a half-rotten skull resembling a man called Snowton, but I know that Snowton died a year ago fighting pirates in the Zandis Belt. Other faces, faces of men who are dead, flit past. There's a thunderous roar and everybody starts rushing around. I realise that the Harpikon guards are firing. Bullets ricochet all over the place, zinging off pieces of machinery and thudding into the flesh of those around me. I try to run, but my feet feel welded to the floor. I look around desperately for somewhere to hide, but there isn't anywhere. Then I'm alone with the security men, the smoking muzzles of their guns pointing in my direction. There's a blinding flash and the thunder of shooting.

I WAKE UP from the dream gasping for breath, sweat coating my skin despite the chill of the large cell. I fling aside the thin blanket that serves as my bed and sit up, placing my hands on the cold floor to steady myself as dizziness from the sudden movement swamps me. Gulping down what feels like a dead rat in my mouth, I look around. There's the usual night-cycle activity – mumbles and groans from the sleepless, the odd murmured prayer as some other poor soul is afflicted by the sleep-daemons. It's always the same once you've dropped into the Immaterium.

I've had the same nightmare every night in warpspace for the past three years, ever since I joined the Imperial Guard. I'm always back in the hive on Olympas, carrying out a wreck-raid on a rival factory. Sometimes it's the Harpikon Union, like tonight; other times it's against the Jorean Consuls; and sometimes even the nobles of the Enlightened, though we never dared do that for real. There's always the walking dead as well. Folks from my past come back to haunt me: people I've killed, comrades who have died, my family, all of them appear in the nightmares. Lately I've realised that there's more and more of them after every battle, like the fallen are being added to my dreams. I always end up dying as well, which is perhaps the most disturbing thing. Sometimes I'm blown apart by gunfire, other times I'm sawn in half by a poweraxe or a chainsword, sometimes I'm burnt alive by firethrowers. Several people have told me that the warp is not bound in time like the real universe. Instead, you might see images from your past or your future, all mixed together in strange ways. Interpreting warp dreams is a speciality of Lammax, one of the ex-Departmento men. I think they threw him into the penal legions for blasphemy after he offered to read the dreams of a quartermaster-major. He says it's my fear of death being manifested.

Suddenly there's a demented screaming from the far end of the cargo hold where we're held, down where the lighting has gone fritzy and its arrhythmic pulsing gives you a headache. Nobody's slept down there for months, not since there was enough room for everyone to fit in at this end. With everyone gathered in one cell now, someone must have had to try to get to sleep down there. I push myself to my feet and pull on my boots over my bare feet. As I walk towards the commotion, I rub a hand across my bared chest to wipe off the sweat. My body tingles all over with a bizarre feeling of energy, the map of scars traced out across my torso feels strangely hot under my fingertips. I look down, half-expecting the old wounds to be glowing. They're not.

I tramp into the gloom, watched by most of the others. The screaming's loud enough to wake up the Navy ratings on the next deck up. I understand their suspicion and morbid curiosity, because sometimes when a man starts screaming in warpspace, it's not with his own voice. Luckily it's never happened to anyone I know, but there are guys here who tell tales of men being possessed by creatures from the warp. They either go completely mad and kill a load of people before collapsing and dying, or they get taken over totally becoming a body for some strange creature's mind, in which case they'll stalk along the corridors calmly murdering anyone they come across. And that's even when the Immaterium shielding is still working. You don't want to know what happens on a ship whose warpwards collapse under the continual assault from formless beings intent on the death of the ship's crew.

'Emperor of Terra, watch over me,' I whisper to myself as I'm halfway towards the source of the screeching. If it is a Touched One, this could be some really serious trouble. They don't allow us anything that can be used as a weapon, so we're virtually defenceless. Still, that's just as well really, because there'd be a hell of a lot less of us left if we were armed. Fights break out a lot, but despite what some people think it takes a while to beat someone to death and somebody usually breaks it up before there's a casualty. That said, if I wanted to kill someone I could, particularly if they're sleeping.

My whole body's shaking, and I'm not quite sure why. I try to tell myself it's the cold, but I'm man enough to admit when I'm scared. Men don't scare me, except perhaps the Colonel. Aliens give me shudders now and then, especially the tyranids, but there's something about the idea of warp creatures that just shivers me the core, even though I've never had to face one. There's nothing that I can think of in the galaxy that's more unholy.

I can see someone thrashing around in a blanket ahead, just where the lights go gloomy. It's hard to see in the intermittent haze of the broken glow-globe, but I think I see Kronin's face twisting and turning. I hear footsteps behind me and turn suddenly, almost lashing out at Franx who's got up and followed me.

'Just warp-dreams,' he tries to reassure me with a crooked smile, his big hands held up in reflex.

'Like that makes me feel better,' I reply shortly, turning back to the writhing figure of Kronin. I can just about make out words in the shrieks bursting from his contorted mouth.

'And from the deeps… there arose a mighty beast, of many eyes… and many limbs. And the beast from the… darkness did set upon the light of mankind… with hateful thirst and unnatural hunger!'

'Don't wake him!' Franx hisses as I reach out a hand towards the struggling figure.

'Why not?' I demand, kneeling down beside Kronin and glaring back at the sergeant.

'Preacher Durant once said that waking a man with warp-dreams empties his mind, allows Chaos to seep in,' he says with an earnest look in his face.

'Well, I'll just have to risk a bit of corruption, won't I?' I tell him, annoyed at what seems like a childish superstition to me. 'If he carries on like that for the rest of the cycle, I'm not going to get any sleep at all.'

I rest a hand on Kronin's shoulder, gently at first but squeezing more firmly when he continues to toss and turn. It still doesn't do any good and I lean over him and slap him hard on the cheek with the back of my hand. His eyes snap open and there's a dangerous light in them for a second, but that's quickly replaced by a vague recognition. He sits up and looks straight at me, eyes squinting in the faltering light.

'Saint Lucius spake unto the masses of Belushidar, and great was their uproar of delight,' he says with a warm smile on his thin lips, but his eyes quickly fill with a haunted look.

'Guess that means thanks,' I say to Franx, standing up as Kronin lowers himself back down onto the blanket, glancing around once more before closing his eyes. I stay there for a couple more minutes until Kronin's breathing is shallow and regular again, meaning he's either really asleep or faking it well enough for me not to care any more.

Why the hell did Green have to get himself killed, I ask myself miserably as I trudge back to my sleeping area? I could do without the responsibility of wet-nursing this bunch of frag-for-brains criminals. It's hard enough just to survive in the Last Chancers without having to worry about everyone else. I guess I'll just have to not worry, let them take care of themselves. Hell, if they can't do that, they deserve to die.

It's A FEW DAYS after the incident with Kronin, and we're sitting down for mess in the middle of the cell, sprawled on the floor with dishes of protein globs in front of us. We have to spoon it out by hand; they won't let us have any kind of cutlery in case it can be sharpened into a blade of some sort. It's this kind of attitude that can really break a man – them not trusting you to even be able to sit down for a meal without being at each other's throats. The food is also picked to grind you down. I know for a fact that they brought hundreds of horn-heads on board from the plains around Deliverance, but do we see any sign of freshly slaughtered meat? Do we ever. No, it's just the same brown, half-liquid slush that you have to shovel into your mouth with your fingers, feeling it slide horribly down your throat with the consistency of cold vomit. You get used to it after a while, you have to. You just shove it in, swallow and hope you don't gag too much. It doesn't even taste of anything except the brackish water it's mixed with. It's cold and slimy, and more than once I've felt like hurling the stuff back into the armsmen's faces, but that'd just get me a kicking and the chance to go hungry. For all of its lack of delights, it certainly fills your stomach and keeps you going, which is all it's supposed to do.

As usual I'm sitting with Franx and Gappo, who are the closest thing to friends that I've got in this miserable outfit. We spend a few minutes cramming our faces with the sludge, before washing it down with reconstituted fruit juice. For some people, fruit juice might seem like an extravagance, but on board ship, where the air's constantly refiltered over and over, and there's only artificial light and close confines, it's the best way of stopping any diseases. There are tales of whole ships' crews being wiped out by Thalois fever or muritan cholettia, and that's too much of a risk to take when you only need to give a man half a pint of juice a day to stave off the worst.

'Ever thought of trying to get out while on board?' Franx asks, using one of his little fingers to wipe the last bits of protein from the rim of his dish.

'I've heard it isn't impossible,' Gappo says, pushing his dish away before digging into his mouth with a fingernail to extract a fragment of protein chunk lodged somewhere.

'Some of the crew reckon there's places a man can hide forever,' I add before pouring the rest of the fruit juice in my mouth and swilling it around to remove the horrid texture left in there from the goop. 'This ship isn't that big, but there's still hundreds of places where no one goes any more, places between the decks, in the ducting and down by the engines. You can creep out and steal what you need to eat, it wouldn't be difficult.'

'Yeah,' Franx says with a curled lip, 'but it ain't exactly bloody freedom, is it?'

'And what would you call freedom?' Gappo asks, lying back onto his elbows, stretching his long legs out in front of him.

'Not sure,' the sergeant says with a shrug. 'Guess I like to choose what I eat, where I go, who I know.'

'I've never been able to do that,' I tell them. 'In the hive factories it's just as much a matter of survival as it is here. Kill or be killed, win the trade wars or starve, it's that simple.'

'None of us knows what freedom is,' Gappo says, rocking his head from side to side to work out a stiff muscle. 'When I was a preacher, all I knew were the holy scriptures and the dogma of the Ecclesiarchy. They told me exactly how I was supposed to act and feel in any kind of situation. They told me who was right and who was wrong. I realise now that I didn't really have any freedom.'

'You know, I'm from an agri-world,' Franx says. 'Just a farmer, wasn't much hardship. Had lots of machines, single man could tend fifteen hundred hectares. Was always plenty to eat, women were young and healthy, nothing more a man could want.'

'So why the bloody hell did you join the Guard?' Gappo blurts out, sitting bolt upright.

'Didn't get any fragging choice, did I?' Franx says bitterly, a sour look on his face. 'Got listed for the Departmento Munitorum tithe when orks invaded Alris Colvin. I was mustered. That was it, no choice.'

'Yeah,' I butt in, 'but you must've settled in all right, you made major after all.'

'Being in the Guard turned out fine,' the sergeant says, leaning forward to stack his dish on top of Gappo's. 'Tell the truth, I liked the discipline. As a trooper, I didn't have to worry about anything except orders. Got foddered and watered, had the comfort that whatever I was told to do would be the right thing.'

'But as you got promoted, that must have changed,' Gappo interjects, leaning back again.

'Did, that was the problem,' Franx continues, ruffling his curly hair with a hand. 'Higher up the chain of command I got, less I liked it. Soon making decisions that get men killed and maimed. All of a sudden it seemed like it was all my responsibility. Colonel was a born officer, one of the gentry, didn't give a second thought to troopers, was just making sure he could sneak his way up the greasy pole of the upper ranks, hoping to make commander-general or warmaster.'

'That's why you went over the edge?' I ask, knowing that Franx was in the Last Chancers for inciting subordination and disobeying orders.

'Right,' he says, face grim with the memory, voice deep and embittered. 'Stuck in the middle of an ice plain on Fortuna II, been on half rations for a month because the rebels kept shooting down our supply shuttles. Got the order to attack a keep called Lanskar's Citadel, two dozen leagues across bare ice. Officers were dining on stewed horndeer and braised black ox, drinking Chanalain brandy; my men were eating dried food substitutes and making water from snow. Led my two companies into the officers' camp and demanded supplies for the march. Departmento bastards turned us down flat and the men went on the rampage, looting everything. Didn't try to stop them, they were cold and starving. What was I supposed to do? Order them back into the ice wastes to attack an enemy-held fort with empty stomachs?'

'That's kinda what happened to you, Gappo,' I say to the ex-preacher, making a pillow out of my thin blanket and lying down with my hands behind my head.

'The haves and have-nots?' he asks, not expecting an answer. 'I can see why Franx here did what he did, but to this day I have not the faintest clue what made me denounce a cardinal in front of half a dozen Imperial Guard officers.'

'Think you were right,' Franx says. 'Cardinal shouldn't have executed men who were laying down their lives for the defence of his palaces.'

'But you had to go and accuse the whole Ecclesiarchy of being corrupt,' I add with a grin. 'Questioning whether there really was an Emperor. How stupid are you?'

'I cannot believe that such suffering could happen if there were such a divine influence looking over humanity,' Gappo replies emphatically. 'If there is an Emperor, which I doubt, the cardinal and others like him representing such a figure is patently ridiculous.'

'Can't imagine being able to carry on if there wasn't an Emperor,' Franx says, shaking his head, trying to comprehend the idea. 'Would've killed myself as soon as I was hauled in by the Colonel if that was the case.'

'You really believe that you have a soul to save?' Gappo asks with obvious contempt. 'You believe this magnificent Emperor cares one bit whether you die serving the Imperium or as a disobedient looter?'

'Hey!' I snap at both of them. 'Let's drop this topic, shall we?'

It's at that point that Poal walks over, face scrunched up into a vicious snarl.

'He's done it again,' he says through gritted teeth.

'Rollis?' I ask, already knowing the answer, pushing myself to my feet. Poal nods and I follow him towards the far end of the prison chamber, where he and what's left of Kronin's old platoon usually eat now. Kronin is sitting there looking dejected.

'I shall steal from the plate of decadence to feed the mouths of the powerless,' the mad lieutenant says.

'That's the sermons of Sebastian Thor. I know that one,' puts in Poal, standing just behind my right shoulder.

'Where's Rollis?' I demand.

One of the men lounging on the ground nods his head to the right and I see the traitor sat with his back to the cell wall about ten metres away. Trust them to leave it up to me. Most of them hate Rollis, just like I do. They're just scared the treacherous bastard is going to do something to them if they stand up to him, and the Colonel's wrath is another factor. Well, I won't stand for it, having to breathe the same air as him makes me want to rip his lungs out. I march up to stand in front of the scumbag. He's got a half-full bowl in his lap.

I stand there with my hands on my hips. I'm shaking with anger, I detest this man so much.

'Slow eater, aren't you?' I hiss at Rollis. He looks slowly up at me with his tiny black eyes.

'Just because I'm more civilised than you animals, I don't have to put up with these insults,' he says languidly, putting the dish to one side.

'You took Kronin's food again.' A statement, not a question.

'I asked him if he would share his ration with me,' he says with a sly smile. 'He didn't say no.'

'He said: "And the bounties of the Emperor shall go to those who have worked hard in his service",' Poal interjects from behind me. 'Sounds like a big "frag off" if you ask me.'

'I warned you last time, Rollis,' I say heavily, sickened at the sight of his blubbery face. 'One warning is all you get.'

His eyes fill with fear and he opens his mouth to speak, but my boot fills it before he can say anything, knocking bloodied teeth across his lap. He clamps his hands to his jaw, whimpering with pain. As I turn away I hear him move behind me and I look back over my shoulder.

'Bashtard!' he spits at me, halfway to his feet, blood and spittle dribbling down his chin. 'I'll fragging get you back for thish, you shanctimonioush shon-of-an-ork!'

'Keep going and you'll need to ask for soup in future,' I laugh back at him. I'd pity the piece of grox crap if he wasn't such a scumbag piece of sumpfloat. He slumps back down again, probing at a tooth with a finger, eyes filled with pure venom. If looks really could kill, they'd be tagging my toes already.

'If he tries it again,' I tell Poal, 'break the fingers of his left hand. He'll find it even harder to eat then, but he'll still be able to pull a trigger. I'll back you up.'

Poal glances back at the traitor, obviously relishing the thought.

'I just hope he tries it again,' he says darkly, glaring at Rollis. 'I just hope he does...'

IN THE DIM ruddy glow of an old star, the tyranid hive fleet drifted remorselessly onwards. The smaller drone ships huddled under the massive, crater-pocked carapaces of the hive ships, the larger vessels slowly coiling in upon themselves to enter a dormant state that allowed them to traverse the vast distances between stars. The clouds of spores were dispersing, scattering slowly on the stellar winds. One hive ship was still awake, feeder tentacles wrapped around the shattered hull of an Imperial warship, digesting the mineral content, the flesh of the dead crew, leeching off the air contained within to sustain itself.

Across the heavens the flotilla of bio-ships stretched out, impelled by instinct to hibernate again until they found new prey and new resources to plunder. In their wake, a bare rock orbited the star, scoured of every organic particle, stripped of all but the most basic elements. Nothing was left of the farming world of Langosta III. There were no testaments to the humans who had once lived there. Now all that was left was an airless asteroid, the unmarked dying place of three million people. All that remained of them was raw genetic material, stored within the great hive ships, ready to be turned into more hunters, more killing machines.

TWO
FALSE HOPE

+++ *Operation New Sun in place, ready for your arrival.* +++

+++ *Operation Harvest preparing to progress to next stage.* +++

+++ *Only the Insane can truly Prosper.* +++

YOU COULD SAY that dropping out of warpspace feels like having your body turned inside out by some giant invisible hand. You could say it's like you've been scattered into fragments and then reassembled in the real universe. You could say that your mind buzzes with images of birth and death, each flashing into your brain and then disappearing in an instant. I've heard it described like this, and many other fanciful ways, by other soldiers and travellers. You could say it was like these things, but you'd be lying, because it isn't like any of them. In fact, you hardly notice that you've dropped out of warpspace at all. There's a slight pressure at the back of your mind, and then a kind of release of tension, like you've just had a stimm-shot or something. You relax a little, breathe just a little more easily. Well, that's how it's always been for me, and nobody else seems to have come up with a more accurate description that I know of. Then again, maybe you don't even actually get that; perhaps it's all in your mind. I know that I'm damned well relieved every time we drop back into realspace, because it's a whole lot less dangerous than on the Otherside. Considering the outfit I'm in these days, that's saying a hell of a lot, because each drop is just a prelude to the next blood-soaked battle.

I'm standing in the upper starboard gallery, along with another two dozen Last Chancers. The row of windows to our right continues for several hundred metres. The wood-panelled wall of the inner bulkhead stretches unbroken on the other side, leaving a massive corridor thirty metres wide where we can run back and forth along its length, but without any nooks or crannies in the featureless room to hide behind. There's only one door at each end of the gallery, each protected by a squad of armsmen with loaded shotcannons. Sealed, sterile, contained. Just like the Colonel wanted it. We're fortunate that we're on exercise when the drop happens. The shutters on the massive viewing ports grind out of sight, revealing a distant blue star. We're too far away to see any worlds yet, we've still got to go in-system under ordinary plasma drives.

Poal strides up to me, sweat dripping off him from his physical exertions.

'Where are we?' he asks, wiping his forehead with the back of his good hand.

'Haven't got a fraggin' clue,' I tell him with a deep shrug. I catch the eye of the naval officer watching over us from the near end of the gallery. He walks over with a half-confident, half-nervous look. Don't ask me how he manages it but he seems to convey a sense of superiority, but the look in his eyes doesn't match it. He glances quickly to check that the armsmen are still close at hand as he stops in front of me.

'What do you want?' he demands, his lip curled as if he was talking to a pool of sick.

'Just wondering where we are,' I say to him with a pleasant smile. I'm in a good mood for some reason, most likely because we're out of warpspace, as I said before, and so I'm not up for any Navy-baiting today.

'System XV/108, that's where we are,' he replies with a smirk.

'Oh right,' says Poal, lounging an arm across my shoulder and leaning towards the naval officer. 'XV/108? That's right next to XV/109. I heard of it.'

'Have you?' the lieutenant asks, jerking himself up straight, clearly startled.

'Oh yeah,' says Poal, his voice totally deadpan, his face radiating sincerity. 'I hear that this place is Grox-country. Nothing but Grox farms as far as the eye can see. They say that folks around here are so keen on Grox they live with 'em, sleep with 'em, even have kids by 'em.'

'Really?' the lieutenant asks, his pudgy little face screwed up with genuine repulsion now.

'That's right,' Poal continues, casting a mischievous glance at me that the Navy man doesn't notice. 'In fact, looking at you, are you sure your mother wasn't a Grox and your father a lonely farmer?'

'Certainly not, my father was a–' he starts back before he actually realises what Poal's been saying. 'Damn you, penal scum! Schaeffer will hear about this insult!'

'That's *Colonel* Schaeffer to you, Grox-baby,' Poal says, suddenly serious, staring intently at the lieutenant. 'You Navy men would do well to remember it.'

'Is that right, trooper?' the lieutenant spits back, taking a step towards us. 'When the lash is taking strips off your back, you would do well to remember that it's a naval rating doing it to you!'

With that, he spins on the spot and marches off, the thick heels of his naval boots thudding loudly on the wood-panelled floor. Poal and I just burst out laughing, and I can see his shoulders tense even more. It's a couple of minutes before we can control ourselves – each time I look at Poal I can see his innocent face and the lieutenant's enraged look.

'Hasn't even got a damned name,' Poal says when he's calmed down a little, standing looking out of the nearest viewport, looking pale against the blackness of the high-arched window that stretches up at least another ten metres above his head.

'That's worrying,' I agree, stepping up beside him. 'Even the newest explored system usually gets a name, even if it's just the same as the ship or the man who found it.'

'No name, no name...' Poal mutters to himself for a moment, before turning to look at me, his hand and hook clasped behind his back like an officer or something. 'I've just had a thought. No name probably means it's a dead system, no life-bearing worlds, right?'

'Could be,' I say, though I wouldn't really know. Unlike Poal who was brought up by the Schola Progenium, my education consisted more of how to work a las-lathe and parry an axe-blow with a crowbar.

'And a dead system is just the place you'd put a penal colony...' he suggests, looking back out of the window, more interested this time.

'You think they're going to offload us?' I ask him with an incredulous look.

'Course not,' he says, still staring out of the viewport. 'But we could be getting some more men in, that'd make sense.'

'I see your point,' I say, turning and leaning back against the thick armoured glass of the port. 'It's been two and half years, and we've not had a single new member.'

'And maybe he's organising us into one big platoon to make room for the fresh faces,' Poal says, his face showing a thoughtful impression.

'Hang on, though,' I say, a sudden thought crossing my mind. 'Wouldn't it be better to have the old-timers in charge of the squads and platoons?'

'What? Have us teaching them all the tricks we've learned?' he says with a laugh. 'The Colonel knows better than that.'

We lounge around and jaw a bit more, strolling back and forth along the gallery after one of the armsmen prompts us to carry on exercising instead of loafing. We're talking about what we'd do if we ever get out of the Last Chancers when there's an interruption.

'Lieutenant Kage!' a voice barks out from behind me and I automatically stand to attention, the parade drills banged into me so hard I still can't stop myself responding to a voice with that much authority.

'Emperor damn me it's the Colonel,' hisses Poal, standing-to on my left. 'That bloody naval bastard has fragged us.'

The Colonel walks up behind us. I can hear his slow, certain steps thudding on the floor.

'Face front, guardsmen,' he says and we both spin on the spot in perfect unison, moving with instinct rather than thought.

'If it's about that naval lieutenant, sir–' I begin to excuse myself, but he cuts me off with a short, chopping motion with his hand, his gold epaulettes swaying with the motion.

'Between you and me,' he says quietly, leaning forward to look at us face-to-face, 'I do not care what the Imperial Navy thinks of you. It could not be any worse than what I think of you.'

We stand there in silence for a moment as he glances sharply at both of us. Clearing his throat with a short cough he stands up straight again.

'Kage,' he tells me, looking past at the other Last Chancers in the gallery, 'you will be escorted to my chambers after exercise to receive briefing about our next mission.'

'Yes, sir!' I snap back, keeping my face neutral, even though inside I feel like dropping to the deck and beating my head against the wooden planks. The relaxation I've felt in the past hour after dropping from the warp disappears totally and tension seeps into my muscles and bones again. So we're here to fight again. No new recruits, no fresh blood. Just here to fight in some other bloody war. To die, perhaps. Well, that's the life of a Last Chancer. It's all there is left for us.

* * *

THE ARMSMAN TAPS politely at the panelled and lacquered door, before opening it inwards and waving me inside with the muzzle of his shotcannon. I step inside, as I've done a dozen times before, and stand to attention, my polished boots sinking into the thick carpet. Behind me I hear the door close and the ring of the armsman's boots standing to attention on the corridor decking.

The Colonel glances up from behind his massive desk and then looks back at the data-slate before him, immediately seeming to forget my presence. He presses his thumb to an identification slate on the side of the data-slate and it makes a whirring noise, which I recognise as the 'erase' function operating. He places the device carefully on the desk in front of him, lying it parallel to the edge closest to me, before looking in my direction again.

'At ease,' he tells me as he stands up and begins to pace up and down behind his high-backed chair for a few moments, hands clasped behind his back. It's then that I realise this was the pose Poal was imitating earlier and I fight hard to hold back a smirk. He stops walking and looks at me sharply and I gulp, thinking for a second that he can read my mind.

'Tyranids, Kage,' he says obtusely, pacing back and forth again, turning his gaze downwards once more.

'What… what about them, sir?' I ask after a moment, realising he was waiting for me to say something.

'Some of them may be in this system,' he tells me, still not looking at me, but from his posture I can tell that somehow every sense he has is still directed towards me.

'So there's probably nothing left for us to do,' I say boldly, hoping that perhaps we'd arrived too late, that for once we'd missed the battle.

'That may be the case, Kage,' he says slowly, stopping now to look directly at me. 'We are here to ascertain why communication with our outpost on the third world has been lost. We suspect that a small scouting fleet from Kraken was heading this way.'

As he turns to his desk to pick up a transparent copy of a terminal readout, I wonder who 'we' was meant to include. As far as I know, we're a bit of a rogue element really, bouncing about across this part of the galaxy and dropping in on any wars we happen to come across. I've not heard anything about who the Colonel's superiors might be, if he has any at all.

'Do you remember the first battle of these Last Chancers?' he asks suddenly, sitting down again, more relaxed than he was a moment before.

'Of course, sir,' I reply immediately, wondering what he meant by 'these Last Chancers'. 'I could never forget Ichar IV. I wish I could, and I've tried, but I'll never forget it.'

He replies with a non-committal grunt and proffers me the transparency. It's covered in lines and circles, and I recognise it as some kind of star chart. There are tiny runes inscribed against crosses drawn in a line that arcs from one end to the other, but it might as well be written in Harangarian for all that I can understand it. I give the Colonel a blank look and he realises I haven't got a clue what I'm holding.

'It seems that defending Ichar IV was not necessarily the best plan in the world,' he says heavily, tugging the readout from my fingers and placing it in a vellum-covered envelope in the centre of his desk.

'Saving a hundred and ninety billion people was a bad plan, sir?' I ask, amazed at what the Colonel is implying.

'If by doing so we cause five hundred billion people to die, then yes,' he says giving me a stern look, a warning not to continue my train of thought.

'Five hundred billion, sir?' I ask, totally confused and unsure what the Colonel is talking about.

'When we broke the tyranid fleet attacking Ichar IV, much of it was not destroyed,' he tells me, leaning forward to rest his elbows on the polished marble of the desk, his black-gloved hands clasped in front of him. 'That part of Hive Fleet Kraken was simply shattered. Much of it we managed to locate and destroy while the tyranids were still reeling from their defeat. However, we believe a sizeable proportion of the survivors that attacked Ichar IV coalesced into a new fleet, heading in a different direction. It is impossible to say exactly where they are heading, but reports from monitoring stations and patrol vessels indicate that its course might lead straight into the heart of the sector we are now in – the Typhon sector. If we had let them have Ichar IV, we might have mustered more of a defence and destroyed the tyranids utterly rather than scattering them to hell and back where we cannot find them and it is impossible to track them down until too late.'

'So instead of losing a planet, we could lose the whole of Typhon sector?' I ask, finally catching on to what the Colonel is implying. 'That's where five hundred billion people might die?'

'Now do you see why it is important that we know exactly where this hive fleet is heading?' he asks, an earnest look on his bony face.

'I certainly do, sir,' I reply, my head reeling with the thought of what could happen. It's so many people you can't picture it. It's far more than a hive, more than an entire hive world. Five hundred billion people, all of them devoured by hideous, unfeeling aliens if the tyranids couldn't be stopped.

THE DREAM'S SLIGHTLY different this time: we're defending one of our own factories, against shapeless green men I've never seen before. They hiss and cackle at me as they charge, their vaguely humanoid bodies shifting and changing, covered with what look like scales.

A sound close by pulls me from my sleep and I glimpse a shadow over me. Before I can do anything something heavy falls on my face and pushes down over my mouth and nose, stifling me. I lash out, but my fist connects with thin air and something hard rams into my gut, expelling what little air is in my lungs. I flail around helplessly for another second; I can hear the other man panting hard, feel the warmth of his body on top of me. The cloth on my face smells rank with old sweat, making me want to gag even more.

Suddenly the weight lifts off me and I hear a shrill titter and gasp. I throw off the thing on my face, noting it's a shirt, and I glance up to see Rollis. Behind him is Kronin, a sock wrapped around the traitor's throat, a knot in it to press hard against his windpipe. The ex-lieutenant giggles again.

'And vengeance shall be the Emperor's, said Saint Taphistis,' Kronin laughs, wrenching harder on the improvised garrotte and pulling Rollis backwards onto the decking. Kronin leans over Rollis's shoulder, twisting the sock tighter, and bites his ear, blood dribbling onto his chin and down Rollis's neck as he looks up and grins at me. Rollis's face is going blue now, his eyes bulging under his heavy-set brow. I clamber to my feet, unsteady, my head still light from being choked.

'Let him go, Kronin,' I say, taking a shaky step towards them. Killing Rollis like this will just get Kronin executed, and me as well probably. The Colonel's ordered it before; he won't hesitate to do it again.

'And the Emperor's thanks for those who had been bountiful in their gifts would be eternal,' he replies, a plaintive look on his narrow face, licking the blood from his lips.

'Do it,' I say quietly. With another pleading look, Kronin lets go and Rollis slumps to the deck, panting and clutching his throat. I put a foot against his chest and roll him over, pinning his unresisting body to the floor. I lean forward, crossing my arms and resting them on my knee, putting more weight onto his laboured chest.

'You haven't suffered for your crimes enough yet, it's too soon for you to die,' I hiss at him. 'And when you do, I'm going to be the one that does it.'

'THIS IS NOT a good idea,' Linskrug says, before he gives a deep sigh and takes a swig from his canteen. We're taking a quick rest break from the march, sitting in the jungle mud. All around birds are chattering, whistling and screeching in the trees. Flies the size of your thumb buzz past, and I bat one away that settles on my arm. Who can tell what I might catch if it bit me. Other insects flit around on brightly patterned wings, and a beetle bigger than my foot scuttles into the light on the far side of the track, three metres away. The air is sultry, soaking us in humidity and our own sweat, which pours from every part of my body even though I'm resting.

'What's not a good idea?' I ask with a sour look. 'Marching through this green hellhole, getting slowly eaten by flies, drowning in our own sweat and choking on sulphur fumes? I can't see why that's not a good idea.'

'No, none of that,' he says, waving a dismissive hand. 'I'm talking about following this trail.'

'Finding this trail is the only good thing that's happened since we made planetfall on this Emperor-forsaken jungle world,' I tell him bitterly, pulling my right boot off and massaging my blistered foot. 'It certainly beats hacking our way through the undergrowth. I mean, we've lost eight men already, in just fifteen hours! Drowned in swamps, fallen down hidden crevasses, poisoned by spinethorns, infected by bleed-eye and the black vomit, bitten by snakes and birds. Droken's lost his leg to some damned swamprat-thing, and we're all going to die horribly unless we can find the outpost in the next day or two.'

'Do you know why there's a trail here?' asks Linskrug, glancing sideways at me as he sits down gingerly on a fallen log, his lean, muscled frame showing through the clinging tightness of his sweat-sodden shirt.

'I don't know. Because the Emperor loves us?' I say, teasing the sodden sock from my foot and wringing out the sweat and marsh water.

'Because creatures move along here regularly,' he says, wrinkling his nose at my ministrations on my feet. 'They travel along here frequently, thus forming the trail.'

'Very interesting,' I tell him dryly, slipping on my damp footwear.

'I learnt that hunting back home, on the estate,' he says sagely, screwing the cap back on the water bottle.

I bet you did, I think to myself. Linskrug was once a baron on Korall, and says that his political opponents fragged him good and proper, stitching him up for unlicensed slaving. He's never even been in the Guard before the Last Chancers, so whoever his enemies were, they must have scratched quite a few backs in their time.

'Why's that so useful for hunting?' I ask, switching feet while I wriggle the toes on my right foot inside my clammy boot.

'Because that's where to look for the prey,' he says with exaggerated patience, turning his hawkish features to look at me across his shoulder, his eyes giving me a patronising look.

'But if you know that,' I say slowly, little gears in my head beginning to whirr into slow life, 'then don't the animals know it?'

'The other predators do...' he says quietly.

'What?' I half scream at him. The other Last Chancers around hurriedly glance in my direction, hands reaching instinctively for lasguns. 'You mean that... things will be hunting along here?'

'That's right,' Linskrug says with a slow, nonchalant nod.

'Did you think of letting the Colonel know that?' I ask, desperately trying to keep my temper in check.

'Oh, I'm very sure he knows,' Linskrug says, taking his helmet off and rubbing the sweat out of his long hair. 'He has the look of the hunter about him, does our Colonel.'

'So we must be safer here than in the jungle,' I say, calming down a little. 'I mean, I remember you saying before that the largest predators need a wide territory so there can't be that many around.'

'I can't say that I've noticed the Colonel being overly conscious of our safety,' laughs the baron, slapping his helmet back on his head.

'I guess not,' I agree with a grimace.

'Rest break over!' I hear the Colonel's shout from further up the trail. We're at the back of the column, keeping an eye out for anyone trying to drop away and lose themselves. That said, the Colonel knows anyone dumb enough to think that they can go it alone on a deathworld like this is better off lost.

'Most animals only kill when they're hungry, isn't that right?' I ask Linskrug, seeking a bit more reassurance, as we trudge along the trail, ankle-deep in mud.

'No,' he says, shaking his head vehemently, 'most predators only eat when they're hungry. Some will kill out of sheer maliciousness, while most of them are highly aggressive and will attack anything they see as a threat to their territory.'

'By threat,' I say slowly, pushing my pistol holster further round on my belt to stop it slapping my sore thigh, 'you wouldn't mean two hundred armed men marching along your favourite hunting ground, would you?'

'Well, I couldn't answer for the local beasts,' he says with a smile, 'but back on Korall there is this massive cat called a hookfang, and it'll attack anything man-sized or larger it sees. I can't see any hunting beast trying to survive on a deathworld being any less touchy.'

We march on in silence, and the clouds open up with a fine drizzle of rain. It's been near-constant since we landed yesterday, except for the past few hours. I let my mind wander, forgetting the fatigue in my legs by thinking about our mission. We've come to False Hope, the rather depressing name of this world, because all contact has been lost with the outpost here, nothing at all from two hundred inhabitants. The place is called False Hope because the men who originally landed here suffered a warp engine malfunction and were unceremoniously dumped back into realspace. The ship was badly damaged by the catastrophe and they thought they were doomed until they happened across a habitable world. They managed to land safely, and set up camp. A Navy patrol vessel came across their auto-distress call seventy-five years later, and the landing party found nothing left except the ship, almost swallowed up by the jungle. Apparently the captain had kept a diary, which told of how five hundred crew had died in about a year. He was the last to go. The final line in the diary went something like *It appears that what we thought was our salvation has turned out to be nothing but false hope.* The name just kind of stuck, I guess.

I learnt this from one of the shuttle crew, a rating called Jamieson. Quite a nice guy really, despite him being Navy. We get on a whole lot better with the regular ratings than we do the armsmen, and a lot better than we do with the officers. I guess it's because most of them never wanted to be there either, just got caught up in the press-gangs. Still, they soon get it bludgeoned into their heads by their superiors that the Navy is better than the Guard. I don't know how long the enmity between the Navy and Guard has lasted, probably since they were split up right after the Great Heresy. That was one of the first things I learned when I joined the Imperial Guard – Navy and Guard don't mix. I mean, how can you respect the Navy when they think that they can deal with anything, just by stopping the threat before it reaches a planet. Half the fraggin' time they don't even know there's a threat until it's too late. And then their answer is just to frag everything to the warp and back from orbit with their big guns. I'm no strategist, but without the Guard to fight the ground wars, I reckon the Navy'd be next to useless. All they're good for is getting us from one warzone to the next relatively intact.

The rain patters irritatingly across my face. There don't seem to be any storms here, but there's an almost constant shower, so it's next to impossible to keep anything dry. Some of the men have complained about finding pungent-smelling mould growing in their packs, it's that bad.

Anyway, we've lost contact with False Hope Station, and the Colonel, and whoever the mysterious 'we' is, think the tyranids might have been here, just a little ship. It's blatantly obvious that nothing as big as a hive ship has got here, otherwise the whole planet would be stripped bare by now. They'd be having a total banquet with all those different animals to eat up and mutate. But the Colonel reckons that where you get a few 'nids, more follow soon after. I know that from Ichar IV and Deliverance. They send out scouts: on planetside they use these slippery fraggers we call lictors to find out where the greatest concentration of prey is. These lictors, they're superb predators, they say. It's been reckoned they can track a single man across a desert, and if that wasn't bad enough, they're deadly, with huge scything claws that can rip a man in two, fast as lightning too. When they find somewhere worth visiting, then the rest of the swarm comes along to join in the party. Don't ask me how they keep in contact with all these scouting fleets and beasties, they just manage it somehow. If there are tyranids here, in the Typhon Sector, it's our job to hunt them down and kill them before they do their transmitting thing, or whatever it is they do. If we don't, the Colonel informs me, then there's going to be upwards of a hundred hive ships floating this way over the next couple of years, gearing up to devour everything for a hundred light years in every direction.

'Kage!' Linskrug hisses in my ear, breaking my reverie.

'What?' I snarl, irritated at him derailing my thoughts.

'Shut up and listen!' he snaps back as he stops, putting a finger to his lips, his eyes narrowed.

I do as he says, slowly letting out my breath, trying to tune in to the sounds of the jungle around us. I can just hear the pattering of the rain on leaves and splashing onto the muddy trail, the slack wind sighing through the treetops around us.

'I don't hear anything,' I tell him after a minute or so of standing around.

'Exactly,' he says with an insistent nod. 'The whole place has been veritably screaming with insects and birds since we landed, now we can't hear a thing!'

'Sergeant Becksbauer!' I call to the nearest man in front of us, who's stopped and is looking at us, probably wondering if we've decided to make a break for it, despite the odds against surviving for long in this place. 'Go and get the Colonel from the head of the column. There might be trouble coming.'

He gives a wave and then sets off double-stepping up the trail, tapping guys on the shoulder as he goes past, directing them back towards us with a thumb. I see Franx is among them and he breaks into a trot and starts heading towards us. He's jogging through the rain and puddles when suddenly his eyes go wide and he opens his mouth to scream but doesn't utter a sound. He tries to stop suddenly and his feet slide out from underneath him, pitching the sergeant onto his back in the mud. I hear a strangled gulp from Linskrug and look over my shoulder. My heart stops beating for an eternity at what I see.

About fifty metres behind us, poking from between the jungle trees, is a massive reptilian head, almost as long as I am tall. Its plate-sized yellow eye is glaring straight at us, black pupil nothing but a vertical slit.

'Stay still,' Linskrug tells me out of the corner of his mouth. 'Some lizards can't see you if you don't move.'

A trickle of sweat runs down my back, chilling my spine and making me want to shiver.

'What the frag do we do?' I asked in a strained voice, slowly edging my right hand towards the laspistol hanging in the holster at my belt.

'Do you think that's going to hurt it?' Linskrug whispers.

The beast stamps forward two paces, massively muscled shoulders bending aside the trunks of two trees to force its way through. It's covered in scales the size of my face, green and glistening, perfectly matching the round, rain-drenched leaves of the surrounding trees. The camouflage is near-perfect, we could have walked straight past it for all I know. It takes another step and I can see its nostrils flaring as it sniffs the air.

'Any chance that it eats bushes and stuff?' I whisper to Linskrug, not particularly hopeful. As if in reply, the creature's huge jaw opens revealing row after row of serrated teeth, obviously used for stripping flesh and crushing bones.

'I don't think so,' says Linskrug, taking a slow step backwards, shuffling his foot through the mud rather than picking it up. I follow suit, sliding my boots through the puddles as we slowly back away.

'What's the delay?' I hear someone calling, but I daren't look around to see who it is.

The enormous reptile's head swings left and right, trying to look with both eyes down the trail at us. It gives a snort and then breaks into a waddling run on its four tremendous legs, its thick hide scraping bark off the trees along both sides of the trail, its tail swinging in a wide arc from side to side and smashing through branches as thick as my arm.

'Can we run now?' I ask Linskrug, my jaw tight with fear, a trembling starting in my legs and working upwards.

'Not yet,' he says, and I can hear him breathing heavily but steadily, as if calming himself. 'Not yet.'

This thing's pounding down the trail at us, gathering momentum and I can feel the ground shuddering under the impact of its huge weight. It's bigger than a battle tank, easily eleven metres long, not including its tail. I can hear its deep breathing, a constant growling, growing louder by the second. It's speeding up, now moving about as fast as a man can comfortably run and still getting faster. It's only about ten metres away when I feel Linskrug moving.

'Now!' he bellows in my ear, shoving me sideways into the treeline, landing on top of me and knocking my breath out. The predator's head swings in our direction and it snaps its jaw at us as it charges past, but it's going too fast to stop. As it thunders along the trail, we pick ourselves up and jump back onto the track – I've already learnt that it's suicide to lie around in the undergrowth on False Hope.

Ahead of us the other Last Chancers are scattering like flies from a snapping greel, leaping in every direction, some of them turning to try to outpace the beast. I see Franx dodging to one side, but the creature's tail lashes out, crashing across his chest and flinging him bodily through the air for a dozen metres before he thumps awkwardly against a tree trunk.

The sound of lasguns crackles up ahead, and I pull my pistol from its holster and begin snapping off shots at the beast's hindquarters, the flashes of laser impacting on its thick hide with little visible effect. Linskrug is snapping off shots from the hip with his lasgun too, as we hurry side-by-side after the giant reptile. The lasgun fire increases in intensity, accompanied by screams of pain and shouts of terror. It's hard to see past the vast bulk of the monster, all I can see are half-glimpses of guardsmen dodging to and fro. Now and then one of them is caught up in the beast's immense jaws, crushed and tossed aside or cleaved in half by its huge fangs. It's still thundering along, and I see a clawed foot descend onto the chest of a trooper trying to crawl into the bushes, flattening him in a explosion of pulverised organs and splashing blood.

'Any smart ideas?' I shout to Linskrug, stopping and trying to level a shot at the beast's head as it snakes from side to side.

'Run away?' he suggests, stopping next to me and pulling the power pack from the bottom of his lasrifle. He glances around as he slams another one home, perhaps looking for inspiration.

'Lasfire isn't having much effect, we need to hit and run,' he says, unhooking his bayonet from his belt and twisting it onto the mounting on the end of his lasgun.

'Hand-to-hand? I thought it was Kronin who'd gone mad!' I shout at him, my heart faltering at the thought of voluntarily going any nearer to that murderous mass of muscles and teeth.

'Work a blade in under the scales, in the direction of the head, and push deep,' Linskrug says with a grin, obviously relishing the whole situation, before setting off again along the track. At least half a dozen mashed corpses litter the trail now, and a few more men lie battered, groaning in pain. The monster has stopped its rampage now and is standing four square in the trail, head lunging forward at the guardsmen in front. Linskrug ducks neatly under its swishing tail and rams his bayonet into the yellowish scales of its underbelly. I see him spread his legs wider and brace himself, and with his teeth gritted with strain he levers the bayonet further into the creature's flesh. It gives a roar of pain and tries to turn round and attack us, but it's too bulky to turn quickly, its massive flanks jamming against trees, its neck not long enough to bend back to attack us. It takes a step back, pushing Linskrug to the ground as it shifts its feet to get into a better position.

'What the frag,' I hear myself saying before I leap forward, grabbing Linskrug's collar in one hand and dragging him free. I can hear the shouts of the other men from across its broad, flat back, bellowed commands from the Colonel cutting through their hysterical yelling. The reptile shuffles forward a little, now almost at right angles to the track, its back hunching up to give it more room. I roll forwards between its legs and make a grab for the rifle still hanging from its midriff. I miss at the first attempt and as the creature shifts its weight the rifle butt cracks painfully against my knuckles. Spitting incoherent curses I duck forward again, narrowly stepping aside as it backs up once again, and manage to get one hand on the lasgun. I put my shoulder to the stock and heave upwards, straining every muscle in my back and legs, my fleet slipping and sliding in the mud. My efforts are rewarded by a plaintive howl of pain and it thrashes around even more violently. Its rear legs become entangled in the thorns of a bush next to the trail and it slips for a moment. The vast bulk of its underside crashes down onto the top of my helmet, knocking me flat to my chest, my face in a puddle. The lasgun slips from my grip once more.

Dark red blood spills freely from the wound now, splashing onto my head and shoulders. The lizard's heaving itself backwards and forwards, left and right, trying to angle its head under, either to attack me or perhaps to pull the bayonet free, I'm not sure which. I roll sideways just as a back foot thuds into the mud where I was lying, spinning out from underneath the monstrous reptile.

I'm covered head to toe in mud and blood, spluttering and spitting dirty water from my mouth. Through grime-filled eyes I see the Colonel leaping through the rain, power sword clenched in his fist, the rain hissing off its searing blue blade. Without a sound he lunges forward, the power sword sheering through the creature's muzzle, a great hunk of burnt flesh flopping to the floor. It rears up, slashing its front claws through the space the Colonel occupied a moment before, but he's already side-stepped to the left. As the lizard lowers its head again, looking for its prey, the Colonel's arm stabs outward with a precise move, plunging the power sword through its right eye. I see the point of the blade protruding a few centimetres from the top of the giant beast's skull and it thrashes wildly for a moment, tearing the sword from the Colonel's grasp and forcing him to take a step backwards. Everyone jumps back hurriedly as its death throes continue, and I have to push myself to my feet and leap aside again as it stumbles towards where I lay. With a thud that reverberates along the ground the monstrosity finally collapses, the air of its last breath whistling out of its ruined face.

The Colonel marches up to the gigantic corpse and pulls his power sword free, as easily as if he were sliding it out of the scabbard, and with no more ceremony either. He looks around at us, slipping the sword back into its sheath. He glances down and, with a casualness I would have thought forced if I didn't know the Colonel, wipes flecks of blood from its basket hilt with a handkerchief pulled from one of his deep greatcoat pockets.

'All right, men,' he says, adjusting how the scabbard hangs against his leg. 'Find out who is dead and who can carry on.'

And with that, the whole incident is over, just a few more deaths in the bloody history of the Last Chancers.

WE STUMBLE INTO False Hope Station later the same day, just as the sun is setting. One minute we're in thick jungle, the next there's a rough pathway and buildings to either side. The whole outpost is covered with vines and trailing leaves, woven around the walls and roofs of the rockcrete shelters in a near-continuous mass. What passes for the roads are little more than mud tracks, the odd slab of stone showing through the dense moss underfoot. There's no sign of life at all, just the normal sounds of the jungle. It looks like a ghost town, deserted for a while, succumbing to the eternal predations of the surrounding plants. It's eerie, and I shiver, despite the boiling heat. It's like the people here have disappeared, snatched up by the hand of an unknown god. Something unholy is at work here, I can feel it in my bones.

Deciding to see if there's anyone around, I force open the nearest door, leading into a square building just to my left. Inside it's dark, but from the fitful light coming from the doorway I can see that the building is deserted. There are a few scattered pieces of furniture, hewn from wood, probably from the surrounding trees. I see a firepit in the middle of the one-roomed quarters, but the ashes inside are sodden with rain dripping from the imperfectly covered chimney vent above. As I skulk around in the darkness my foot sends something skittering along the floor. I flounder around for a moment to recover whatever it was that I disturbed, and my hand comes to rest on something vaguely oval and leathery.

I bring it outside to have a look, where Kronin and Gappo are waiting, supporting the half-dead form of Franx. The sergeant didn't seem too badly hurt from his encounter with the lizard, just a bruised back and a few broken ribs, but a couple of hours ago he began to get feverish. The lacerations on his chest have begun to mortify; you can smell the disease from several paces away. He's only half-conscious, his moments of lucidity separated by fever-induced delusions and mumbling. He keeps asking for food, but I don't think it's because he's hungry, more likely memories of his time on Fortuna II coming back to life in his head. He sounds stuck in the past at the moment, replaying what was probably the most important event in his life over and over again.

The object in my hands is about thirty centimetres long, and looks very much like a bunch of dead leaves connected together at one end in a small bundle of fibres.

'What is that, a plant or something?' Gappo says, peering over my shoulder.

'Whatever it is, it can wait,' I tell the ex-preacher. 'We need to get the wounded to the infirmary as soon as possible.'

Dropping the strange object into the mud, I grab Franx's legs and heave them onto my shoulder, the other two have an arm each around their necks and we carry him towards what looks like the centre of False Hope Station. The Colonel is there, directing squads to fan out and search the ghost settlement, which is what it looks like at the moment. The other two wounded, Oklar and Jereminus from Franx's squad, have been propped up against the wall of the largest building, Oklar nursing the stump of his right leg, Jereminus holding a ragged bandage to what's left of the side of his face. We left the corpses of seven other men back where we fought the giant lizard.

'Where's Droken, sir?' I ask the Colonel as we step out of a side street into the central square.

'He died of blood loss just before we arrived,' he says calmly. He nods to the building where Oklar and Jereminus are. 'That should be the station's main facility, where you will find the infirmary, communications room and supplies store. Get the wounded sorted out and then see what you can find that might tell us what has happened here.'

It's with a start that I realise that I'd completely forgotten we were hunting 'nids down here. And there was me just barging into a place without even checking what was inside. I almost deserved to have my head clawed off for being so stupid. I see now that the Colonel's ordered a firesweep of the settlement to make sure there isn't anything nasty still lurking around, and he expects me to sort out the control centre. I shout for the five survivors of Franx's squad to follow me, before touching the open rune on the door control panel. With a hiss the portal slides out of sight, letting the twilight spill into the corridor beyond. I pull my laspistol from its holster and peek around the corner, seeing nothing out of the ordinary, just a plain rockcrete-floored corridor stretching away into darkness, a couple of doors in the wall about five metres down on either side.

'Well, power's still working,' I hear Crunch say loudly from behind me. I curse inwardly when I realise he's one of the men still alive. We call him Crunch for his total inability to sneak around anywhere. He'll always find a twig to tread on, a piece of razorwire to get snagged in or a glass crucible to knock over, even in the middle of a desert. Just the man I need to slip undetected into a potentially hostile building!

'Crunch, you stay here and watch the entrance,' I tell him, motioning the others inside with a wave of my laspistol. He nods and stands to attention by the side of the door, lasgun in the shouldered-arms position.

'At ease, trooper,' I say to him as I step past, and hear him let out a sigh and relax. Shaking my head in irritation, I sneak down the corridor in a half-crouch. I can see artificial light under the door to the right, while a quick check of the left-hand door shows that the lock has been activated. I haven't got time to worry about that right now and signal the four men with me to go through the right-hand doorway. Inside is a small administration room, illuminated by a yellow lightstrip halfway up the far wall. A portable terminal is next to the door on a rickety-looking wooden table, its screen blank, the interface pad carefully stowed in the recharging pouch on the side of the storage banks. I make a mental note to come back and try to start the machine up once we've ensured the rest of the building is clear. There's a rack of record scrolls on the other side of the doorway, and I take out the one nearest the bottom, which should be the most recent. It's written in what looks to be Techna-lingua, the code used by the tech-priests, but I recognise the date in the top left corner. It's about forty days old, give or take a few days, so it's safe to assume that whatever happened occurred roughly six weeks ago, unless there's another reason why they stopped making records before then.

Remembering the crew of the ship that discovered False Hope, I wonder if the people in the research station weren't just killed by the denizens of the horrible world they lived on, rather than there being any tyranids involved. But that didn't make a careful sweep of the building any less necessary.

The next five rooms we check turn out to be dormitories, each with four bunks, though there's no actual bedding to be found. There's also no sign of any personal belongings at all, reinforcing the spookiness of the abandoned settlement, making the hairs on the back of my neck stand up as we look around, like in a graveyard or something. All we keep finding are the same fibrous pods that I picked up in the first building on the outskirts. By the time we've exhausted our search along the corridor, there's a pile of twenty or so by the main entrance. I don't know why they've been left behind when everything else has gone, but that's a puzzle to sort out another time, there's more urgent matters, like making sure I'm safe.

All the other routes explored, I turn my attention back to the locked door. I study the locking mechanism, which is a numberpad next to the door, and it looks like there's no chance of trying to work out what the cipher is.

'Ah, frag it!' I declare to the galaxy in general and loose off a bolt from my laspistol at the panel, which explodes in a shower of green sparks. I hear the noise of something heavy dropping on the other side of the wall and make a push at the door, which swings inwards easily. I peer inside, laspistol held ready, crouched to duck back out of sight in an instant. Inside are more terminals, although these appear to be wired in, standing on rockcrete plinths along the walls of a room roughly twenty metres long and ten wide. There's another door at the far end, already open, and through it I can see more lights, and two rows of beds. Everything is totally still, no noises except those filtering in from outside, no signs of movement or any kind of life. Dead, a worried part of my mind tells me.

There's a closed door to the right, and I decide to check in there first, not wanting to leave a potential hiding place behind me. The large room we're standing in is obviously the main control chamber, probably where the communications array is. We slip through the door to the right, lasweapons at the ready, but there's nobody inside. The side door leads us into a wide space, filled with metal cages on wheels, each full of boxes marked with an Imperial eagle and notations of shipping dates and so on. This is the store room, obviously, and it appears that there's the usual combat rations, water purification tonics, spare uniforms and some technical equipment. The cages are all still closed with simple padlocks and so it doesn't look like anything was taken by force. That probably rules out pirates, which is one of the thoughts that had occurred to me when

looking into the sleeping chambers, which seemed as if they
might have been looted.

'Okay, let's check out the ward,' I tell the men, pushing my way
past them and back into the control room. Two of them hang
back, covering us with their lasguns, while the other pair and me
stand either side of the door. I take a quick peek inside and see
that the beds are all empty, ten of them each side of the narrow
room. I duck through the doorway and scuttle behind the nearest to the right, waving the other two with me, Donalson and
Fredricks, to the left-hand side. Glancing behind me to check
that the troopers behind have followed us to the door, I begin to
creep along the space between the two rows of beds, keeping
bent, laspistol pointed in front of me. We're about halfway
along, seven or eight metres from the door, when a movement
to my right catches my attention. At the far end of the room,
there's an archway leading into some kind of ante-chamber and
I think I can see something moving about inside.

I shuffle to my left to get a better view and can see a high desk
inside the small room, in front of a tall bookshelf filled with
tomes and rolled parchments. I can hear something scraping
on the floor, perhaps something trying to keep out of sight
behind the desk. I gesture with my thumb towards the archway
and Fredricks gives a nod and begins to slink very slowly
towards it, lasgun cradled across his chest. My breath is coming
in shallow gasps at the moment, my whole body tensed and
ready for action. I can hear my heart beating, the blood coursing through my ears like the rush of a waterfall. It seems like an
eternity is passing as Fredricks makes his way crabwise towards
the other room.

There's movement in there again and we all react at the same
time, a sudden torrent of las-fire flashing through the archway
into the room. The air is filled with the crackling of energy. My
heart is hammering in my chest, glad for the sudden release,
and I can hear myself growling between gritted teeth. There's a
shrill screech from the room and we fire another volley,
Donalson spitting incomprehensible curses between gritted
teeth as he fires, an incoherent yell bursting from my own lips
as I pull repeatedly on the trigger of my laspistol.

'Stop shooting, Emperor damn you!' I hear a high-pitched,
strained voice cry out from the ante-chamber. The three of us
exchange startled glances.

'Who are you?' I shout back, aiming my pistol into the far room in case a target should present itself.

'I'm Lieutenant Hopkins,' the voice calls back and he shuffles into view, hands held high above his head. He's a little older than me, scrawny-looking with lank hair and a straggly beard on his cheeks and chin. He's wearing a crumpled uniform of some sort: dress jacket a deep red with white breeches and knee-high black boots. He has a slightly tarnished epaulette on one shoulder, the frogging hanging from it frayed and lacklustre. I relax only a little and stand up, still pointing the laspistol at him. He grins when he sees our uniforms, lowers his hands and takes a step forward.

'Stay where you fraggin' are!' I shout, taking a step towards him, laspistol now levelled at his head.

'Are you Imperial Guard? Which regiment are you from?' he asks, voice trembling. I can see his whole body shaking with nerves, obviously distressed that the people he thought were his saviours might still turn out to be his killers.

'It's okay,' I tell him, lowering my laspistol, although I leave the safety catch off and don't holster it. 'We're from the 13th Penal Legion. Colonel Schaeffer's Last Chancers.'

'Penal legion?' he says vaguely, lifting his peaked cap and scratching at his head. 'What the hell are you doing here?'

'I think that's a question you should be answering,' I tell him.

DONALSON BRINGS Lieutenant Hopkins from where he's been guarding him in the administration room. I'm sat with the Colonel and Sergeants Broker and Roiseland in the command centre. He looks around curiously, seeing the terminals we've managed to reactivate. It's pitch dark outside; all I can see through the small slit windows are reflections of the interior of the command room. Even through the thick walls I can hear the constant chirruping of insects and the occasional screech of some nocturnal bird or whatever.

'You are Lieutenant Hopkins, of the False Hope garrison company,' the Colonel says. 'I am Colonel Schaeffer, commanding the 13th Penal Legion. I would like an explanation of what has happened to False Hope Station.'

Hopkins gives a quick salute, fingers of his right hand hovering by the peak of his cap for a moment, before his arm drops limply back by his side.

'I wish I could offer one, colonel,' he says apologetically, darting a longing look at an empty chair next to Broker. He seems all but dead on his feet, there's darkness around his eyes and his skin hangs loosely from his cheeks. The Colonel nods towards the seat and Hopkins sits down gratefully, slouching against the high back of the chair with visible relief. I wave Donalson away, and turn my attention to the Colonel. His ice-blue eyes are still fixed on Hopkins, looking right inside him, trying to work out who the man is.

'Records show that at the last count there were seventy-five Guardsmen and one hundred and forty-eight civilians in False Hope Station,' the Colonel says, glancing at a datasheet in his hands. 'Now there is only you. I think you would agree that this situation demands investigation.'

Hopkins looks helplessly back at the Colonel and gives a weak shrug.

'I don't know what happened to the others,' he says miserably. 'I've been stuck here on my own for thirty-five days now, trying to work out how to get the communications assembly working.'

'Tell me what you remember before then,' the Colonel says sternly, handing the datasheet to Roiseland.

'I was ill in the infirmary,' Hopkins tells us, looking through the doorway towards the ward, where Franx and the others are now safely tucked in. We broke into the medicine chest to get more bandages and stimm-needles. None of us is a medico, so it's down to the Emperor whether they live or die. 'I'd come down with blood poisoning, a local plague we call jungle flu. I'd been leading an expedition through to the sulphur marshes about twenty kays west of here and I caught a dose. The men brought me back, I remember Physician Murrays giving me one of his elixirs and then I must have fallen unconscious. When I woke up, the place was as you find it now.'

'Before the expedition,' the Colonel asks him, gaze never wandering for a second, 'was there anything untoward happening? Was there any sign of danger to the settlement?'

'Our commander, Captain Nepetine, had been acting a bit strangely,' Hopkins admits with a frown. 'He'd been doing some exploration towards the Heart of the Jungle with twenty of the men, and came back alone. He said he'd found a better location for a settlement, one that wasn't as hostile as the area we're in.'

'The Heart of the Jungle?' I ask before I can stop myself, earning myself a scowl from the Colonel.

'Yes,' Hopkins says, not noticing the Colonel's annoyance. 'It's the thickest part of the jungle on the whole planet, about three days march further up the equatorial ridge. It was stupid, because there's nowhere near there at all that could be any more hospitable than where we are. I mean, the whole planet is virtually one big jungle, right up to the poles. Every acre is solid with trees and plants, horrible insects, giant predators and countless hideous diseases. I said so, and the other officers, Lieutenants Korl and Paximan, agreed with me.'

'Do you think that Captain Nepetine may have persuaded the others to leave while you were comatose?' the Colonel asks, absent-mindedly tapping a finger on his knee.

'It's unlikely, sir,' Hopkins says with a doubtful look. 'They were both in vehement agreement with me the last time we spoke about it.'

The Colonel gestures to Sergeant Broker, who pulls one of the empty pod things from a sack under his chair and passes it to Hopkins.

'What is this?' the Colonel asks, pointing towards the object in Hopkins's hands.

'I haven't seen anything like it before,' the lieutenant says. 'I'm no bio-magus, but it looks similar to the seed pods that some of the trees around here use for reproducing. I'm afraid that Lieutenant Paximan was liaison to our Adeptus Mechanicus comrades, I had little to do with the study itself. It's a lot bigger than anything I've seen though, I'm sure I would remember a specimen of this size. If it really is a seed pod, the tree or bush it came from must be enormous. Even the pods from trees over thirty metres tall are only the size of my hand, a quarter of the size of this one.'

'Could it be offworld in origin?' the Colonel asks, his face as neutral as ever. I look at him sharply, realising that he thinks it might be some kind of tyranid organism. I feel the urge to glance over my shoulder, wondering what else is lurking in the jungles out there, as well as all the native killers of False Hope.

'I suppose it could be, but I can't say for sure one way or the other,' Hopkins tells us with a sorrowful look. 'I'm not a specialist in plants or anything, I just run, I mean ran, the camp.'

'Can you take us to the Heart of the Jungle?' Schaeffer asks, finally standing up and beginning to pace back and forth. I wondered how long it would take him before being confined to a chair made him too fidgety. He's obviously concocting some kind of plan, otherwise he'd be content just to sit and ask questions.

'I could lead the way,' Hopkins admits with a shallow nod of the head.

'But?' the Colonel adds.

'All the heavy-duty exploration equipment has gone,' he says with a grimace. 'I checked before, thinking the same thing you do, that I could go after them. But without that sort of gear, one man on his own won't last the first night out in the trees.'

'Well,' the Colonel says, looking at each of us in turn. My heart sinks, knowing what he's going to say next. 'We are more than one man, so I am sure we will survive.'

'Sir?' I interject. 'What about the wounded? They won't be able to make another trip into the jungle.'

'If they can march by tomorrow morning, they come with us,' he says meeting my anxious gaze without a hint of compassion in his eyes. 'If not, we leave them here.'

I'VE BEEN ASLEEP only a short while when sounds of footsteps padding across the rockcrete floor wake me up. Someone's coughing violently from the furthest beds, near the chamber where we found Hopkins. I'm bedded down in the control room with Kronin and a couple of the sergeants, ready to act if any communication comes down from our transport in orbit. In the pale glimmer of the moonlight streaming through the narrow windows of the infirmary I can see a shadow gingerly stepping towards me. Thinking it may be Rollis out for some revenge, I put my hand under the pillow, my fingers closing around the grip of my knife. As the figure gets closer, I can see it's too tall to be Rollis and I relax.

'Kage!' I hear Gappo's terse whisper. 'Franx has woken up.'

I sling my blanket to one side and get up. I see Gappo, barefoot and wearing only his fatigues, leaning on the doorframe and peering into the gloom of the control centre. It's sultry inside the command centre, the rockcrete trapping the humidity and heat of the False Hope day, and I'm covered in a light sheen of sweat. I follow Gappo along the row of beds, towards the intense coughing.

'Kill 'im now,' I hear someone murmur from the darkness. 'That coughin's kept me awake for ages.'

'Drop dead yourself!' I snap back, wishing I could identify the culprit, but it's too dark.

Franx looks a state, his face doused in perspiration, his curls plastered across the tight skin of his forehead, his cheeks hollow. Even the gleam of the moonlight cannot hide the yellowish tinge to his features. His breathing comes in wheezes through his cracked lips. Every few seconds he erupts into a spasm of coughing, blood flecks appearing on his lips. But his eyes are brighter than before, with an intelligent look in them that I haven't seen during the past day.

'You look rougher than a flatulent ork's arse,' I tell him, sitting on the end of the bed. He grins at me, and I can see the reddish stains on his teeth from the blood he's been coughing up.

'Nobody's going to paint portraits of you either, scarface!' he manages to retort before his body convulses with more racking coughs.

'Do you think you'll be able to walk, come the morning?' Gappo asks, concern on his face.

'Fresh air will do me good. Hate infirmaries; always full of sick people,' the sergeant jokes.

Gappo looks at me, his expression one of worry. He's a caring soul at heart, I'm amazed he's managed to survive this long, but in battle he's just as steady as the next man.

'Course you can march in the morning,' I say to Franx. 'And if you need a little help, there are those who'll give you a hand.'

He nods without saying anything and settles back into the bed, closing his eyes, his breathing still ragged.

'What about the other two?' I ask Gappo, who appointed himself chief medico as soon as he heard about the Colonel's decree to leave behind anyone who couldn't make the march.

'Oklar's got one leg left. How do you think he's doing?' the former preacher snaps bitterly. 'Jereminus will be fine, he's just badly concussed.'

'Can we pump Oklar full of stimms before we leave, set him up on some kind of crutch?' I ask, trying to figure a way to deny the Colonel another corpse.

'It might work, providing we can take a bagful of stimm-needles with us to keep him and Jereminus going,' Gappo agrees, looking slightly dubious.

'Well, sort it out,' I tell him. 'I'm going back to bed.'

OKLAR SAVED GAPPO the trouble: stabbed himself through the eye with a stimm-needle left by his bed. The point drove into his brain and killed him instantly. We set out just after dawn yesterday, following Hopkins and the Colonel. Turning westward as soon as we left False Hope station, we climbed up onto a high ridge that Hopkins tells us runs the whole length of the planet's equator. We're marching at the front – me, Kronin, Gappo, Linskrug and Franx's squad, taking it in turns to give Franx a shoulder to lean on. He's stopped coughing blood, but is continuously short of breath. Broker's squad is looking after Jereminus, the sergeant taking custody of a dozen stimms smuggled out of the infirmary by Gappo.

The jungle hasn't been too thick, finding it harder to grow on the dense rock of the volcanic ridge. The air gets even hotter, more choked with sulphur and ashes, as we progress. We can't see them through the jungle canopy, but Hopkins tells us that there's two massive volcanoes a few kilometres away to the south, called Khorne's Twins by the False Hope settlers, named by the original ship's crew after some unholy and violent god. Heresy and blasphemy, but I guess they were getting pretty low on faith at the time. The lieutenant assures us they've been dormant recently, but knowing our luck they'll both blow any moment, just so things don't get too easy for us. My head filled with these gloomy thoughts, I sense somebody falling in beside me and glance right to see Hopkins walking alongside.

'He's Sergeant Franx, is that right?' he asks, glancing towards where the sergeant's stumbling along hanging on to Poal. I nod.

'He must have the constitution of a grox,' Hopkins adds, still looking at the half-crippled Franx.

'He used to,' I say, not being able to stop myself. 'But this sodding sump of a planet of yours might kill him yet.'

'It may yet,' agrees Hopkins with a disconsolate look. 'He's got lungrot, and there's not many survive that.'

'Any more encouraging news?' I ask sourly, wishing he'd frag off and leave me alone.

'He's still alive, and that's half a miracle,' he tells me with a smile. 'Most men don't last the first night. He's lasted two, both of them after days of marching. He won't get any better, but I don't think he'll get any worse.'

'If he was any worse, he'd be dead,' I say, looking over at the wasted figure almost draped over Poal's sunburnt shoulders. 'And looking at him, I'm not sure that would be worse.'

'Don't say that!' Hopkins exclaims.

'What?' I snap back at him. 'You think he's going to survive for long in the Last Chancers while he's in that state? Even if he gets out of this cess tank, the next battle'll kill him, that I'm sure.'

'How long does he have left in the penal legion?' Hopkins asks, pulling a canteen from his belt and proffering it towards me. I irritably wave it away.

'We're all here until we either die or get pardoned by the Colonel,' I tell him, my voice harsh.

'And how many people has he pardoned?' asks Hopkins innocently.

'None,' I snarl, quickening my step to leave the annoying lieutenant behind.

DAWN ON THE third day of the march sees us on the ridge above the area Hopkins calls the Heart of the Jungle. From up here it doesn't look any different from the rest of the Emperor-forsaken jungle, but he assures me that inside the undergrowth is a lot thicker, the trees are a lot bigger and closer together.

'That's where our captain was exploring,' he tells me as we stand in the orange glow of the rising sun, pointing southwards at an area that might be a slightly darker green than the surrounding trees.

'This captain of yours, was he a bit mad or something?' I ask, taking a swig of dentclene from a foil pouch and swilling it around my mouth before spitting the foamy liquid into a puddle by the lieutenant's feet.

'Not really,' he says, stepping back from the splash and giving me an annoyed glance. 'As far as I know, he was perfectly stable.'

He hesitates for a second as if he's going to say more, but closes his mouth and turns away to look at the sunrise.

'What is it?' I ask. He turns back, takes his cap off and scratches his head, a gesture I've noticed him using whenever he seems to be worried about something.

'Do you really think that those seed pods could be some kind of tyranid weapon?' he asks, crumpling the top of his cap in his hand.

'I've seen stranger things,' I tell him, leaning closer, as if confiding something secret to him. 'On Ichar IV, the tech-priests are still trying to eradicate swarms of tyranid bugs, which eat anything organic they come across. I've seen bio-titans twenty-five metres tall, great four-legged things that can trample buildings and crush battle tanks in their huge claws. You ever seen a tyranid?'

'I've seen sketches,' he says hesitantly, placing his creased cap back on his head.

'Sketches?' I laugh. 'Sketches are nothing! When you've got a four-metre tall tyranid warrior standing in front of you, then you know what tyranids are like. Its carapace oozes this lubricant slime to keep the plates from chafing, it's got fangs as long as your fingers and four arms. They stink of death, when they're really close it's almost suffocating. They use all kinds of symbiote weapons to blast, tear, cut and grind you apart.'

I remember the first time I saw them, on Ichar IV. Three warriors jumped us as we were doing a firesweep of some old ruins. I can see clearly now their dark blue skin and reddish-black bony plates as they stormed forward. The shock and fear that swept over us when we first saw them, unnatural and unholy in every way. They had guns we call devourers, spitting out a hail of flesh-eating grubs that can chew straight through you, worse than any bullet. Our lasgun shots just bounced off them, and those who didn't fall to the devourers had their heads ripped off and limbs torn free by their powerful claws. It was only Craggon and his plasma gun that saved us, incinerating the alien monstrosities as they carved through us. As it was, those three tyranid warriors killed fifteen men before they were brought down. I remember Craggon died later on Ichar IV, his blood soaking into the ash wastes when a tyranid gargoyle dropped from the skies and tore out his throat.

Hopkins is visibly shaken, his face pale under his deep tan. I point towards my face, or rather the maze of scars criss-crossing it. I still don't think he understands the horror of the tyranids and decide to press the point. People have to know about the abominations we face out here in the stars.

'I got these from a tyranid spore mine,' I say fiercely, wishing he'd never brought up tyranids, wishing that of all the horrors I've faced, I could forget about the carnage of Ichar IV and the terrifying, bowel-loosening horror that the tyranids represent. No one who wasn't there, hasn't fought them, can really understand what they're like, it's like trying to describe the ocean to a blind man. 'Damn thing exploded as close to me as you're standing now, threw me to the ground with the burst of gasses. Bits of razor-sharp carapace shrapnel damn near tore my face off! Franx bound my head up with his shirt to stop the bleeding. I was in agony for weeks, even on regular stimm doses. I'm lucky I've still got both my eyes, Franx tells me. There were men in my platoon who had limbs ripped off in that explosion, had holes punched straight through them. Others lost their skin and muscles to acid from the spore mine, burning through clean to the bone. Do you know what it looks like, a man with bio-acid searing through his body, eating away at him? Do you know what his screams sound like?'

'I… I…' he stutters, looking at me in a new, horrified way.

'Next time you look at one of those sketches,' I tell him scornfully, 'just you remember that, and just you try to imagine it.'

He stands there, mouth hanging open, eyes blank. I snarl wordlessly and stalk off up the ridge, wishing he hadn't reminded me about Ichar IV.

POAL CURSES CONSTANTLY as he hacks with his bayonet at the branches and vines around us. Hopkins wasn't exaggerating when he said this was the worst part of jungle on the whole of False Hope. It's nearly dusk, and we've travelled perhaps two kilometres down the ridge. We're nearly at the bottom, that much I can tell, but if we have to keep going like this for more than another day or two, we're all going to starve or die of thirst. We found one pool, but it was tainted with sulphur from the volcanoes. Franx thought of catching the rain in canteens, but Hopkins told us there are certain plants, parasites way up near the treetops, which dissolve their spores in the rainwater, so that the stuff cascading down through the trees carries a deadly curse.

One man didn't believe him and tried it anyway. His throat swelled up within an hour and he choked to death. We lost another trooper to poisoned thorn bushes, the lacerations on the guardsman's legs filling with pus almost in minutes. I shot him, after he begged me to. Hopkins agreed, saying that the infection would pass through his bloodstream into his brain, driving him insane before he died. I began to feel a little more respect for Hopkins after that, when I realised he must have seen his fair share of horrors in this place.

'We need to find a campsite for the night,' Hopkins tells the Colonel as we wait for the men to cut a path through the wall of vegetation in front of us.

'We will look for somewhere when we reach the ridge bottom,' he says, dabbing at the sweat on his cheeks with the handkerchief still stained with the giant lizard's blood. At a shout from Poal we turn our attention back to the troopers, who seem to have found some kind of trail. I spy Linskrug among the throng and we exchange a knowing glance. Trails mean bad news in the jungle. Still, the Colonel steps through the opening and I follow, Hopkins close behind. It's almost like a living tunnel, the foliage curves above us to form a solid canopy, and the closeness of the trunks, intertwined with vines as thick as your arm, make a near-impenetrable wall to either side. With a glance back to check we're following, the Colonel sets off and we file after him.

IT'S ALMOST impossible to tell how long we've been in the labyrinth of plants. The only real light is a kind of glow from the dying sun seeping through and reflecting off the leaves around us. A few patches of luminous fungi, which grow more frequent the further we press on, cast a sickly yellow aura across the path and fill the air with a decaying smell. Side tunnels, or that's what I'd call them, branch off now and then, and it soon becomes obvious we're in an extensive network of paths. The roots of the trees higher up the ridge jut out of the ground around us, twisting about each other in the centuries-long fight with each other for sustenance. There is no sound at all except our own laboured breathing, because if it was hot before, we're being boiled in our uniforms now. Sweat constantly runs from every pore in my body, soaking my fatigues and shirt, making them stick in wet folds to my body.

The air is still, no chance of a breeze through the layers of greenery surrounding us. My mouth is full of salt from my own sweat, drying on my lips, making me want to keep licking them clean. My eyes are gummed up with sweat as well, forcing me to squint in the half-light as I shuffle along, trying not to trip on the roots snaking across the path. Franx is just behind me, recovered enough to be walking on his own now, but just barely. The moisture in the air is playing hell with his lungs, making him cough constantly. Still we stumble on, following the stiff-backed outline of the Colonel forging ahead.

All of a sudden we find ourselves in an open space. It's like a massive amount of pressure is lifted, the air seeming to clear slightly. There's movement in the branches around us, like the wind, and as the rest of the troopers trudge in behind us, we drop to the floor. I close my eyes and take a deep lungful of air. The humidity isn't so bad, but there's another tinge to the atmosphere in here. I take a deep sniff, trying to identify where I know the scent from. It's like rotting flesh or something. Perhaps there's a dead animal nearby.

'Kage…' croaks Franx, and I sit up and look over to where he's lying flat out a few metres to my right.

'What?' I ask, seeing a disturbed look on his face.

'I think I'm having delusions,' he tells me, pointing straight up. 'I can see people up in the trees.'

I follow his gaze upwards, squinting to look into the canopy that arches about thirty metres above our heads. I see a tremor of movement and stare even harder, blinking the sweat from my eyes. A shiver of fear courses through me as I pick out the shape of a woman directly above me, half-cocooned in a nest of leaves and vines.

'C-colonel…' I stammer, seeing more and more bodies hanging in the branches overhead, mind balking at how they could have got there.

'I know,' he says grimly, pulling his power sword from its scabbard, the blue glow of its blade casting shadows in the leafy cavern. The others have noticed too, and they're stumbling about, looking upwards and pointing in disbelief.

'Kage!' shouts Linskrug. I look back. I see what he's seen – the entrance to the chamber has disappeared, there's just a solid wall of branches and leaves all around us.

'Get those flamers burning!' I call out to the men, noticing as I do that about a quarter of them are missing, presumably cut off on the far side of the vegetation.

'Some of them are alive,' hisses someone to my left, and I look up. I see an arm stretched out, withered as if drained of blood or something, but the fingers are slowly clenching. As I look around, I see that the movement in the leaves isn't caused by the breeze, it's more people, almost out of sight, writhing in their torment. I snatch my knife from my belt and run towards the nearest, hacking away at the leaves in between.

My eyes meet those of a young girl, pale grey and staring, her blonde hair covered in mud, twirled around the branches entombing her. She's trapped a metre from the ground. I rip at the leaves around her face with my spare hand and saw at a thick branch curled around her waist. She croaks something, but I can't understand what she's saying. Her face is pinched, the skin dry as parchment. To my left and right, others are tearing at the tree-prison, trying to pull people free. I manage to work my arm around the little girl's waist, trying to avoid her staring, pitiful gaze. I heave and she gives a gasp of pain. Pulling harder, I manage to get her head and chest out of the cocoon, but as she pitches forward I see thorns as long as my forearm but as thin as a finger are imbedded into her back. Her blood is leaking down her backbone. I grab the nearest spine and try to pull it free, but as I do so I feel something slithering around my left leg.

I look down and see a tendril pushing out of the ground, wrapping around my ankle. It tugs and I fall backwards, slamming hard into the mulchy ground, the knife jarred out of my hand. I curl forwards and grab the vine with both hands, trying to wrench my foot free, but the thing is incredibly strong. Suddenly Franx is there, sawing away at the tendril with his bayonet. Between the two of us, we manage to yank my foot free and we both stumble away from the plant. Others are doing the same, congregating around the Colonel where he stands in the middle of the green chamber. Some are too late, I can see them being enveloped by leaves, pushed upwards along the branches until they're a good few metres off the floor.

There's an explosion off to my right where a flamer cylinder is crushed, spewing flames over the branches and suddenly the area around the detonation is thrashing madly, tossing the burning canister away.

'We have to get out,' shouts Poal, glancing around for some avenue of escape. As far as I can see, there isn't one: we're trapped. We're in an unbroken dome of branches, vines and leaves, about sixty metres in diameter. All around us is a solid mass of vegetation, slowly creeping closer and closer, forcing us back to back in a circle. Men start firing their lasguns at the approaching vines, shearing through the tendrils with bolts of compressed light. But for every one that's blasted, another seems to snake forward, the whole of the cavern constricting around us. Something darts past my face and I hear Warnick scream, a fanged leaf slashing at his neck. His blood sprays over me and more of the horrid tentacles fasten on to him. I step away from him, only to feel someone bumping into my back, obviously avoiding something else. Glancing over my shoulder I see that it's the Colonel, teeth gritted, chopping through attacking tendrils with sweeps of his power sword. I'm gripped by a sudden desperation to get out, overwhelmed with the feeling of being trapped like a fly in a web.

Someone else jogs my elbow and I see that it's Hopkins, eyes wide, staring around at our leafy tomb.

'Treacherous bastard!' I spit, my fear suddenly turning to anger. I pull free my laspistol and push it against his temple, forcing him down to his knees. 'You knew what was here! You led us into a trap! You were the bait, weren't you? I'm gonna see you dead before I'm taken!'

He gives a shriek and throws himself down, curling up on the floor. I can hear him sobbing.

'Don't kill me,' he pleads. 'Don't kill me, I didn't know any of this. Please don't shoot me, I don't want to die. I don't want to die!'

It's obvious from his horror that he's telling the truth, that he wasn't left in the station to lure us here. He's just as dead as the rest of us, as well, so there's no point shooting him.

As the living chamber grows smaller, ten or perhaps twelve metres across now, I can see more and more of the poor souls captured inside. Some of them are corpses, that much is obvious from their sunken features and empty eyes. Others are still alive, their mouths opening and shutting with wordless pleas, their eyes full of terror, staring at me, imploring me to do something, but I'm just as helpless as they are.

'That's the captain!' I hear Hopkins shout, and I look to where he's pointing. There's a man in an officer's coat the same colour as Hopkins's jacket, his brown eyes staring intelligently at us, just a few metres away. His skin is almost glowing with health, in stark contrast to the wasted faces of the others trapped by the plant. I take a step towards him, but suddenly there's a dense fog in the air, a cloud of something that fills my mouth and nostrils. It's like the heavy incense the Ecclesiarchy use, almost making me gag. I see brown shapes in the leaves around me, ovals bigger than my head, and recognise them briefly as the same as the seed pods we found back at the station. My head feels stuffed with bandage gauze, I can't think straight with all of the stuff clogging up my throat. It's then that I hear a voice, almost like it's inside my head.

'Don't fight it,' it tells me, strangely melodic. 'The god-plant will make you immortal. Embrace the god-plant and it will reward you. Embrace it as I did. See its divine beauty, become part of the god-plant's great benevolence.'

Around me I dimly see many of the men stop struggling, staring in rapturous awe at the leaves curling down towards them. The air has a purple tint to it, like a haze across my vision, glittering slightly. My limbs feel leaden and I have to fight hard not to lose my grip on the laspistol.

'There is no point struggling,' the voice continues calmly. 'There will be no pain, the god-plant shall see to your needs. It will sustain you, even as you sustain it. Provide for the god-plant and it shall provide for you in return.'

The cloud of spores is thicker than ever, a purplish mist swirling around my head, fogging my vision and mind. I sense a leafy tendril sliding up my arm, curling towards my face. I feel weak at the knees, it would be so easy just to give in. To become one with the god-plant. I can feel its magnificence, spreading out all around me, its alien life coursing through roots and branches for many kilometres in every direction.

I feel tiny pinpricks of sensation on my neck and dumbly look down, seeing a red liquid seeping into the collar of my shirt. Somewhere in the back of my mind a distant voice tells me it's my own blood, but I don't really take any notice. My throat and neck are warming up, building in heat, like relaxing tonic spreading through my body.

The voice – *my* voice, I realise – is nagging at me to wake up, to shake off the plant. I feel very tired, but from deep within me I start to feel a surge of energy, welling up from my stomach. I feel my fingers twitching into life and my head clears a little. I gaze around, trying to look through the haze that has dropped over my eyes. I can see vague outlines of other people, as if through a fog, some of them standing still, others struggling violently. Noises, real noises from outside, filter through the dull humming filling my ears, strangled shouts and violent cursing.

Like waking from a deep sleep I rise to consciousness again, startled awake by the sharp pain in my neck. Shaking off the last vestiges of the dream-like state, I snatch the tendril biting into my neck and tear it free, my blood scattering in crimson droplets over its greeny-yellow leaf. With a snap I'm fully aware of what's going on again. The Colonel is standing to one side of me, slashing back and forth as vines snap towards him. Franx is on the other side, fallen to one knee, both hands fending off another leafy tentacle lunging for his face.

Without actually thinking about it, I begin snapping shots off from my laspistol, bolts of light flaring into the plant around us, severing tendrils and slashing through leaves.

'Kage!' the Colonel barks over his shoulder at me. 'Hold these off. I will deal with Nepetine.'

He takes a step towards the captain and I jump to fill his place, my laspistol spitting bolts of energy into the green, writhing mass still slowly constricting on us. There's a lull in the attack, the god-plant concentrating its alien limbs on picking up the men who are standing around in dumb acquiescence, pulling them away and into the branches above our heads, their limbs dangling lifelessly like dolls. I see the Colonel fighting with Nepetine, the captain's arms flailing weakly at Schaeffer as the Colonel pushes his hands deep into the leafy folds surrounding Nepetine.

'Step back,' orders the Colonel, pushing me and some of the others away from the captain. A second later and there's a roaring noise, a flame blossoms around Nepetine, shredding the god-plant, throwing pulpy vegetation and human flesh all over us, covering us in blood and sticky sap. The god-plant suddenly recoils, the branches thrashing madly as they rapidly draw away into the distance. The dome retreats slightly, giving us room to spread out a little.

'Anybody still got a flamer?' I shout out, casting my gaze over the few dozen of us left, keen to grab the offensive while we still have the chance. 'Repentance' Clain, murderer of seventeen women, steps forward, the ignition flame on his weapon burning with a piercing blue light in the gloom of the god-plant's bowels.

'Burn a way out!' I snarl viciously, pointing vaguely in the direction where we came in. Repentance gives a grim smile and jogs up to the receding walls. With a torrent of flame that hurts my eyes to look at he opens up, the flammable liquid splashing across the leaves and branches, turning them into an instant inferno. He blasts gout after gout of fire into the retreating vegetation, the whoosh of the flamer accompanied by the crack of burning branches and the staccato popping of exploding seed pods. The leafy wall draws back even more rapidly, trying to get away from the deadly flames. The rest of us join him, firing our own weapons around the flames, forcing the god-plant to open up even further. After we've blasted our way a good hundred metres clear of the chamber, there's still no sign of the men who were cut off, presumably they're already dead.

A few tendrils half-heartedly snake towards us from the ceiling, but the Colonel easily hacks them apart with his power sword. Slowly but steadily we push forwards, the god-plant relenting before our ferocious attack, closing behind us but too far away to be dangerous. I don't know how I can tell, but the god-plant seems to be getting more and more desperate, something in the uncoordinated way it flings biting leaves at us, something about the gradually yellowing, sickly colour of its foliage. We press on, letting the flamers do the work.

The air is filled with the stench and smoke of burning plant, choking me and stinging my eyes as I stumble after the flamer teams. Franx is coughing up so hard now that Poal and one of his men have to carry him again. The green light, tinged with sudden bursts of red and yellow from the flamers, is making me feel sick as well. For what seems like half a lifetime, we push our way forwards through the depths of the god-plant, fending off its ever weakening attacks. I feel the ground rising and I realise we are starting up the ridge. I'm surprised by how far this thing extends, how long we were wandering around inside it, oblivious to the peril as it let us get closer and closer to its centre, where I suppose it thought we would never escape.

It's with a shock that we burst through onto the open rock of the ridge. Glancing behind me, I see the others come stumbling out, some turning around to open up with a fusillade of lasfire to drive back the god-plant's alien limbs as they creep towards us. Gasping and cursing, we haul ourselves up the rocky slope. There's no other vegetation around, obviously devoured by the god-plant to make room for itself.

After a few minutes we're far enough away, half way up the ridge, the going a lot easier without the twisting confines of the god-plant's outer reaches to ensnare and misdirect us. I turn and look back and I can see the god-plant contracting. Its outer edges are a sickly yellow colour by now, looking like grass in a drought. It leaves bare, grey dirt in the wake of its retreat, drained of all nutrition.

'Sergeant Poal,' I hear the Colonel saying behind me as I continue to stare at the plant monstrosity, 'get your comms-operator to call down the shuttles, and order a bombardment of that… thing.'

It's the first time I've ever heard the Colonel almost lost for words. Dragging my gaze away from the strange beast, I push myself a few more steps up the ridge to stand next to the Colonel. Hopkins is there, blood pouring down from a cut above his right eye.

'Well, that was something,' the lieutenant pants, gazing in amazement at the god-plant.

'What the hell was it?' Franx asks, flopping down exhaustedly on a patch of mud in front of me. Others are collapsing around us, staring vacantly at the sky. Some fall to their knees, hands clasped in front of them as they offer up thanks to the Emperor. The Colonel steps forward, gazing intently towards the god-plant.

'Whatever it was,' he says with a hint of satisfaction, 'it is going to be dead soon. I am tempted to request this whole world be virus bombed, just to make sure.'

'What did you do, sir?' Hopkins asks, dabbing a cuff gingerly to the cut on his forehead.

'Frag grenades,' the Colonel replies, breaking his gaze from the view to look at the lieutenant. 'I have heard tales of such symbiotic creatures, though I have never heard of them taking plant form. They lie dormant for centuries, perhaps even millennia, until they can ensnare an alien mind. They form a link with their victim, somehow using their intelligence. Captain Nepetine seemed the conduit for that connection, so I blew him apart with fragmentation grenades. I think we were right at its centre, the damage we did was considerable.'

He looks over all of us, before fastening his gaze on me.

'Those we left behind were weak,' he says sternly. 'To give in to alien domination is one of the greatest acts of treachery against the Emperor. Remember that well.'

I remember how close I came to succumbing and say nothing.

It's with a good feeling in the pit of my stomach that I look out of the shuttle window as we roar up into the sky of False Hope. Out of the window I can see a raging fire, setting light across hundreds of square kilometres of jungle. Another bright flash descends from orbit into the ground with an explosion as our transport ship, the *Pride of Lothus*, fires another shot from its plasma driver into the god-plant.

'Burn, you alien piece of crap,' I whisper, rubbing the fresh scabs on my neck. 'Burn!'

THREE
BAD LANDINGS

THE FEELING IN the cell is even tenser than normal. Everybody's shaken up by what happened on False Hope, the memory of our fellow Last Chancers being eaten by the god-plant fresh in our memories. To make matters even worse, there's been no sign of the Colonel for the past three weeks. Talking to the ratings, it seems he disappeared on a rapid transport two days after we left False Hope orbit, taking Hopkins with him.

Not wanting to think about the future, determined to leave the past behind, I try to lose myself in the day-to-day drudgery. I've had to reorganise the men again: there are only forty-seven of us left. I've made an ad-hoc command squad out of Franx, Kronin, Gappo, Linskrug, Becksbauer and Fredricks. The other men are organised into four squads, with Poal, Donalson, Jorett and Slavini as the sergeants. Everyone's getting really shaky now; I need the calmest heads in charge if I'm ever going to survive this whole mess. With less than fifty of us left, we're a below-strength platoon, not even a full company of men. There's an unspoken feeling floating around the unit, a feeling that the end is getting very close. Roughly three thousand nine hundred and fifty Last Chancers have died in the past two and a half years, I can't see forty-seven of us surviving the next battle. Not if the Colonel comes back.

The thought of the Colonel's not returning doesn't leave me too optimistic either, I can't help feeling he's dumped us. There are too few of us to do anything useful that I can think of. I mean, given time the Departmento Munitorum can muster regiments numbering thousands of men, so what can four dozen Last Chancers do? In my gossiping with the ratings I've also learnt that we're heading to a system called Hypernol for re-supply. On the face of it, there seems nothing particularly odd about that. On the other hand, I can remember some of the men, dead now, who had been drafted in from a penal colony in the Hypernol system. The Colonel leaving and us being shipped to a penal colony – coincidence? I don't think so. He's left us to rot, I'm sure of it.

I'm not the only one to add two and two. As usual, Franx and Gappo are sitting with me during the sludge-eating gala they call meal time, a few cycles after dropping back into warpspace, some three weeks after leaving False Hope.

'Can't believe that's it,' Franx says vehemently, his voice a ragged whisper since his infection on the deathworld. 'Four thousand men dead, all over? Just like that, all finished? Doesn't make sense. What have we done? Fought in a bunch of wars, lots of men have died, but we haven't achieved anything. Can't believe this is the end.'

'You think there's some grander scheme?' laughs Gappo. 'Don't be naive! We're just meat in the Imperial grinder, nothing more.'

'What do you mean?' I ask the ex-preacher, slightly disturbed at his words.

'Sitting on a prison hulk or in some penal colony, we were just dead meat, carcasses hanging from the body of humanity,' he replies after a moment's thought. 'We're all criminals, according to the Colonel, who have wasted our chance to serve the Imperium. It doesn't matter if we live or die, as long as we're doing something useful. So they give us guns, put us into a war and let us hurl ourselves at the enemy.'

'That's stupid, too,' argues Franx, shaking his head. 'If we're such a waste, why bother sending us anywhere? Why not just kill us? Men are hung and beheaded and shot, all punishments listed in the Codex Imperialis. Having a naval transport at our beck and call is unheard of. Those resources don't come cheap, somebody owes the Navy.'

'That isn't normal, I'll grant you,' Gappo concedes with a thoughtful look. 'Then again, we've all heard the Colonel. He genuinely believes in our Last Chance, in giving us an opportunity to save our souls from Chaos by allowing us to serve the Emperor again.'

'Can't see how the Colonel has enough clout to have a Navy transport seconded to us,' counters Franx, wagging a finger at Gappo. 'For all the Colonel believes in his mission to save our souls, I don't think it's enough of an argument to convince the

Lord Admirals to give him a ship that can carry stores for fifty thousand fighting men, to ferry around a few hundred. Logistics don't make sense.'

'It's not just logistics, though,' I tell them, looking at Gappo then Franx. 'If you knew this was going to happen to you, would you have still defied the cardinal or let your men revolt against your superiors?'

'Not sure,' answers Franx, gnawing at his bottom lip in thought. 'Never really thought about it.'

'I know what you mean,' Gappo exclaims excitedly, as if he's just stumbled on some secret truth about the galaxy. 'It's the deterrent, you're saying?'

'We've been in twelve war zones now,' I remind them. 'How many other regiments have we come in contact with? There were at least thirty on our battlefront on Ichar IV; there's the Perditian Outriders from Octo Genesis, the Choreks at Deliverance, and about another ten from other places. They all saw or heard about the dirty jobs we have to do, the massive casualties we suffer. I know for a fact that if I'd seen this coming, my knife would have stayed firmly in my belt that time.'

'Still doesn't explain why there's a few dozen of us left,' Franx argues, his voice rasping and quiet. Gappo's about to answer back but Franx holds up his hand to stop him. He takes a sip of his juice before continuing. 'Throat feels on fire… Anyway, it would make sense to round up convicts as we travel. Four thousand men are as much a deterrent as fifty, much more useful military force.'

'So perhaps that's where the Colonel's gone,' I suggest with a smug smile. 'He's gone ahead to the penal colony to organise some new recruits. They'll be waiting for us when we arrive.'

'I don't know which would be worse,' Gappo laments, looking thoroughly miserable again. 'Getting locked up in a prison somewhere for the rest of my life, or dying on a battlefield.'

'I want to go down fighting,' I tell them firmly. 'Whether the Colonel's right or not about my immortal soul, I want to die doing something that's worth a damn. I joined the Guard to fight for the Emperor, I ain't gonna rot in a cell, be sure about that.'

'With you on this one, scarface,' Franx laughs. 'Give me a gun, a googly-eyed alien to shoot it at, and I'll die a happy man.'

* * *

IT'S ANOTHER TWENTY cycles before we drop from warp space into the Hypernol system. The tension and uncertainty is almost tearing us apart. A trooper called Dress was shot by the arms-men when he attacked a Navy warrant officer during unarmed combat drill. Another, Krilbourne, got a broken arm from a fight with Donalson, and everyone, including me, has a few bruises and cuts from flaring tempers. I've tried everything to ease the men: drilling them hard so they're too exhausted to scrap, organised a meal time rotation system so that everyone eats with everyone else and the squads don't get too isolated, stuff like that. None of it seems to be working too well, but then again maybe things would be a whole lot worse if I hadn't.

I'm not sure why I'm bothering, to be honest. Actually that's not true, when I think about it. On the face of it, I could quite happily let them strangle each other in their sleep, even Franx and Gappo, and I wouldn't shed a tear. Nearly four thousand in the regiment have died, and I hardly ever give them a second thought, except perhaps in my warp-dreams. No, it's not a concern for them individually that I'm worried about. It's my survival that bothers me. If the Last Chancers are going to keep going, which means I get to keep breathing, they need to stay sharp, need to keep it together as a fighting force. They always fight and bicker, more than even your normal Guardsmen, but in a fight they watch out for each other.

There's something about battle that unites men like us, whether it's for a common cause or, like us, just for survival. You're all in the same crap, and that makes a bond stronger than friendship or family. But as soon as the battle's finished, the cause is gone and they fragment again. I've come to realise a lot about these men, and myself along with them, over the past thirty months. They're born fighters, men who are at their best in combat. Any other situation and they're not worth a damn, but with a knife or a gun in their hands they seem a whole lot happier somehow. I know I am. I like to know that the man in front of me is the enemy and the one behind me is an ally. I can handle that without any problem. It's the rest of it that I can't stand: the politics and personalities, the responsibilities and the frustration and helplessness of it all. If you haven't been there, you might have some clue what I'm talking about, but to really understand you can't just watch, you have to take part.

* * *

I<small>T'S WITH CONFUSION</small> and trepidation that we're herded back into the cell after exercise; rumours are flying everywhere that the transport the Colonel left in has come back. My feelings are mixed, and I'm just waiting to see who's come with him, if anyone, before I start worrying about the future.

Sure enough, an hour later the cargo hold door opens and the Colonel steps in. I bark orders to the Last Chancers, forming them up for the unexpected inspection. The Colonel walks along the five ranks, looking intently at each of the men, before standing next to me.

'The men appear to be combat ready, Lieutenant Kage,' he quietly says to me.

'They are, sir,' I reply, keeping my eyes firmly directed forwards as my drill sergeant instructed me back in basic training.

'You have done well, Kage,' he tells me and my heart skips a beat. I barely stop my eyes flicking to the right to see his face. That's the first word of praise I've ever heard slip from the Colonel's lips. It's stupid, I know, but to hear him sound pleased makes me feel good. The praise of this murderous bastard, this unfeeling tyrant, makes me happy. I feel like a traitor to the other Last Chancers, but I can't stop myself.

'You will have to reorganise the squads again,' he tells me. 'You have some new troopers.' He takes a couple of steps back towards the door and gestures to the armsmen waiting in the corridor. Two figures walk into the cell chamber and I stare in amazement at them.

The two of them are almost identical. Both are tall and slender and dressed in urban camouflage fatigues. Even in the yellow light of the cell their skin is incredibly pale, almost white, and so is their hair. Not silvery grey with age, but pure white, cropped about two centimetres long. As they march into the hold and stand to attention in front of the Colonel I can see their eyes, strikingly blue, a lot darker than the icy colour of the Colonel's, but still very disturbing. Looking more closely at them, I see that the one on the left is a woman. I can see the roundness of small, firm breasts under her shirt, and a curve to her hips which is altogether quite pleasing to the eye. There were about forty women in the Last Chancers when we first started out, but the last of them, Aliss, was killed on Promor about a year ago. The only women I've seen since then were the Battle Sisters at Deliverance, and they were always wearing power armour.

'See that they settle in, lieutenant,' the Colonel orders, snapping me from my contemplation of the finer points of the female form. He strides out and everybody relaxes.

'Names?' I ask, walking up to the new pair, my eyes still drawn to the woman.

'I am Loron,' the man says, his voice quiet, almost feminine. He indicates his companion. 'This is Lorii, my sister.'

'I'm Kage. You two will join my squad,' I tell them, pointing towards where Franx and the others are lounging. Without a word they walk off, sitting next to each other near the wall, in the vicinity of the squad, but not really with them. Franx waves me over.

'Who are they?' he asks, staring at the two troopers.

'Loron and Lorii,' I tell him, pointing each one out. 'Twins, I reckon.'

'Not exactly your normal guardsmen, are they?' Linskrug mutters, stepping up beside Franx, his eyes following our gaze.

'What do you call a normal guardsman, baron?' Franx asks with venom in his voice. There's always been a bit of a thing between the two of them. I blame Franx's experience with the officers of his regiment for his distrust of anyone from the Imperial aristocracy. Linskrug didn't help himself; he was a bit off-hand when he first arrived a couple of years ago. But since then I think he's realised he's up to his neck in crap, just like the rest of us. Franx doesn't seem to have noticed the change, though.

'One with a bit of colour, I guess,' Linskrug chuckles, slapping Franx jovially on the shoulder. 'They do seem a bit distant though,' he adds.

'Quit staring, the pair of you!' I snap, tearing my own eyes away. 'They'll soon warm up, once they've shared a few meals and exercise periods. They certainly won't settle in with everybody giving them the wide-eyed treatment all the time.'

'Gives me a strange feeling,' Franx says with a mock shudder before strolling off. Linskrug wanders away after another few seconds, leaving me standing there with my own thoughts. I glance at the two again. It's odd, you'd think that combat fatigues would make a woman look more masculine, but to my eye the manly clothing only emphasises her female attributes even more. Giving myself a mental slap to clear my thoughts, I march away, hollering for Poal and Jorett's squads to report for exercise.

* * *

'WITCHERY, IT MUST be!' says Slavini, dropping to a crouch and bending his head forward to stretch the muscles in his back.

'I don't think they'd taint us with a thaumist,' I reply casually, continuing my own warm-up exercises.

'But nobody's heard them utter a word to each other,' protests the sergeant, standing up again. 'Twins are more prone to magical infection than others, everyone knows that.'

'Well, they keep themselves to themselves,' I admit, 'but I'd prefer that to more gossiping old women and bad-mouths like you.'

'Ah,' he says with a triumphant look, 'that's something else as well. In the week they've been here have they given you any trouble at all? Any fights started? Tried to steal anything?'

'No,' I tell him, rolling my head back and forth to loosen my neck. 'I wish you were all like them, in that respect.'

'So it stands to reason, doesn't it?' Slavini says emphatically, looking at me for some sign of agreement.

'What stands to reason?' I ask him irritably, wishing he'd talk sense for a change.

'Twins, perfectly behaved,' he says in a frustrated fashion, as if his point is obvious. 'Is there any other reason that they'd end up in the Last Chancers you can think of? Witchery, it has to be.'

'It doesn't have to be anything of the sort!' I argue. 'Perhaps they're cowards, that's why they're so quiet. Maybe they refused the order to attack or something.'

'They certainly don't come across to me as cowards,' Slavini counters, leaning against the wall and pulling a leg up behind him with his free hand. 'There's something hard-edge in there, not fear, when they meet your gaze.'

'Okay,' I admit, 'they don't seem to be cowards, but that doesn't make them psykers.'

'Does to me,' Slavini exclaims, getting the last word in before jogging off along the gantry. Shaking my head in disbelief at his stubbornness, I run after him.

LIKE EVERYONE ELSE, I gaze open mouthed as the albino twins walk back into the cell after their exercise break. Lorii is stripped from the waist up, displaying her perfectly formed chest to all and sundry, a sheen of sweat glistening on her alabaster skin. She's talking quietly to Loron, their heads leaning together as they walk, totally oblivious to all around them.

'Okay, put your eyes back in!' I snap at the men close by, and most of them avert their gaze. I notice Rollis still staring from where he's sat with his back against the wall, and I begin to walk over to remind him who's in charge when I see something even more pressing. Donovan, a real snake from Korolis, is sidling towards the twins, rubbing sweat from his hands on his combats. I head off to intercept him, but I'm too slow and he stands in front of Lorii, stopping her. My stomach gives a lurch of anxiety, because I know that whatever happens next, this is going to turn out bad.

'That's a fine showing, Lorii,' Donovan says with a leer. He reaches forward and places his right hand on her chest, gazing into her eyes.

She snarls, slapping his hand away angrily and trying to step past, but he wraps an arm around her waist and pulls her back with a laugh. I don't see exactly what happens next – they've both got their backs to me – but half a second later Donovan starts screaming his head off and drops to his knees, clutching his face. Lorii spins apart from him and starts to walk away with Loron. I call out Lorii's name and she stops and walks over to me. She smiles sweetly, holding her right hand out, closed around something.

'I don't like being touched by perverts,' she says lightly, her blue eyes staring straight into mine. I feel her place something wet in my hand before she turns and walks off. Looking down, I see one of Donovan's eyes staring back at me from my palm. My interest in her body immediately drops to below zero.

GAZING OUT THROUGH the small round port in the Colonel's office, I can see the world we're orbiting. It's grey and cloudy, not particularly remarkable. The Colonel is watching me intently, as always, and I self-consciously avoid meeting his eyes.

'Hypernol penal colony is on the moon of the planet below us,' he says, confirming my earlier suspicions. 'We will be travelling to the surface at the start of the last pre-midcycle watch. The *Pride of Lothus* will be re-supplying at the orbital marshalling station. When we reach the penal colony, I will be dispensing with the services of certain members of your platoon who have failed to perform satisfactorily.'

'May I ask who, sir?' I inquire, curious about this change of attitude. The Colonel's never mentioned expelling anyone from the Last Chancers before. Up until now the only options for getting out have been death or a pardon. It seems to me we can die just as well as anyone.

'You may not,' the Colonel replies sternly, reminding me that I'm still gutterfilth in his eyes, for all of the recent increases in my responsibilities. He turns to look out of the port, and as I look away from his back I notice something out of the corner of my eye, on Schaeffer's desk. It's a picture of Loron on a file, and with the Colonel's attention elsewhere I lean forward a little to try to sneak a look.

'You could just ask, Kage,' the Colonel says without turning around.

'Sir?' I blurt out, startled.

'You could just ask what crimes Loron and Lorii have committed,' he replies, looking over his shoulder at me.

'What did they do?' I ask uncertainly, wondering if this is some kind of trap or test being set by the Colonel.

'Disobedience,' the Colonel says simply, turning around fully. 'They refused an order.'

'I understand, sir', I assure the Colonel, crowing inside because I was right and Slavini was wrong. Witches indeed!

'I am sure you will, lieutenant,' the Colonel says with an odd look in his eyes. 'Prepare for embarkation on the shuttle in one hour's time,' he adds before dismissing me with a waved hand.

'OKAY,' ADMITS SLAVINI when I tell him as soon as I get back to the holding pen. 'But that doesn't mean that's what really happened, just because that's what the record shows.'

'Emperor, you're a suspicious man, Slavini,' I say sourly, annoyed that he still won't admit that he's wrong. 'Come with me, we'll settle this once and for all.'

I grab the sergeant's arm and drag him over to where Loron is sitting against the wall, staring at the floor. I put him and his sister on different exercise details in the hope that it would force them to communicate more with the others, but it just seems to have annoyed and upset them. Well, I've had it with their introverted ways, they're going to become a part of the unit whether they like it or not.

'What are you in for?' I demand, standing with my hands on my hips in front of Loron. He looks slowly up at me with those deep blue eyes of his, but doesn't say a word.

'As your lieutenant, I'm ordering you to tell me,' I snap at him, furious at his silence. 'Or is that another order you're gonna refuse?' I add viciously. He stands up and looks me straight in the eye.

'It isn't what you think,' he says finally, his glance moving back and forth between me and Slavini.

'So tell us what it really is,' I insist. He looks at us both again and then sighs.

'It's true that Lorii disobeyed an order,' he tells us slowly. I look smugly at Slavini, who scowls back. 'It was an order to retreat, not an order to attack,' he adds, and we both stare at him in astonishment.

'Ordered to withdraw, you refused?' Slavini says incredulously. 'You'll fit in nicely with the Last Chancers. Are you suicide freaks or something?'

'I was wounded in the leg,' Loron explains, face sombre. 'Lorii refused the order for general withdrawal and came back to get me. She carried me over her shoulders for the kilometre back to the siege lines. They said she had disobeyed orders and dishonourably discharged her at the court martial.'

'They didn't get you on some crappy conspiracy or complicity charge, did they?' I ask, wondering how Loron had ended up joining his sister.

'No,' he replies. 'I insisted I be discharged with her. They refused, so I punched the captain of my company. They were only too happy to throw me out after that.'

'To stay with your sister, you punched your captain?' laughs Slavini. 'No mistake about it you're fragging weird, man.' I look at the albino's sincere face, seeing an odd look in his eyes that makes me wonder even more about them. About where they're from.

'Very well,' I tell him. 'I'll keep you and Lorii together from now on, if that makes you feel happier.'

'It does,' Loron replies with a slight smile. He takes a step to walk past Slavini and then stops. He looks back at the sergeant and the smile on his face is gone.

'I would suggest you don't use words like freak and weird around Lorii,' he says, his voice dropping to a menacing tone. 'She is more sensitive and less reasonable than me.'

I bet she is, I think to myself as Loron walks off, leaving Slavini visibly shaken. In an unconscious gesture, the sergeant rubs his eye with a knuckle and then wanders off, thoughts obviously somewhere else.

'SO, LORII,' LINSKRUG says, leaning as far forward as the shuttle safety straps will allow to talk across Kronin's chest, 'I bet you didn't think you'd be going back to the penal colony this soon!'

'We've not been in a penal colony,' she corrects him. The twins have begun to lighten up finally, as everybody gets used to them and gives them some space. For their part, they've started talking a bit more, as if the both of them have resolved that they're not going anywhere, so they better at least try to get along with some of the others. In fact, I'd say Lorii has got a soft spot for Linskrug, though I can't think what she sees in the handsome and once wealthy and well-connected baron. Kronin's asleep between the pair of them, snoring gently, as the shuttle takes us down to the moon.

'Sorry?' I say, catching on to what she said. I look over to my right where she's sitting next to the aft bulkhead. 'You mean the Colonel hasn't just picked you up from the penal moon we're going to?'

'No,' she says with a fierce shake of her head. 'We've been fighting with a punishment battalion on Proxima Finalis for the past eighteen months.'

'Why has the Colonel singled you out?' I ask.

'We weren't singled out,' Loron says, and we turn our heads to the left to look at him. 'We were the only ones left.'

'Only ones?' Franx croaks beside me. 'How'd that happen?'

'Cluster bombs from ork fighter-bombers dropped straight into the middle of the battalion as we made an assault,' says Lorii and everyone's gaze shifts back to her. 'Blew apart two hundred troopers – everybody except my brother and me.'

'Woah,' Broker says from the other side of the shuttle, shock showing on his face. 'That's pretty awesome.'

'What happened then?' I ask Lorii, curious as to how they ended up with us.

'The commissars weren't sure what to do with us,' Loron continues the story, dragging our eyes to the other end of the shuttle. 'That's when Colonel Schaeffer turned up again, had a word with the commissars and then brought us here.'

'Turned up again?' Gappo asks, before I get the chance. 'You'd seen him before?'

'Yes,' Loron replies with a nod. 'It was over a year ago, when the punishment battalion was first formed. He came and met the captain. We don't know what they talked about.'

I'm trying to work out what we were doing roughly a year ago. It's not that easy, for a number of reasons. For a start, in the past year or so we've been to five different worlds, and they all blur into one long war after a while. Added to that, what was a year ago for Loron and Lorii might not be the same for us, what with warp time and the rest. It's like this: a ship in the warp can travel so fast because time there doesn't flow the same as it does in the real universe. Well, that's how a tech-priest tried to explain it to me on my first trip off Olympas. In our universe, time passes normally, so the people on the ship might experience only a week to a month, while three months have really passed them by. I've not had any reference to, for want of a proper term, normal time since Ichar IV two of my years ago. For all I know, ten years might have really passed me by in that time.

The shuttle suddenly lurches, slamming my head back against the hull and wrenching me from my reverie. Everybody's glancing about at each other, wondering what's going on.

'What the frag?' I manage to bark out before the shuttle dips to the right sharply, hurling me forward into my harness.

'Turbulence?' suggests Linskrug, the calmest among us. I twist my head over my shoulder to look out the viewport behind me. I can see the circle of the moon below us, too far away for us to be in its atmosphere yet.

'Nope,' I growl, pulling the release on my straps and hauling myself to my feet. 'Stay here!'

I try to work my way to the front bulkhead, leaning on people's knees as I pull myself along. The shuttle shudders and banks the other way, tossing me sideways and pitching me to my hands and knees. Clawing my way forward, I pull myself up the bulkhead and lean against the wall next to the comms-unit connecting us to the forward chamber where the crew and Colonel are. Pushing the switch to activate it, I steady myself some more as the shuttle seems to waggle from side to side for a few seconds.

'What's happening Colonel?' I shout into the pick-up. The link crackles for about a second before I hear the Colonel, his voice distant and tinny.

'Get back to your seat, Kage,' he orders. 'The pilot has suffered a synaptic haemorrhage. Prepare for crash landing.'

Everybody's looking at me, and they've heard what the Colonel said. Almost all of them seem to start talking at once, I can't make out a word they're saying.

'Shut up!' I bellow, flicking the comms-unit off again and leaning with my back to the bulkhead. 'Check your harnesses are tight. Really tight. When we hit, get your arms over your face and keep your ankles and knees together. If we have to ditch after we land, Broker's squad goes first, followed by Donalson, Jorett and Slavini. I'll follow up. Until then, don't say anything.'

The next few minutes pass agonisingly slowly as I stumble back to my place and strap myself in again. We're utterly help-less, just hoping that the pilot's back-up can regain some kind of control. The moon's got enough of an atmosphere to burn us up if we enter wrong, and even if we survive that we'll slam into the surface at something like a thousand kilometres per hour if the landing thrusters don't fire. Even if the thrusters do slow our descent, we could be spun around like crazy, smash-ing side or top first into the ground. Assuming the plasma chambers don't explode on impact and incinerate all of us, some of us might just get out of this alive.

It's about ten minutes after the first sign of trouble when I feel the hull vibrating with the constant burning of attitude adjusters, altering our roll and pitch as we plunge towards the moon. That at least is a good sign, because it shows that some-one's regained some manoeuvrability. Looking out the port again, the moon is looming large, filling it up. It's a sandy yel-low colour, orange wisps of cloud drifting through its atmosphere. The anti-glare shutters snap up, blocking my sight, protecting us from the blinding light caused by entry into the atmosphere. Half a minute later and the shuttle starts shaking violently, bouncing me a few centimetres or so up and down on the bench, despite the fact that my harness is biting painfully tight into my gut and shoulders. I hear the whine of the engines turn into the customary roar as the turbo-jets kick in, and I realise we're not going to burn up. That still doesn't help the fact that we were going twice as fast as we should have been. If the pilot hits the retros too hard he could snap the shuttle in half; if he goes too late we'll be flattened on impact.

The warning lights snap on, glowing a constant red, indicating imminent landing.

'Get ready everyone!' I shout. I wait a moment to check they're all braced properly before wrapping my arms across my face, cupping my hands over my ears to stop my ear drums being blown out by any explosive change in pressure. My heart is hammering, my knees trembling as I try to press them together. This has to be the most terrifying experience of my life, because I'm totally helpless to do anything. There's not a single fragging thing I can do to alter whether I live or die, except protect myself and try not to tense up too much. That's easier said than done when you know you're plummeting groundwards at high speed.

The air fills with a high-pitched whistling as we scream down through the air. I grit my teeth until I remember that you're supposed to keep your mouth open. I can hear some of the troopers praying to the Emperor, and I offer a silent one of my own. Please don't kill me this way, I ask him. Keep me safe and I'll never doubt you again, I promise.

With a near-deafening crash we hit, and the impact hurls me backwards. I feel like we're skidding, the shuttle is jumping and lurching, yawing wildly left and right.

'Fragfragfragfragfrag!' I hear Franz wheezing next to me, but I'm relaxing already, realising that we're down and still alive. Then suddenly I feel light again and can sense us plummeting downwards, like we slipped over the edge of a cliff or something. I pitch towards the front of the shuttle as we go into a nose-dive, and a wild screech forms in my throat, but I manage to bite it back in time. Everything is spinning wildly, making me dizzy and sick. There's a sudden jolt and the spinning changes direction. Across from me, Mallory gives a high pitched yelp and then throws up across my boots. Then there's a sudden moment of calm and I can still hear Franx's cursing.

'Fragfragfragfragfragfrag!' he's spitting. I glance at him and see his knuckles are pure white, he's clenching his fists so tightly. It's then that I notice a pain in my palms and realise I've been digging my fingernails into my hand, even through the cloth of my gloves. Forcing myself to unclench my hands, I stare fixedly at my knees, trying to ignore the nausea sweeping through me.

The next impact smashes my knees together and is accompanied by the wrenching sound of torn metal. And then we've stopped. Suddenly it's all over; there's no sense of motion at all.

'Frag me!' Slavini shouts, breaking the silence, punching a fist into the air, his voice shrill, a wild grin across his face. I'm grinning like a madman too. Someone starts whooping, I burst out laughing, other people are crying out with joy. Feeling hysteria threatening to overwhelm us all I bang my head sharply back against the fuselage, the pain jarring some sense back into me.

'Stow the celebrations,' I bark. 'Is everybody okay?'

There's a series of affirmatives, and then I hear Lorii's melodic voice.

'There's something wrong with Crunch,' she says, indicating the burly guardsman on her left. I release my harness and make my way over to him, telling everybody to stay sitting in case the shuttle shifts or something. Crunch is flopped in his seat, his head against his chest. I crouch down in front of him and look up into his open eyes. There's no sign of consciousness in them. As I stand up again, I notice a massive bruise on the back of his neck. Fearing the worst, I put a finger to his chin and lift his head up. As I suspected, there's no resistance at all.

'Damn,' I curse to no one in particular. 'His neck's snapped.' Letting Crunch's face flop back to his chest, I go along to the comms-panel.

'Everything all right up there, sir?' I ask.

'The pilot is incapacitated, that is all,' the Colonel tells me, his voice crackling from the comms-panel. 'What is your status?'

I glance around for another check before replying.

'One dead, probably a few dislocations, sprains and bruises, but that's all,' I report.

'We seem to have broken through the surface into a cave,' the Colonel's metallic voice tells me. 'Organise ten men for a survey party, I will be with you shortly.'

Switching off the comms-unit I turn back to the cabin. Everyone seems to have got over their initial delight, realising that we're stuck somewhere on this moon. We don't even know if the air outside is breathable, or anything else about this place. There could be a fire in the engines for all we know, still threatening to blow us to the warp.

'Jorett, how's your squad?' I ask, stepping between the benches towards the sergeant. He glances back at them before replying.

'All present and able, Kage,' he tells me with a relieved smile. 'Fraggin' lucky us, eh?'

'Okay, when the Colonel gets here, we'll see where the frag we've ended up,' I say, dropping into the empty place next to Jorett and sighing heavily. Something always happens; the curse of the Last Chancers always manages to strike when you least expect it. Not even a simple shuttle run can go right for us.

'WHAT'S THAT BLOODY noise?' Jorett asks as I hand out the rebreather masks and photolamps. I listen for a moment, brow furrowed, and hear it as well. It's like a scratching on the hull, an intermittent scraping noise.

'Haven't a clue,' I tell him with a shrug, pulling on the headband of my own mask. Apparently the moon's atmosphere isn't breathable, but other than that, and the darkness of being in an underground cave, everything else is tolerable. The Colonel's watching over the men as we attempt some rudimentary repairs to the engines; the power relays were punctured during the crash. The tech-priest pilot is phasing in and out of consciousness, and from his scattered mumbling it's clear we're not going to go anywhere until the engines are back on-line, and a few other things are fixed up. The warrant officer who took over piloting says his last navigational contact placed us about thirty kilometres from the penal colony, well out of marching range. We've only got enough rebreathers for a dozen people, and even if we had one for everybody the tanks last for only half an hour or so before they need refilling from the shuttle's filtering system, and that's at full stretch at the moment, running on auxiliary power. We're going outside to check for any damage to the exterior, but there's been no hull breach as far as we can tell. If the shuttle's contaminant detection systems are working, that is.

We're running on secondary power with the engines offline and so have to hand-crank the ramp down. It's a laborious process, because two sealing bulkheads have to be lowered first to form an air-lock. It's sweaty work and the air circulators in the small boarding cabin are almost at overload with the eleven of us puffing and panting, making the air stale and thin. After about an hour's work we're ready to get the ramp into position.

'Okay, get your masks in place,' I order, pulling down the mouthpiece of my own. I take a few experimental breaths to check it's working properly and then push the two nose plugs up my nostrils. I pull the visor down from my forehead, settling it across the bridge of my nose, and then check everybody else is ready. I get three of the men on each crank wheel, and they start turning, lowering the ramp centimetre by centimetre. I feel the wisp of a breeze blowing in as the air outside flows fitfully inside. Five minutes later the ramp's down and I march down into the cave, switching on my photolamp. In its harsh red glare I can see the strata of different rocks in the jagged wall of the cave. Looking up, the beam disappears into the darkness, so the roof must be more than ten metres above us. I wave the rest down and set off towards the engines, the most vital part of the shuttle at the moment. Grit crunches underfoot, the floor littered with shards of rock brought down by our crash. I can hear the strange scratching noise again as I near the engine pods. The heat emanating from the thrusters makes me break out in a sweat as I approach closer.

I run the beam of the photolamp over the nozzles of the thrusters, looking for any cracks or dents, but don't see anything. I see Jorett walk past me, playing his photolamp over the engine housing on the other side. He takes a step forward for a closer look and then straightens up, a frown on his face.

'Kage,' he says, voice muffled by the mask, waving me over, 'have a look at this.'

Stepping up beside him I look carefully where his photolamp is pointing. In the ruddy glare I can make out a shadow about halfway up the engine housing, just above my head. It looks like a hole and I curse inwardly. If the housing is punctured, it'll need patching up before the men inside can go through to reconnect the relays. Then the hole seems to move, changing shape slightly.

'What the frag?' I hear Jorett murmur. Pulling myself up the grab rail a little, I peer closer. The hole isn't a hole at all. It's some kind of many-legged creature about the size of my hand. I can see its eyes glittering in my photolamp beam. Its ten legs splay outwards, hooking on to the hull of the shuttle. Its three centimetre mandibles work in and out and I see a kind of froth by its mouth. It seems totally oblivious to my presence. I prod it with the photolamp but it doesn't even move. Something else catches my eye and I look further up the fuselage. I can see another two dozen or so of the things clamped to the hull. Bubbling rivulets run down the hull, leaving metallic trails through the heat-blackened paintwork.

'Send two men to the weapons locker in the boarding bay, and bring every flamer we've got,' I order Jorett. He hesitates for a second. 'Now, Jorett!'

'They're eating the shuttle,' I tell the sergeant after he's sent a couple of his guys heading back to the ramp. 'Have a check up front, see how many more of them there are. If they penetrate the fuselage, the air will bleed out and everyone inside will choke to death…'

As he walks off, I turn my attention back to the alien bugs spread across the shuttle. Walking around to the far side of the shuttle, I count twenty more. I guess they must be like the ferro-beasts on Epsion Octarius, digesting metal ore from the rocks. The shuttle must be one hell of a banquet for them, that's for sure.

'There's about forty of the fraggin' things down here!' I hear Jorett's muted shout from the front of the shuttle. The two men sent inside return, each carrying a couple of flamers. I take one from each of them and tell them to get forward with the sergeant.

'Help me burn the little fraggers off,' I say, passing the flamer to Lammax, the dream interpreter. I take a step back and push the firing stud on the ignition chamber, the blue flame springing into life. Tossing my photolamp to one of the others, I take a firm grip of the flamer in both hands, bracing my legs apart, pointing the nozzle up at the top of the shuttle. I pull the trigger and let flames spray out six metres across the shuttle for a couple of seconds. In the pause between bursts I see flickering orange from ahead and know that Jorett's doing the same up front. Lammax opens up and I can see patches of steaming grease where the alien beasties used to be. Lammox redirects the flow of fire and burning flamer fuel slides down the hull, splashing a metre or so to my right.

'Watch where you're fraggin' pointin' that thing!' I cry out and the flames disappear. Opening up the flamer again, I send an orange jet of fire washing over the thrusters, making sure none of the creatures are hiding inside the nozzles. For another minute I make my way sideways along the shuttle sending bursts across the roof every few metres. Patches of flamer oil carry on burning, stuck to the fuselage, illuminating the cave with a flickering orange light.

'Okay, cease fire!' I call out. Swapping the flamer for my photolamp again, I clamber up the grab rails to stand on top of the shuttle. Playing the beam of the photolamp across the roof, I can see blistered, melted paint and nothing else. I turn to call back to the others that it's all clear, when a strange noise starts echoing around the cave, a low continuous scraping. Scanning around with the photolamp, I see that there's a tunnel leading off about twenty metres from the rear of the shuttle. As I look, I see a shadow moving down the tunnel towards us, accompanied by the same scratching sound we heard inside the shuttle, only getting much louder.

'Oh frag,' I whisper as the tide of aliens sweeps into the chamber, spreading across the cave floor like a living carpet.

'Flamers!' I bellow to the oblivious guardsmen below, pointing to the approaching mass of aliens. Jorett comes running back from the front of the shuttle as once more blazing fires illuminate the cave. He sets himself up next to Lammax and fiddles for a moment with the nozzle of the flamer before sending a wide sheet of fire arcing towards the tunnel. I hastily clamber back to the ground, constantly looking over my shoulder to see what's going on.

'We're bloody holding them,' declares Jorett as he unleashes another burst.

'Yes, but not forever, they're spreading out,' adds Lammax, pausing to point to his left. I see that it's true, the creatures are spilling around the flamer fire, threatening to surround us.

'Darvon! Thensson!' I call out to the troopers with flamers. 'Get yourself over there and push them back to the tunnel.' As they do as I ordered, I step up between Jorett and Lammax. 'We've got to keep the little fraggers contained within the tunnel, where they can't get around us.'

As we force them back, step by step, something else occurs to me.

'Did you see any other tunnels down the front?' I ask Jorett, casting a panicked glance behind me.

'Rest up,' he replies. 'That was the first fraggin' thing I checked.'

Breathing a sigh of relief I step back and let them carry on with their work. A couple of minutes later and we're stood at the mouth of the cave. It's about two and a half metres across and the same high, almost circular.

'I'm out,' calls Thensson, pulling the flamer up to his shoulder.

'Get to the weapons locker, there should be spare canisters inside,' I tell him.

'They've stopped!' exclaims Darvon. Pushing past, I see he's right. There's no sign of them for the twenty metres we can see up the tunnel, before it curves away out of sight.

'They'll be back,' I say heavily. 'They must have a nest or something close by, for that many to get here so quick. We'll go and hunt them down.'

'Are you fraggin' sure?' asks Jorett. 'We've already been out here ten minutes. We've only got twenty minutes of fraggin' air left.'

'Emperor alone knows how many of those things are up there,' I tell them. 'The flamers are almost out of fuel already. Who can tell how many more attacks we can stave off. No, we hit the lair, get them all in one place at the same time.'

'I'm not sure…' Jorett continues, squaring up to me.

'I'm in charge,' I growl at him and he backs down, shaking his head.

I WAS RIGHT: the tunnel led direct to their nest, about two hundred metres from the shuttle. There's a massive cavern, the far wall too distant to see in the light of the photolamps. There's one more refill for each of the flamers, which might not be enough, because there's thousands of the creatures. They seem to be in some disarray, swarming haphazardly all over the place, covering the floor and scuttling along the walls and roof. Like before, they're not paying us any attention and I lead the squad further into the chamber. I can see another four tunnels leading off this cave, some heading up, others heading down, it's quite a network they've chewed themselves out down here. I wonder if the authorities at the penal colony know what's right under their feet.

'Sir,' Jorett attracts my attention with a terse whisper, jerking his head to one side. Looking over in that direction I see a mass of yellow alien eggs, little fleshy sacs about the size of your thumb. They stretch across the floor in a rough circle, spreading beyond the beam of the photolamp, tens of thousands of them. In the ruddy glare of the photolamps I can make out a larger, darker shape. It's about a metre tall, bloated atop dozens of spindly legs, sitting on a pile of eggs at the centre of the nest.

'I reckon that's the breeder,' Darvon says with a meaningful look.

'Let's torch it!' I snarl, grabbing Darvon's flamer and heading towards the mother bug. It turns its head towards us as we reach the edge of the egg-pile, a cluster of eyes staring back at me, a look of intelligence in them. I raise the flamer and point it directly at the breeder, smiling grimly inside my mask. Just then I notice movement to my left and right. The other guardsmen have noticed it too and start backing away from the eggs. From the side tunnels, another sort of creature is scuttling into view. They stand waist-high on ten many-jointed legs, with vicious-looking horns jutting forward from their insect-like heads. More and more of them are pouring in, hastening behind us to cut off our retreat.

'Run for it!' I bellow, pulling the trigger of the flamer, engulfing the mother alien in flames, seeing it writhe for a moment in the fires before collapsing in on itself. The air is filled with a hissing sound and the soldier bugs, I guess that's what they are, rush towards us, moving rapidly on their many legs. The others are already heading for the tunnel and I pound after them, jetting the flamer to my left and right a couple of times as the aliens get too close.

One of the soldiers scuttles up the wall around the tunnel entrance and hurls itself at Jorett, landing on his shoulders and clamping its legs around his face. He screams as it drives its horns into his throat, spraying blood as the sergeant falls to the floor. In his death-spasm the sergeant's finger tightens on the trigger of his flamer sending a gout of fire searing across the back of one of the other guardsmen, Mallory. Mallory flounders for a moment as the flames lick up his fatigues and his hair catches fire. He comes flailing towards me, his skin melting and bubbling around his rebreather mask, eyes staring wide through the visor, and I have to leap to my right to stop him grabbing hold of me. He falls flat on his face, a gurgling shriek issuing from his lips. He claws at his face for a moment as his mask melts into the flesh, before collapsing and lying still. I haven't got time to give him a second thought, two of the soldiers are between me and the tunnel, legs constricting, ready to jump. A flame whooshes out from the tunnel, incinerating the aliens in an instant, ashes wafting around in the heat of the fire. I see Thensson standing there, waving me on. Leaping over the charred, smouldering corpses of the soldiers, I head into the tunnel.

WE MAKE A fighting withdrawal down the passage towards the shuttle. Thensson, Lammax and I take it in turns to hold back the pursuing aliens before falling back past the next flamer man. It takes us another ten minutes to get back to the cave, where we make our stand again at the tunnel entrance. Lammax is on point when I see that he's aiming too low; some of the soldiers are scuttling along the roof of the passage. I shout out, but it's too late, one of them drops on to him, spikes piercing his shoulder. Darvon grabs the thing and flings it away and I drag Lammax out of the way as Thensson steps up to take his place, the first burst from his flamer scouring the ceiling.

Lammax is trying to scratch at the wound, but I hold his hand away, kneeling on his chest to stop him thrashing around too much. The puncture is deep, but doesn't look too bad until I see a thick, tar-like substance smeared with the blood – poison probably. Lammax recognises the look on my face and glances at his shoulder, eyes wide with horror. Tears of pain roll down his cheek, pooling at the bottom of his visor. With a lunge, he pushes me off his chest, wrenching the knife from my belt. I make a grab to get it back, but I'm not quick enough; he rams it into his chest up to the hilt.

'Right!' I shout, standing up and pushing the others away from where they've clustered around Lammax's body. 'Everyone share a rebreather and get back on the shuttle. Leave the rest for me.'

'What the frag are you talking about, sir?' demands Thensson over his shoulder.

'We don't know how long it's going to take to fix the shuttle engines,' I explain hurriedly, jabbing a finger down the tunnel to remind Thensson to keep watch. 'One man can hold this tunnel just as well as all of us, and if you give me your masks I'll be able to stay longer than if everyone stands out here together.'

'You get back on board,' insists Darvon, picking up Lammax's flamer, 'and I'll hold 'em off.'

'Don't even think about arguing with me on this one,' I snap back. 'This ain't self-sacrifice crap, I just don't trust you not to get yourselves killed. Now give me that flamer and get your sorry hide onto that shuttle.'

They exchange glances with each other, but when they see the determined look in my eye, I see them give up the fight. Thensson backs away, firing a final burst of fire down the tunnel, before hooking the strap of the flamer off his shoulder and leaning the weapon up against the wall.

'Soon as you run out of fuel or air, get inside,' he says fiercely, staring at me, daring me to contradict him.

'Get out of my sight,' I say, shooing him away with a wave of the flamer.

I'm left on my own, with three flamers and about an hour's worth of air. I just hope it's enough because one way or the other, if either isn't enough I'm a dead man.

I'VE FENDED OFF another half a dozen attacks over quarter of an hour when Thensson comes running up beside me. I've already had to swap masks once, and the tank on the one I'm wearing is getting low.

'What the frag are you doin' here?' I demand, pushing him back towards the shuttle.

'The Colonel sent me to tell you that main power's been restored,' he says, batting my arm away. 'It'll be another half an hour before we can ignite the take-off thrusters. Do you reckon you can hang on that long?'

'This flamer's almost out, the others are both half full,' I reassure him. He nods and heads back to the shuttle, glancing once more over his shoulder. My attention is back on the tunnel as I see another wave of aliens scuttling towards me. I fire the last shot from the flamer and then toss it to one side, grabbing another from beside me and opening up again straight away. It's going to be a long half hour.

I RECKON THERE'S four, maybe five, shots left in the last flamer. I'm onto the last rebreather as well, and I glance back towards the shuttle to see any sign that they've succeeded in fixing the thrusters. There isn't. Looking back down the tunnel, I can see a mound of twisted, burnt alien bodies, half-filling it. The creatures are amazing, throwing themselves time and time again into certain death. I can't understand why they do it. They don't look intelligent enough to be out for vengeance for killing their breeder, and the shuttle isn't worth the hundreds of dead they've suffered. Then again, people have asked me why I don't just kill myself rather than stay in the Last Chancers, fighting battle after battle. They've got a point, because if I did it myself I could make sure it's quick, clean and painless, rather than risking agony and mutilation on the battlefield. But for me, that isn't the point. I am not going to die for the Colonel.

Once, I was willing to die for the Emperor and the Imperium, but the more I've seen of what they represent, the more I've decided they aren't worth it. I've been around a fair bit in the last three years, since I signed up for the Imperial Guard, and I've not seen anything that makes me think all the sacrifices are any use. Millions of guardsmen and Navy guys are dying all the time, and for what? So that ingrate planetary commanders, cardinals and officers can notch up another pointless victory? So that some Departmento Munitorum or Administratum clerk can make a notation on a star chart to say that a worthless lump of rock is still under Imperial control? So that I can be stood here on this stupid moon, facing a swarm of alien beasts on my own so that I can go off and risk my neck in some other damned war?

I'm starting to feel dizzy now; the air from the mask has almost run out. I wipe a hand across the visor of the mask a few times before I realise the spots are in my eyes not on the plastisteel lenses. There's movement on the heap of dead and I see the aliens pouring towards me once again. I lift the flamer up once more, the gun feeling heavier than it did a moment ago. I pull the trigger and a sheet of fire roars down the tunnel, scorching the live aliens into ashes.

I gasp when I try to take my next breath and I realise with panic that the tank's empty, there's just what's left in the mask itself. More of the aliens are streaming down the tunnel and I manage to fire again, my throat tightening as I try to breathe non-existent air. The dizziness floods up into my head and my legs just collapse underneath me. I can hardly move, but I can see the darker shadow of the alien wave getting closer. I'm choking, my chest tightening, but I manage to angle the flamer in front of me and fire again, forcing the soldiers back a final time. All life goes from my fingers and I see rather than feel the weapon slipping from my grasp. I try to push myself up, to find some last reserve of strength, but there's none there this time. There's a roaring in my ears and blackness swirls around me.

I JAR AWAKE, feeling something touching me. Flailing around weakly with my arms, I try to fend off the soldier aliens. One of them rips the mask off and I feel something clamping down on my face. Suddenly my lungs fill with fresh air, and I can feel myself being dragged across the ground. As my vision returns, I see Thensson firing a flamer up the tunnel before grabbing it by the stock and hurling it down the passage, shouting something I can't hear. As I'm bundled up the ramp, I see a wave of blackness pour over and around the guardsman, flooring him. Spikes rise and fall, stabbing repeatedly into his body, blood spurting from deep wounds. With a whine the ramp begins to close, obscuring the scene.

'We're in!' I hear someone behind me call out. I'm laid flat on my back and I stare at the glowglobe in the ceiling, entranced by its yellow light. It seems blindingly bright after the cave, but I keep staring at it. The floor beneath me begins to shake violently and I feel the increase in weight that indicates we've taken off. Out-of-focus faces cluster into my vision; people talk, but their voices are just a mixed-up burbling. I close my eyes and concentrate on filling my lungs as much as possible.

THE JURY-RIGGED shuttle managed to make it the score of kilometres to the penal colony, where the Colonel commandeered one of theirs to take us back to the *Pride of Lothus*. The tech-priest died from his feedback injury before we reached the colony, and we left the body there. As we're disembarking into the transport's shuttle bay, I approach the Colonel.

'You didn't leave anyone behind, sir,' I point out.

'You are right, I did not,' he replies, watching the guardsmen plodding exhaustedly down the ramp.

'And we're not getting any new recruits, either?' I suggest, watching his face for some betrayal of what he might be thinking, but there's nothing there at all.

'You are not,' he confirms, finally turning to look at me.

'Why, sir?' I ask after a moment, wondering if I just need to ask, like he said with Loron and Lorii's history.

'None of them were good enough,' is all he says, looking straight at me and then turning to walk away.

'Good enough for what?' I ask, trotting after him.

'You are full of questions today, Kage,' he says, striding across the mesh decking. He looks over his shoulder at me, sizing me up, and then seems to reach a decision. 'Come with me back to my chamber, the armsmen know how to get your men back to the holding pen.'

We walk in silence, my head spinning with thoughts. What was he going to show me? Or was he going to give me a dressing down in private, not wanting to spoil discipline by taking a few lumps off me in front of the troopers? Then again, it's never stopped him before.

The Colonel keeps glancing at me as we ascend through the decks on the ironwork escalator. This sudden turn of events both worries and excites me. As we walk down the corridor towards his study, one of the robe-shrouded flunkies approaches from the other direction. He gives me a startled look but doesn't say anything. We both follow the Colonel inside and he closes the door behind us.

'Show Lieutenant Kage the documents,' Schaeffer tells the clerk, sitting down behind his desk. The robed man pulls a bundle of parchments from a voluminous sleeve and hands them to me.

I unroll the top one and place the others on the corner of the Colonel's desk. It's written in a large, flowing script. It's in High Gothic, so I can't understand much of what's written. However I do recognise the title. It says *Absolvus Imperius Felonium Omna*, which I take it means 'The Emperor absolves all your sins'. At the bottom is a heavy wax seal with the mark of the Commissariat and above it I see Jorett's name. Startled, I look at the others, and they are for Lammax and the rest of them.

'Pardons for dead men?' I ask, confused.

'Absolution can be awarded posthumously,' the clerk tells me with utter sincerity. 'As easily as commendations and medals.'

'Does everyone get one of these?' I ask, turning to the Colonel. He just nods once, staring intently at me.

You really are mad, I think to myself as I look at him, sitting in his leather-bound chair, fingers steepled in front of him.

'Only the Emperor can grant eternal and unbounded absolution,' the scribe murmurs behind me.

'You all know my promise,' the Colonel says, the first words he's uttered to me since we left the shuttle hangar. 'I give you a last chance. If you die in my service, you have earned the right for absolution. It means a number of things; it is not just sophistry. Your name can be entered into the Imperial annals as serving the Emperor and doing your duty. If we know who they are, your children will be cared for by the Schola Progenium; your families will be contacted and told the manner of your death.'

'And if you don't die?' I ask, suddenly worried.

'Everybody dies, lieutenant,' the clerk says quietly from behind me. I whirl around and glare at him. 'Sooner or later,' he adds, completely unfazed. I turn back to the Colonel, about to demand why he wants us all dead, but he speaks first.

'That will be all, Lieutenant Kage,' he says, no hint of emotion at all. I snap my mouth shut and salute, fuming inside. 'Clericus Amadiel here will summon an armsman to return you to your men,' the Colonel finishes, indicating the door with an open hand and a slight tilt of the head.

THE SOUND OF the constant bombardment was dull and muffled inside the command centre, reduced to a distant thudding. Inside the operations room everything was organised chaos as scribes and logisticians scurried to and fro carrying information detailing the latest enemy offensive. In the centre of the room, amid banks of dials and tactical displays, a hololithic projector showed a schematic diagram of the fortress, red blinking icons indicating the positions of enemy formations. Blue symbols represented the defenders, mustering to their places to fend off the assault. Two officers stood beside the hololith, resplendent in their deep blue frock coats and gold braiding. One, with the five studs of a commander-general on his epaulettes, pointed to an area to the south west.

'This looks like a diversionary attack,' he commented to his fellow officer, whose rank markings showed him to be a captain. 'Bring Epsilon Brigade back to the west wall, and push forward with the 23rd along their flank.'

The captain called over a scribe with a wave of his hand and passed on the order in clipped tones. He turned back to his grey-haired superior, his face a picture of worry.

'How can we continue to fight, sir?' he asked, fingers tapping nervously on the golden hilt of the sword hanging against his left thigh. 'They seem to have limitless numbers, and are willing to throw in thousands just to test our reactions.'

'Don't worry, Jonathan,' the commander-general assured him. 'Help is on the way, and when it arrives we shall be safe.'

'And what of the other problem?' the captain inquired in an agitated fashion, voice dropping to a terse whisper. 'What of the enemy within?'

'There is only one of them,' the commander-general replied in the same hushed tones. 'They will be caught and removed, and the small threat will pass. Nothing is going to stop us now.'

FOUR
TREACHERY

+++ *Operation Harvest entering Final Stage. What is status of Operation New Sun.* +++

+++ *New Sun entering pivotal phase. Operation Harvest must be completed as soon as possible, time is short.* +++

+++ *Will make all speed for New Sun location.* +++

I'VE NEVER SEEN the Colonel so angry before. I thought I'd seen him get mad, but that was just mild annoyance compared with his current performance. His eyes are so hard they could chip rockcrete and his skin is almost white, his jaw is clenched so tight I can see the muscles twitching in his cheeks. Captain Ferrin isn't all that happy either. The ship's commander is flushed and sweating, scowling at the Colonel. And there's me, caught in the middle of it. I'd just been reporting the latest weapons stock check to the Colonel when the captain came in and told him we were altering course to respond to a general alarm call. The Colonel told him flat that they weren't going anywhere and to bring us back on to our original heading, and then things started getting ugly.

'You know my standing orders, Colonel Schaeffer,' hisses the captain, leaning on the front of the Colonel's desk with balled fists, his thick shoulders level with his chin.

'May I remind you that this vessel has been seconded to me for transportation, captain,' Schaeffer spits back, standing up from his big chair and pacing to look out of the viewport.

'It is a high treason offence not to respond to a general alarm signal,' the captain barks at his back. 'There is no over-riding situation or a countermanding order from a superior officer.'

'This vessel is at my disposal,' the Colonel says quietly, and that's when I know things are getting really dangerous. The Colonel's one of those men whose voice gets quieter the nearer to going over the edge he is. 'I am giving you a countermanding order, captain.'

'I am still the most senior officer on this vessel, colonel,' the captain tells him, pulling himself up stiffly, clenching and unclenching his fists behind his back. 'This is naval jurisdiction. *I* am in command of this ship.'

'I have the highest authority! You know what I am talking about, captain!' yells the Colonel, spinning on his heel to confront Ferrin. 'I am giving you a direct order, with all of that authority behind it. You will return us to our original course for Typhos Prime!'

'Your authority does not extend to over-ruling the Naval Articles of War, colonel,' the captain says with a shake of his head. 'After we have reported for duty at Kragmeer, I will reconsider. That is my final word on the matter. If you don't like it, you can get out of the nearest airlock and make your own way!'

With that the captain storms out of the study, the heavy door slamming shut behind him. I can't shake the image of the Colonel lining us up and marching us out of an airlock, like Ferrin suggested. He's probably mad enough to do it. The Colonel looks as if he's going to go after Captain Ferrin for a moment before he pulls himself up short. He takes a deep breath, straightens his greatcoat and then turns to me.

'What do we have in the way of cold weather equipment, Kage?' he asks suddenly. I hesitate, taken aback, and he points to the dataslab with the inventory on it in my hand.

'I– er, what for?' I stammer back, regretting it instantly when he glowers at me.

'Get out, Kage!' he snaps at me, snatching the dataslab from my hand and waving me away with it. I give a hurried salute and bolt for the door, glad to be out of the Colonel's sight while he's in this murderous mood.

ANOTHER TWO WEEKS of warp-dreams end when we drop into the Kragmeer system. We're here to fight orks, the Colonel tells me. On an ice world, unfortunately. Locked in a permanent ice age, Kragmeer is one huge tundra, scoured by snow storms and covered in glaciers and jagged mountains. Fighting orks is bad enough, but fighting them in those harsh conditions is going to be damn near impossible. I've fought orks before, when a group of slavers tried raiding the world I was garrisoned on before I became a Last Chancer. They're huge green monsters, not much taller than a man because they stoop constantly, but really broad and muscular, with long, ape-like arms. They could bite your head off with their massive jaws and they have sharp claws too. They've also got pretty good guns, though their armour usually isn't worth a damn.

Then again, they don't need much armour; they can survive injuries that would cripple or kill a human. I don't know how they do it, but they hardly bleed at all, they don't seem to register pain very much and they can be patched, bolted and stapled back together in the crudest fashion and still fight with almost full effectiveness. I've seen warriors with rough and ready bionics, huge hissing pistons in their arms or legs, actually making them stronger, with guns or slashing blades built into the limb. No mistakes, even a few orks are bad news, and apparently a few thousand dropped onto Kragmeer several weeks ago.

We've still got a week of in-system travel before we reach orbit, so I go through cold weather survival with the few dozen Last Chancers left on board. Once again, the conversation has turned to just how useful we can be, with less than a platoon of men. Apparently there's another penal legion on the surface already, three whole companies. That's about five hundred to a thousand men, depending on the size of the companies. Who knows: maybe the Colonel will just wedge us into their organisation and leave us there?

Somehow, I don't think that's going to happen, though. The more things happen, and Franx agrees with me on this, the more it seems that the Colonel's got something in mind for us. I mean, if he's just trying to get us all killed, Kragmeer is as good a place as any so why the big fight with the ship's captain? And what's this authority he says he has? As far as I know, the only non-naval rank who can command a ship to do something is a warmaster, and that's because it takes the nominations of at least two admirals to make you warmaster to start with. Well, so they told us when they explained the local ranking system when I joined up. And there's also the Colonel's comment about the convicts from the last penal colony not being good enough. It all makes me wonder what's going on.

WE'RE DOWN IN the main launch bay driving Chimera infantry fighting vehicles onto the shuttles ready for transport down to the surface. The steady chugging of well-tuned engines echoes off the high vaulted ceiling, the tang of diesel fumes filling the air. Rating work parties clamber around on the cranes and gantries, preparing them for when they have to launch the shuttles. The Colonel had a Navy tech-priest look over our

Chimeras, bearing in mind the freezing conditions they'll be operating in. We've got vegetative processors loaded on board the Chimeras in case we need to chop down trees to fuel them. Blizzard filters have been installed over the intakes and exhausts and double-graded ignition systems fitted to the chargers to make sure they won't ice over. I, for one, wouldn't like to have to foot it across Kragmeer to get wherever we're going. Apparently we're going to have to land near one of the Imperial bases and then get to the frontline from there. The storm season is just starting, making any air travel impossible except right out on the plains where we're landing, some forty-five kilometres from the fighting.

A piercing shrill echoes out across the rumbling of engines, bringing everybody to an instant standstill.

'Attack alert!' shouts one of the ratings helping us with the loading, my half-friend Jamieson. 'Kage! Get your men over to the gantry if they want to see something interesting.'

Everybody crowds up the metal steps to get a view through the massive armoured windows. I can't see anything yet except for the plasma trails of the two frigates that jumped out of the warp just after us. Apparently on the other side of us is the cruiser *Justice of Terra* but I've never had the chance to see her.

'There!' hisses Jamieson, pointing at a movement to his left. I cup my hands around my face as I push my nose against the armaglass, trying to block out the light so I can see better. Then I can see it, nothing more than a shooting star at this range, sweeping past the furthest frigate.

'I hope there aren't too many of the eldar,' Jamieson mutters, shaking his head. 'We're not built for combat; transports usually act as part of a convoy.'

'How the hell do you know it's eldar?' asks Gappo incredulously from my right.

'Watch how they turn,' Jamieson tells us, nodding towards the window. I strain my eyes for a few minutes before I can see the orange-red spark again. Then I see what Jamieson means. The pinprick of light slows for a second or two and then speeds off in another direction entirely. Even burning retros and working the manoeuvring thrusters to maximum, one of our ships could never turn that tightly. Nowhere near that tightly, in fact.

As I watch, I see a tiny flicker of blue erupt around the blob of light that I identified as one of the frigates. The frigate seems to glow a little bit brighter as its shields absorb the attack. I can feel the engines of the *Pride of Lothus* forcing us away from the battle, a rumbling that seems to react with the pulsing of the ship to create a stomach-churning vibration.

'Frag me...' whispers Franx, looking up. I glance through the uppermost part of the window and see lights moving across my field of vision. I realise it's the *Justice of Terra* powering across us, over the top of the transport just a few kilometres away. She's immense: gallery after gallery, rows and rows of gunports moving into view. Even through the blast-filter tint of the arma-glass I can see the directional engines burning briefly into life along her port side, pushing her a bit further from us. Her plasma drives start to come into view, huge cylinders criss-crossed by countless kilometres of massive pipes and cables, feeding vital power from the plasma reactors deep within her armoured hull. The brightness of the plasma trails is almost blinding even through the darkened glass, white hot energy spilling from her engine tubes, hurling her through space at an incredible speed, although her size and weight make her look ponderous. No, not ponderous, it's more stately, a serenity that belies the awesome amounts of energy she's using. She's an inspiring sight, there's no doubt about that, and I can see why many a young man fantasises about growing up to be a ship's captain, commanding one of those deadly behemoths.

Watching the cruiser forging her way towards the eldar, I feel a sense of security. Surely nothing could stand up to the atten-tions of that gigantic engine of destruction. The Navy may have some strange ideas about strategy and defence, but you have to hand it to them, they know a hell of a lot about firepower. Their anti-ordnance defence turrets have weapons larger than those carried on Titans, their barrels over ten metres long, dozens of the point-defences studding the hull of a ship the size of a cruiser. Their broadsides vary, sometimes they have huge plasma cannons capable of incinerating cities, other times it's mass drivers that can pound metal and rock into oblivion. Short-ranged missile batteries can obliterate a smaller foe in a matter of minutes, while high-energy lasers, which Jamieson tells me are called lances, can shear through three metres of the toughest armour with one devastating shot. Most cruisers carry huge torpedoes as well, loaded with multiple warheads charged with volatile plasma bombs, carrying the power to unleash the energy of a small star on the enemy. It makes my humble laspistol look like spit in an ocean. More like a hundred oceans, actually.

When the *Justice of Terra* becomes nothing more than another spark in the distant battle, we begin to lose interest. There's the flickering of gunfire, but from several thousand kilometres away, it's hard to see anything really happening. I'm sure up on the gun decks and on the bridge they've got ocular sensors and stuff that allows them to have a better view, but down here it's just an incredibly distant and faint light show.

'Okay,' I tell the men as they begin to wander away from the window gallery, 'let's finish loading the Chimeras.'

WE HAVE THREE of the Chimeras on board one of the dropships and are getting ready to take another two onto the other when the ratings start hurrying around us, a sudden panic stirring them into activity. I grab a warrant officer by the arm as he tries to dash past.

'What's going on?' I demand, looking at the naval men as they converge on the lockers at the rear of the shuttle bay.

'We've got the order to prepare for boarders,' he tells me, pulling my hand off his arm with a snarl. 'One of the eldar pirates has doubled back and is coming straight for us. They lured the cruiser away and now we're on our own. Look!' He points out of the windows and I see a swirling shape approaching us speedily. I can't see the ship clearly, it's defended by what we call holo-fields, which twist and bend light so you can't see the exact location and sends augurs and surveyors haywire. Another example of the infernal witchcraft the eldar use in their weapons and machines.

I'm about to ask somebody to get in contact with the Colonel when I see him walking through the blast doors at the far end of the shuttle bay. He glances out of the windows as I hurry over to him.

'We need to get armed, sir,' I tell him. 'They're expecting a boarding action.'

'I know,' he replies turning his attention to me. I see he has his power sword hanging in its scabbard from his belt, and a holster on his other hip for his bolt pistol. 'I have informed the armsmen. They will issue you with weapons when they have finished assembling the naval parties.'

'Where should we be, sir?' I ask as we walk back towards the platoon. 'The Navy boys seem to know what they're doing. Where can we help out?'

'You are right. They can manage without us interfering,' he agrees, pulling his bolt pistol out and cocking the safety off. 'We shall act as a reserve, behind the Navy teams. If they look like they are faltering, we will advance and support them.'

That seems sensible. I'm all for staying behind the ratings and armsmen. After all, they're the ones trained for this sort of thing, in short-range firefights and close melee, and they've got the heavy duty armour to keep them safe in that sort of scrap. While we're waiting for the armsmen to dish out the weapons, I order the dropships secured, more to keep the men busy than because of any fears that having them open will help the eldar.

We're just finishing that when the armsmen bring over a trolley of weapons. They start handing out shotguns and shell bandoleers to everyone. I grab one and sling it over my shoulder and then snatch a bundle of electro-gaffs, calling over the squad sergeants to take one each and keeping one for myself. Looking back out of the windows I can see fire from our measly batteries flaring towards the miasma of colour that is the eldar ship. It doesn't seem to be damaged at all; it changes course to come alongside us, slowing its speed to match ours.

The whole ship shudders violently as the captain orders evasive manoeuvres and retro-jets spring into life, cutting our speed suddenly and hurling us sideways. This gives us a respite for only half a minute or so before a livid purple stream of energy pours out of the cloud of shifting colours, striking us somewhere near the aft section and causing the ship to tremble under detonations.

'They have disabled the engines,' the Colonel says from beside me, his face grim as ever. 'Now they will board.'

I see smaller shapes detach themselves from the multi-coloured fog, heading towards us. They must be using assault boats, I deduce. I can see half a dozen of them, and they seem to be heading straight for us. I think it must be an illusion but then I perceive that they are actually heading straight for us. They grow larger and larger in the windows and I hear the clattering of boots on the metal decking as more men pour into the shuttle bay from the surrounding areas of the ship. I push half a dozen cartridges into the chamber of the shotgun and pump them ready to fire. Holding the electro-gaff under my left arm, I herd the platoon back towards the wall, away from the windows and launch doors.

'Wait for the Colonel's order and follow my lead!' I shout out to them. I see a few of them glancing around, looking to see if there's an opportunity to get away, but as I follow their gazes I see that the doors have all been shut again. Glancing overhead I notice a trio of Navy officers in the control tower, looking out through the massive plate windows at their men below.

'They're here!' I hear someone bellowing from the front of the bay. I can see the sleek, menacing shapes of the assault boats dropping down past the windows, each patterned in strange, flowing stripes of black, purple and red. A few seconds later, patches of the walls to either side of the launch doors glow blue as the assault boats use some kind of energy field to burn their way through. With an explosion of light the first breach is made to my right, throwing sparks and debris onto the decking. Almost at once other detonations flare to my left and right and the Navy parties begin to open fire, the thunder of their shotguns resounding around the large chamber. The flare of gunfire flickers across my vision, joined by the odd burst of light from a lascannon or something similar.

From where I am I can't see anything of our attackers, but I can see men being hurled to the floor by blasts of dark energy, or torn to shreds by hails of fire. Right in front of me I see a pulsing star of blackness burst through the Navy ranks, smashing through a handful of men, tossing their charred bodies into the air and flinging severed limbs and heads in all directions. Everybody seems to be shouting at once, adding to the cacophony of the gunfire. Hoarse screams of agony or panic echo off the walls and the clatter of spent shell cases rings from the decking. The air stinks with the cordite from two hundred shotguns, the stench of burnt flesh and abattoir smell of dismembered and decapitated bodies. As I glance around trying to work out what the hell is going on, everything is in anarchy, flashes of lasfire mixing in with the bark of shotguns and the shrill, whickering noise from the eldar's splinter rifles and cannons.

It's impossible to see how many we're facing, or whether we're holding them back or not. I can see mounds of dead everywhere, men crawling away holding onto mutilated limbs or clasping wounds on their bodies and heads. Another explosion rocks the grates of the decking, a fireball blossoms far to my left where a generator or something goes up. Shots are whistling overhead now, impacting on the ironwork of the control tower support, hissing and bubbling as they melt through the girders holding the control room a dozen metres above the deck. A shuttle to my right bursts into a huge fireball, a hail of shrapnel scything through the men around it, cutting them down with a cloud of sharp-edged debris.

'It is time,' the Colonel says, stepping forward, the pulsing blue of his power sword illuminating his face from beneath. He nods his head towards the right where I can just see the first alien warriors through the thinned ranks of the Navy ratings and armsmen. They're wearing armour striped in the same colours as their attack ships. Their armour is plated and covered in blades and spikes, which glisten in the erratic light of the firefight. They stand about a head taller than the men around them, but are slim to the point of being emaciated. They move with a graceful, flowing motion that seems entirely effortless. With a speed that the most hardened human fighter would find difficult to match, I see them cutting left and right with close combat weapons made of exotic blades and barbed whips. A man's head spins to the ground as one of them tears through his throat with a backhand slash from its sword, before turning on its heel to plunge the blade through the stomach of another Navy man. There's an aura of malice about them, a ruthlessness betrayed by the odd shrill laugh or extravagant gesture.

There's a moment when the aliens in front of us stand on their own, about two dozen of them, with dead and dying Navy men littering the deck around their feet. Without any order being needed everybody opens fire at once, the heat from the volley washing over me and causing sweat to jump out of my skin. I pump the shotgun and fire again, the haft of my gaff wedged between the top of the breach and under my arm, and I see one of the eldar thrown back by the impact, bright blood spattering into the air. To our left, more come leaping towards us, easily cutting through the few men in their path.

There's a thudding of booted feet to our right and a squad of armsmen rush up and join us.

'They're breaking through towards the main corridor!' their petty officer screams, gesturing towards the far end of the bay with his assault shotgun. His visor is pushed back and I see his hate-filled snarl as he opens up with the shotgun, a dozen shots crashing through the approaching eldar in the space of a few seconds. Pulling the drum magazine from the shotgun and flinging it aside, he leads his men past us. I see Donalson leading his squad after them, and I let them go. The Colonel stands to my left, power sword in one hand, bolt pistol levelled at the enemy in the other.

'Fighting withdrawal to the command tower,' he snaps over his shoulder at me before firing a burst of rounds into the eldar as they head towards us.

'Fall back by squads!' I bellow over the din of the fighting. 'Jorett and Command squad up front!' I see the other men falling back towards the rear of the bay as I kneel to slam another six shells into the shotgun. Getting to my feet again I see the other Last Chancers are in position and I begin to walk backwards, firing round after round from the shotgun, the other squad's covering fire blasting past me into the aliens. The dead are heaped everywhere now, ours and theirs, bloodied body parts scattered across the metal decking, the deep crimson of human blood mixing with the brighter red of alien life fluid. I can't tell how many of them are left, but as I pull back past the other squad I can see that fighting is still raging fiercely to my left as the eldar attempt to break through the main doors and into the ship's interior.

'If they get out, they have an almost direct route to the bridge,' the Colonel informs me as he ejects the magazine on his bolt pistol and slides another into place. 'We must stop them getting out of the shuttle bay.'

Glancing over my shoulder I see that we're at the steps to the command tower now. You can follow the trail of our retreat, five dead Last Chancers lie among more than two dozen alien bodies and a swathe of shotgun cases and bolt pistol cartridges litters the floor. A few eldar manage to dart through our fusillade, almost naked except for a few pieces of bladed red armour strapped across vital body parts. Almost skipping with light steps, they duck left and right with unnatural speed. In their hands they hold vicious-looking whips and two-bladed daggers that drip with some kind of venom that smokes as it drops to the metal decking. Their fierce grins show exquisitely white teeth as they close for the kill, their bright oval eyes burning with unholy passion.

The Colonel counter-attacks, followed by Loron and Lorii. Schaeffer ducks beneath a venomed blade and opens fire with his bolt pistol, blasting the face of his attacker. Loron spins on his heel to send the butt of his shotgun crashing into the midriff of another, grabbing the gun double-handed and bringing the muzzle up into the alien's face, snapping its neck with the blow. Lorii side-steps between two of them, weaving to her right as one makes a lunge at her, grabbing the female eldar's arm and whipping it around, sending the slender creature tumbling into the blade of its comrade. One-handed, she fires the shotgun into the stomach of another, spraying shredded entrails across her white skin, dying her hair with bright red blood.

'Get the men to the control tower,' the Colonel orders me, bounding past me up the metal steps. The aliens continue to fire as we hurry up the open stairwell, cutting down two men from Slavini's squad and pitching them over the railing. I see the sergeant turn around and push his squad back down a few steps, returning fire to hold back the aliens as they race across the open deck towards us. My breath explodes out of my mouth in ragged gasps as I pound up the spiral stairs, forcing my aching legs to keep going, pushing at the back of Franx in front of me to keep him moving. Below us I can see that the eldar have almost reached the main gateway. Only a couple of dozen armsmen stand between them and the locked doorway.

It's with a sense of enormous relief that I tumble through the door of the control room, other men piling after me and pitching me onto the floor. The Colonel grabs me by the shoulder of my flak jacket and hauls me to my feet.

'Seal that,' he tells someone behind me, using his spare hand to point over my shoulder at the control room door. The door closes with a hiss of air and a dull thud. Three dazed naval officers stand looking at us with a mixture of surprise and horror.

'How do you blow the launch doors?' the Colonel demands, letting go of me and stepping up to the nearest one.

'Blow the doors? There's men still fighting down there!' the officer responds, his face a mask of horror.

'They will be dead soon anyway,' the Colonel snarls grimly, pushing the man to one side and stepping up to the next. 'The doors, lieutenant?'

'You can't just flick a switch,' he tells us. 'The crank wheel on the back wall is the gateway pressure release valve.' He points to a wheel about three metres across, with twenty spokes. It's connected by a huge chain to a massive series of gears that disappear into the ceiling. 'It's locked into the barring mechanism that keeps the doors shut. Open up the valves and the internal pressure within the bay will blow the doors out completely. This tower is on a separate system, it should be able to maintain pressure balance.'

'Do it!' the Colonel hisses at us over his shoulder, before looking back out at the shuttle bay.

'Slavini and Donalson's squads are still out there!' I argue, a lump in my throat. 'You can't order me to kill my own men.'

'I am giving you a direct order, Lieutenant Kage,' he says as he turns to me, his voice very low, his eyes glittering dangerously. 'We are all dead if they reach the bridge.'

'I… I can't do it sir,' I plead, thinking of Slavini and his men going back to hold off the Eldar to make sure we got up here.

'Do it now, Lieutenant Kage,' Schaeffer whispers, leaning very close, right in front of my face, those eyes lasering their way through mine into my brain. I flinch under that terrible gaze.

'Okay, everyone grab a spoke at the wheel!' I call out to the others, turning away from the Colonel's murderous stare. They start to argue but I soon shut them up, using the butt of my shotgun to smash Kordinara across the jaw when he starts shouting obscenities at me.

'Maintain discipline, Kage,' barks Schaeffer from behind me.

'You have five seconds to turn that wheel before I shoot you myself,' I growl at them, wondering if my eyes are filled with the same psychopathic glare I'd just seen in the Colonel's.

Without a further word they hurl themselves at the valve wheel. It creaks and grinds as they turn it; on a panel above their heads the needles on the dials begin to drop. With a sudden release of tension the wheel spins rapidly, throwing them to the floor in all directions. As they get to their feet an ominous creaking noise resounds around us. I look back out of the window and see the launch doors beginning to buckle under the strain. The huge doors, three metres thick, give way with a loud screeching, each one weighing several tons, ripped off their massive hinges and flung into the darkness. All hell breaks loose on the shuttle bay deck as shuttles, dropships, Chimeras, men and eldar are sucked into the air by the escaping atmosphere.

Men are whirled everywhere. Someone who looks like Slavini bounces off the hull of a spinning shuttle, his blood spraying wildly and violently from his face in the low pressure, sucking the life out of him in an instant. I can't hear their screams over the wild rushing of wind, a howling gale tearing around the shuttle bay throwing men and machines into oblivion. It's one of the most horrific sights I've ever seen, seeing everything rushing out of the jagged gap in the far wall, pitching them into the vacuum to a horrible death. Ice begins to form on the outside of the control tower, frosting over the glass, condensation from our breath beading quickly on the inside. I give a worried glance at the Navy officers, but they're staring in a horrified fashion at the carnage in the shuttle bay. I hear several of the Last Chancers behind me swearing and cursing. I look at the Colonel and he's stood there, totally immobile, watching the destruction outside with no sign of any emotion.

Rage boils up inside me. He knew this was going to happen. As soon as the eldar attacked, he knew it'd come to this. Don't ask me how he knew, or how I know that he knew, but he did. I drop the shotgun and electro-gaff and ball my hands into fists. Like a warm flood the anger flows through me, into my legs and arms, filling them with strength, and I'm about to hurl myself at the Colonel when he turns to look at me. I see the twitch of muscles in his jaw and a resigned look in his eyes, and I realise that he's not totally without compassion. He might have seen this coming, but he doesn't look happy about it. The anger suddenly bleeds away into the air around me, leaving me feeling sick and exhausted. I drop to my knees and bury my face in my hands, rubbing at my eyes with my knuckles. Shock sweeps over me as I realise that I killed them. The Colonel made me kill all of them: the aliens, the ratings, the armsmen and the Last Chancers. He made me do it, and I made the others do it. I hate him for that, more than I hate him for anything else he's done to me. I truly wish he was dead.

* * *

WE WERE SHUT UP in that control tower, twenty-four of us in that horrid room, for the next six hours while pressure-suited repair teams brought in heavy machinery to clamp and weld a solid plate over the breaches. No one said anything for the whole time, just the odd muttered whisper to themselves. When we get back down to the shuttle bay deck, there is nothing to mark the death that had taken place only a watch and a half earlier. Everything has been swept out into space. Every loose machine, every corpse, every living man, every spent shell and piece of debris, all of it blown to the stars. Only the scorch marks from the explosions show there was any fighting at all.

As we walk back to the holding cell I catch snippets of conversation between the armsmen, who I note have different names from those who have escorted us for nearly the past three years. Our regulars must have been in the launching bay. The eldar attack was unerringly accurate. They seemed to know that the shuttle bay would be weakly defended and that they would be able to get access to the main corridors by going through it. The eldar are very smart, of that I'm sure, but this feat of planning seems unlikely even for them.

I ruminate more on this course of events as we settle back into our prison. Nobody says anything at all, the massive open space seems even emptier than the loss of twenty men would suggest. I've never seen them like this before. For that matter, I've never felt this way myself about any of the other Last Chancers. We all expect to die; we learn that after the first battle. It's only twenty men out of four thousand, so what's the big deal this time? It's because they didn't stand a chance. That's what we're here for – our Last Chance. If we fight well, we survive. If we fight poorly, we die. It's that brutally simple. It's like the law of the downhive – the strongest survive, the weak are killed and eaten. That reminds me again of the Colonel's comments about other convicts not being good enough. There is something going on, and I'm almost there, but I can't quite fit the pieces.

My thoughts veer back to the dead men that started the train of thought. But this time, there was no Last Chance. They were just in the wrong place at the wrong time. And we killed them. The other Last Chancers and I turned that wheel and blew the doors. We killed our own comrades and that's treachery of the highest order. The eldar pirates left us no option, left the

Colonel no option, but to blow our fellow soldiers into the heavens. None of us wants to think about that. None of us likes to think that we're that lowest of soldiers, the basest of creatures: a killer of comrades, a cold-blooded traitor.

Except one of us, perhaps. One of us has done it before. One of us could do this sort of thing, betray us to monstrous aliens, betray his fellow men. A man who has had his punishment forestalled for a long time. A man who doesn't share an ounce of common humanity that even the most crazed psychopath in the Last Chancers may feel. A man who tried to kill me in my sleep for standing up to him. A man who has slinked, skulked and slithered his way through life, a slimy sump-toad of the worst order. I feel myself filling with righteous anger. I've held off from this moment for so long, but as I dwell on what happened in the launch bay my fury at the Colonel suddenly returns, but this time directed elsewhere, more focused and backed up by three years of loathing and hatred. I almost hear something in my brain snap.

'Never again,' I whisper to myself, and a few others nearby look up at me, their faces worried when they catch the look in my eye.

Fuelled by a sudden ire I dash across the floor of the cell, looking for Rollis. I see him on his own, in his usual place sitting down with his back against the wall. Trust him to survive when better men die. His eyes are closed, his head drooping against his chest. He gives a startled cry as I grab the front of his shirt and haul him to his feet, slamming him back against the bulkhead with the ring of his head against metal.

'Kage!' he splutters, eyes wide. 'Get the frag off of me!'

'You treacherous bastard!' I hiss back at him, grabbing his throat in one hand and forcing his head back. 'You sold us out! You betrayed us to the eldar!'

'What's this?' asks Loron from behind me, and I glance round to see that everybody has gathered around us.

'He's a traitor,' Linskrug speaks up, pushing through the throng to stand next to me. 'That was with eldar as well.'

'I haven't done anything,' gasps Rollis, twisting out of my grip and pushing me backwards a step.

'He was a comms-operator,' continues Gappo, eyes fixed on the traitor scum. 'He deliberately transmitted unciphered orders, letting the aliens know where our troops were moving.

He got his whole company killed in an ambush. Everyone except him. Seems a bit strange, doesn't it?'

Lorii then steps forward, a puzzled look on her pretty face.

'How the hell did he tell them anything this time?' she asks. Everyone is quiet for a moment, trying to work it out.

'I know,' wheezes Franx ominously. 'He was driving one of the Chimeras onto the dropship while the assault boats closed. Was still inside while we were battening it down. Could have used the on-board transceiver. Good for fifteen kilometres, plenty of time to send a quick message to his alien accomplices.'

'This is just so fragging crazy!' Rollis spits at us, sneering in contempt. 'You're all deluded.'

There's an angry growl from some of the men as we absorb this theory. I realise I'm among them. I see Slavini's face exploding in blood against the side of the shuttle again and something inside me snaps. Without a thought, I grab Rollis by both shoulders and ram my knee up into his groin. He gives a choked cry and tries to pitch sideways, but my grip is too tight. I butt him between the eyes, my forehead crashing into the bridge of his nose with the crunch of shattering cartilage. I step back, panting with anger, and let go of him. He stands there swaying, stunned from the blows, blood trickling across his lips and down his chin.

'You stupid bastard!' snarls Rollis, lashing out suddenly with his right fist, catching me on the cheek and knocking my head back. He staggers forward a step and raises the other hand, but I react quicker than he can strike, jabbing the fingertips of my right hand into his reddened throat, driving them into his windpipe. As he doubles over gasping for breath, I grab his greasy hair and smash my knee into his face. In a flash of blood-red I can see Slavini's face again, exploding, slowed down in my mind's eye. I see bodies and men tossed into the air like discarded ration packets. I ram my knee into his stomach. Again and again, over and over, crushing his ribs to a pulp with the repeated hammering until he vomits a gout of blood over my fatigues. But I can't stop; I keep getting flashes of those men sucked into the darkness, blood turning to thousands of sparkling crystals in the freezing void. I claw my left hand and rake it down his face, punching the fingers into his eye sockets.

It's then that I realise that I'm not the only one beating him. Fists and feet are pitching in from all around, pummelling him this way and that, driving him to the floor. I stagger back as others force their way into the fray, and all I can see is Rollis writhing under a storm of kicks and stamping boots. A thin trickle of blood oozes out between Kronin's legs as he stands over Rollis, hands on hips, watching the man bleeding to death.

'And they smote the enemies of the Emperor with a righteous fury, for they knew they were doing His work,' the insane lieutenant says, a vicious grin on his face, his eyes lit with madness. He plunges his teeth into the man's fat cheek, sending droplets of blood splashing through the air. Another flurry of blows descends on the traitor, accompanied by the crack of breaking bones.

There's not a sound from Rollis, not even a hoarse breath. It's then that everyone realises that it's all over. Without another word spoken everybody disperses, each making their way back to their regular spots. I look at the broken, battered corpse of Rollis, and I feel nothing. No hate any more, no contempt. I don't feel sorry either. He was a total bastard, and whether or not he betrayed us to the eldar, he had this coming a long time.

Feeling more exhausted than any time in the past three years, I drag myself over to my bedroll and throw myself down. A few minutes later the lights go dim for sleep cycle and as I lie there my stomach grumbles, empty. I realise that in all the excitement that's been going on, they've forgotten to feed us this evening. Ignoring the hunger pains I try to get some sleep.

I WAKE FROM a nightmare of blood and screaming, with the Colonel laughing at us as we die in front of him. As I roll my neck back and forth to ease out a kink, it dawns on me that I've been woken by the day cycle lights coming back on. It's then that I see the crumpled shape further along the wall, and realise that the part of the nightmare about Rollis wasn't a dream at all. I push myself to my feet and stroll over to have a look at him. Scrawled across the wall in blood over his head is the word 'Traitor'. As I stand there, I feel someone lean on my shoulder and glance round to see Lorii standing there, looking down at him. She turns and looks at me.

'Do you really think he did it?' I say, half-horrified and half-gladdened by what we had done last night.

'Does it matter?' she asks back, her fabulous blue eyes looking deep into mine.

'No,' I decide. 'He never deserved a last chance; he should have been executed a long time ago. Some things are beyond forgiveness. I'm surprised it took a bunch of criminals like us to realise that.'

'Last Chance justice,' she says with a sweet smile.

'ADMIRAL BECKS, your plan is totally unacceptable,' the wizened warmaster said, smoothing the folds in his long black trench coat. 'It is impossible to reduce Coritanorum from orbit.'

'Nothing is impossible to destroy, Warmaster Menitus,' the fleet admiral replied with a smug grin creasing the leathery skin of his hawk-like face. 'It may take a decade of bombardment, but we can annihilate that rebellious fortress and everyone in it.'

'That is not an option, and you know it,' Warmaster Menitus snapped back irritably. 'By ancient decree, as long as Coritanorum still stands, Typhos Prime remains the capital world of the Typhon Sector and the Typhos Supreme Guard are excused off-world duties. My superiors will do nothing to endanger that privileged position.'

'Then you will send in another ten thousand men to be slaughtered in yet another hopeless assault?' Admiral Becks answered sharply. 'If you cannot keep your own house in order, perhaps your privileged position should be reviewed. After all, who could trust a high command that allows their capital to fall to rebels?'

'You should concern yourself with keeping track of Hive Fleet Dagon, admiral,' the warmaster retaliated. 'Or have you lost track of it again? Leave the ground war to us and just make sure you get us more troops here safely.'

'Don't worry about Dagon, general,' Becks assured him with a sneer. 'The Navy will make sure you are well protected. We are the best line of defence, after all…'

'Best line of…' Menitus spluttered, face going red with anger. 'If you spent half the resources getting Imperial Guard regiments into place as you spend shuttling worthless diplomats across the galaxy, there would be no Hive Fleet Dagon left.'

'You dare suggest that the magnificent Imperial Navy should be nothing more than a glorified ferry service?' snarled fleet admiral Becks. 'You Guard have no idea, no idea at all, about just how big the galaxy is. Without the Navy, even mighty Terra itself would have fallen thousands of years ago.

'Well, so be it. You can waste as many Imperial Guard lives as you care, that's your stupidity and not my responsibility.'

FIVE
COLD STEEL

+++ *Operation Harvest nearing completion.* +++
+++ *Good. I expect you soon.* +++

I CAN SEE for about five metres in front of me, then my vision is blocked by the swirling snow. I pull the hood of my winter coat tighter around my face with heavily gloved hands, trudging slowly but steadily through the knee-deep snow. It seems our Chimeras are useless down here after all; the locals use a transport built from a Chimera chassis on top of a set of skis and driven by a giant turbofan engine. It's only a kilometre or two's march from the heated landing pad to the entrance to Epsilon Station, where we're joining up with the other penal legion, but I'm exhausted by the effort. From Epsilon Station we're marching to hold a mountain pass against the orks, more than fifty kilometres from where we are at the moment. We're not expected to survive. We're just here to buy time for the defenders to organise. Two stations have already been overwhelmed by the greenskins' attacks, and we're being thrown in the way to stall their advance.

The going isn't too difficult, it's downhill along the valley to the main entrance to the station. Just ahead of me, the black of his long coat almost obscured by the swirling flurries, the Colonel pushes his way through the snow drifts. Beside him rides Captain Olos of the Kragmeer Imperial Guard, riding on top of a bulky, long-haired grey quadruped which he keeps referring to as a ploughfoot. I can see why: the massive paws on the end of its four legs have horny protrusions that carve through the piled snow. The captain is swathed head to foot in thick dark furs, strapped and belted with gleaming black leather bands around his waist, thighs and biceps. He leans over in the saddle from the ploughfoot's high back to talk to the Colonel and I push myself forwards a little quicker to hear what he's saying.

'I've just sent one of my men on ahead to tell Epsilon we're almost there,' Olos yells against the fierce wind. His face is hard-worn by constant patrols in the harsh conditions, the skin tanned, heavy and thick from constant exposure to the freezing environment.

'How far is it?' the Colonel shouts back, cupping a hand to his mouth to be heard over the howling gale. He's wearing his thick black dresscoat, a heavy scarf wrapped around his chin and cap.

'About five hundred metres,' the captain replies loudly. 'Half an hour's march at this pace.'

'Why send a rider? Why not let them know by comms message?' I ask from behind them, jabbing a thumb over my shoulder at the rider on my left who is wearing a bulky comms set on his back.

'It's the storm season,' Olos bellows back. 'The southern polar regions kick up some weird element that fritzes comms transmissions over any distance greater than about two hundred metres. Every station has an astrotelepath to communicate with relay satellites in orbit. In the summer it isn't so bad, but the timing of the ork invasion couldn't have been worse for us.'

Someone else shuffles up beside me and I glance over to see Loron, his pale face almost blue with the cold, peering out of his fur-lined hood. Like the rest of us, he's wearing the long, dun-coloured coat we were given when the shuttle touched down. He cradles his lasgun in bulky mitts fashioned from the same material.

'Why the hell would anyone want to live in this place?' he demands, teeth chattering.

Olos jabs a finger down at the ground a couple of times.

'Ansidium ninety!' he tells us with a grin. 'There's millions of tons of ansidium ore beneath the rock.'

'What's so damn useful about ansidium ninety?' I ask, wondering what could be so important that three million people would live in such an inhospitable environment.

'It produces a catalyst agent used in plasma reactors,' he says, pulling a plasma pistol from its holster among his snow-covered saddlebags. 'It's one of the most stable ignition elements for plasma weapons, for a start. They say a plasma gun made with Kragmeer ansidium has only a forty-five per cent malfunction rate.'

'You seem very comfortable talking to convicted criminals,' the Colonel remarks. I can't see his face but I expect he's giving the captain one of his sternest looks.

'They are serving their punishment?' the captain asks, pushing the plasma pistol back where it came from.

'Yes,' the Colonel answers after a moment's thought, 'they are atoning for their sins.'

'Then they're all right by me,' Olos says with a laugh. 'It's the criminals wandering around unconvicted and unpunished that worry me! At the moment, we're so shafted by the orks I'm happy for any help we can get!'

'You think that twenty-two men can make a difference?' Loron asks, pulling himself free from a particularly deep drift.

'The last time Kragmeer was attacked, about seven years ago,' he tells us, 'ten men held the main gate of Gamma Station for six days against corsairs. In the right situation, ten men are better than a hundred.'

'I'll take your word for it,' I hear Loron mutter as he drops back behind us.

A FEW DOZEN men are working in the entrance chamber when we pass through the large double gates of the station. Half of them stop what they're doing to look at us. If there's one thing that annoys me more than anything else, it's the stares. I don't know why, call it irrational if you like, but why is everyone so Emperor-damned curious when we're around? Okay, so having the Last Chancers on your doorstep isn't an everyday occurrence, but do I gawp like some sloping-browed idiot whenever I see anything I haven't seen before? Of course I don't. I mean, I've got some self-respect. Our reputation seems to precede us more and more these days. I'm not sure if that makes the Colonel happy or annoyed. On the one hand, the more people hear about us, the greater our deterrent value. On the other hand, some people are seeing us just a bit like heroes, and he certainly doesn't want your average guardsman to think that this is some kind of glamorous career move. They'd be damned stupid if they do. Personally, I don't give a frag either way, as long as they don't stare at me like some kind of freak show.

Even inside the walls of Epsilon Station, hewn from the bare rock of the mountains, it's cold. Damn cold. Outside, they say, you'll freeze in five minutes without a proper suit. I can damn well believe it too, my toes are still numb from the short trek from the landing pad at the top of the valley. We're resting up here tonight and heading off in the morning. As I lead the men to the part of the barracks the Colonel's requisitioned for us, Franx falls in beside me.

'Planet's going to kill me, Kage,' he says sombrely, gloved hands clumsily unfastening the toggles down the front of his heavy winter coat.

'If False Hope didn't get you, this place is a walk in the plaza,' I reassure him.

'False Hope might get me yet,' he says with a grimace. 'Cold is playing havoc with my chest, can hardly breathe.'

'You'll survive,' I say with feeling. 'It's what we're good at.'

'Maybe,' he admits, still looking unconvinced. 'Just a matter of time before we're all dead. If the weather doesn't kill me, orks might. How long can we keep surviving?'

'As long as we want to,' I tell him emphatically, gripping his shoulder. 'Look, my philosophy is that if you give up, you've had it. You need something to hang on to. Me, it's the Colonel. Every time I see him I convince myself again that he's not going to get me killed. I don't want to give him that pleasure. It's worked so far.'

'You believe him about our chance at redemption?' asks Franx, hopefully.

'It ain't what I believe that matters,' I tell him with a shrug. 'It's what you believe that's important. We deal with it in our own way. Linskrug thinks that if he can just survive he'll be able to return and reclaim his barony and get revenge on his enemies. Kronin's gone mental, but he thinks he's the voice of the Emperor now and that's what gets him through. Everyone's got their own thing. The ones who died just didn't believe it enough. If you want to fight for your soul, that's fine by me.'

'EMPEROR, YOU'RE bloody scalding me!' Gappo shrieks at the young boy by the water temperature controls. Steam rises from the massive pool, condensing in droplets on the light blue tiles of the walls. He pulls himself up the side so that just his legs are dangling in the bath.

'Keep it nice and hot, boy,' argues Poal, the former storm trooper. 'This weather's bitten clean through to my heart, I need to let the heat seep in.'

'Don't rust your hook,' Gappo sneers back, gingerly lowering himself back into the water.

'Best damn wash I've had in a long while,' I tell them, reaching for one of the bottles of cleansing tonic. 'This ansidium stuff must bring in a good price, they live pretty well here on Kragmeer.'

'By the sounds of it, the Cult Mechanicus give an arm and a leg for the stuff,' agrees Poal, sliding further into the water until it's up to his chin. 'Think what kind of energy it takes to heat water to this when it's freezing cold topside.'

'Push over, give a weak man room!' calls Franx, padding gingerly across the floor, his bare feet reluctant to touch the cold tiles. He's right, he is looking really haggard, his once ample frame clings to his bones now. There's still plenty of muscle there, but the weight's fallen off him completely. He dips a toe in and whips it back with a hiss, much to everyone's amusement.

'Too hot for your delicate skin?' laughs Poal, splashing water at the sergeant. Franx puts a foot on Poal's head, forcing it under the water. When he surfaces again, spluttering and cursing, Franx jumps in beside him.

'Aieee,' he winces, biting his lip. 'Bastard hot!'

'You get used to it!' I reassure him, pouring some lotion into the stubbly growth on my head that passes for hair.

'Don't forget to wash behind your ears,' Gappo chuckles, grabbing the bottle from me, his lunge forward causing waves to lap against the side and splash up onto the floor. I hear someone else coming in and look up to see Kronin, treading cautiously across the water-slicked tiles.

'And there shall be space in the Emperor's heart for all true believers,' he tells us, waiting at the edge, peering suspiciously into the pool.

'That means shift up, Last Chancers,' I tell them, pushing Poal to one side to clear a space on my right. Kronin takes a deep breath and steps off the edge; the small man splashes in and goes completely under. A few seconds later he bursts into view again, face split by one of the widest grins I've seen.

'Could easily stay here for days,' Franx rasps, closing his eyes and leaning his head back against the pool edge. 'Can see why Kragmeerans don't mind cold patrols up top if they come back to this.'

'I think it's Kragmeerites,' Gappo corrects him, tossing the lotion to Poal.

'Kragmeerans, Kragmeerites, whatever,' Franx croaks back sleepily.

'And I'm sure the novelty wears off after a dozen sweeps in the early morning frost,' the ex-preacher continues. 'I met a sergeant from one of their long-range scouting groups. Even the most experienced men die quite regularly. Frostbite, hidden crevasses, ice bears, all kinds of nasty things waiting for the unwary out there.'

'Can't be any worse than False Hope,' I remind them. 'Now there was a hellhole, with no redeeming features.'

'Amen to that,' Franx agrees. He's got more reason than any of us to want to forget that deathworld.

'There was a great light, and all around was the beauty of the Emperor,' chips in Kronin, chasing after a piece of soap as it slithers through his thin fingers.

'Eh? What's that mean?' asks Poal. Our synchronised shrugs cause more ripples to spread across the water, and Kronin looks around, brow furrowed in thought.

'There was rejoicing upon the Square of the Evernight, for the darkness had passed and the light had returned,' he tries again. He sighs in frustration when we shake our heads.

'Try something from the Articles of Thor,' suggests Gappo. 'I studied them. Wrote a treatise published in the Magnamina Liber, actually.'

'I always thought the Articles of Thor were dull,' argues Poal, dropping the lotion bottle over his shoulder onto the tiled floor. 'Give me some stirring hymns from the Crusade Verses.'

'You even think about singing, I'll drown you,' Franx laughs. We all have to put up with Poal's atonal bellowing in the ablution block aboard ship.

'Ah!' exclaims Kronin suddenly, raising a finger excitedly in the air like some ageing scholar who's just discovered the secret of eternal health, youth and attraction to the opposite sex. 'The people gathered about Thor, and fell to their knees in adoration, for they realised that all that had come to pass was gone, and that all that remained was the future, and it was filled with the love of the Emperor!'

'Thor five-six-eight,' Gappo tells us, biting the corner of his lip in thought. 'It's all about how the people of San Sebacle survived the horrors of the Reign of Blood.'

'Going to be all right!' exclaims Franx suddenly, opening his eyes and turning to Kronin. 'Got a good feeling?'

Kronin grins widely again and nods, his thin face bobbing up and down in the water.

'That's comforting,' Poal says. 'Last time Kronin had a good feeling about a mission was on Harrifax. I ended up jumping bunks with Morag Claptin after that one!'

'You mean Lieutenant Claptin? That's how you made sergeant so fast, you wily dog!' Gappo says, his face a picture of shattered innocence. I duck under the water and rinse my head as Poal expands on the details of his conquest. I've heard them before. We've all heard all the stories before, but it doesn't stop us telling them, or listening to them again. Two and a half years together, there isn't that much we don't know about each other. Or anything new to say.

'Damn it!' I hear Poliwicz cursing as I rise up again. He's been busily scrubbing away on the far side of the pool. 'I knew it wouldn't work.'

'What's that?' Poal asks, swimming a few strokes to cross the three or so metres to the other side.

'Wondered if these fancy cleansers might work on the tattoo,' Poliwicz admits, lifting his shoulder out of the water to show where he's rubbed his upper arm raw. He's talking about the penal legion marking we all got tattooed with when we were 'recruited'.

'Ain't nothing gets rid of that,' Poal assures us. '"Cept perhaps the worms. Just ask Kage here, look what happened to his,' he adds, swimming back and prodding his hook into my right upper arm. You can't see that much of my tattoo now, there's a scar from a too-near miss of an eldar splinter rifle slashed across it.

'You remember Themper?' I ask them and they nod. 'Remember how he used his bayonet to slice off about three fingers of flesh to get rid of his?'

'That's right!' exclaims Poal. 'Bled like some fragged bastard for weeks, then they just tattooed another one onto his other arm and the Colonel told him if he cut that one out the next one would be across his face!'

'Should've said it'd be on his crotch,' Poliwicz laughs loudly. 'There'd be no way he'd take a blade anywhere near there!'

'He still died of blood poisoning though,' Gappo finishes the sorry saga of Themper. 'That's what happens when you don't change dressings.'

'And that is the importance of cleanliness and hygiene,' I say to them like a stern tutor. And then I grab a wet flannel floating in the pool and fling it at Franx, landing it square across his chin. Franx hurls it back, then Kronin ducks under the water and grabs my leg, pulling me under, and everything devolves into soaking wet anarchy as the others pile in on top.

As we get further into the mountains, the weather gets worse, if you can believe it. The wind gusts so strongly at times the only thing keeping me upright is that I'm standing thigh-deep in snow. The going is really slow sometimes, as we have to force our way up a ridge or slope. They're expecting the orks to reach the pass we'll be defending in about five days, and we've got to cover more than forty-five kilometres in that time. Not only that, we've got to bring all our camp equipment with us. A few dozen ploughfoots haul sledges for the heaviest gear, but the rest of it we're humping on our backs. I've never been so bone-tired before in my life. The past two nights I've just collapsed in my bedroll and fallen asleep almost straight away. At least we're getting some fresh food, roasted snow-ox, Kragmeerian pod-wheat and other such basics. It's good wholesome stuff. The Colonel realises that we wouldn't be able to carry on in these conditions on a bowl of protein slop a day.

The worst problem is the broken monotony. You can march for an hour or two, happily getting into your stride and letting your mind wander away from all this crap so that you don't notice the biting cold or the continuous aches in your spine and the backs of your legs. But then you have to scale a hill or something, or the snow gets soft and shifts under your feet, or you almost stumble into an ice crevasse, and it breaks your rhythm entirely and you have to work really hard to get back into your comfortable, numbing rut again.

The whole comms-blockage is playing on my mind too. I've been thinking about it while I've been plodding along. No communications with the base or even an army in the next valley. We're totally isolated. We're marching out here just to fight and die. Nobody's expecting us to return, they're just hoping our deaths will make the orks falter for a day or two while they build more barricades and bring in more troops from other stations. Fodder, that's all we are. Fodder for the orks to chew on for a while, maybe to choke on a little, and then it's over. Emperor knows what Kronin was so happy about. The hot bath seems a thousand kilometres and a year ago, though it was only three days.

Kragmeer is two different worlds, if you ask me. There's the one inside the stations. Nice, civilised, heated. Then there's the surface where snow twisters tear across the ice plains, blizzards can rip the skin off a man, and predators the size of battle tanks fight with each other for morsels of precious food. One planet, two worlds. And we have to get stuck in the nasty one.

I've been watching the Colonel closely these past few days and he seems to have changed. He seems more agitated than usual, urging us on with more than even his normal uncaring relentlessness. This whole business about us getting redirected to Kragmeer has unsettled him for some reason, and that worries me. If there's something that unsettles the Colonel, it probably should make me very, very worried. Still, there doesn't seem to be anything that can be done about it, whatever it is, so I try not to get overly concerned. Problem is, just trudging along I've got too much time to think, and that's when I get depressed. I don't like to think about the future, because I never know when I won't have one any more. Not that I've got much of one at the moment either.

BRAXTON DIED TODAY. The stupid fragger slipped out of his tent and tried to make a run for it. He headed the wrong way for a start, legging even further into the wilderness. We found his body a couple of hours along the march. He'd slipped down a narrow ravine, jagged icicles tearing his coat to ribbons. His body was frozen solid just a couple of metres down the crevasse, his face looked very serene considering his blood had frozen in his veins. He must have passed out before he died, that's what Gappo reckons.

It's the end of another long day. Not just in terms of hard work, it really is a long day here. It lasts about half as long again as a Terran day, which is what they use for the shipboard wake and sleep cycle. In the middle of winter, that's still twelve hours of straight slog; you can't really even stop for proper meals or anything, because once you stop, it's so hard to get going again. I'm getting blisters on my feet the size of eyeballs, and Poliwicz reckons he's going to lose a toe or two to frostbite. I told him to check with the Kragmeer guides, to see if he can get some better boots or something. They told him to put ploughfoot crap in his boots, for added insulation. Poal thought they were messing Poliwicz around, but I'll give it a try tomorrow, see if it works. If it gives me another edge, something else that helps keep me alive in this place, I'll do it.

There's self-respect, and there's pride, and some people can't see where the line is drawn. For me the difference is between doing something you don't want to but is necessary, and just plain refusing to do anything unpleasant at all. I won't let anyone tell me I'm worthless, even if I am a criminal. But I'll still put crap in my boots if it means it'll keep my feet warm. That's self-respect, not pride.

Kragmeer's star looks very distant and almost bluish as it sets over the mountains. Everything about this place is cold, even the light. I turn and watch the others rigging up our three storm tents – long, dome-like shapes of reinforced animal hide, designed to let the wind flow over them rather than push them over. Everything has to be done inside, the cooking, cleaning. Even emptying your bowels, which is quite unpleasant for everyone involved because snow ox is quite rich, if you understand me. Better that than freezing your butt off in a blizzard though.

With the camp set up, I tell Gappo to break out the stove. Huddled under the low roof of the tent, a few of us try to get as close as possible to the portable cooker, desperate for any warmth. The others huddle down in their bedrolls instead. Like everything else on Kragmeer, the stoves have been chosen for their suitability for the conditions, using a hot plate rather than an open flame that could set light to the tent. Its red glow is the only illumination, reflecting off the flapping walls to cast ruddy shadows, one moment making the tent seem warm and cosy, the next turning it into a blood-hued vision of hell. I try to concentrate on the warm and cosy look.

'I can't remember the last time I was this cold,' mutters Poal, his good hand held over the hotplate while Gappo digs around in the ration bags.

'Sure you can,' says Poliwicz, pulling back his hood to reveal his flat cheeks and broad nose, a classic example of Myrmidian ancestry. 'It was when you were in bed with Gappo's sister!'

'I don't have a sister,' Gappo says distractedly, pulling a hunk of flesh the size of my forearm from a saddlebag and dusting it off with his sleeve.

'Do they remove your sense of humour in the Ecclesiarchy?' asks Poliwicz, pushing past me to help Gappo with the food preparation.

'Hmm? No, they just bludgeon it out of you,' Gappo replies sincerely. 'Keeping the souls of humanity pure is a serious endeavour, you know.'

'I guess you're right,' Poliwicz concedes, pulling another piece of meat free and slapping it sizzling onto the stove.

'Not as serious as filling the coffers with donations and penances, of course,' Gappo adds darkly.

'Stop it right there!' I snap, before anyone else can say anything. 'Can we talk about something else? I'm too tired to stop you killing each other over religion.'

Everyone sits quiet, only the wind and the sputtering of the food on the stove break the silence. The tent flaps and flutters, the gale singing across the guy ropes in a tuneless fashion. I hear laughter from one of the other tents, where I put Franx in charge. The Colonel's on his own, keeping his solitary counsel as usual. It's been said before that he practises ways of killing himself in case he gets captured. I guess we all occupy our minds during these quiet moments in our own ways. Well, if the orks get him, all he'll have to do is strip naked and he'll be a lifeless icicle in minutes. The smell of the grilling snow ox fills the tent with its thick scent, reminding my stomach how empty it is. Someone else's guts gurgle in appreciation, so I'm not alone.

'I've got a sister,' Poal says finally.

'Oh, yeah?' I ask, expecting this to be the lead up to some crass joke.

'No, seriously,' he tells us. 'She was, is still I hope, in one of the Orders Hospitaller, from the Sisterhood.'

'Patching up wounded soldiers?' Gappo asks.

'That's right,' Poal confirms. 'Last I heard from her, before my unfortunate encounter with that two-timing serving wench, she was in a field surgery over near Macragge.'

'Say what you like about the Ministorum and their tithes, you get it back really,' says Poliwicz.

'In what way?' asks Gappo, the question half an accusation.

'Well,' explains the Myrmidian, settling down among the bags of grain, 'they fund the Schola Progenium abbeys. That's where we get the Sisterhood, the Commissars, the Storm Troopers, the scribes and so on. That's got to be worth something.'

'There are bounties and treasures aplenty for those of the true faith,' Kronin points out, the first thing I've heard him say today. He says less and less these days, I think he's getting more and more isolated, unable to talk properly with the rest of us. This vast, bleak world probably isn't helping him, it's easy to feel unimportant and lonely when faced with such harsh and eternal elements as the ones that rage outside. I can feel a melancholy mood coming on, fuelled by frustration and exhaustion.

'And of all those bounties,' Gappo says, 'we end up with bloody Poal!'

'So there is a sense of humour in there!' exclaims Poliwicz with a laugh as the rest of us chuckle stupidly.

'Shut the frag up, and turn those steaks over, I don't like mine burnt!' Poal snaps, causing another fit of giggles to erupt.

'I wonder if Franx has killed Linskrug yet?' I speculate idly, as Gappo busies himself with handing out mess tins.

'Why did you put them together then?' asks Kyle, sitting up from where he was lying in a bedsack at the far end of the tent.

'Don't you know?' I say, suddenly feeling bitter about being stuck out here in the middle of nowhere, an ugly and painful death lurking not far away. 'It's the same reason we're all here – torment is good for the soul.'

TWO DAYS WE'VE waited for the orks on this Emperor-forsaken mountainside. Two days sitting on our hands, so to speak, in the freezing snow and bone-chilling wind. We're set up just beneath the cloud line, sometimes it drifts down on us and you can't see your hand in front of your face. The air is so thin up here too, causing sickness and dizziness, the lower pressure making your body expel its gases pretty continuously. That caused some laughs the first few times until it became plain uncomfortable. Some of the men have already died from exposure to the elements, killed by sheer altitude.

The only way to cross onto the plains is over a ridge at the top end of the valley, or that's what the guides reckon. A few brave souls have tried to navigate the routes to the north and west, but none ever returned. We've got some explosives rigged up to bring down a good sized chunk of snow and rock on the greenskins, but I expect that'll just get their attention more than anything. I hope these Kragmeer guys know what they're doing because I don't want to get caught up in that mess when it comes tumbling down.

Now that we're here you might be fooled into thinking that the hard slog was over, but you'd be wrong. We've been kept really busy digging trenches in the ice. If you ever thought snow was soft, you're sorely mistaken. The stuff round here has been packed solid for centuries and I swear is harder than the rock. We've only been able to get the trenches maybe a metre and a half deep. Also, the bulky mitts you have to wear make it hard to grip the haft of a pickaxe or a shovel handle, and Poliwicz almost took his foot off earlier this morning. The watery light of the sun is just about above the clouds now, and for once the snow seems to have slackened off. Well, relatively speaking – it's just coming down continuously in big chunks now, instead of almost horizontally in a blizzard.

'The wind's shifted to the south,' one of the guides, Ekul, explains when I ask him about the calming weather. 'But that's actually bad news.'

'Why so?' I ask, wanting to know the worst before I get caught out by it. He looks to the south for a moment, showing the pointed, sharp profile of his nose and chin from out of the grey and white furs he's wearing. Like the rest of the Kragmeerites, his face is battered and weathered, and his dark eyes seem to gaze into the distance as if remembering something. He looks back at me, those eyes regarding me slowly, set above high cheekbones that seem to have been chiselled rather than grown.

'There's a kind of funnel effect in the valleys and that stirs up the storm a lot,' he replies eventually, bending down to draw a spiral with his finger in the snow. 'It builds up and builds up and then whoosh, it breaks up and over the mountaintops and comes rushing up here. We call it the Emperor's Wrath. A bit poetic, but you understand the idea.'

'Bad news to be caught out in it,' I finish for him.

'Seen men blown easily thirty metres clear off the ground, and that's no lying,' he tells me with a sorry shake of his head.

We stand there looking down the pass at the zigzag of trenches being built. We've taken up position on the western side of the valley, the shallower face. The other penal regiment has been split into two contingents, forming a first line and a second line. The plan is for the orks to crash against the first line and when they're thrown back the surviving defenders will pull back and reinforce the second line. I thought it would have been better on the eastern slopes, where the going is steeper and would slow down the ork assault. But of course the Colonel has looked at everything and pointed out a good kilometre of defilade further along the valley, where units on the eastern slope wouldn't be able to target the valley floor. All the orks would have to do would be rush the gauntlet of fire for the first kilometre and then they'd be in the defilade and in cover. Once they were clear of that they'd be out of range. That said, I've fought orks before, and I can't see them refusing the challenge of six thousand guardsmen shooting at them without trying an assault. It's the way their minds work – they're brutal beasts, without much thought, just an unquenchable hunger for war and bloodshed. Emperor knows, nature has certainly built them for battle. As I said before, you can shoot them, stab them, chop them, and they don't go down.

I see someone striding up through the snow and it's not difficult to recognise the Colonel. I watch him as he pushes up through the drifts, hauling himself along the rocks towards us at some points where the going is really treacherous. He pulls himself over the lip of the ledge we're standing on and stands there for a moment, catching his breath, glancing back down towards the entrenchments.

'How much warning can you give me?' he asks Ekul, looking around, towards the guide.

'Depends on how fast the orks are moving, sir,' he replies with a shrug. 'A ploughfoot can cover the ground from the pickets in a couple of hours, and assuming the cloud stays up, you should be able to spot a force that size a good ten kilometres away.'

'About five or six hours, then?' the Colonel confirms and the guide nods. 'Why are you here, Kage?' he adds suddenly.

'I was surveying the layout of the trenches, sir,' I reply quickly. It's the truth. I made the back-breaking climb up here with Ekul to get a feel for the lay of the land.

'You would not try to get away, would you lieutenant?' he says darkly.

'And go where?' I can't stop myself answering back. 'Go live with the orks?'

'And what are your conclusions, lieutenant?' the Colonel asks, thankfully ignoring my insubordination this time.

'We need to extend the front trenches on the left flank,' I tell him, indicating the area with a sweep of my arm. 'They should overlap the secondary position by a few hundred metres.'

'And how did you become such a student of military theory?' he asks quietly, looking straight at me.

'Because that's what we ran into when you led us on the for-lorn hope assault into Castle Shornigar on Harrifax, sir,' I point out, keeping the bitterness from my voice.

'I remember,' he says back to me. 'There was quite a deadly crossfire, if I recall.'

'There was, sir,' I concur, keeping my tone level. Three hundred and eighteen men and women died in that crossfire, you murderous bastard, I add mentally.

'I will talk to Colonel Greaves about extending his works,' he says with a nod. 'Thank you, lieutenant.'

I think about Greaves, the man in charge of the other penal regiment, as I clamber awkwardly back down the slope. He's a bull of a man, a few centimetres shorter than I am, but with chest and shoulders that would put an ogryn to shame. He constantly lambastes his men, shouting and swearing at them, cursing their heathen souls. He even has some wardens with him – Adeptus Arbites bullies who like to use their shock mauls. Unlike the Last Chancers, the other poor souls on this barren mountain are all civilians, sentenced to serve a term in a penal legion by the judges and magisters.

Their commander couldn't be any more different from ours either. I've never seen Schaeffer hit anyone who hasn't tried to attack him first. There's been a few over the years, and they ended up spitting teeth, let me assure you. He despises us all as criminals on principle, but doesn't seem to hate us as individuals. Unlike Greaves, who seems to delight in broadcasting his charges' shortcomings and inadequacies to everyone. If I were to sum it up, it's a completely different philosophy. Greaves's poor bastards only have to survive a certain length of time and they're out, so he tries to make their lives as miserable as possible while he can. Schaeffer, on the other hand, thinks he has a higher purpose. He does not act as our judge, he leaves that to the Emperor. And that means getting us killed, of course. It's like comparing False Hope to Kragmeer. One is very obviously a death-trap, full of instant death. The other is subtler, slowly leeching your life from you with a thousand tests of strength and endurance. Both are just as deadly of course.

'MOTHER OF DOLAN,' Poal curses from where he's sitting on the lip of the trench. 'There's thousands of them.'

I pull myself up the trench wall and stand next to him. The air has cleared a lot, part of the build-up for the Emperor's Wrath storm brewing to the south, and I can see what he means. At the mouth of the valley, about two kilometres to the south, the ork horde is spilling towards us. There seems to be little organisation or formation, just a solid mass of green-skinned devils marching solidly through the snow. Among the horde are a few tanks, battlewagons we call them. It's hard to make out any details at this range; it's just a dark mass against the snow.

More than a kilometre away, I make out the shapes of Dreadnoughts among the mobs of ork warriors. These giant walking war engines are twice to three times the height of a man, armed with a wild variety of heavy guns and close combat blades, saws and fists. The walls of the valley begin to echo with the noise of their approach. It's like a dull rumbling of thunder, a bass tone of war cries and bellows all merged into one cacophonous roar. As the horde gets closer, I can see that they're mainly wearing dark furs, with black and white checked banners fluttering in their midst, their vehicles picked out in places with the same patterning, oily smoke gouting from noisy engines that add to the gloom and racket.

The orks aren't stupid: they see the trenchlines and slowly the army begins to wheel up the slope, advancing along a diagonal towards us, making less of the slope's incline. The detachment in the primary trenches open fire with their heaviest weapons at about eight hundred metres, the crack of autocannons reverberating off the valley sides. I can see the sporadic flash of fire from the gun pits dug into the trenchlines, about three hundred metres further down the slope from where I am. The orks respond by starting a low chant, which slowly rises in volume as they advance, until it drowns out the fire of heavy bolters and lascannon.

'Waa-ork! Waa-ork! Waa-ork! Waa-ork! Waa-ork! Waa-ork!' they bellow at us, the mountainsides echoing with the battle-cry as it gathers in pace and the greenskins work themselves up for the final charge.

Their shouts are joined by a series of muffled detonations. Huge fountains of snow erupt to our right, just above the ork army. As a single mass, an enormous crescent of snow billows out. The slope begins to slide down towards the aliens, boulders rolling along amongst the wave of whiteness, the sparse trees on the mountainside ripped up as the avalanche quickens, its momentum accelerating rapidly. The orks' cries of dismay are swallowed up by the roaring of tons of snow and rock bearing down on them, the slope turned into a death-trap by the cascading ice.

The ork march falters immediately and the army tries to scatter as the snowslide bears down on them. The ground trembles violently, as it does under a bombardment, and I cast a nervous glance up the slope above, to make sure the effect isn't wider than planned. I must admit I breathe a sigh of relief when I see no movement at all, the glistening ice stretches up the mountain completely undisturbed. Ekul and his scouts did well. The gunners in the front trenches continue firing into the panicked horde even as the avalanche hits the orks. One moment there's a dispersing ork horde, the next there's just a solid whiteness, flecked with darker patches as orks and vehicles are hurled skywards, before being engulfed and disappearing from view.

Secondary slides pile up on top of the hill of snow now filling the valley floor, layering more death onto the orks buried under the packed snow. Greaves's men start cheering, their cries of joy replacing the thunder of the avalanche. I notice that none of the Last Chancers join in, they're all watching the valley floor with determined expressions. I know what they're thinking. It's not going to be that easy, one quick avalanche and the orks are dead. It's never that easy for a Last Chancer. Sure enough, as the swirl of scattered snow begins to clear in the air, I can see a sizeable proportion of the ork army left. Stunned and dazed for the moment, but still more than enough to over-run our defences once they gather their wits again. And now they'll be even madder for the fight, eager to even the head count.

In the front trench, Greaves gets his poor charges to continue the fusillade into the orks, giving them no respite. A smart tactic, but I can't help but think that it's just Greaves wanting to shout at his penal troopers some more. A bright orange explosion lights the centre of the ork mob as a Dreadnought's fuel is detonated by a lascannon. A couple of other Dreadnoughts and a single battlewagon survived the avalanche, but Greaves is directing his men well and the lascannons and autocannons soon reduce them to burning wrecks.

An odd thing occurs to me as the orks forge their way back up the slope. Vehicles need fuel, and there's little to be found out in this icy wilderness. The Kragmeerites have one-in-three of their ski-based Chimeras converted into fuel carriers for long range work, and it stands to reason that orks would need some kind of support vehicles. Not only for fuel, but for transporting ammunition and food. It's hard to see how this army, small as it is, relatively speaking, could take a single Kragmeer station, never mind the three that have already fallen. And it's eight hundred kilometres across unbroken ice plains from the nearest to these mountains. Even if they looted everything they could from the fallen stations, they'd have to move it around somehow. Orks are good looters, they can scavenge pretty much anything, and I was half expecting them to turn up in captured, specially modified Chimeras. It doesn't make sense that several thousand orks, hardy as they are, could survive this long without that kind of backup. I don't know what the explanation is, but I start to feel uneasy about this. I'd speak to the Colonel, but I don't have any answers, and I'm sure he's made the same observations.

Lasgun salvoes join the heavy weapons fire as the orks close. The greenskins begin to return fire, flickers of muzzle flare sparkling across the darkness of the horde as it breaks into a charge. Once more, they break into their war chant, faster and louder than ever. The las-fire is almost constant now; Greaves has ordered the troopers to shoot at will rather than volley fire. Orks tumble into the snow in droves, but the rest keep coming on, surging up the mountainside in a living tide of bestial ferocity.

'They won't hold,' Poal says from beside me, his lasgun whining as he powers up its energy cell.

'They might,' I reply, keeping my gaze firmly fixed on the front trench. The orks burst onto Greaves's soldiers like a storm, the poorly trained penal guardsmen no match for the orks' innate lust for close quarters combat.

'Pull them back now,' I hear Poal whispering insistently. 'Pull them back before it's too bloody late!'

I see what Poal means as more and more orks pour into the trenchline. If Greaves makes a break for it now, we can give enough covering fire to keep the orks off his back. If he goes too late, they'll be all mingled up and we won't be able to pick out friend from foe.

'Now, you fragging idiot!' Poal bellows, clambering to his feet.

For a moment I think that hard-headed Greaves is going to fight to the last man, taking his criminals into hell with him. But then movement from our end of the front trench, the left flank, shows men and women clambering up the back walls before the orks can fight their way along the trench to them. I reckon Greaves's own instincts for self-preservation must have kicked in. I can see him urging his troopers on, waving his arm towards us as he hauls himself through the snow.

'Covering fire!' the order is shouted from further up the trench. Poal starts snapping off shots to our right, spotting a few dozen orks that have broken from the trench and are charging after Greaves's men, trying to cut them off. The staccato roaring of a heavy bolter joins the snap of lasguns, and a hole is torn in the crowd of orks.

Colonel Greaves leads his men to our left. We're on the right flank of the second trench, about five hundred of them, half of the first-line force. The orks don't pause to consolidate their position in the front trench; they pour over the fortifications and spill up towards us. I pull my laspistol free and start snapping off shots – the orks are densely packed, I can't miss, even at this range with a pistol. The greenskins begin to disperse, trying to attack along a wider frontage, some of them breaking to our left in a bid to get around the left flank and encircle us.

Return fire starts sending up sprays of snow and Poal and I jump back down into the trench for shelter. The orks are spread into a thinning line now, concentrated more in front of us, but stretching out to the left and right.

'Prepare for hand-to-hand combat!' The wardens' bellows carry up the trenchline.

'We cannot hold the trench,' I hear Schaeffer say next to me.

'Sir?' I ask, turning to look at him.

'One on one, these men cannot fight orks,' he explains quickly. 'Once the orks are in the trench, we cannot concentrate our numbers on them. And they will be very hard to get out again.'

'Counter-attack, sir?' I suggest, reading the Colonel's mind, horrified by the thought of hastening any confrontation with the brutal aliens, but seeing there's little hope otherwise. 'Hit them in the open?'

'Pass the word for general attack,' the Colonel shouts up the trench to our left. A moment later and he's grabbing the rungs of the trench ladder and hauling himself out. I follow him, and feel the ladder vibrating as others follow.

There's shouting and screams all around as the orks and guardsmen exchange fire. We're about fifty metres from the orks, charging full speed towards them, men slipping and floundering in the snow, the greenskins encountering similar difficulties. I start firing with my laspistol again, dismayed to see the flashes of energy striking targets but not having too much effect against the tough aliens. They continue roaring their guttural cries as they close, a wave of sound accompanied by the crack of shells and zip of lasguns. A change in the wind wafts their stench over me, and I gasp for breath, hauling myself through the folds of snow. It's a mixture of death and unwashed bodies, utterly foul.

As we close the gap, I can see the greenskins are armed with a variety of crude-looking guns and hefty close combat weapons. Blazes of muzzle flare punctuate the ork mass, and the silvery light glitters off blades lovingly honed to cleave through flesh and bone with a single stroke. I pick out one to engage, pulling my knife from my belt when I'm twenty metres from the greenskin. It's dressed in black mainly, bits of ragged fur stitched onto a kind of jerkin, white checks painted onto metal pads on its broad shoulder and a roughly beaten breastplate which is gouged and dented from previous fighting. I notice with dismay the two human heads dangling from its belt, meat hooks plunged through their lifeless eyes to hold them on. The alien seems to read my thoughts, its red eyes glaring back at me as we close. Everyone and everything else is forgotten as I focus all my attention on the ork, noting the bulge of muscles under its furs, the ragged scar stretching from its wide chin across its fanged mouth and over its left cheek, passing its pug nose. Its skin is dark green and leathery looking, pocked with scars and warts, obviously impervious to the biting cold that would kill a man. It opens its mouth and bellows something, revealing a jawful of yellowing tusks – tusks that can rip through muscles and crush bones with one bite.

At five metres it levels a bulky pistol and fires, but the shots are way off, screaming past my head at least half a metre to my left. In its right hand is a blade like a butcher's cleaver, its head easily a metre long. It pulls back the cleaver and swings at my chest but I dodge to my left, feet slipping in the snow as the blade arcs past. I take a lunge with my knife but the ork easily bats it away with a strong arm, chopping down with the cleaver at the same time. Once more I wriggle sideways, though not quite quick enough, the crude chopper slicing a strip from the left sleeve of my coat. Cold air swirls onto my arm, causing my flesh to prickle all over with the chill, but that goes unnoticed as I bring my pistol up to its face. It ducks to avoid the shot, straight onto my waiting knife, which I jab upwards, plunging the tip into its throat, twisting with all my strength as dark blood, almost black and very thick, gushes into the white snow and over my legs.

I step back and another ork leaps at me, two serrated knives glittering in the cold light. The las-bolt from my pistol takes it squarely in the left eye, smashing out the back of its head, flinging the creature down into the snow.

Poal's fending off another ork with his hook, slashing at its guts with the point, jumping back as it punches back with knuckle-dusters fitted with a couple of short blades. I reverse my knife and plunge it backhanded into the ork's neck, feeling it deflected off the thick bones of its spine, tearing a gash up into the base of its skull. The ork backhands me, knocking me to my knees, and turns around snarling, blood spraying from the open wound. It kicks out, scattering snow, a metal toe-capped boot connecting with my thigh, almost snapping the bone. Poal's hook flashes up, slashing into the ork's mouth and ripping out its cheek. Spitting blood and teeth, the greenskin rounds on Poal, but his next swipe smashes into the ork's nose, the point ramming up its nostril, lacerating its face and plunging into the brain. The ork twitches spasmodically as it crumples to the ground, but neither of us spares it a second glance as we check on how the fight is going. Most of the orks are falling back towards the other trench, taken off guard by the counter-attack. The few that fight on are hopelessly outnumbered and quickly overwhelmed. Hundreds of greenskin corpses, and more humans, lie twisted and ragged, the snow churned up and red with blood. Severed limbs and decapitated bodies are piled waist high in places where the fighting was most fierce.

'CAUGHT OUT BY a pretty simple trick,' Poal says as I describe the fight with the first ork, the two of us collapsed in the trench with the others. 'I thought the orks were smarter than to be caught out with a straightforward feint.'

'Oldest trick in the bloody book,' chips in Poliwicz, cleaning his bayonet in the snow.

'Yeah, the simplest of tricks…' I murmur to myself, an unsettling thought beginning to form in my mind. I look around for the Colonel and see him not much further along the trench, talking to Greaves and Ekul. I push my way through the tired guardsmen, turning a deaf ear to the groans and moans of the wounded as I barge them aside.

'Sir!' I call to the Colonel as he's about to walk away.

'Yes, Kage?' he asks sharply, turning on his heel.

'I think we've been tricked, sir,' I tell him quickly, glancing back over my shoulder to see what the orks are doing.

'Tricked?' Greaves says from behind the Colonel, disbelief written all over his face. 'What do you mean?'

'This attack is a feint, a diversion,' I explain hurriedly, waving my hands around trying to convey the sudden sense of urgency that fills me. 'It makes sense, now I think about it. They crossed the plains with the support of the main army and then split off.'

'What nonsense is this?' Greaves demands. 'Get back to your place.'

'Wait a moment, colonel,' Ekul says, stepping up beside the Colonel, looking intently at me. 'A diversion for what, Kage?'

'This isn't the main ork army, it's a diversionary attack sent to fool us and keep us occupied while the main force goes around

us.' The words spill out quickly, my mind racing with the impli-
cations of the situation.

'You could be right,' the Colonel says with a nod. 'This army
bears little resemblance to the one in the reports. I thought it
might just be a vanguard.'

'Where else can they go?' asks Greaves disdainfully. 'Ekul says
no man's ever survived the other passes in this region.'

'No man, sir,' Ekul agrees, 'but the lieutenant may have a
point. We are not fighting men. It is possible the orks could
forge another route towards Epsilon Station, circumnavigating
this valley altogether.'

'What can we do about it? Our orders are to hold this pass,'
Greaves says stubbornly. 'And Kage is probably wrong.'

'It is still a distinct possibility,' the Colonel replies, eyes narrowed as he thinks. 'You and your regiment will continue to
hold this pass. The loss of my force does not greatly affect that.
We must get to Epsilon Station and warn them.'

My hopes rise at the thought of going back to Epsilon. Much
easier to survive a siege than an open battle. And we'll be
inside, out of this forsaken cold and snow.

'My few mounted men can travel much quicker,' Ekul points
out, dashing my hopes to the ground. 'And we know the terrain
better.'

'Wouldn't it be better if you and your scouts went looking for
the main force?' I suggest, thinking quickly, trying to keep the
desperation from my voice.

'They're coming again!' a warden shouts from back down the
line.

'We go now!' the Colonel says emphatically. 'Pack what provisions you can, Kage, and muster the men here.'

FIVE MINUTES LATER and the surviving Last Chancers are gathered
with me, stowing what we can onto a couple of the ploughfoot
sleds. The wind's picked up again, tossing the snow around us,
and over its keening can be heard the rattle of autocannons and
snap of lasguns as Greaves's soldiers try to hold off the orks as
they pour from the forward trench. The Colonel appears
through the snow.

'Are you ready?' he asks, glancing back over his shoulder
towards the trenches a few dozen metres away. The odd stray
ork shot zips past, but not that close. Greaves soon appears too,

stamping through the snow to stand in front of the Colonel with his hands on hips.

'You're disobeying orders, Schaeffer,' Greaves says hotly, jabbing at the Colonel with an accusing finger. 'You're abandoning your position.'

'If you get the opportunity, follow us,' the Colonel replies calmly, ignoring the accusation.

'You're a coward, Schaeffer,' the bulky man counters, prodding a finger into the Colonel's chest. 'You're no better than these scum we have to lead.'

'Goodbye, Colonel Greaves,' the Colonel says shortly, and I can tell he's holding his temper in check. 'We probably will not meet again.'

Greaves continues cursing us as we trudge off through the snow, Franx and Loron leading the ploughfoots at the front, the Colonel at the rear.

As we near the top of the ridge again the wind starts to really bite, managing to push its way onto my face despite the thick fur lining of my coat's hood. Already my legs are beginning to feel tired, after just a couple of kilometres. The Colonel pushes us hard, not saying a word, just giving us a scathing look when one of us falters or slows down. I trudge on, concentrating all my thoughts on lifting my feet and taking the next step, my eyes focused on Lorii's back in front of me, letting me detach my mind from the real world.

The light begins to fail soon after, the sun dipping beneath the mountains and casting a red glow across the summits. It would be quite beautiful if I hadn't seen the snow back in the valley stained red and black with blood. Now all the sunset reminds me of is hacked limbs and dismembered bodies. It seems there's nothing left that isn't tainted by bloodshed now. I see children and they just remind me of the pile of small corpses we found in Ravensbrost on Carlille Two. Every time I think of something like flowers, I just remember False Hope and the alien beast of the Heart of the Jungle. A sunny day just takes me back to the crushing heat of the Gathalon ash wastes, where two hundred men sank into the shifting ash dunes, the corrosive dust eating away at them even as they were sucked down. As for any kind of bugs, well I guess you know what they remind me of. There are no pleasures left anywhere except the company of my fellow Last Chancers, and those moments are few and far between. Why does everything have to remind me of a war or battlefield somewhere? Does the Colonel realise this? Is this part of the punishment, to have everything stripped away from you? All my comfortable illusions have been torn apart over the past three years. When I joined up, I thought I'd be able to make a difference. Hah, what a joke. I've seen battle with ten thousand men killed in an afternoon, the rockets and shells raining down like explosive hail for hour after hour. I've shot, strangled and stabbed more enemies than I can remember. There's not a sensation I can feel now that hasn't been stained somehow. Even jumping in the tub back in Epsilon Station, my first thoughts were memories of a river crossing on Juno. Mangled bodies floating past as we tried to swim across, men being dragged down by the swift undercurrents, tracer fire screaming through the night towards us.

IT'S AROUND midnight before the Colonel calls a stop. We don't even bother setting camp or cooking, everybody takes a few bites of salted meat and then collapses with their blankets wrapped around them. I drift into an exhausted sleep, woken occasionally by the Colonel, who's doing the rounds, making sure the cold hasn't got to anyone too much. It must only have been a couple of hours when he kicks us all awake again. It's still pitch dark as we flounder around getting ready, the Colonel snarling at us to get a move on. Once more the march starts, forcing my aching legs to work, at points literally hauling myself through the snow on my hands and knees, sinking into the cold white layer up to my elbows.

A sudden scream of panic has everybody reaching for their guns, but Gappo comes hurrying back to tell the Colonel someone's wandered into a crevasse in the dark. I push myself after the Colonel as he forges ahead, Gappo guiding us to where the hole is. I can see frag all in the dark, and the Colonel asks who it is. There's just a groan in reply, and we do a quick name check of everybody else and find that bloody Poal is missing.

'We cannot afford the time for a rescue,' the Colonel announces, stepping away from the crevasse's edge. 'There is no way of telling how far down he is and we do not have the proper equipment.'

There's a few discontented murmurs, but everyone's too cold to really argue. Gappo stays by the edge after everyone else has gone. When he turns and looks at me, there's a blank look in his eyes.

'It only takes a few minutes,' he says, to himself I think. 'He'll just fall asleep. He won't know what's happening.'

'If it's deep, he's probably out of it already,' I say, laying a hand on his shoulder and pulling him away. He takes a couple of steps, then stops again.

'We have to keep going!' I snap at him, dragging him forward again. 'We reach Epsilon or we *all* die.'

THE COLONEL PUSHES us without a break for the whole of the next day as well. I walked past someone lying in the snow in the afternoon. They were face down, I couldn't tell who it was and didn't have the energy to try to find out. I try to see who's missing when we stop, but my eyes are crusted up and sore, and everyone looks the same in their heavy coats with the hoods pulled tight across their faces. I force myself to gulp down some more preserved meat. Nobody says a word to each other, and even the Colonel is quieter than usual. I sit there shivering, hands clasped across my chest, feeling an ache in every single bone and muscle. My head's just nodding as my body gives up the fight against the cold and sleep begins to take over, when someone's shaking me awake again.

'What the…?' I snarl, slapping the hand away.

'It's Franx,' says Gappo.

That's all he needs to say. He helps me to my feet and we make our way over to where he's lying. I crouch down beside him and peer inside his hood. His face is crusted with ice, and looks extremely pale. A moment later and Lorii joins us, bending close, her cheek next to his mouth.

'Still breathing,' she tells us, straightening out. 'Barely.'

'I can't leave him,' Gappo declares, and I nod in agreement. I kind of promised myself that Franx was going to survive this one. 'What can we do? I'm too tired to carry anything other than this coat.'

'Put him on the sled,' Lorii suggests.

'The ploughfoots are already pulling as much as they're supposed to,' Gappo cautions, stamping his feet to keep himself warm.

'Well, they'll have to work harder. We'll get them to do it in shifts,' I decide. Nobody argues.

THERE'S A STRANGE whinnying of pain from the ploughfoot at the head of the diminishing column. Two men didn't wake up, another two collapsed this morning. The midday sun glares off the snow, making it as difficult to see during the day as it is at night.

'Kage!' I hear the Colonel bellowing, and I shuffle forward. The ploughfoot is lying in the snow, its left hind leg at an odd angle and clearly broken. The sled is over-turned on a rock nearby.

'Sir?' I ask as the Colonel stands up from where he was kneeling next to the stricken animal.

'Organise the men into teams of six, and rig up the harness into drag ropes,' he says. He pulls his bolt pistol from its holster, places the muzzle against the side of the ploughfoot's head and blows its brains out. My first thought is the fresh meat it could provide, but a glance at the Colonel reminds me that we won't be wasting a second. Then I'm filled with a sudden surge of hatred.

'You wouldn't do the same for us,' I snarl at Schaeffer, pointing to the still-smoking bolt pistol.

'If you had also served the Emperor well, you might have deserved some mercy,' he counters, holstering the pistol. 'You have not, and you do not deserve anything.'

THERE'S TWELVE OF us left now, not including the Colonel, and we take it in turns to drag the sled on two-hour stints. The Colonel tried to get me to leave Franx behind, saying the additional weight was unnecessary, but Gappo, Loron, Lorii and Kronin volunteered to team up with me and we've been swapping him between our shift and the remaining ploughfoot's sled.

I soon lose track of the time, even the midnight stops have gone beyond counting, so we might have been going for only three days or for a whole week, it's impossible to say. The wind's really picked up now, and the snow is getting heavier again. I remember Ekul's warnings about the Emperor's Wrath storm, and fear the worst. I let the others know what's coming and everybody redoubles their efforts, but it's getting to the point where it takes everything out of you just to stay awake, never mind keeping walking and pulling the sled. Soon we've emptied one sled of provisions and we decide to dump the tents, nobody's had the strength to put them up since we started. The going gets a little quicker then, with the two teams and the ploughfoot taking turns with the remaining sled.

'If the orks are up against anything like this, they may never make it across,' Kyle suggests one evening as we gnaw on half-frozen strips of meat.

'Don't you believe it,' I say. 'They're tough bastards, you know that. Besides, they'll have looted and built Emperor knows what before trying the crossing. If their warlord's smart enough to come up with the feint, it's definitely got the brains to come prepared. They've probably got vehicles and everything as well.'

'What if we're too late?' exclaims Kyle, suddenly veering from optimism to total depression in a moment. I've never noticed him having mood swings like this before, but then I guess we're all swinging wildly from hope to despair and back again at the moment.

'Then we're bent over backwards, good and proper,' Poliwicz says, tearing at his salted meat with his teeth.

'Whole Emperor-damned planet looks the same,' curses Kyle. 'I can't tell where we are, how far we've got to go.'

Nobody bothers replying; it's hard enough to concentrate on the next few minutes, let alone worry about the next day. I toss the remnants of my rations aside, too tired to chew, and lie back, willing sleep to claim me quickly and take me away from the pain in every part of my body.

HOARSE SCREAMING up ahead snaps me out of my fatigue-induced sleepwalking.

'What now?' I ask sleepily when I reach the half-dozen Last Chancers clustered up ahead.

'One of the station's pickets,' the Colonel says. 'I have sent him back with the warning about the orks.' I realise they were shouts of joy, not screams, but in my befuddled state I'd just interpreted them as more pain and misery for some poor soul.

'We're still going on to Epsilon, aren't we?' I ask hurriedly, fearing the Colonel might be about to order us to turn around and go back the way we came.

'Yes we are. This has gone on long enough,' he reassures me, and for the first time I notice how thin and drawn he's looking.

There are massive dark rings around his eyes from the sleepless nights, and his whole body looks slumped, like the rest of us.

It takes another two hours' trekking before we reach the gate-houses. A small delegation of officers from the Kragmeer regiments waits for us. Their mood is grim, but they don't look too unkindly on us when, at a word from the Colonel, we fall to the snow a few metres away from them, completely exhausted.

I don't hear what they're saying; my ears have been numb for the past few days, even with the fur-lined coat pulled protectively over my head. They seem to be having some sort of argument, and I'm wondering if they've taken the same line as Greaves, accusing the Colonel of abandoning his command. I see Schaeffer shaking his head violently and point up into the sky. I hear a scattering of words, like 'siege', 'time', 'important', and 'orbit'. None of it makes any sense. One of the Kragmeer officers, bloody high-ranking by all the finery on his uniform, steps forward and makes negative cutting gestures with his hand before pointing over his shoulder back into the station. There are more heated exchanges and the Colonel turns on his heel and stamps over to us.

'On your feet, Last Chancers,' he snaps, before marching off, up the valley and away from the gates.

'Where the frag are we going now?' asks Poliwicz.

'Perhaps we're defending the shuttle pad?' Gappo guesses with a shrug.

After the brief flood of energy once we knew we were close to Epsilon, my tiredness returns with a vengeance. My brain shuts down everything except the bits needed for walking and breathing for the trek up to the shuttle pad, and everything from the past couple of weeks condenses into a blurry white mess.

We reach the shuttle pad to find the gate closed. Peering through the mesh of the high fence, I can see our shuttle still out on the apron, kept clear of snow by the attendants.

'That's a direct order from a superior officer,' I hear the Colonel say and I focus my attention back on him. He's standing at the door of the little guardhouse next to the gate, and there's a Kragmeer sergeant shaking his head.

'I'm sorry, Colonel,' the sergeant says, hands held up in a helpless gesture, 'but without the proper authority I can't let you take the shuttle.'

My brain suddenly clunks into gear. *Take the shuttle?* We're leaving?

'Lieutenant Kage!' barks the Colonel and I quick march over to him, standing to attention as best I can. 'If this man does not open this gate immediately and clear the pad for launch, shoot him.'

The Kragmeerite starts babbling something as I pull my pistol out and point it at his head. I really don't give a frag whether I blow this guy's brains out or not. For one thing, I'm just too tired to care. For another, if this frag-head is stopping me from getting off this ice-frozen hell, I'll happily put a slug in his skull.

He relents under my not-so-subtle coercion, stepping back into the hut to pull a lever which sets the gate grinding open. Klaxons begin to echo off the hills around us, and people start scurrying from the hangars and work barracks.

'We're leaving,' the Colonel announces, stepping through the gateway.

'Leaving?' Linskrug asks. 'Going where?'

'You'll find that out when we get there, trooper,' the Colonel says mysteriously.

SIX
TYPHOS PRIME

+++ *Operation Harvest complete. Preparing to commence Operation New Sun.* +++

+++ *There can be no more delays. New Sun must go ahead on schedule or all will be lost.* +++

COMPARED WITH SOME of the places I've been with the Last Chancers, and considering that it's been torn apart by bloody civil war for the past two years, Typhos Prime seems very civilised. After touching down at one of its many spaceports, a Commissariat squad escorts us through busy city streets, with people coming and going as if there weren't battles being fought less than two hundred kilometres away. There are a few telltale signs that everything isn't as cosy as it seems, though. There are air raid warning sirens at every junction – huge hailers atop six-metre poles – and signs marking the route to the nearest shelters. Arbitrators patrol the streets, menacing with their silvered armour over jet-black jump-suits, wielding shock mauls and suppression shields.

As we pass along a wide thoroughfare, there are shuttered windows amongst the stores along both sides of the wide road. There are a few people around, swathed against the autumnal chill and damp in shapeless brown coats and thick felt hats, trailing brightly coloured scarves from their necks. A smog hangs above the city, visible over the squat buildings to either side, mixing with the cloud that stretches across the sky to cast a dismal gloom over the settlement. A column of Chimeras led by two growling Conqueror tanks, resplendent in blue and gold livery, grumbles past along the road, horse carriages and zimmer cars pulling aside to let them pass. In a reinforced underground staging area, we embark on a massive eight-wheeled roadster designed for long-haul troop movements, and the twelve of us spread out, trying to decide in which of the three hundred seats we want to sit. The Colonel parks himself up front with the driver, intently ignoring us.

'Reminds me of tutelage outings,' jokes Franx. 'Head up the back where bad boys hang out!'

I'll take his word for it, I never had that kind of education. I was brought up as part of an extended family, with a dozen brothers, sisters and cousins, and my first memories are of chipping at slag deposits with a rusted chisel and mallet, trying to find nuggets of iron and steel. The roadster jolts into life, the whine of the electric engines soon being relegated to the back of my mind, out of conscious thought. Linskrug and Gappo join us and we sprawl happily, each across a three-wide seating tier.

'This is a bit of a royal treatment, is it not?' suggests Linskrug, peering out of the tinted windows at the low buildings blurring past outside. A faint rain has started, speckling the windows with tiny droplets of moisture. 'It's much more what I'm accustomed to.'

'He wants to keep us contained,' I point out to him. 'Of all the places we've been, this is the best one to get lost in. Billions of people live on Typhos Prime; a man could quite happily disappear here, never to be seen again.'

'Hey!' whispers Gappo urgently from the other side of the aisle. 'There's an emergency exit down these stairs!'

We cluster round and have a look. It's true, there's a small door at the bottom of a flight of four steps.

'Reckon it's locked?' asks Franx in his now-familiar wheeze. I test the handle and it turns slightly. I look at the others and grin widely. Gappo glances over the top of the surrounding seats and then crouches down again.

'No one's paying the blindest bit of notice,' he says with a smile and a mischievous look in his eye. 'I don't think anyone will miss us.'

'We're moving at a pretty rate,' Linskrug says, pointing to the blurred grey shapes of the outside whizzing past the windows.

'Hell,' coughs Franx, rubbing his hands together with glee. 'I can live with a few bruises!'

I look at each of them in turn, and they meet my gaze, trying to gauge my thoughts. They know my track record on escape attempts, and how I keep nagging them not to get stupid. I guess I've been half-hearted in my own attempts to escape, because I think a part of me agrees with the Colonel. Perhaps I have wasted the opportunity the Emperor gave me, reneged on my oaths. I never intended to, of that much I'm certain, I joined up with the purest of intentions, even though I wanted to get the hell off Olympas. But as they say, the road to Chaos is paved with good intentions. But then again, how much blood does the Emperor want from me? It's kind of a tradition that an Imperial Guard regiment serves for a maximum of ten years at which point it can retire, maybe returning home or going off to join the Explorator fleets and help claim a new world for the Emperor. A lot of them won't spend half that time fighting. I've been up to my neck in blood and guts, seeing men and women and children dead and dying, for nearly three years now. Haven't I had my fair share of war? I think I have. I think I've made the most of my Last Chance. The Colonel's never going to let us live; he wants us all dead, that much I'm sure. I'll let the Emperor be my judge, when I die, hopefully in the not so near future.

'Frag, let's do it!' I whisper hoarsely before twisting the door handle fully. The emergency exit swings open and I see the black of the road tearing past the opening. Somewhere at the head of the roadster there's a shrill whining. The door must have been alarmed. I take a deep breath and then drop out of the doorway feet first. Thudding down onto the road, my momentum sends me rolling madly, pitching me into a shin-high kerbstone. Glancing up the road I see the others bailing out after me, slamming uncomfortably to the ground. I jump to my feet and set off towards them at a run.

'We did it!' screams Linskrug, eyes alight with joy. There's a few people walking past on the pavement, swathed in high-collared raincoats. A couple turn to look at us. 'Schaeffer will never get that thing turned around in time to catch us.'

Just then there's a screech of airbrakes and a black-painted armoured car slews to a halt in front of us, twin cannons on its roof pointing in our direction. A man jumps out of the back hatch, bolt pistol in hand, dressed in a commissar's uniform. His face is pinched, thin-lipped mouth curled in a sneer.

'Please try to run,' he growls as he walks towards us, bolt pistol held unwaveringly in front of him. 'It would save me lots of problems.'

None of us make a move. Ten black-clad troopers pour from the armoured car, thick carapace breastplates over their uniforms, faces hidden behind dark visors. The Commissariat provosts have us surrounded in a couple of seconds and our brief moment of freedom is over. I take a deep breath, loving the smoke-tinged air, the feel of the gentle rain splashing down onto my upturned face. I don't want to relinquish this feeling that easily. I can't believe the Colonel will have us in his grip again. I look at the provosts, at the bulky laser carbines pointed at us, and I wonder if we might not still get out of this. The four of us are hardened fighters. These guys are bully-boys, used to guardsmen being scared of them. But I can see their faces set grimly underneath the black visors of their helmets and I can tell they're not going to hesitate for a second. The commissar had the truth of it – they'd rather we tried something, giving them the excuse to open fire.

'I can't believe that Schaeffer had an escort following us,' Gappo moans as we're shoved into the back of the armoured car. We have to squat in the middle of the floor between the provosts, there's not enough room for everyone to sit or stand. The commissar leans down towards me and grabs my chin between a finger and thumb, turning my face towards him.

'I am sure Colonel Schaeffer will be very pleased to see you again,' the commissar says with a cruel smile. 'Very pleased indeed.'

TRUDGING THROUGH the mud, rain cascading off my helmet, I realise that perhaps Typhos Prime isn't so nice after all. The roadster dropped us off about sixteen kilometres from the front line, or where they think the front line is, leaving us to foot it the rest of the way. The war's dragged on for a couple of years now, ever since a first abortive assault against the rebel fortress failed, and both sides have drawn up trenchlines a few kilometres from Coritanorum's walls and have since tried to shell each other into submission.

Alongside us is a Mordian marching column, trying to look smart and trim in their nice blue uniforms. The effect is somewhat spoilt by the mud splashes, and the peaks of their caps are starting to lose their stiffness under the downpour of rain, drooping towards their noses in a pathetic fashion. They've steadfastly ignored us for the past eight kilometres as we sauntered forward alongside them. The Colonel didn't even bother shouting at us when Kyle tried to provoke them by calling them toy soldiers and officers' pets.

He seems very distracted at the moment, the Colonel I mean. Franx and I have agreed that this is what we've been building up to, for a year at least, anyway. He's brought us here to do something particularly horrid, of that we're sure, but we can't suss what it might be yet. A dozen Last Chancers isn't a whole heap of a lot in a war where each side has supposedly already lost half a million men.

'Incoming!' shrieks Linskrug and a second later my ears pick up what the baron's sharp ears heard a moment earlier – the whine of an aircraft's engines in a screaming dive. We scatter, hurling ourselves into water-filled craters and behind rocks, peering up into the clouds for a sign of our attacker. I look astonished as the Mordians continue their formed march and then I realise that they won't break formation until one of their officers tells them to. I see a swathe of them knocked to the ground and an instant later the chatter of heavy guns can be heard. Glancing up I see the rebel stratocraft sweeping low, four flashing bursts along its wings showing where light autocannons are spitting out a hail of death. The Mordians march relentlessly on and the aircraft wings over and banks round for another pass. Once more the guns chatter and two dozen or more Mordians, all the men in two ranks of troopers, are torn apart by the fusillade.

'Get down, you fragging idiots!' screams Gappo, the first time I've ever heard him swear. The Mordians don't pay him any notice though and the aircraft makes another attack run, the trail of bullets sending up splashes of mud and water as the hail zigzags towards the marching guardsmen. It passes over the column and as it does so I realise with horror that it's heading towards us. Before I can react I feel something slamming across my forehead, pitching me backwards into the puddles and stunning me.

'Emperor-damn, we've got men down! Kage is down! The lieutenant's down!' I dimly hear someone screaming, Poliwicz by the broad Myrmidian accent. People splash around me, soaking me further, but I just lie there, still. Dead still. Two opportunities in one day must mean the Emperor approves.

I feel someone wiping the blood from my forehead and hear them curse bitterly – it's Linskrug. He grabs my arms and I try to go as limp as possible. As he folds my arms across my chest someone else pushes my helmet down across my face.

'The Colonel's says we've got to keep going,' I hear Gappo shouting hoarsely, choking back a sob by the sound of it.

Sentimental idiot, I think to myself. Linskrug disappears and another shadow falls across my eyelids.

'Unto death, I shall serve him,' says Kronin. 'Unto life again, shall he serve the Emperor.'

I WAIT UNTIL I haven't heard voices for a long time before opening my eyes. Darkness is falling and I can't see anyone around. The rain's still drizzling down from the overcast sky, but I pull off my flak jacket and fatigues, grabbing the uniform from a dead Mordian only a few metres away. It isn't an exact fit, but it'll do. Cramming the cap onto my head, I try to work out which way to go.

It's then that I see Franx, half buried in slick mud at the rim of the crater he was sheltering in. He hangs loosely over the edge of the shell hole, one arm outstretched. I can see three holes in his chest where the bullets from the aircraft hit him, and a dribble of blood from his mouth shows that they punctured his already overworked lungs. I pause for a moment, shocked that Franx is actually dead. He seemed unkillable, all the way through. And this is how it ends, a random victim of a rebel strafing run. No heroics, no glory, just a few bullets from the skies and it's all over. It saddens me, the way it happened, more than the fact that he's dead. He didn't have a chance. Not much of a Last Chance at all, taking on stratocraft. Still, I hope dying like this counts, and that his soul is safe with the Emperor. Poliwicz and Kyle are lying spread-eagled in another pool, not far from where I fell, their rain- and blood-soaked sleeves clinging tightly to their arms. Poliwicz has half his face blown away, shattered teeth leering at me from his exposed skull. At first I can't tell where Kyle's been hit and I roll him over, finding four holes through the back of his flak jacket, right at the base of his spine. They both look like they died quickly, which is a blessing of sorts, I guess.

Pushing thoughts of Franx and the others from my mind to concentrate on my own survival, I try to figure out which way we were heading in. The rain's obscured all the tracks, and I can see lights in almost every direction, so it's impossible to tell which way is the rear area and which way is the front line. Deciding that it's better to be moving than not, I pick a direction at random and start walking.

* * *

I'VE WALKED FOR about an hour in the gathering darkness of the night, when I hear voices nearby. Dropping to my belly, I lie very still, ears straining to work out which direction the conversation is coming from. It's just to my left and a little ahead of me. Moving my head slightly, I look in that direction. Sure enough, I can see a faint light, of a cooking stove or something. I worm my way a little bit closer, and after about ten metres can just make out the outline of a couple of men sitting around a dimly glowing camp cooker.

'Emperor-damned rain,' one curses. 'I wish this Emperor-damned patrol were over.'

'You always moan 'bout the weather. Only another two days on this tour,' replies the other in a conciliatory tone. 'Then we can head on back to old Corry and rest up awhile.'

'Still, trust us to draw a sentry roster that gets us four damned shifts outta three,' the other one whines. Their conversation drifts out of my thoughts as my subconscious tries to attract my attention with an important thought. 'Back to old Corry,' one of them had said. They must mean Coritanorum, the citadel under siege. And that means they're rebels! And here's me a few metres away in a Mordian, in other words loyalist, uniform! Oh frag, I've managed to sneak all the way through our own front line without noticing and now I'm at the traitor picket. How the frag did I manage that?

I'm about to shuffle away again when I hear something that adds to my disturbance.

'I hope Renov's commandos get here on time,' one of the rebels says. 'Once we've scouted out the eastern flank, we can tell 'em the route through the traitors' lines and get back home.'

'Yeah, if this weak spot leads right back to their artillery lines, Renov's boys'll have a field day,' the other says with a laugh.

They must be a scouting party or something, and they've found a chink in our siege line. If they can break through, who knows what hell these commandos they're talking about can play? I push myself further into the darkness to have a think, finding a bit of shelter under the blasted stump of a tree. I'm no hero, anyone will tell you that, but if these rebels can carry on with their mission, who knows what damage it could do to the Imperial lines? It's strange, but if the Colonel had ordered me to do something about it, I would have tried everything I could to get out of it. Now I'm on my own, I wonder whether I

should try to break up this little party. After all, I joined the
Imperial Guard to fight in defence of the Emperor's domains,
and though I have strayed a long way over the years, that's still
an oath I took. Knowing I would be guilty of a gross treachery
if I heard that an incursion by the rebels had been a powerful
setback to the siege, costing thousands more lives, I draw the
Mordian knife hanging from my belt and rise up into a crouch.

I circle to my right for a bit, until I find the faint glow of the
sentries' position again. Slowly, meticulously, I place one foot
in front of the other, easing myself towards them, trying not to
make a sound. I make my breathing as shallow as possible,
though I'm sure they can hear my heart as it hammers in my
chest. Step by step, I get closer. In the near-blackness, I can
barely make them both out. The one nearest me is heavy set.
The other I can't make out at all. Realising they might be able
to see my face if I get any closer, I grab a handful of mud and
smear it over my skin, covering my face and hands in the stuff.
Fat-boy seems to be napping, I can hear his regular, deep
breathing, and I circle round some more so that the other one
is closest. I gulp down a sudden feeling of fear and then spring
forward, wrapping my left hand across the mouth of the rebel
and plunging the knife point-first into his throat. He gives a
brief spasm, and I feel warm blood splashing across my fingers
as I ease his still shuddering body to the ground.

A glance at the other one shows that he hasn't stirred at all. I
step over and drop to a crouch in front of him. Leaning closer,
I put the blade of the knife against the artery in his throat and
blow softly up his nose. His eyelids flutter open and his eyes
flicker for a moment before fixing on me and going wide with
terror.

'Say anything,' I whisper harshly, 'and I'll slice you to pieces.'

He gives a jerky nod, eyes trying to peer around his blubbery
cheek to see the knife at his throat.

'I'm going to ask you some questions,' I tell him, nicking the
skin of his throat a little with the dagger to keep his attention
as his eyes wander from mine. 'Answer them quickly, quietly
and truthfully.'

He nods again, a kind of panicked squeak sounding from the
back of his throat.

'How many of you are near here?' I ask, leaning very close so
I can hear the merest whisper.

'One squad... twelve men,' he breathes, body trembling all over.

'Where are the other ten?' I say.

'Fifty metres that way,' he tells me, slowly raising a hand and pointing to his right. I notice his whole arm is shaking with fear.

'Thank you,' I tell him with a grin and he begins to relax. With a swift flick of my wrist the knife slashes through his neck, arterial blood spraying from his throat. He slumps backwards, raised arm flopping to the floor.

As I expected, everyone else in the squad is sleeping, murmuring to themselves in their dreams, perhaps imagining themselves to be at home with loved ones and friends. Some people might say cutting their throats in their sleep would be a cruel thing to do, but I don't care. If these bastards hadn't renounced the reign of the Emperor, I wouldn't be here now, soaked with rain and blood, Emperor-knows how far from where I was born. To think of them betraying the oaths they must have sworn makes me sick to my stomach. They deserve everything they get, and I'll enjoy giving it to them. They're the enemy. It's a matter of moments to tread carefully along the lines of men in their waterproof sleeping sacks, jabbing the knife under ribcages and slicing throats. As I plunge the point of the knife into the eyeball of the ninth one, a movement to my left grabs my attention.

'Wass 'appenin'?' someone says sleepily, sitting up slowly in his nightsack. With an inward curse I pounce towards him, but not quickly enough. He rolls to his left and grabs the lasgun lying next to him in the mud. I dodge sideways as the blast of light sears past me and then kick the barrel of the gun away as he lines up for another shot. He tries to trip me with the gun but I'm too sure-footed, dancing past his clumsy attempt, kicking him in the face as I do so. I fall on top of him and he drops the lasgun and grabs my right wrist with both hands, forcing the knife up and away from his face.

I punch him straight in the throat, the knuckle of my middle finger extended slightly to crush his windpipe. He gives a choked cry and his grip weakens slightly. I wrench my knife hand free and plunge it towards his throat but a flailing arm knocks the blow slightly and the blade gouges down one side of his face, ripping across his cheek and hacking a chunk off his ear. He's still too short of breath to scream and I bring the knife back, smashing it through the thin skull at his left temple, plunging it into his brain. He convulses madly for a second with system shock and then goes limp.

Glancing around to make sure nobody else is about, I wipe the knife on the dead rebel's nightsack and snatch the lasgun from the mud, wiping the slushy dirt off with the Typhon's tunic. I don't know why I didn't grab one of the Mordians' lasguns. I guess I was keen to get away.

'Right,' I say to myself, getting my bearings, 'which way now?'

Looking around, I see a break in the gathering storm clouds back from where I came from. In the hazy scattering of stars I can see moving lights, going up and down, instantly recognisable as shuttle runs. Well, where there's shuttles, there's a way out of this warzone. Putting the knife back into its sheath, I set off at a run.

EVER BEEN TEN strides from death? Not a nice feeling. The trench is seventy strides away and in sixty the snipers will trace me and I'm gonna get a bullet trepanning. I was always fast, but you can't outrun fate, as my sarge used to say.

Fifty strides from safety and the first shot whistles past my ear. At forty I drop my lasgun in the mud. Light as they are, they don't let you pump your arms properly for the type of speed I need if I'm going to get myself out of this. If I'm too slow now, having a gun ain't gonna help me a whole lot.

At thirty strides someone calls in the mortars and suddenly there's explosions all around throwing up water and muck, spattering me with dirt. Luckily I'm dodging left and right too, so only luck will help them out, you can't correct a mortar that quick. There's a tremendous roar of thunder, making the ground under my feet shake, and lightning crackles across the sky. Great, all I needs is more light for the snipers to see me.

Something else, larger than a bullet, goes crashing past me and sends up a plume of debris as it explodes. Oh great! Still twenty strides to go and some smart frag-head has grabbed a grenade launcher. Fifteen strides from life, five from death, bet nobody would give me odds on surviving now!

A ball of plasma roars past me, almost blinding me as it explodes against the shattered hull of an abandoned Leman Russ. I'm eight strides off when I feel something punch into my shoulder from the left. Instinct takes over and I dive forward.

Oh frag! I'm at the trench! Double frag! I land head first in the mud and I swear I hear my shoulder snap as I hit the ground two metres further down than I thought I would.

A CROWD HAS gathered, rain-blurred faces peering curiously at me as I sit there in the mud at the bottom of the trench. I hear someone bark an order and the throng dissipates instantly revealing a tall man in his early twenties, wearing the uniform of a Mordian lieutenant. The flash on his breast says Martinez. There must be regiments from half a dozen worlds fighting on Typhos Prime, and I fragging have to land in one full of Mordians! Considering I'm wearing a stolen Mordian uniform, this is not a good situation to be in.

Martinez looks at me with distaste, and I can't blame him. My face is caked in mud and blood, and his precious Mordian uniform is worse off than an engineer's rag.

'On your feet, guardsman!' the lieutenant snaps.

I give him a surly look and push myself to my feet to lean against a trench support batten, seeking shelter from the incessant downpour. Martinez gives me an odd second glance when he sees my face.

Hey, I feel like shouting, I know I'm not that pretty, but have some manners! His eye lingers on the bullet graze across my forehead, which reminds me that I must wash it out or risk getting infection.

'Name, guardsman!' barks Martinez, false bravado in his voice.

Nausea sweeps through me as I try to straighten out a little, jerked into action by their parade-ground drilling. I haven't slept for a day and a half, let alone eaten.

'Kage,' I manage to mumble, fighting back a wave of dizziness.

'What is the meaning of this?' demands the Mordian. 'You look a total state! I don't know how discipline is maintained in your platoon, guardsman, but here I expect every soldier to maintain standards appropriate to the regiment. Get yourself cleaned up! And you will address me as "sir", or I'll have you flogged for insubordination. Is that clear?'

'Yes… sir,' I snarl. You don't even want to know about discipline in my regiment, lieutenant, I think, knowing his strait-laced attitude would have got him killed ten times over if he'd spent the past three years with me.

* * *

THIS FRAGGING jumped-up nobody lieutenant is beginning to grate on my nerves. Still, I only have myself to blame. I know these damned Mordians are really tagged up on being smart and shiny. I should've looked for a corpse more my size rather than grabbing the first uniform I came across. On the other hand, I've made it to the trench in one piece. That's phase one of my plan complete.

Suddenly, I catch the distinctive scent of gun oil close by, hear the snick of a safety being released and feel a cold metal muzzle poking into the back of my neck. I slowly turn round and face a jutting chin big enough to bulldoze buildings with. Glancing up I pass over the face and focus my attention on the commissar's cap, resplendent with its braiding and solid gold eagle. Frag me, this guy looks almost as mean as the Colonel!

'Kage? Your flash says "Hernandez", guardsman. Just who are you and what are you doing?' The commissar's voice is gravelly, just like all commissars' voices. Do they train them to speak like that, making them chew on razor blades or something? I can't believe I hadn't checked out the dead guy's name before putting on his uniform! Frag, this is getting too hot!

'Lieutenant Kage, sir! I'm special ops, covert operations kinda thing,' I say, thinking on my feet.

'I was not aware of any special units in this sector,' he replies, clearly unconvinced.

'With respect, sir, that's the idea,' I tell him, trying to remember what normal guardsmen act like. 'Hardly covert if everyone knows you're around.'

Well, I hadn't lied. You don't get much more special than my unit.

'Who is your commanding officer?' he demands.

'I'm sorry, but I cannot disclose that to anyone outside of the unit, sir,' I tell him. Okay, that was a lie, but he's bound to have heard of the Colonel.

'I'm placing you under armed guard, pending confirmation of your story by command headquarters,' the commissar announces. 'Lieutenant Martinez, detail five men to watch this prisoner. If he so much as looks out of this trench, shoot him!'

As the lieutenant nominates a handful of men to watch me, the commissar strides off towards the comms bunker I'd seen when I'd been waiting for the storm to cover my dash. The lieutenant disappears too, ordering everybody back to their duties, leaving me with the five hopeless cases standing around me.

I SLUMP BACK to the bottom of the trench, ignoring the mud and filth that splashes around me. For the first time I check out my shoulder. It's just a flesh wound: the bullet has left a small furrow about a thumb's length across my left shoulder. Flexing it hurts like hell, but I can tell it isn't actually dislocated, just jarred. I pluck a needle and some wire thread from the survival pack inside my left boot and begin stitching, gritting my teeth against the pain.

My guards look on aghast and it's then that I first realise what's been nagging at my brain since I'd first splashed down in the trench. These soldiers are young. I mean really young; some of them look about sixteen years old, the oldest must be twenty at the most. A bunch of wet-backs, freshly drafted in to fight. I then notice a satchel just off to my left, gold-tinged foil packages stuffed in its pockets. With a flick of my head in its direction, I quiz the youngest soldier.

'That a ration pack?' I ask, already knowing the answer. 'Sure looks like one. Do you get fed regular here? Frag, you don't know how grateful I'd be for just a bite to eat. Any chance?'

With a worried look to his comrades the raw recruit shuffles over to the satchel and pulls out a can. With a twist he opens it up and passes me the hard biscuit inside

'Eat it quick,' he says. 'The rain gets them soggy in no time and they're awful if that happens.' His voice is high-pitched and quivering and he shoots a nervous glance over his shoulder at the others and then up the trench. I laugh.

'You mean "Eat it quick before Lieutenant Frag-Brain or that dumb commissar come back", don't you?' My imitation of his nasal whine makes the others grin before they can stop themselves.

The young guardsman is silent as he steps back and squats down on the opposite side of the trench, his lasgun cradled between his legs. The oldest one speaks up, his voice a little firmer, a little harder.

'Between us, why are you here? Are you really special ops? What's it like?' he asks, eyes curious.

I stare into his narrow brown eyes, sparkling with moisture. Rain runs down his cheeks and makes me realise how thirsty I am. But I wouldn't trust the stuff pouring out of the sky right now. 'You dig out a canteen of water and I'll clear this smoke out of my throat and tell you,' I offer. The flask is in my hand almost instantly and I grin stupidly for a moment as the cool liquid spills down my parched throat. Without handing it back, I flip the cap shut again and wedge it into the mud next to me.

'Oh. I'm definitely very special, boys,' I say with a grin. 'I don't know if you wet-backs have ever heard about us, but you're about to. You see, I'm with the Last Chancers.'

As I EXPECT, this statement is met with blank incomprehension. These rookies don't know anything outside their platoon, but I'm gonna change that, for sure. 'Your lieutenant, he's very keen on discipline, isn't he?' Nods of agreement. 'I expect he's made it very clear what the different punishments for various infractions are. Flogging, staking, firing squad and all the rest. Has he told you about Vincularum? No? well it's a gulag, basically. You're sent to some prison planet to rot away for the rest of your life. Now, there's one of those prison planets, it doesn't have a name, down near the southern rim. That's where I was sent.'

One of the guards, a slim youngster with ridiculously wide eyes, speaks up. 'What had you done?'

'Well, it's kind of a long story,' I say, settling down against the trench wall, making myself more comfortable. 'My platoon were doing sentry on some backwater hole called Stygies, down near Ophelia. It was a real easy number, watching a bunch of degenerate peasants grubbing around in the dirt, making sure nothing nasty happened to them. In those situations you have to provide your own excitement, know what I mean?'

Again the blank stares. Never mind.

'Well,' I continue regardless, 'back on Stygies they have this contest, called the Path of Fate. It's like one of those obstacle courses you must have gone over a thousand times during your training. Only a lot worse. This was one mean fraggin' test, make no mistake. Every month the bravest locals all line up for a race over the Path. There's a pit of boiling water to swing across, deadfall traps, pitfalls with spikes, not to mention the fact that in the final stretch you're allowed to attack the other contenders, right? Anyway, after watching this go on for a few months, my sergeant, he starts running a book on each race. After all, the contenders have to announce their intentions well in advance, and going on past experience he could work out the odds according to their previous form and their local reputation. I mean, these fraggers were hard as nails, but some of them were just rock, you know?'

A few nods this time. Lucky old me...

'We used to gamble rations, that sort of thing,' I say, settling in to the story I'd told two dozen times back on the transport. 'But that kinda gets boring after a while. Then we moved onto more valuable stuff, picked up from the local artisans. Things like gold necklaces, gems and stuff. I mean, all we did was give 'em a few ration packs and they would sell their daughters, it was amazing. Well, speaking of young ladies, I had my eye on one particular sweet little thing.' I grin at the memory. 'The sarge was soft on her too and rather than contest with each other, neither of us liked the idea of sharing you know, we gambled first rights on the next Path of Fate. I won, but the sarge got sour. Fat people often get like that, and he was immense what with all the easy living and free rations. Anyway, he bawls me out one day, threatening to report me to the lieutenant for something he'd made up unless I gave him the wench. That was it, I just pulled my blade and gutted the fat fragger there and then. Course, they hauled me off of there quicker than you can say it and I end up out on this gulag.'

Their open-mouthed astonishment is hilarious. One of them stutters something incomprehensible and continues staring at me like I've grown an extra head or something.

Then the older one pipes up. 'You murdered your sergeant over a woman?'

'Yeah, and I didn't get to have her in the end anyway, did I?' I take another swig of water to moisten my tongue and then cock my head to one side to listen to what's going on outside the trench. 'You boys better move over to this side of the trench.'

They look at me, Wide Eyes frowning, the older one with his mouth half-open, the others not really paying attention.

'Move it! Now!' I snap, seeing if I can pull the parade ground trick as well as any real officer.

The commanding tone in my voice makes them act instantly, leaping across to my side and thudding down in the muck as well. The sound of explosions gets rapidly closer and suddenly the whole trench line is engulfed in a raging torrent of shells. Red fire explodes everywhere, plasma shells spewing a torrent of molten death onto the far side of the trench where the recruits had been lounging.

Stupid fraggers, did nobody tell them to use the lee of the trench to protect themselves during an artillery attack? And it goes without saying that they hadn't heard the pause in the gunfire that suggested a change of aiming point, or the whistle of the first shells heading our way. Emperor's blood, I would have made a brilliant training officer if I didn't have such a lousy temper!

STRANGE AS IT seems, even the thunderous tumult of a barrage soon gets relegated to being background noise, and you learn to ignore the shaking ground.

It's Wide Eyes who speaks first, pulling his collar up as a gust of wind sends the rain spraying beneath the overhang of the trench.

'Why are you here if you're supposed to be on this prison planet?' he asks. First sensible thing anyone else has said so far. 'Did you escape or something?'

'If I'd escaped, do you really think I would end up in this grave-bait war?' I reply with a sour look. 'I don't think so! But I did try to get out once. You have to understand that this world wasn't a prison like the brig aboard ship. There were only a few guards, and they had this massive fortified tower out on the central plains. Apart from that, you were just kicked out into the wastelands and forgotten. I mean, really! It's just like any other world, there're empires and lords and stuff. The meanest fraggers get to the top and the weak are just left by the wayside or killed and preyed upon. If you're strong, you survive, if you ain't...' I let it hang.

'Anyway, I gets into the retinue of this guy called Tagel,' I tell them. One of the many people I've met and wish I hadn't. 'Big fragger from Catachan, and they breed 'em really big deep in that hellhole. He'd directed an artillery barrage on friendly troops 'cause his captain had called him names or some equally petty stupidity. He was fighting against a rag-tag bunch from across the other side of the valley, who had a nice little still going brewing up some really potent juice. Anyway, I kinda led some of Tagel's guys into an ambush on purpose, but before I can get to the other side they're hunting me. It may be a big planet, but when you've got that red-faced fragger chasing you everywhere you start getting the idea that this planet isn't the best place to be, know what I mean?

'Anyway, there's this supply shuttle every few months. I holed up long enough until one was due and then forged my way across the plains. I hid for a few days, waiting nice and patient. Then the shuttle comes in, as I'd hoped. I sneak real close to the station while they're all excited about getting their visitors. Then the gates open so they can let out the latest bunch of sorry malcontents. In the confusion I scrag one of the guards and swipe his uniform. I slip into the complex just as the gates are closing and then it's time to head for the shuttle. I'd just bluffed my way to the landing pad when the body's spotted and the alarm's raised.'

Their eyes are fixed to me like a sniper's sight, hanging on each word. Can I tell a story or what?

'So, I knife a couple more frag-heads to clear a way through and I'm up the ramp and inside. Just as the door's about to close there's someone up ahead of me. Without thinking I thrust with my stained blade into this guy's shoulder. He just takes it, can you believe that? A span of mono-edge in his arm and the guy just takes a pace back. I look up into his face, 'cause this guy is one big meatgrinder, if you take my meaning, and there's these cold blue eyes just staring at me, icy to the core. He backhands me, breaking my jaw as I later find out, and I go down. I get a boot in the crotch and then a pistol butt to the back of my head. Last thing I hear is this guy laughing. Laughing! I hear him say something which I'll never forget.'

Their eyes ask the question before their mouths can move.

'"Just my type of scum!" is what he says!' That's me, the Colonel's scum through and through.

THE BARRAGE FROM Coritanorum has moved on, dropping its payload of death and misery on some other poor souls, not that I give them a second thought. Rations Boy asks the obvious question. 'Who was he? How did he get you here?'

'That was the Colonel,' I say with due reverence. 'Colonel Schaeffer, no less. Commander of the Last Chancers.'

Wide Eyes jumps in with the next obvious question. 'Who are the Last Chancers?'

'The 13th Penal Legion,' I inform them grandly. 'Of course, there's been hundreds more than thirteen raisings, but we've always been called the 13th on account of our bad luck.'

Wide Eyes is full of questions at the moment. He takes his cap off and flicks water from the brim into the trench, revealing his close-cropped blond hair. It's smudged with brown and black from the dirt and muck that this whole Emperor-damned world is covered in.

'What bad luck?' he asks.

'Our bad luck to have the Colonel in command,' I say with a grin. 'We get the dirtiest missions he can find. Suicide strikes, rearguards, forlorn hope for assaults. You name the nastiest situation you could ever imagine and I'd bet a week's rations the Colonel has been in it. And survived, more importantly. We get a hundred guys gunned down in the first volley and he'll walk through the entire battle without a scratch. Not a fragging scratch!'

One of the others, silent until now, opens his thin-lipped mouth to ask one of the most sensible questions I'd heard in a long time. 'So why are you here? I know I've not had much experience of battle, but I know this isn't a suicide run. I mean, we're new here; why bother raising a whole new regiment just to throw them away?'

'You so sure it ain't a suicide run?' I say back to him, eyebrows raised. 'You seen the lights, flares heading up, to the west?' Nods of agreement. 'They ain't flares. They're landing barges evacuating this battle-zone. There are twenty or thirty transports up there in orbit, waiting to pull out. Guess they've decided to wipe out everything from space – virus bombs, mass drivers and all the rest. Coritanorum is a lost cause now. The rebels are too well dug in. In the past eighteen months, there've been thirty-eight assaults and we haven't advanced one pace. They're pulling back and guess who's left to hold the front line…'

'But we're behind the front, so what're you doing back here?' Thin Lips points out.

There's a distant whine behind us, getting louder and louder. The recruits duck into shelter, but I know what's coming and take a peek over the trench to see the show. Suddenly, there's a howling roar directly overhead and a squadron of Marauders streak across the sky, Thunderbolt fighters spiralling around them in an escort pattern. While the others cower in stupidity, I see a line of fiery blossoms blooming over the enemy positions. Our own artillery has set up a counter-barrage and the incoming fire suddenly stops. Then the attack run of the Marauders hits, sending up a plume of smoke as their bombs detonate and the blinding pulses of lascannon smash through the enemy fortifications and explode their ammo dumps. The ground attack is over in an instant as the planes light their afterburners and scream off into the storm.

'Hey boys!' I call down to them. 'Take a look at this, you won't see another one for a while!'

The recruits timidly poke their heads out, and give me a quizzical look.

'Bombardment, air attack – next comes the orbital barrage.' I tell them. I've seen it half a dozen times, standard Imperial battle dogma. 'Those damned rebels are in for some hot stuff tonight!'

Just as I finish speaking, the clouds are brilliantly lit up in one area and a moment later an immense ball of energy flashes towards Coritanorum. The fusion torpedo smashes into the citadel's armoured walls, smearing along the scarred and pockmarked metal like fiery oil. Several more salvoes rain down through the storm, some shells kicking up huge plumes of steam as they bury themselves in the mud before detonating, others causing rivulets of molten metal to pour down Coritanorum's walls like lava flows.

Then the rebels' anti-strike batteries open up, huge turrets swivel skywards and blasts of laser energy punch through the atmosphere. For almost a minute the return fusillade continues, dissipating the clouds above the fortress with the heat of their attack. The ship in orbit must have pulled out, as no more death comes spilling from the cloud cover.

Half a minute later a siren sounds along the whole trench. Rations Boy looks up, face suddenly pale and lip trembling. 'That's the standby order. Next one sounds the attack,' he tells me.

This is my big chance. In the confusion of the attack, it'll be easy to slip out the other side of the trench and get myself out of here. As stimulating as their company is, I don't want to be anywhere near these recruits for more than another half-minute.

'I'd wish you luck, but I'm afraid I'm hogging that all to myself just for now.' I smile, but they don't look reassured. Never mind.

Just then the grim-faced commissar comes striding round the corner of the trench, his beady eyes fixed on me. 'Bring the prisoner with you when we advance. Let him go and I'll have all of you up on a charge of negligence!'

Frag! Still, an order's one thing, but execution's another.

Then the attack siren sounds. I'm being pushed out first, so I guess my new friends have learnt one thing, at least. I start sprinting cross the open killing ground to the next trench line. The enemy snipers, who I'd avoided so nimbly before, get a second chance at skinning my hide. There's a yell and Wide Eyes goes down as a bullet smashes through his neck, spraying spine and blood over my stolen uniform. I snatch up his lasgun and send a volley of shots from the hip into the sniper's probable hiding place. No more shots ring out for the moment.

Then something grabs my leg. Looking down I see the hard-headed commissar down on his knees coughing blood, broken. He looks at me with those hard eyes and whispers, 'Do something decent with your life for a change, treacherous scum!'

Without a thought I turn the lasgun round and grant him his wish. The beams of murderous light silencing him forever. I must be getting soft. I've never bothered with a mercy killing before now, especially this knee-deep in trouble.

WITH THE COMMISSAR down, this is my chance to break for it. I just have to turn round and run straight back the way we came. I don't think the rebels are going to bother shooting at someone running in the opposite direction. Just then I notice something, probably the enemy, casting a shadow in the lightning, just ahead of us to the right. Damned snipers must be laughing it up tonight. I look about as a shot plucks at my tunic – maybe I was wrong about an easy getaway. There's a ruined farmstead on the left and I head for it. With the resumption of sniper fire, some of the rookie platoon is face down in the mud, hiding or dead, I don't know. The rest are standing around, milling about in confusion. Someone I don't know gets in my way, his eyes strangely vacant with desperation as more and more of the rookies are gunned down by hidden foes. I slam my fist into his weasel face and as he stumbles out of my way he goes down, his chest blown out by a bullet that would have hit me. Another couple of heartbeats and I'm over the wall of the farm and kneeling in some kind of animal pen.

Right, now that I've separated myself from those no-hopers, time to formulate my escape plan. Then there's the thud of boots all around me and I realise that the platoon has followed me into cover instead of carrying on their planned advance to the next trench! A journey, I might add, that they would have never finished.

One of the little soldier boys grabs my collar and shouts in my ear. 'Good thinking, sir! We'd have been butchered if you hadn't brought us here!'

Frag! 'Brought you here?' I almost scream. 'I didn't fraggin' bring you here, you dumb rookies! Frag, you stupid wetbacks are gonna get me killed, hangin' around here with "target" written all over you as badly as if it was in bright lights five metres high! Get outta my face before I skin you, you stupid little fragger!'

Chips of masonry are flying everywhere now as the snipers bring their high-powered rifles to bear on us. Well, as long as these space-heads are around, I might as well use them to my advantage. As Tagel used to say, an iron ball around your leg can still be used to smash someone's head in. Actually, that was probably one of the longest sentences the dumb brute had ever used, so I figure he'd heard it from someone else. Pulling my thoughts back to the problem in hand, I point through the downpour towards the escarpment where the snipers are lying in cover.

'Suppression fire on that ridge!' I bellow.

Drilled for months while in transit to this hellhole, the platoon reacts without thought. The guys around me open up with their lasguns, a torrent of light pulsing through the darkness. I find the shattered casing of a solar boiler and use its twisted panes to get some cover from the shells knocking chunks off the plascrete wall of the outhouse. Little did my boys know, but the shuttles wouldn't hang around forever, and I've still got every intention of warming my behind on one of those seats.

There's a shouted greeting and the remnants of another squad joins us, two of the guardsmen carrying grenade launchers. They start fiddling with their sights to get the correct trajectory but by this time there's more incoming fire as the snipers behind the ridge get reinforcements. I snatch one of the launchers, select a frag round and send the charge sailing through the air. I grin madly, along with others I note, as three bodies are tossed into view by the explosion. Casting the launcher back to the guardsman, I draw the concealed knife from my right boot and charge. Not too far now.

As I LEAP OVER a mound of bodies, I see the rest of the platoon on either side of me, pouring over the ridge. Stunned by the sudden attack the traitors are soon hacked down in a storm of lasgun fire and slashing bayonets. I gut two of the rebel swine myself. From there it's just a matter of half a minute's jogging to the forward trench line. As the others set off I turn on my heel and start heading back to the second line, which now would hopefully be empty. I see the grox-breath lieutenant to my right. He sees me too. But before he can say anything, him and his command squad are knocked off their feet in a bloody cloud by a hail of fire. I see shadows moving up on the left, cutting me off from my route to the shuttles – for now at least.

As I splash down in the front-line trench, I hear the sergeants crying out the roll-call. Lots of names get no reply and I guess they've lost about three-quarters of the men. The others are gonna die as soon as the rebels counter-attack, and I'm gonna make damn sure I'm not around to suffer a similar fate. Suddenly I notice everyone's looking at me, expectation in their eyes.

'What the frag is this? What're you looking at, for Emperor's sake?' I snarl at them. It's the oldest one of my guards who makes the plea.

'Lieutenant Martinez is dead! The command squad are all dead!' he says, high-pitched voice wobbling with fright.

'And?' I ask.

'And you saw to Commissar Caeditz!' he replies.

'Yeah, and?' I ask again. I don't like the sound of this at all. I dare not believe it, but I have a feeling something bad is happening.

'We're stuck here until another command squad gets sent up,' he explains. 'There's no one in command. Well, except you. You said you were a lieutenant.'

'Yeah, of a fraggin' penal legion platoon!' I spit out. 'That don't mean nothing in the real world.'

'You got us this far,' pipes up another nuisance, his face streaked with rain and blood, his lips swollen and bruised.

'Look, no offence, but the last thing I need right now is a bunch of wet-backed brainless fraggers like you weighing me down,' I explain to them. 'I got me this far. You guys have just tagged along for the ride. There's a seat on one of those stellar transports with my name on it, and I fully intend to sit in it. Do you understand?'

'But you can't just leave us!' comes the call from someone at the back.

The pitiful misery in their eyes is truly galling. There's no chance in creation I'm gonna lumber myself with this thankless task. I set about rummaging through the packs they've dumped in the trench to see if I can scrag some rations. I feel a faint tremor in the ground and look up. I see movement in the darkness, and as the wind subtly changes direction it brings the faint smell of oil smoke. Out in the rainswept darkness of the night I can make out the silhouette of a rebel Demolisher siege tank rumbling forwards. By its course I can tell the crew haven't seen us yet, but as soon as they pass a clump of twisted concrete columns to our right, we'll be easy targets. Bad news, bad news indeed.

'Listen up!' I call out, getting their attention. 'I am not in command! I am going to leave you to your fate! Make no bones, but there's a Demolisher on the prowl out there and he's gonna blow me to little pieces with that big gun of his if you give him the chance.'

I'm thinking really hard now. Maybe this would give me the chance I need to get away. I've survived for years on my wits, and I'm not going to give up that easily now. Being alive is a hobby of mine, and I don't feel like giving it up right now.

'Do exactly what I say and I may just get out of this with my skin,' I say to them, brain working overtime.

They listen intently, staring up at me with expectant eyes as I detail the plan. I check they understand and as they all nod I send them on their way. As the Demolisher rumbles forward

someone switches on the turret's searchlight. The tank's hull
glistens with rain and the steady sheet of water pouring from
the sky reflects along the beam's length. Damn! I hadn't
thought of that! Still, it's too late now, the plan's in motion and
to shout now would be asking for death. I signal my bunch of
guys to hunker down more as the others move out into position. I watch the Demolisher constantly as it slowly grinds its
way through piles of bones, smashing aside small walls, its
bulldozer blade creating a furrow in the deep mud. The searchlight is swinging left and right, but we're slightly behind it now
and the commander isn't checking every angle. If he spots us,
that turret is going to turn round on us, slow as he likes and
drop one of those massive Demolisher shells right on top of
my head!

Suddenly the searchlight is swinging my way, sweeping over
the ground and harshly illuminating the piled bodies of the
dead, ours and theirs. It swings onwards and I find myself holding my breath, but a few heartbeats before it's shining in my
face it swings back the other way, moving fast. Looking down
the beam – the tank's about forty strides from where I'm
crouched – I see the other attack party standing rigid. I feel like
screaming 'Run, don't stand there!' but when it comes down
the line, if I shout I'll be dead just as surely as them. And as I
say, I ain't ready to die for a long, long time.

As I had predicted, the turret turns with a slow grinding and
the huge Demolisher cannon, wide enough for a man to crawl
inside, tilts upwards. With a blossom of flame and a wreath of
smoke the tank fires. A moment later the searchlight is outshone
by the explosion of the shell. I fancy I see bodies flung into the
air, but it's unlikely since Demolisher shells don't usually leave
enough of you to be thrown about. As the flames flicker down,
the searchlight roves left and right and the heavy bolter in the
hull opens up with a flash from its muzzle. In the searchlight
beam I see the survivors being kicked from their feet by the
attack, blood spraying from exit wounds as the explosive bolts
punch through skin, muscle and bone as if they were paper.

I snap back to the job in hand. Raising my fist I signal the
charge. We run silently towards the tank, no battle cries, no
shouts of defiance, just nice and quiet. However, the first guys
are still about twenty strides from the tank when the sponson
gunner on our side wakes up and opens fire with his heavy

flamer. A raging inferno pours out from the side of the tank, turning men into charred hunks of flesh and quickly silencing their screams.

The searchlight swivels around towards us, but I level my lasgun and open up on the run, sending two shots into the wide lens and shattering it. I hear a faint cry of alarm as I dodge behind the tank. Its tracks churn wildly as the driver tries to turn it round to bring its weapons to bear.

As those huge steel tracks rumble round, so close to my face I could reach out and touch them, I leap up, grabbing onto the engine cover. I pull myself onto the tank's hull and wrench the panel loose to expose the oily, roaring mass of the engine. As the other survivors pile on board, blasting into the engine compartment with their lasguns, I make a jump for the turret.

The commander's shocked expression makes me laugh as I smash the butt of my gun into his chin, breaking his neck. I fire a couple of shots into the hatch and jump inside. The crew look at me in horror: daubed as I am in blood and mud I must seem like some hideous alien come for their hearts. And I have. My knife tears into them, I've always prided myself on my knife-fighting skills, and in a matter of a few breaths it's over.

Suddenly somebody's shouting down the hatch to get out.

I WATCH IN satisfaction from the trench as the charges go up, turning the siege tank into a storm of whirling metal debris and tangled wreckage. Right, now the coast is clear, time to head for those evacuation landing bays. Someone grabs my shoulder as I turn to head back across no-man's land. It's someone I don't know, a long scratch across his face and his left side and leg smouldering from a close encounter with a heavy flamer.

'You can't go, Kage – I mean, sir!' he begs. 'We need you, and you need us!'

'Need you? *Need you?*' I'm almost screaming in frustration. 'Look, I'm heading back. Any of you dumb fraggers tries to follow me and I'm gonna start shooting. I don't need you, you're all liabilities. Is that perfectly clear?'

There's silence. I think a couple of them are gonna start crying, their lips quiver so much. Well tough luck, it doesn't work on Kage, not one bit. I turn and start climbing up the back wall of the trench, towards our own lines. Someone says, 'Give you a hand up, soldier?'

I grab the proffered hand without thinking and get hauled out of the trench by strong arms. As I kneel there in the mud my spine tingles with horror as my mind catches up with events. I look up. Blazing back at me are two pits of coldness, ripping into my soul. The Colonel stands there, bolt pistol pointed directly between my eyes!

'Deserting scum!' he snarls. 'You had your last chance. It is time to pay for your crimes!'

Just then he looks away and my fuddled brain suddenly identifies a rush of clicks and whine of power cells. Glancing over my shoulder I see the platoon, the whole sorry, bedraggled mess of them, all with their weapons trained on the Colonel, a wall of lasgun barrels, plasma gun muzzles and even the tube of a grenade launcher. I fight down the hysterical urge to laugh. Some of them are shaking with fear; others are rock-hard and steady. Each one of them is staring at the Colonel with a silent ferocity. It's a scary feeling, like a herdbeast suddenly sprouting fangs. Rations Boy braves the Colonel's wrath with words.

'I– I'm sorry, sir, but Kage doesn't deserve that,' he tells Schaeffer. 'If you shoot, we will too.'

'Yes, sir,' someone else chips in their two-cred worth, his lasgun cradled over the ragged, bloodied mess of a broken arm. 'We'd all be dead three times over if it wasn't for him. We're not going to let you kill him!'

They're all focused now. Their guns are steady, and I can see their eyes filled with bloodlust. The adrenalin is pumping and they're so hyped up they could kill just about anyone right now. Flushed with victory, I heard someone call it once. I can see it, and the Colonel can too. For what seems like an eternity he just stands there, turning that icy stare of his onto them. Each one in turn takes the full force of the Colonel's look, but not one of them breaks off, and that's saying something! Still, the Colonel is the Colonel and he just sneers.

'This wretched piece of slime is not worth your time,' he barks at them. 'I recommend you use your ammunition on something more worthwhile.'

No one moves and the sneer disappears. 'Very well. You have proved your point, guardsmen,' the Colonel almost spits the words out.

The bristling guns are as steady as ever.

The Colonel's voice drops to a whisper, a menacing tone that even us in the Last Chancers dread to hear. 'I am ordering you. To lower. Your weapons.'

Still no movement.

'Have it your way,' he says finally. 'You will all be mine soon enough.'

It's several more long, deep breaths before the first of them lifts his gun away, finally convinced by the Colonel's sincere look. For me, I still think he's gonna blow my brains out.

'On your feet, Kage!' the Colonel snaps. I stand up slowly, not daring to breathe. 'Get that uniform off this instant – you do not deserve to wear it!'

As I begin unfastening the tunic, Colonel Schaeffer turns me around so I'm looking at Coritanorum, the heart of the rebel army. Even before the traitors had turned against the Emperor, the stronghold had a reputation for being nigh-on impregnable. Wall upon wall stretch into the hills, gun ports blazing as the artillery barrages a point in the line a few kilometres west of us. Searchlights roam across the open ground before the fort, showing the rows of razorwire, the mass of plasma and frag minefields, the tank traps, death pits, snares and other weapons of defence. As I watch, a massive armoured gate opens and a column of four Leman Russ tanks spills from a drawbridge across the acid moat, heading south.

'What happens now, sir?' I ask quietly.

The Colonel points towards the inner keep and whispers in my ear.

'That is what happens now, Kage. Because that is where we are heading.'

Oh frag.

THE MAN'S RAGGED breathing echoed off the condensation-covered pipes that ran along both corridor walls, his exhalations producing a small cloud of mist around his head. A dismal, solitary yellow glowstrip illuminated his freshly shaven face from the ceiling, bathing it in a sickly light. He glanced back nervously, bent double catching his breath, hands resting on his knees. A flicker of movement in the distant shadows caught his attention and he gritted his teeth and started running again, pulling a stubby pistol from inside his blue coveralls. The clatter of something hard on metal rang along the corridor floor after him, accompanied by a scratching noise like rough leather being drawn along the corroded steel of the piping.

'Emperor's blood, the hunter has become the hunted,' he hissed, looking back again.

There was a blur of movement under the glow strip, an impression of bluish black and purple dashing along the corridor towards him. He raised the pistol and pulled the trigger, the muzzle flash almost blinding in the dim confines of the passageway, the whine of bullets passed into the dim distance. With preternatural speed the fast-approaching shape

191

leapt aside, bone-coloured claws sinking into the rusted metal to pull itself out of the line of fire. The pipes rang with the sound of scraping on metal as the monster continued its relentless advance, its chase moving effortlessly onto the wall.

The man broke into a sprint again, his legs and arms pumped rapidly as he sped down the passage. His eyes scanned the walls and ceiling as he ran down the twisting corridor, desperately seeking some avenue of escape. He had run another thirty metres, the creature bearing down on him all the while, when he noticed an opening to his right. Jumping through the doorway, his eyes fell on the lock-down switch, which he slammed his fist into. With a hiss the blast door began to descend rapidly, but a second later it was only halfway down when his inhuman hunter slipped under it. It pulled itself up to its full height right next to him, its dark, alien eyes regarding him menacingly.

He blasted randomly at the monstrosity with the pistol as he dived back underneath the door, rolling under its bottom edge and to his feet on the other side. Half a second later the door slammed shut, sealing him off from the voracious predator. Breathing a deep sigh of relief, he could hear the sound of powerful limbs battering at the other side of the portal, broken by the screech of long claws shredding metal. The noise of the futile assault ceased after a few seconds, replaced by the clicking of claws disappearing along the side tunnel.

'Emperor willing, I'll catch you yet,' he said with a wry smile to the entity on the other side of the doorway, before he turned and carried on running down the corridor.

SEVEN
NEW SUN

+++ Commencing Operation New Sun. +++
+++ I look forward to seeing you. +++

THE COLONEL AND I approach a sizeable bunker complex, four or five large modules connected by enclosed walkways. The hatchway he leads me to is flanked by two of the commissariat provosts, the black plates of their carapace armour slick in the continuing rain. Their look of disgust bites more than the cold wind and bitter rain on my bare flesh, making me fully aware of the pitiful state I'm in. My teeth are chattering with the cold, my naked body chilled with the rain, my feet numb from walking through the puddles and mud barefoot. Half my face is covered in grime from where I slipped over a while ago, and there are scratches along my lower legs from stumbling into a half-buried coil of razorwire. I've got my arms clasped tightly across my chest, shivering, trying to keep myself a little bit warmer. Their stares follow me as the Colonel opens the door lock and the hatchway cycles open, and he waves me inside. A few metres down a short corridor is another door to my left, and at a gesture from the Colonel I open it and step inside.

Within the small bunk room on the other side of the door are the rest of the Last Chancers: Linskrug, Lorii, Loron and Kronin. The Colonel told me on the way here that just after they left me Gappo managed to find a plasma charge minefield, the hard way, and was scattered liberally over a wide area. That was a blow to hear, though I suspect Gappo would be glad that his death warned the others of danger.

They look at me with astonished gazes. They've seen me nude before, every day on the ship during daily post-exercise ablutions in fact, but my bedraggled state must be pretty extraordinary.

'And Saint Phistinius went unto the enemy unarmed and unarmoured,' jokes Kronin and they all burst out laughing. I stand there humiliated for a moment before I find myself joining in with the laugh, realising that I must make for a particularly pathetic spectacle.

'Not that unarmed,' I quip back, glancing meaningfully down past my bare stomach, getting another laugh from them.

'More of a sidearm than artillery…' Lorii sighs with mock wistfulness, eliciting another round of raucous cackles from us all. As we subside into childish sniggers I hear someone come in behind me and turn to see the Colonel. He's carrying folded combat fatigues, shirt and flak jacket and dumps them on one of the bunks. Behind him a provost carries in a pair of boots and a standard issue anti-frag helmet, which he adds to the pile.

'It's bad luck not to put new boots on the floor,' I say to the provost as he leaves, but I can't tell his reaction past the dark visor of his helmet.

'Be quiet, Kage,' the Colonel tells me, nodding with his head to a door leading off the bunkroom. 'Clean up through there and get in uniform.' Inside the small cubicle beyond the door is a small showering unit. I find a hard-bristled brush and a misshapen lump of infirmary-smelling soap in a little alcove and set to scrubbing myself clean under the desultory trickle of cold water that dribbles from the showerhead when I work the pump a few times.

Cold, but clean and invigorated, I towel myself off back in the bunkroom and get dressed, feeling more human than I've done in the past day and a half since I made my bid for freedom. The Colonel's gone again and the others sit around with their own thoughts as I ready myself.

'I knew you weren't dead,' Linskrug says as I'm finishing, 'but I figured out what you were up to. Sorry it didn't work out.'

'Thanks, anyway,' I reply with a shrug. 'How the hell did the Colonel know, though?'

'When we got here, there were some odd reports floating around,' Loron says, sitting on the edge of one of the bunks and kicking his feet against the floor. 'The provosts told the Colonel that a storm trooper patrol found an enemy infiltration squad dead in their camp, about three kilometres past the front trenchline. Nobody was supposed to be in that area, and the Colonel said that you were the only one stupid enough to be out there. He left us here and headed off to look for you.'

'Did you kill that squad, Kage?' the Colonel asks from the doorway, causing us all to glance towards him in surprise.

'Yes, sir,' I tell him, sitting down on the floor to lace up my boots. 'I'm glad I did, even though it helped you catch me. This whole place might be swarming with rebels otherwise.' He just nods and grunts in a non-committal fashion.

'I have someone new for you all to meet,' he says after another moment, standing to one side and waving somebody through the door. The man who steps through is swathed in a dark purple robe, a skull and cog emblem embroidered in silver onto the top of the hood over his head, instantly identifying him as a tech-priest of the Cult Mechanicus.

'This is Adept Gudmanz, lately from the forgeworld of Fractrix,' the Colonel introduces him. 'To save tiresome speculation on your part, I will tell you now that he is with us for supplying Imperial armaments to pirates raiding Navy convoys. A most extreme abuse of his position, I am sure you will agree.'

Gudmanz shuffles over towards us, pulling back his hood to reveal a tired, withered face. His scalp is bald, puckered scars across his head show where implants have been recently removed. His eyes are rheumy and as he looks at us listlessly, I can hear his breath is ragged and strained.

'Make him feel welcome,' the Colonel adds. 'I will be back shortly.'

With the Colonel gone, we get down to the serious business of questioning our latest 'recruit'.

'Bit of a bad deal for you,' says Linskrug, slouched nonchalantly along a bed at the far end of the long bunkroom.

'Better than the alternative,' Gudmanz replies with a grimace, easing himself cautiously down onto one of the other bunks, his voice a grating, laboured whisper.

'You look completely done in,' I say, looking at his tired, frail form.

'I am two hundred and eighty-six,' he wheezes back sadly, head hung low. 'They took my enhancements away and without regular doses of anti-agapic oils I'll suffer increasing dysfunctions within the next month owing to lack of maintenance.'

We sit there absorbing this information for a moment before Loron breaks our contemplation.

'I think I'd prefer just to be hanged and get it over and done with,' he says, shaking his head in amazement.

'They would not have hanged me, young man,' the tech-priest tells him, eyes suddenly sharp and aware as he looks at each of us in turn. 'My masters would have had me altered to be a servitor. I would have my memory scrubbed. My biological components would be permanently interfaced into some menial control system or similar. I would be cogitating but not alive, simply existing. I would know in my subconscious that I am a living, breathing thing, but also denied the ultimate synthesis with the Machine God. Not truly alive and not truly dead. That is the usual punishment for betraying the great Adeptus Mechanicus. Your Colonel must have some good influence to deny the Cult Mechanicus its vengeance.'

'Don't I know it,' Linskrug says bitterly. Further questions are interrupted by the Colonel's reappearance, accompanied by the scribe I'd seen several times in his chamber aboard the *Pride of Lothus*, Clericus Amadiel. Amadiel is carrying a bundle of scrolls, which I immediately recognise as the pardons the Colonel had shown me before.

'And now you all learn what I really intend for you,' says the Colonel gravely, taking the pardons and placing them on the bunk next to Loron, everybody's eyes locked to him as he walks across the room back to the door. 'This is the time when your careers in the Last Chancers will soon be over, one way or another.'

There's a tangible change to the atmosphere inside the bunkroom as everybody draws their breath in at the same time. If I'm hearing right, and the reaction of the other Last Chancers suggests I am, the Colonel has just told us we can get out of the 13th Penal Legion.

'Those,' the Colonel continues, jabbing a finger towards the pile of parchments, 'are Imperial pardons for each and every one of you. I will sign and seal them once we have completed our final mission. You can refuse, in which case the provosts will take you to another penal legion.'

'And the Heretic Priests of Eidoline came forth, bringing false images for the praise of the lost people,' Kronin says, frowning hard.

'What?' says the Colonel, taken aback by the madman's statement.

'He means this is far too simple,' translates Lorii. I know what she means, the offer seems too good to be true. And then I understand that it isn't, that I know what the Colonel has in mind.

'You were serious when you said we're going into Coritanorum,' I say slowly, making sure the other Last Chancers understand the statement.

'Of course I was serious, Kage,' the Colonel answers brusquely. 'Why would I not be serious?'

'Well,' puts in Linskrug, leaning forward, 'there is the small matter that Coritanorum is the most impregnable citadel in the sector, the most unassailable fortress for a month's warp travel in every direction.'

'No citadel is impregnable,' the Colonel replies, radiating self-confidence and sincerity.

'The fact that five hundred thousand Imperial Guard, backed up by the Imperial Navy, haven't been able to take the place doesn't vex you?' blurts out Linskrug, highly perturbed by what the Colonel is proposing.

'We shall not be storming Coritanorum, that would be ridiculous,' the Colonel tells us in an irritated voice. 'We shall be infiltrating the complex and rendering it inoperable from the inside.'

'Assuming you can get us inside – which is a hell of an assumption – there's about three million people living in that city,' I say, brow knitted as I try to work out what the Colonel's whole plan is. 'We're bound to be discovered. Frag, I couldn't even hide among people on my own side, on my own.'

'Then we shall have to endeavour to do better than your recent exploits,' the Colonel replies curtly, obviously getting impatient with our reluctance. 'Make your decisions now. Are you coming with me, or do I transfer you?'

'Count me out,' says Linskrug emphatically, shaking his head vehemently. When he continues he looks at each of us in turn, forcing himself to speak slowly and surely. 'This is so insane, so reckless, it's unbelievable. It's sheer suicide trying to attack Coritanorum with seven people. I am going to survive this and get my barony back, and marching into the middle of a strongly held rebel fortress is not going to help me do that. Do what you will, I'm not going along with this suicide squad deal.'

'Very well,' the Colonel says calmly, strolling over to the bed with the pardons on. He sorts through them for a moment, finds Linskrug's and holds it up for all to see. Then, slowly and deliberately, he begins to tear it up. He tears it lengthways down the middle and then puts the two halves together and tears it across its width. He does this a couple more times until sixteen ragged pieces nestle in his hand. With the same deliberation he tips his hand over, the scraps of parchment fluttering to the floor around his boots. He treads on the pieces, twisting his foot on top of them to scrunch them up and tear them even more. We watch this in horrified silence, and to me it's like he's torn up and scuffed out Linskrug.

He bends over and picks up another pardon, holding it up for us to see. I read *my* name across the top and my heart flutters. Linskrug has got a good point: the whole idea of going into Coritanorum is suicidal. I have a philosophy about staying alive, and that's to do it for as long as possible. Going into the enemy fort isn't going to help that at all. But for all this, that's my life the Colonel has gripped between finger and thumb. If I say yes, and I survive this ridiculous mission, then I'll be free. I'll be able to do whatever I want. Stay in the Guard possibly, make a home for myself here on Typhos Prime, or perhaps be able to work my way back to where I was born on Olympas.

If I survive…

The Colonel looks at me with those ice-shards he has for eyes, an expectant expression on his face. I think about all the pain, misery and danger I've been through in the past three years, and consider the whole of my life being like that. I can tell that this is the only chance I've got to get out of the penal legions. If I'm transferred, I'm dead, sooner or later. That'll be the whole of my fate, for perhaps another three years if I'm lucky; just more wars and death and wondering when that bullet or las-bolt will finally get me. Perhaps I'll end up like Kronin, head snapped with the enormity of his destiny. And will there be someone around to watch my back the same way I look out for Kronin? Maybe, maybe not, but do I want to risk it? One choice, almost certain death, but the chance for freedom. The other choice, death almost as certainly, and no escape. I had my best bid for getting out the easy way here on Typhos Prime, and that wasn't good enough, and besides, do I really want to spend the rest of my life wondering if I could have done it the proper way?

All these thoughts are whirling round my head at the speed of a las-bolt, everyone else seems to be caught in some kind of stasis loop around me, the universe pausing in its slow life to let me make my decision. And through it all there's a recurring voice at the back of my head. You're an Imperial Guardsman, it says. This is the chance to prove yourself, it tells me. This is where you show them all that you're worth something. This is where the Colonel sees what kind of man you are. A man, it repeats, not a criminal scumbag.

'I'm in, Colonel,' I hear myself saying, my mind feeling like it's floating around a hand's breadth above my head, letting some other part of me take control for the moment. The others give their answers but I don't register what they actually say, my mind is still racing around and around, trying to catch up with itself. I hear Gudmanz muttering how dying in Coritanorum will be a release for him. Then, with a slamming sensation in my consciousness it hits home.

If I survive this, I'm free to walk away.

I have no doubt that the Colonel will keep his promise. All I need to do is survive one more mission, one more battle. Okay, it's Coritanorum, but I've been through some real crap lately and I'm still here. Who knows, this could be easy in comparison, if the Colonel's got it figured right.

With this realisation seeping into my thoughts I manage to turn my attention to the others. There's still only one torn-up parchment on the floor, so that must mean all the others accepted as well. They're looking at me, including the Colonel, and I realise that someone was speaking to me but I hadn't heard them, my mind was so engrossed in its own thoughts.

'What?' I say, forcing myself to try to think straight. It's going to be essential to think clearly if I'm going to get to see that pardon again.

'We said that we were going with you, not the Colonel,' repeats Lorii, looking encouragingly at me.

'What?' I snap, angry because I'm confused. 'What the hell does that mean?'

'It means that if you think we can make it, we're willing to try,' Loron explains, his pale face a picture of sincerity.

'Okay then, guardsmen,' the Colonel says. 'We move out at nightfall. You have two hours to prepare yourselves.'

THE STORM SEEMS to be passing, the thunder rumbling away to be replaced by the roar of distant artillery batteries. We're sitting on a rocky hillock, about eight hundred metres past the current Imperial trenchline, as far as I can tell. A plain stretches out for a few kilometres in front of us, swarming with rebels. It seems to be a kind of staging area, the open ground buzzing with activity. In the distance I can just about make out a sally port of Coritanorum. Two gatehouses flank a big armoured portal dug into an outcrop of rock from the mountain into which most of the citadel is dug. It's that mountain that makes it so easy to defend, rendering it impervious to all but the most sustained and concentrated orbital bombardment. Who knows how deep its lowest levels go? The parts that are above ground are rings of concentric curtain walls, each metres thick and constructed of bonded plasteel and rockcrete, making it hard to damage with shells and energy weapons, their slanted shape designed to deflect attacks towards the dead ground between them. That open space is a killing ground too, left clear and smooth to give no cover for any foe fortunate enough to get over one of the walls. I can see why half a million guardsmen have thrown themselves against this bastion of defiance with no effect.

I'm distracted as a cluster of starshells soar into the air over to the west, to our left, exploding in a blast of yellow blossoms.

'That is the signal we have been awaiting,' the Colonel says from where he's stood on the lip of an abandoned rebel trench.

The fighting's moved away from this area now, and the communications trench along this ridgeline gives us perfect cover from the scrutiny of Coritanorum's defenders. The forces being assembled before us are probably for a push along the southern flank of the Imperial line, hoping perhaps to turn the end of the line and pin a large part of the Emperor's troops between this sally and the walls of Coritanorum.

'The diversionary attack will have begun,' the Colonel informs us, clicking shut the case of a gold chronometer that he procured from the commissariat, before we left the relay outpost where he'd given us our ultimatum. Placing the timer into a deep pocket of his greatcoat, he looks around, seemingly at ease. Very at ease, actually, considering this is the most important and riskiest mission we've ever been involved in.

The sound of small stones skittering over the rocks above us gets everybody swinging round with weapons raised – except the Colonel, who's still stood there gazing towards Coritanorum.

'Good evening, Lieutenant Striden,' the Colonel says without looking, and we see a young man scrabbling down from the ridgeline, his thin face split with a wide grin.

'Good to see you, Colonel Schaeffer,' the man says pleasantly, nodding politely in greeting to each of us as well. He's swathed head to foot in an elaborate camouflage cape, patterned to blend in almost perfectly with the grey-brown rocks of the hills around Coritanorum. He jumps over the narrow trench to stand next to the Colonel, the cape fluttering around him.

'Now, Colonel Schaeffer?' Striden asks excitedly.

'When you are ready, Lieutenant Striden,' the Colonel affirms with a nod.

'What's happening, sir?' Lorii asks, looking suspiciously at Striden.

'Lieutenant Striden is going to call down some fire on these rebels, to clear a path to the sally port,' the Colonel replies, dropping down into the trench.

'You're going to need some big guns to shift that lot,' I say to the lieutenant. He turns his permanent grin towards me.

'Oh, we have some very large ordnance, Mr Kage,' he says, pulling a complex-looking device from beneath his cape. He squats down and opens up a shutter in the fist-sized box, holding it up to his eye. His fingers travel back and forth along a row of knobs down the side of what is evidently a range-finder or something, making small adjustments. Pulling the box away from his face, Striden looks down and I see a series of numbers and letters displayed on a digi-panel. He nods with a satisfied look and then looks upwards into the cloud-filled night sky.

'Wind's sou' sou' west, wouldn't you say, Mr Kage?' he says suddenly.

'Wind?' I blurt back, taken completely by surprise at this unusual question.

'Yes,' he says, glancing at me with a smile, 'and it looks as if there is a counter-cyclic at about six thousand metres.'

'Your guns must lob their shells a hell of a long way up for that to matter,' comments Loron from the other side of the lieutenant.

'Oh no, they don't go up at all, they just come down,' he replies amiably, pressing a stud on the bottom of the gadget and holding it up above his head.

'Doesn't go up…' murmurs Gudmanz. 'This is coming from orbit?'

'That's right,' Striden affirms with a nod. 'I'm ground observation officer for the battleship *Emperor's Benevolence*. She'll be opening fire shortly.'

'A battleship?' I ask incredulously. My mind fills with memories of the cruiser that was with us in the Kragmeer system, and the rows of massive guns along her broadside. Emperor knows how much firepower this battleship has!

'Here it comes,' Striden says happily, directing our eyes upwards with his own gaze.

The sky above Coritanorum begins to brighten and a moment later I can see the fiery trails of ten missiles streaking groundwards. As they approach, movement on the ground attracts my attention as the rebels begin to scurry around in panic when they realise what's happening. With a vast, thunderous roar the torpedo warheads impact into the plain, and `a ripple of explosions, each at least fifty metres across, tears through the assembled traitors, tossing tanks thirty or more metres into the air with great balls of fire. I don't see any bodies flung around, and I assume the men are completely incinerated. The ground is engulfed in a raging inferno, and then the blast wave hits us, from a kilometre away, causing the Navy officer's cape to flutter madly as the blast of hot air sweeps over my face, stinging my eyes. The air itself seems to burn for a few seconds, blossoms of secondary explosions filling the skies. Striden taps me on the arm and nods upwards and I can just make out a series of streaks in the air, reflecting the light of the flames around Coritanorum. The Colonel climbs out of the trench to watch, his eyes glittering red from the burning plain.

The shells' impacts are even more devastating than the torpedo fire as they explode in four parallel lines towards us, each one ripping up great gouts of earth and hurling men and machines in all directions. The roar of the detonations drowns out their screams and the screech of sheared metal. The blasts from the shells extinguish the murderous fires from the plasma warheads; a black pall of smoke drifts into the night sky, silhouetted against the twinkling lights of distant windows in Coritanorum. The salvo continues, numerous explosions creeping closer towards us across the plain. For a full minute the shells impact nearer and nearer and I start to worry that I'll go deaf with the intense, continuous pounding in my ears.

This is replaced by a more urgent fear as the bombardment carries on into a second minute, and it seems as if the battleship is going to go too far. When shells start exploding at the bottom of the ridgeline and keep coming, panic grips us, and everybody starts hurling themselves into the trench. As the bombardment continues I begin to fear for my life. I wouldn't trust ground artillery to shell that close to me, never mind a battleship more than a hundred kilometres above my head! The Colonel jumps in after us, a concerned look on his face, but Striden just stands there on the lip, gazing in raptured awe as the devastation approaches. Rock splinters are hurled into the sky by an explosion no more than fifty metres away and in the bright glare of the detonation, I see Striden raising his arms above his head and just make out shrill laughter over the tumult of the barrage. His cape is almost being ripped from his shoulders by the successive blast waves, but he stands there as solid as a rock.

Then everything goes silent and dark, my ears and eyes useless for a few seconds as they adjust to the sudden lack of violent stimuli. Striden's still laughing like a madman, and the Colonel gives a scowl and brushes down his coat before climbing out of the trench. The Navy lieutenant drops his hands to his sides and looks back over his shoulder, his eyes wide with excitement.

'Emperor help me, it doesn't matter how many times I see that, Mr Kage, I still get a tingle watching it!' he exclaims passionately, bright teeth showing in the darkness.

'That was a little fraggin' close!' I shout at him, pulling myself up over the rim of the trench and striding over to him.

'Orders, I'm afraid,' he says apologetically. 'Usually we'd bracket a target first to make sure of our positioning, but we weren't allowed to do that this time. This time, we're here, so we don't want anything unfriendly dropping on us, do we? And we were requested to miss the gatehouses too, which is a bit strange, but orders is orders. There's no need to worry, though: we've had quite a lot of practice at this.'

'I guess we won't be able to get in if the gate is fused into a molten lump,' says Lorii, vaulting gracefully over the top few rungs of the ladder out of the trench. I survey the scene as it is now, not even five minutes have passed since the starshells went up. The plains are pockmarked with hundreds of craters, at a rough guess, and from here, with my eyes still reeling, I can just about make out tangled heaps of wreckage scattered around. For about six kilometres in every direction, the plain has been bodily ripped up and dumped back down again. A haze of smoke floats a metre or so above the ground, dispersing slowly in the sluggish wind. The tang of burnt shell powder is almost asphyxiating, the air is thick with it. Nothing could have survived that, nothing that ever walked, crawled or was driven across the face of a world, at least.

'Going inside?' says Striden suddenly, Lorii's words filtering into his over-excited mind. 'Emperor's throne, that sounds damned exciting. More exciting than standing here waiting for my next target orders. Mind if I join you?'

'What?' I exclaim. 'Have you totally lost it?'

He gives me a pleasant smile and then looks towards Coritanorum, eyes staring with fascination.

'He can come,' I hear the Colonel say heavily from where he stands, further down the ridge, looking at the devastation wrought by the *Emperor's Benevolence*. I can tell that even he's impressed by the magnitude of the slaughter – there must have been near on ten thousand men down there a few minutes ago, and upwards of a hundred tanks. Now there's nothing. 'I do not think we could stop him, in fact,' says the Colonel meaningfully. I understand what he's saying – Striden'll follow us anyway and short of killing him, which the Navy won't appreciate one little bit, there's nothing we can do.

PICKING OUR WAY across the ruined landscape is a time-consuming process. We need to move quickly, but the route to Coritanorum is littered with burning tanks and mounds of corpses, not to mention the fact that the ground has been torn up and in places the rims of the shellholes are six metres high and fifty metres across. As we get nearer, within a few hundred metres of the gate, a thick layer of ash carpets the ground, in places piled up in drifts which go knee-deep. I remember that this is where the plasma torpedoes impacted.

'Do you know what happens to someone who gets caught in the noval centre of a plasma warhead explosion?' Gudmanz asks nobody in particular as he hauls himself up the slope of another impact crater, his robes covered with flecks of grey ash. We all shrug or shake our heads. Gudmanz bends down and grabs a handful of the dusty grey ash and lets it trickle through his fingers with a cruel, rasping laugh.

'You don't mean...' starts Lorii and then she groans with distaste when Gudmanz nods.

'Emperor, I swallowed some of that!' curses Loron, spitting repeatedly to clear his mouth.

'Silence, all of you!' barks the Colonel. 'We are almost at the gates.'

I STEP THROUGH the small portal into the left watchtower with lasgun ready. When I'm inside I understand how the Colonel could lead us through the gate with such confidence. Inside the tower men and women are strewn haphazardly across the floor and up the spiral stairs, their faces blue, contorted by the paroxysms of death.

'Airborne toxin, I suspect,' mutters Gudmanz, peering closely at one of the bodies, a young woman perhaps twenty years old, dressed in a Typhos sergeant's uniform.

'From where?' Striden voices the question that had just popped into my head.

'Keep moving,' the Colonel orders from further up the stairwell. When we reach the top, the whole upper level is a single chamber. There are gunslits all around, and a few emplaced autocannons, their crews lying dead beside their guns.

'Gudmanz,' the Colonel attracts the tech-priest's attention and nods towards a terminal in the inner wall, facing away from the gate. The tech-priest lurches over and leans against the wall. He reaches up and pulls something from behind his ear. It's like a small plug, the size of a thumbnail, and as he pulls it further I see a glistening wire stretching between it and Gudmanz's head. Punching a few runes on the terminal he inserts the plug into a recess in the middle of the contraption and closes his eyes. The display screen flickers into life, throwing a green glow onto the ageing tech-priest's craggy features. A succession of images flickers across the screen, too quick to see each one individually but giving an overall impression of a map or blueprints. Then a lot of numbers scroll up, again too fast to read, a succession of digits that barely appear before they are replaced by new data. With a grunt, Gudmanz steps back, the plug being ejected from the port and whipping back into his skull.

'Just as well that I checked,' he tells the Colonel. 'They have changed some of the security protocols in the inner areas and remapped the plasma chamber access passages.'

'You have a map of this place?' asks Lorii in amazement. 'How can you remember all that information? This place is over forty kilometres across!'

'Subcutaneous cerebral memograph,' Gudmanz replies, tapping an area of his skull just above his right ear. 'They did not take all of my implants.'

'I'm not going to even pretend I understood a word of that,' I butt in, 'but I take it you have an exact copy of the latest schematics in your head now?'

'That is correct,' he affirms with a single nod before pulling his hood up over his head. I turn to the Colonel.

'He mentioned plasma chambers, Colonel,' I say to him. 'What are we actually going to do here?'

'Coritanorum is run by three plasma reactors,' he explains as everyone else gathers around. 'We will get into the primary generators and disable them. Every system, every defence screen and sited energy weapon, as well as many of the major bombardment turrets, are linked into that power system.'

'I can see that,' agrees Lorii. 'But how do we get in?'

The Colonel simply points to the nearest body.

'GETTING INTO THE next circle is going to be harder,' Gudmanz warns the Colonel.

With our stolen uniforms, chosen to fit us better than my scrappy attempt with the Mordian outfit, getting around hasn't been too difficult. Everybody seems to take it for granted when an officer and a bunch of guardsmen, accompanied by a tech-priest, walk past. They've been on a war footing for two years now, I suspect the security is a little bit lax. After all, nobody would be stupid enough to come in here without an army. Except us, of course.

With their extraordinary hair concealed beneath Typhon Guard helmets, and their faces partially obscured by the high collars of the blue jackets, even Lorii and Loron have gone unnoticed. I'm not sure what uniform the Colonel procured for himself, but it seems to be one that makes the Typhons look the other way lest they attract his attention. It's black, without any decoration at all, and I wonder if it isn't some local branch of the commissariat. Even in stolen clothes he's managed to come up as someone everyone else is scared stiff of. Typical. With his camo-cape discarded, Striden is revealed as a skinny young man of about twenty, almost painful in his lankiness, though he doesn't walk with the gawkiness you might reasonably expect.

I'm beginning to understand even more now about how impossible it would be to take Coritanorum by open attack. Even if a sizeable enough force could gain access, the layout of the lower levels is roughly circular, a series of four concentric rings according to Gudmanz. Each is only linked to the next by a single access tunnel, which are on opposite sides of each ring so that to get from one to the next you have to get around half the circumference of the ring. The builders even made the air ducts and power conduits circular, so there's no quick route through there either. It's taken us a day and a half just to get around the outer circle. We grabbed a few hours sleep in an empty barracks block during the morning, and it's about midday now, and we're in a small chamber leading off from the passageway that goes to the next security gate.

'What do we need to do?' asks Schaeffer, dragging a chair from behind a chrome desk and sitting down. The plain, white room is bare except for the desk and chair, obviously disused now.

'We have to get one of the security officers – a senior one, I mean,' Gudmanz tells us. The Colonel looks over at me where I'm lounging against the wall.

'Kage, take Lorii and get me a senior security officer,' he says, as calmly as if asking me to pop out and get him some fresh boot polish or something. Lorii and I exchange glances and head out of the door. The corridor smells faintly of disinfectant and gleams brightly from a recent cleaning. The main tunnel is quite high and wide, its rhombic cross-section five metres tall and ten metres wide at the base with gradually sloping walls. Every surface is sheathed in shining metal panels, like steel planks, riveted into the naked rock. A few people go this way and that, paying us almost no attention at all. Most of them are guardsmen, but the odd Administratum scribe goes past now and then. Lorii and I wander along the corridor a bit until we come to a junction, much narrower and leading off in a curve to our right. We lean against the wall and start chatting, eyes looking over each other's shoulders for a sign of someone who might be the sort of man we're looking for. To everyone else, we just look like we're loafing, merely off-duty guardsmen passing the time.

'Do you think we can pull this off?' Lorii asks, keeping her voice low, a gentle purr in fact.

'If anyone can, it's us,' I assure her, scratching at an itch on my thigh caused by the coarse material of the white Typhon trousers.

'It's still not going to be easy taking this place, even with the power down,' she says with a wry look.

'I've been thinking about that, and I don't reckon there'll be anything to take after we've done,' I reply, voicing a suspicion that's been growing in my mind since the Colonel outlined his plan.

'I don't get you,' she says with a little frown creasing her thin white eyebrows.

'This idea about getting to the plasma chambers and shutting them down...' I start but fall silent when she gives me an urgent glance and then flicks her gaze over my shoulder along the main corridor behind me. I push myself off the wall and glance back. Walking towards us are three men, two of them in security uniforms that we've seen before – deep blue jumpsuits, metal batons hanging off leather belts, peaked caps instead of helmets. The man between the two security officials wears a similar outfit, but with red piping running the length of his sleeves and legs. He carries a short cane under one arm, like a drill sergeant I guess, and his stern demeanour shows that he's nobody to mess with. As they walk past we fall in a few metres behind them. I slip a short-bladed knife into my hand, procured from a kitchen we raided for food last night, and we quicken our step. Looking around to check we're alone, we make our move.

The security man on the right, in front of me, hears our footsteps and turns. Lorii and I pounce at the same time, my knife slamming into the left eye of the one who's looking back at us. Lorii wraps her arms around the head and neck of the other like a snake and with one violent twist and a hideous cracking noise, snaps his neck in two. The officer reacts quickly, lashing out at me with his cane. It just brushes my left arm but must be charged or something, because it sends a shock of pain up to my shoulder. Lorii's in too fast for him to get a second blow, bringing her knee up into the elbow of his outstretched arm and chopping down on his wrist with her right hand, breaking his arm and sending the cane clanging to the floor. His gives a shout of agony and Lorii brings her left arm sharply back, slamming the outside edge of her hand across his nose, snapping his head back. His legs buckle as blood streams down his face and she lashes out with a kick that connects with his chin and poleaxes him to the ground, completely out of it.

We're just recovering our breath, wondering what to do next, when from the next side corridor appears a clericus, staring intently at an opened scroll in his hands.

'Frag!' I spit, and he looks up, eyes widening comically as he sees the two of us crouched over what looks like three dead security men. I go to leap after him but my whole left side is going numb with the shock from the cane and I slump to one side. The adept gives a shriek, drops the parchment and turns to run, but Lorii's up and after him, five strides from her long, slim legs propelling her right up to him. She leaps into the air, her right foot striking out, smashing perfectly into the base of his skull and pitching him onto his face as she lands lightly on her feet. She grabs his head in both hands, and as with the security guard, breaks his spine as if wringing the neck of some fowl for dinner.

Luckily for us nobody else comes along and we find an empty terminal room behind the first door we open. Piling the dead men inside, I shut the door and then ram the blade of my knife into the lock on the door, snapping it off with a twist of my wrist.

'Hopefully nobody'll be too bothered about getting in there,' I say as we grab an arm each of the officer and start dragging him along the corridor.

'Those were some pretty special moves you had there,' I comment as we get to the junction, and Lorii peeks around the corner.

'Special training,' she replies, waving me on.

'What *was* your unit before you were sent to the penal battalion?' I ask, realising that everything we knew about the twins starts from after they were discharged.

'It was a special infiltration force. Fifty of us,' she tells me, returning to pick up her end of the unconscious Typhon officer. 'I can't really talk about it.'

'Were you... special in that outfit?' I ask, picking my words carefully considering Loron's earlier warning about remarks concerning their outlandish appearance.

'Oh no,' she says, glancing at me with a smile. 'We were all like that. It was part of our unique, erm, preparation and training.'

The feeling is returning to my left arm now and I heft the unconscious rebel over my shoulders and we run for it. We get to the door where the others are waiting and I knock on it with my foot.

'Yes?' I hear the Colonel saying from inside.

'It's us, you stupid fraggers, let us in!' I snap tersely through the gap between the door and the frame, my face resting against the cold metal of the door, my shoulder beginning to ache from its oblivious burden. The door opens a crack and I barge it open, throwing Striden to the floor, a pistol in his hand. I unceremoniously dump the security officer at Gudmanz's feet with vocal relief, as Lorii kicks the door shut behind us.

'This one do?' I ask Gudmanz. 'Cos if it don't, you can fraggin' well get your own one next time!'

'He is alive?' the Colonel asks as a groan escapes our prisoner's lips and he begins to move sluggishly.

'Oh, that's not necessary,' Gudmanz assures us, laboriously kneeling down beside the prone traitor, his fingers doing something to the man's neck that I can't quite see. When the tech-priest has finished, our captive has become a corpse, his face flushed red with blood.

'What did you do then?' asks Striden bending for a closer look, curiosity and excitement flashing across his face.

'I merely manipulated the flow of blood in his carotid artery and jugular vein to create a haemorrhaging effect in his brain,' the tech-priest explains, in the same matter-of-fact tone I can imagine him using to describe how to operate a comm-link frequency dial. I give an involuntarily shudder and step away.

'What do we do with him now?' asks the Colonel, still sitting where he was when we left a few minutes ago. Gudmanz looks at me as he pushes himself to his feet, joints cracking loudly in protest at this harsh treatment.

'We need a saw of some kind,' he says, looking expectantly at me, withered head cocked to one side.

'Oh, bugger off,' I reply miserably.

CONSIDERING THE trouble we had to go through to get everything Gudmanz wanted in the end, it might have been easier just to single-handedly storm the accessway. As we march purposefully up the main access corridor towards the two guards stationed by the portal to the next ring, I offer a silent prayer to the Emperor that this ridiculous scheme works. In the end we decided it would be best to break into an infirmary to get all the items on Gudmanz's list. The Colonel, Loron, Striden and me back-tracked to a traumarium a couple of kilometres back the way we came. We knew it'd be impossible to find any medical facility in the citadel that wasn't crammed with war wounded, and decided just to go for the nearest one. So it was that Striden was dragged by us, kicking and screaming enough to be heard across the system, into the infirmary, clasping his hands over his face.

'Plasma blindness,' the Colonel said curtly as the medicos clustered around.

I dropped Striden and made my way into the next room, where there's about fifty wounded soldiers, some of them in beds, most on rough pallets strewn across the floor. The ward stinks of blood and infection, tinged with the bitter smell of old hygienic fluids. Back in the other room, Loron covered the door into the medical centre. I didn't see what happened next, but the Colonel strode into the ward, a bunch of brass keys in his hand. He detailed me to dispose of the bodies while he fetched the surgical tools Gudmanz needed. I went back into the other room and saw Loron and Striden looking strangely at each other. I glanced down at the two dead medicos and see that their faces are contorted as if shouting but can't find any other mark on them. I asked the other two what the Colonel did, but they refused, saying some things were best forgotten.

And that's how we get here, the Colonel dressed up in the security officer's uniform, boldly walking towards the two guards. They straighten up as they see us approach, exchanging a quick glance with each other. Neither of them says a word as the Colonel and Gudmanz step up to a red glass panel set into the wall on the right side of the door. Gudmanz is standing between the guards and Schaeffer, hands held innocently behind his back, so that they can't see what I can.

The Colonel pulls the security officer's severed hand from the darkness of Gudmanz's sleeve and deftly fits the tube projecting from its sutured wrist into the intravenum Gudmanz inserted into his arm earlier. With his own pulse stimulating a fake heartbeat in the dead hand, the Colonel places it against the screen and a beam of yellow light plays between the fingertips, apparently reading the pattern on the end of the fingers. The screen changes to green and a tone sounds from a speaker set in the ceiling. As expertly as he attached it, the Colonel disconnects the hand from himself and passes it back to Gudmanz.

The two security men salute as we walk through the opening gates, standing to attention with their laser carbines along the seams of their right leg, their faces staring obediently into the middle distance. It's a position I learnt well when on garrison duty.

'Hurry up,' hisses the Colonel between tight lips when we're a few metres further down the tunnel. Walking next to him, I look over with a puzzled look. He notices my stare and glances down at his right hand before fixing his look ahead of him again. I surreptitiously look down and a lump appears in my throat when I realise an occasional droplet of blood is running down his wrist, gathering on his fingers and sporadically dripping to the floor. I glance back over my shoulder and luckily the two guards are still in their parade ground position, but it won't be long before one of them looks our way and sees the faint trail of blood on the metal flooring. We take the next quiet turning, the first couple had some people in them, and break into a run, sending Lorii ahead to check it out first. She comes back and guides us along a deserted route until we find an empty hab-complex. The floor is patterned with red and white triangular tiles, I guess the Typhons must really like triangles. The underground houses show signs of being in use, but no one seems to be around at the moment. Loron starts checking the twenty or so glass-panelled doors around the circular communal area at the centre of the little complex, and the third one he tries is unlocked.

'I remember the days when you could leave your door unlocked without fear,' jokes Lorii.

Hurrying through, we find ourselves in a dining chamber, a small kitchen area at one end. There's more tiling on the floors and walls, in two different shades of blue. The Colonel rips the intravenum from his arm and flings it into a waste grinder beside the small cooking stove.

'I thought these were supposed to seal up without the tube inserted!' the Colonel barks loudly at Gudmanz, who flinches from Schaeffer's anger.

'There must have been some flow-back from the rebel's hand,' he explains with his hands raised slightly in a placating gesture. 'They were not designed for this kind of procedure, please remember.'

The Colonel calms down slightly and we nose around the hab-pen. There are two small bedrooms off the living space, and they have their own ablutions area, complete with a basin and bathtub.

'Lucky bastards,' I say to Striden as he splashes cold water over his face. 'My barracks were never like this.'

'These are not barracks, Kage,' I hear the Colonel correct me from the front chamber. 'The second and third rings are the factory areas. This is where the civilians live.'

'Civilians?' says Lorii, popping her head round one of the bedroom doors, a dark red floppy felt hat on her head.

'Yes, civilians,' repeats the Colonel. 'This is the capital city of Typhos Prime, it is not just a fortress. And take that stupid thing off!'

Lorii disappears again, muttering something about the hat suiting her. Loron, who's by the front door keeping watch, gives an urgent hiss.

'Someone's coming!' he whispers, backing away from the glass panel.

When a figure appears right outside the door, we bundle into one of the bedrooms, while the Colonel peers out through the living space. I can hear the front door opening and closing and the Colonel ducks back inside, face screwed up in consternation. It's strange to note how much more alive he seems to have become since we got inside Coritanorum. It's like this is the only thing he lives for. Perhaps it is.

The door to the bedroom opens and a plump, middle-aged woman steps in. Quick as a flash, Kronin grabs her from behind the door, clamping a bony hand across her mouth.

'And the Emperor sayeth that the meek and silent shall be rewarded,' he whispers gently into her ear. Her eyes are rolling left and right, looking at the strangers in her bedroom, terror in her mad glances.

'What the frag do we do with her?' I ask the Colonel, as Kronin leads her over to the bed. He puts a finger to his lips and she nods understanding, and he lets her go. She gives a fearful whimper but doesn't scream.

'We can't take her with us, and she'll be discovered if we leave her here,' says Lorii, eyeing our captive with a frown.

'You can't just kill her!' Striden exclaims, stepping protectively between the Colonel and the woman.

'She's already dead,' Gudmanz says quietly in his grating voice. The Colonel looks at me and gives a slight nod. With his attention fixed on the Colonel, Striden doesn't see me cross to the side of the bed. The woman is also staring at the Colonel, probably wondering why a security officer is in her home.

I lean across the bed and before the woman knows what's happening I grab her throat in both hands. She gives a stifled cry, and lashes out blindly, her fingernails clawing at my face. She writhes and squirms as I squeeze tighter, her eyes locking on mine, alternating looks of pleading and anger. I feel someone grabbing at my shoulders, Striden shouting something in my ear, but my whole universe is just me and the woman. Her thrashing grows sluggish and her arms drop to the bedclothes, which have been rucked up around her with her struggling. With a final effort I squeeze the life out of her, her dead eyes looking at me with a mixture of confusion and accusation. I feel someone dragging the Navy lieutenant off my back, and I let go of her throat slowly. I look down at her pleasant face, purple from the choking now, and I don't feel anything. No guilt or remorse.

Inside, another human part of me seems to die.

'That was too extreme,' Loron says with a doubtful look, as I pull myself off the bed.

'Like Gudmanz said, she's already dead,' I tell them. 'They're all dead if we succeed, all three million of them.'

'What?' asks Lorii, walking over to the bed and closing the dead woman's eyes with her fingertips.

'We're not going to shut down the plasma reactors, are we, Colonel?' I say, turning to face Schaeffer.

'No,' he says simply, shaking his head.

'I'm not a tech-priest, but the hive I'm from ran on plasma reactors,' I tell them, flopping down onto a plastic chair in front of what looks to be a dressing table. 'Once they start, you don't shut them down, it's a self-fuelling process. But you can make them overload.'

'We're going to overload one of the plasma reactors?' asks Loron, turning on Gudmanz and the Colonel, who are standing by the door.

'All three of them, actually,' replies Gudmanz. 'They are omaphagically linked, if one of them fails, they all fail.'

'Call me stupid,' says Lorii, sitting on the edge of the bed, 'but I still don't see where this is going. We kill the power by over-loading the reactors, not shutting them down, so what?'

Gudmanz sighs heavily and lowers himself onto the bed next to Lorii, weariness in every movement.

'Let me try to explain in terms you might understand,' he says, looking at all of us in turn. 'A plasma reactor is, in essence, a miniature star captured inside graviometric and electromagnetic force walls. If you remove the Machine God's blessing from those shields, the star goes into a chain reaction, resulting ultimately in detonation. Three plasma reactors fuelling each other's chain reactions will create an explosion roughly sixty kilometres in every direction.'

'Nothing but ash will be left,' adds the Colonel, 'and at the heart, not even the ash will survive.'

'Sounds like an extreme way to win a war,' offers Striden, who's not calmed down at all.

'It has to be done this way. I will not tell you any more,' the Colonel says insistently. 'We must get moving, I want to find another terminal, so that Gudmanz can check what the security teams are doing. I expect at least one body has been found by now, and I want to know if they suspect any kind of enemy infiltration. We will have to proceed even more carefully.'

ABOUT HALF AN hour later and we're walking along what appears to be a main thoroughfare across the factory area. Massive shut-tered gateways fill one wall, indicating closed sites, to provide workers for the munitions works, I suspect. The ceiling and walls here are brick-lined rather than metal, but the now-famil-iar Typhon fondness for different colours in geometric patterns can be seen in a huge mosaic that covers the floor of the twenty-metre wide passageway. Apart from Gudmanz who wears his robe as normal, tech-priests are a frequent sight around here by the look of it, we're dressed in civilian garb looted from the hab-pens where I strangled the woman. Lorii has a rather fetching light blue dress, and the hat she was so fond of, while her brother, Striden and myself are dressed in dun-coloured worker's coveralls.

The Colonel, rot his soul, managed to find what might have been a wedding suit or something, tight black breeches and a long-tailed dark blue coat. It's not as out of place as you might think, it seems the sort of outfit the higher-ranking civilians wear around here. Kronin found a rough-spun jerkin and some leggings that fitted his short, wiry frame and from the tools we found in that home, I guess they used to belong to a spanner-boy. We used to have them back on Olympas, well they still do I guess. Their job is to crawl into the bowels of machinery and tighten up gears and chains. It's a dangerous job, because you can't afford to stop the machines running, and you can easily lose a limb or your head to some whirling arm or pumping piston. One of the cruellest things I saw was to send in a couple of other spanner-boys to remove a body that was clogging up a transmission mechanism. Of course, during a full trade war, their job is the opposite – they sneak into the enemy factories for a bit of sabotage.

We're almost unarmed, we ditched our captured guns into a waste grinder in the hab complex. I've got a knife secreted in my coveralls though, I'm not totally defenceless. There's a lot more people around here at the moment. I think it must be a shift change, a klaxon sounded a few minutes ago and the streets, well I call them streets but they're just wide corridors really, are packed with the throng. I feel more at home here, underground. When I've been in other towns I always have the strange sensation that someone's stolen the roof. Being brought up on a hive makes you like that, I guess. We've split up a bit so as not to attract too much attention, after Gudmanz told us to keep heading anti-clockwise around the second ring.

Gudmanz found another terminal to plug into, and says that the security forces have been wildly sending reports around. Some smart officer has realised there's a connection between the flurry of murders in the outer ring and the bloodstains found near the gate to the next circle. There's also the question of the dead troopers at the gatehouse, and they've tightened up security on the third ring, the one we've got to get into next. Gudmanz assures us that there's a lot more through-traffic between the second and third circles, as they are both civilian areas, but if the guards are getting itchy, there could be all kinds of problems.

Strolling along with Striden, who's been in a silent, tetchy mood since I had to kill the woman, I catch snippets of conversations from the people around. Most of them are chatting about usual stuff – how the boss is having an affair with some wench from the factory floor, what the plans for the wedding will be, how the food in the factory kitchens has been getting worse lately. Day-to-day life that denies the raging conflict only a short distance away.

But they do talk about the war a bit, and that's what's started confusing me. They keep talking about the 'damned rebels' and 'traitor army' camped outside their walls. These people seem to think that we're the rebels, not them. They accuse the rebels, I mean the Imperium actually, of starting the war, of attacking without provocation. I'd ask the Colonel about it if I thought there was any point, but I don't reckon he'd give me a straight answer.

As the people around disperse a bit more, I catch a glimpse of Kronin ahead of us, looking like he's having an argument with a couple of the locals. He must have got separated from Loron, who was supposed to be looking after the headcase. Cursing to myself I hurry forward.

'Just asking for an apology, I am, ' one of the factory workers is saying angrily, hands on hips. His face is pitted with burn scars and his head is beginning to go bald. Kronin's not a tall man, but he's still a couple of centimetres taller than this tiny fellow.

'And all were blessed in the sight of the Emperor,' says Kronin, getting worked up, frustrated that he can't make himself understood.

'Stop saying that stuff,' the other worker snarls. 'You a preacher or something, you think?'

'Why don't we all settle down!' calls Striden as we jog up to them.

'Who the hell, off-worlder, are you?' demands the first, turning to confront us. His friend steps up next to him, offering support with his threatening posture. He's more my height, and his thick biceps and solid forearms show he's no stranger to heavy manual labour. He looks like he can handle himself, but then again so can I.

'Bad news for you, if you don't frag off this instant!' I hiss at them, squaring up to the pair of them.

'You're all the same, coming down here, to tell us how to run them factories!' the second one says, pointing an accusing finger at me. 'Treats us like we just fell outta the sky, you do. 'Bout time somebody's put in their place, ask me.'

I just laugh, I can't stop myself. It's so ridiculous, the irony is outstanding. I've fought in a dozen wars and now I'm about to get in a fight with a couple of factory workers because I talk with an off-world accent. There's a manic edge to my laugh that makes them stare closely at me, suddenly wary.

'All mad, you are!' spits the first one, throwing his arms up in disgust. 'All of you off-worlders.'

'Mad enough,' I say, putting every ounce of menace I can into those two words. The tall one realises the threat isn't empty and grabs his friend by the shoulders, pulling him away. The short one keeps looking back at us, hurling abuse back at us, causing some of the passers-by to look.

'You!' I snarl at Kronin, grabbing the front of his coveralls and dragging him up to his toes. 'You keep next to me and don't say nothing!'

Pushing the two other Last Chancers ahead of me, I cast one final look around. There's a security team, three men, walking further along the corridor, and I see a young woman hurrying over towards them. I start to walk faster, trying to hurry but be inconspicuous at the same time, which is some feat I'll tell you. I hear a shout to stop from behind.

'Frag!' I curse, breaking into a run and grabbing the other two as I run between them. 'Get your legs moving, we're in trouble!'

THE PAST TWO hours have been the worst in my life. I've seen neither hide nor hair of the Colonel, Loron, Lorii or Gudmanz, and the three of us have been ducking and diving like mad as security teams poured into the factory area. At one point we rounded a corner and walked slap-bang straight into five of them. Luckily, Kronin and me were quicker on the uptake and took them down with only a short fight. These ones were armed as well, which was a first, carrying heavy automatic pistols, which the three of us relieved their unconscious bodies of. Which all leads up to where I am now, crouching with a pistol in each hand at the top of a ladder while Striden and Kronin are behind me trying to prise the grille off a ventilation duct. It was a stroke of pure luck that we took the turning that led here, a district of abandoned factories. Another fortunate twist brought us to this air filtration plant, and from there it was an easy choice to decide to get off the streets for a while. We're not totally alone though, I can hear security men shouting to each other in the distance. I've got no idea what's happening outside, but I can see nobody's entered the building yet.

There's a clang as they drop the grille to the floor and I wince, wondering if anyone else heard it. Turning, I see Striden grinning back at me.

'You two in first, go left and keep heading that way, don't turn off at all until we can work out some kind of plan,' I tell them, peering down the ladder again to check no one's nearby. The rockcrete-floored plant is as deserted as it was a moment before. Satisfied that it's safe, I push myself up through the grille and follow the other two.

'FRAG IT!' I SHOUT, slamming my fist against the metal lining of the conduit. 'For Emperor's sake, give me a break!'

I slump to the ground, teeth gritted with frustration. For half an hour we've crawled along this duct, and when it widened out I thought we were getting somewhere. I was wrong. About twenty metres ahead of us, a massive fan is spinning, blocking any route forward. Crawling around in the darkness, never sure if you're going to pitch down some hole in the blackness, my nerves have started to jangle. And this is all I need, to have to backtrack a couple of hundred metres or so to the last turning.

Pulling myself together I stand up and walk closer to the extraction fan. It isn't going that fast, too fast to jump past though, and beyond its blades I can see an area that looks like the communal foyer of a hab area. Like most of Coritanorum, the area is tiled with different colours and shapes, a stark contrast to the grimy, dull metal of the hive factories where I'm from. I can see two children sitting in the middle of the open area, playing some kind of game with their hands. All in all, it doesn't look like an unpleasant place to be brought up, even with a war raging outside the walls. Studying the fan itself, it seems to be made of some kind of ceramic, about twice as wide as my outstretched arms. There's a thin metal mesh on the far side, clogged up in places with bits of dirt and stuff, so I guess it's there to stop the fan being jammed.

'Back up a bit,' I tell the others as I pace back from the fan, drawing the pistols from where they're rammed into the belt of my coveralls.

'What are you doing?' asks Striden, looking at the pistols.

'Taking the initiative,' I tell him, aiming both pistols down the duct. The muzzle flare is blinding as it reflects off the metal of the air shaft and the conduit rings with the roar of firing. As I hoped the fan shatters into shards which fly in all directions. With my ears recovering, I hear shouts from the end of the duct. I push myself forwards past the wreckage of the fan drive system. There's about two dozen people clustered into the communal area now, all looking up at me standing at the end of the duct, pistol in each hand. I kick out the grille, forcing some of them to jump back as it clatters to the ground.

'Anyone moves, I kill them,' I tell them, keeping my voice calm and steady. I mean it as well. I look down at their dumbfounded faces, and all I can see in my mind's eye are little piles of ashes. They're all dead if we succeed. They're walking corpses. Kronin and Striden crowd in behind me and I lower myself the couple of metres down the wall, whipping round with the pistols to make sure nobody gets too close. The two children are clinging to their mother, a slim young woman dressed in red coveralls, their eyes wide with fear. But they're not two children really, just two tiny, pathetic piles of ash. I hear the other two dropping behind me and Kronin steps up next to me, a pistol in his hand.

As we walk forward, the crowd parts around us, everybody's attention fixed with grim fascination on the strange men who have dropped into their lives so violently and unexpectedly. We've almost reached the corridor leading off from the hab-pens when some idiot hero makes a lunge for Kronin's gun. The pistols in my hand spit death, flinging his ragged corpse into the crowd, who immediately break into hysterical screaming, fleeing towards the safety of their homes. Breaking into a run of our own, we hurry off. I don't even spare a second thought for the dead man in the plaza.

* * *

DITCHING THE GUNS into a waste shaft – they'd be no use really and are far too conspicuous – we make our way towards the next gate. Well, as far as I can tell, my sense of direction is somewhat turned on its head by the time spent in the air ducts. We come across some kind of market place, a huge open space full of stalls, many of which seemed to be closed down. I guess there isn't too much to sell really, as Coritanorum is under siege. An immense bronze statue, of Macharius I think, dominates the centre of the plaza, stood upon a marble pedestal a clear three metres taller than me. The place is quite busy though, and gives us plenty of cover to avoid the few guards prowling around, ducking into the crowds if they get too close. Most of the people around are women and young children, I assume the older children and men are working hard in the factories and struggling to maintain this huge citadel as the noose of the Imperial forces outside tightens even more. I wonder what the hell has happened to the rest of the Last Chancers, and I'd happily let them go off and finish the mission while we hole up somewhere. That isn't an option, though – unless I fancy being fried by a plasma explosion.

We manage to get back onto the main corridor eventually, running in a wide circle around the second ring. From there it's easy to get my bearings and we hurry as much as possible. I've got no idea what we'll do once we get to the accessway, or how we're going to link up with the Colonel, but I decide that we need to worry about one thing at a time for the moment. An increase in the frequency of the guards warns when we start getting close to the linking tunnel, and we walk straight past it, getting a glance at how well manned it is. I can't stop and count without arousing too much suspicion, but I reckon on a dozen men at least. We walk about another hundred metres down the corridor when we come across what looks like a guardhouse, the symbol of the security forces blazoned onto the solid double doors. No one is around, not even a security team, and I saunter closer for a better look, the other two trailing dumbly behind me, quite content just to follow my lead. Realising that there's nothing to be done here, I turn to walk away. At that moment I hear the doors grinding open behind me and a shiver runs down my back as I hear someone walking out.

I hear the Colonel's voice behind me. 'Get in here, you idiot!'

* * *

TWENTY DEAD SECURITY guards lie inside the station, which doesn't appear to be anything more than a terminal room, with a few cells to one side. Once more, there's a mosaic, this time a representation of some battle from the past rather than abstract shapes. I can't tell what it is, the bodies of the dead security men obscure too much of it. Their bloated faces match those of the guardsmen in the gate tower, reminding me that we're not the only ones fighting against the rebels from within.

'You took your time,' Loron says as we stroll in.

'What happened here?' Striden asks, looking at all the corpses.

'Dead when we arrived,' answers Lorii with a shrug. 'I guess our invisible helper from the gatehouse is still watching over us.'

'Have you been deliberately trying to get caught, Kage?' demands Schaeffer, closing the doors behind us. He gestures towards Gudmanz, who is sitting at the largest terminal, plugged in again. 'We have access to the whole security network from here and have been monitoring the comm-channels. We have been tracking reports of your whereabouts for the past four hours. Luckily for you, Gudmanz managed to conjure up some false reports and a fake fire emergency to lead them off the trail.'

'So how do we get past the next gate?' asks Striden. 'They'll be extra cautious now.'

'We will just walk through, as we did last time,' the Colonel tells us, gesturing to the uniformed men lying around us. 'Security teams have been going through each way for the past two hours, one more will not arouse any undue attention.'

Everyone's attention is drawn to Gudmanz when he gives a gasp, and as I look at him the neural plug whips back into his head and he slumps further into the chair.

'What is it?' asks the Colonel, going over to lean on the back of the chair and stare at the half dozen screens on the terminal face.

'I cannot use the terminal network any more,' he tells us slowly, recovering from some kind of shock. 'They realised what I was doing and other tech-priests started scanning the network for me. I manage to eject just before they found me, but only because I have had more practice at this type of thing over the past two days. They will find me straight away if I go in again.'

'What was the last thing you found out?' asks Schaeffer, turning his head from the screens to look at the tech-priest.

'There has been nothing to suggest that they know we are heading for the plasma reactors,' he reassures us. 'They suspect we might be trying to get to one of the turret clusters in the central keep. They have no idea that we are here for something far more unpleasant than disabling a few cannons.'

'Good, then we will press on,' the Colonel says, standing up and passing an eye over the dead security men in the room. 'We should be able to get to the last access tunnel before night, the third ring is not very big at all.'

'And then what?' Loron asks, crouching down to strip the coveralls from a likely sized guard.

'We finish our mission,' the Colonel replies grimly.

'I'VE BEEN THINKING about our mysterious guardian,' says Lorii as we walk down a flight of steps that take us away from the main corridor in the third circle. 'Why didn't they blow up the reactors?'

'It is a very complex process, to curse a containment field of the type we are talking about,' explains Gudmanz as he hobbles down the rockcrete steps in front of us. 'The bulk of a plasma reactor is dedicated to creating wards and heligrams to make sure the Machine God's blessing remains. Many failsafes will stop you, you cannot just touch a rune and say a few canticles to turn them off. It takes one of my order to do it.'

'And I can see why you couldn't be sent in alone,' adds Loron from above, referring to the tech-priest's increasing frailty. It's as if he's ageing a year every hour, he's slowed down that much since we met him three days ago. He said he would last a month, but looking at his current condition, I can't imagine him seeing the end of the day after next. The Colonel's gone tight-lipped on us again, obviously tensing up the closer we get to our goal. He was almost human for a while, but has reverted to man-machine mode now.

The third ring is similar to the second, terraces of factories interspersed with mazes of hab-pens. There's the strange mix of metal panelling, brickwork and tiling that can be found in the outer rings. Trying to imagine the pattern of different styles in my head, with what little I know of Coritanorum's layout, it

seems to me that originally this area was in fact several
different citadels, which over time have slowly been joined
together, with the central access tunnels constructed to link
them all together at some later point.

As nightfall approaches outside, things start to get a lot quieter. We see fewer people, many of them security guards who
we swap salutes with before hurrying on. As we approach the
final accessway, the sprawling rooms become more military
looking, with lots of terminal chambers, and what appear to be
barracks. I can feel everyone getting more nervous as we march
along the twisting corridors, and I try to distract the other Last
Chancers to stop them getting too jumpy.

'I wonder how Linskrug is doing?' I ask in general.

'Glad he isn't here, I bet,' Lorii ventures, casting an edgy
glance down a side tunnel.

'He's dead,' the Colonel informs us quietly from where he's
walking ahead of us.

'How can you possibly know that?' asks Loron.

'Because the penal legion he was sent to was the one ordered
to make the diversionary attack when we came in through the
sally port,' he explains, not looking at us.

'And turning from the flames Saint Baxter leapt from the
cliffs,' says Kronin, half to himself.

'He might still have survived,' Loron says, grasping at a shred
of hope for our departed comrade.

'No,' the Colonel tells us. 'I personally gave Commissar
Handel strict instructions that they were to fight to the last
man. He will have carried out his orders to the letter.'

We walk on in silence for another couple of minutes, pon-
dering this turn of events.

'What would you have done if we all refused this mission?'
asks Loron as the Colonel takes us down a left turn, leading us
across a gantry that passes over what looks to be a metalworks,
the furnaces dead at the moment. 'You'd be fragged if at least
half of us had turned you down.'

'I admit that I did not expect Linskrug to refuse,' says the
Colonel, still facing forward. 'I thought that none of you would
turn down the opportunity I presented you with. Linskrug had
less character than I credited him with.'

'Why so certain that we'd come along?' Loron persists, hurrying forward to fall into step beside Schaeffer.

'Because that is why you are still here,' he replies. 'You have a lust for life that defies the odds. I knew that if I offered you the chance for freedom you would take it.'

'But Linskrug didn't accept,' crows Loron victoriously. We fall silent for a minute as we reach the end of the gantry and turn into another metal-walled corridor, a couple of scribes coming towards us, giving us suspicious looks as we pass them by.

'That must have rattled you,' Lorii says when the Typhons have disappeared from view. 'You must have been a bit shaken up when Linskrug said no.'

The Colonel stops abruptly, turning on his heel to face us.

'I did not choose to have Linskrug in the Last Chancers, he was forced upon me,' he snarls at us. 'The rest of you, I personally recruited. I studied your files, watched you in battle, and weighed your personalities. I did not wage war on a dozen worlds over three years for no reason. I had to be sure of you.'

With that he turns and stalks away. We exchange stunned glances for a couple of seconds before hurrying after Schaeffer.

'You mean you've known this is what we'd be doing all along?' I ask, amazed at the concept.

'Yes,' is all he replies.

'You mustered four thousand men, when you knew that only a handful would be able to get into this place?' I press on relentlessly.

'Yes,' is all he says again, and I can feel the anger radiating from his body.

'Why?' I demand. 'Why the hell do all that?'

'Because we needed the best, Kage,' he says through gritted teeth. 'Like it or not, the Last Chancers produce the best fighters and survivors in this part of the galaxy. You have all shown the combat skills and qualities of personality needed for this mission. I have tested you to destruction, but I have not been able to destroy you.'

'Tested?' I almost scream at him, curbing my anger at the last moment in case it attracts unwanted attention. It's easy to forget we're in the middle of an enemy stronghold. The off-white lighting of the glowstrips set into the ceiling flickers as we pass into another area, and the corridor seems dimmer than the others. Problems with energy distribution, I reckon. If we're successful, the Typhons' power supply problems are going to get a lot worse.

'It is true,' the Colonel admits, pinching the bridge of his nose like he's got a headache or something. 'Many of the events over the past three years have been chosen or engineered to focus on different parts of your military ability and personality traits. They have tested your initiative and resourcefulness. They have examined your determination, sense of duty, discipline and responses to fear. I admit it is not a precise process, but I think you will agree that I have managed to turn all the situations to my advantage, and along the way we have helped win a few wars. Is that so bad?'

'Not a precise process?' I spit angrily. 'I guess the Heart of the Jungle was a little bit unexpected, wasn't it? And what about the eldar attack on the transport? Inconvenient was it? And the shuttle crashing in Hypernol?'

He doesn't reply, simply keeps marching resolutely along the corridor. Then my brain catches up with the rest of me as his earlier words sink in.

'You said engineered,' I say, surprised that I can get even angrier at what this man has done to us.

'Yes,' he admits, glancing back over his shoulder at me. 'Mostly I chose situations that would provoke the required conditions, but some had to be set up deliberately. The shuttle crash was one of those situations. You cannot just hope for that sort of thing to happen, can you?'

That's the final twist, something inside me snaps. I jump forward and lay a hand on Schaeffer's shoulder and spin him around. Before I can do anything else, he slaps me backhanded across the face, almost knocking me from my feet. I'm stunned by the act as much as by the pain – I've never before seen him hit a Last Chancer who didn't attack him first.

'Maintain discipline, Lieutenant Kage,' he says coldly, staring at me with those glitters of ice he has for eyes. 'I will no longer tolerate this insubordination.'

I'm half-shocked and half-not by this news. Our suspicion had been growing over the past few months in particular, but the extent to which the Colonel has created and manipulated events is almost unbelievable. I begin to wonder how often he's done this before. How many times has he killed thousands of soldiers to see who were the best, the greatest survivors? How many times more would he do it? It seems such a merciless, uncaring thing to do, but part of me can see his reasoning. It's a merciless, uncaring galaxy we live in, and if other missions were as important as this one, to save whole worlds, I could just about forgive him. Just about. It still doesn't explain why he was still so secretive about the mission goals. Did he really think we'd back down when we realised what was at stake? Does he think so little of us he doesn't believe we have at least that much decency and courage we'd be willing to fight for the sake of a world of people, for the hundreds of thousands of guardsmen and Navy personnel who'd lose their lives trying to take the place by force?

We walk on in resentful silence.

FINDING WHAT LOOKS to be a deserted archive room, we hide out and formulate the next part of our plan. Rows and rows of parchments, dataslabs and crystal disks surround us on endless shelves. Hidden among the teetering mass of information, we cluster around a battered wooden table, looking intently at a copy of Coritanorum's innermost layout, brought forth like magic from one of Gudmanz's voluminous sleeves.

'Our benefactor have anything lined up for this one?' asks Loron, leaning across the schematic at the far end of the table.

'We will have to work this out ourselves,' the Colonel replies, shaking his head. All eyes turn to Gudmanz.

'This will not be easy,' he says heavily, taking a deep sigh. 'To open the gate requires a retinal scan.'

'A what?' asks Lorii, looking across from where she's perched on the edge of the table, bent over the map.

'Remember at the first gate, the scanner read the skin indentations of the security officer's fingertips?' he asks, and we all nod in agreement. Who could forget that macabre episode? 'Well, this portal has a device that can map the blood vessels within your eyeball.'

'An eye?' exclaims Striden, looking thoroughly disconsolate. He had been starting to cheer up again, getting over the grisly episode with the woman, I guess. 'That's going to be even trickier than getting a hand!'

'Forget about eyeballs,' says the Colonel quietly and we turn to look at him, sat a little away from the table in a padded armchair, right elbow resting on the arm, fingers cradling his chin. 'We will do this the easy way.'

* * *

Now, I wouldn't say that the Colonel's way was going to be easy, but it's certainly a lot more straightforward. There's two guardsmen stood outside the armoury as we approach, lasguns held at the ready. They ease up slightly as they see the Colonel, in his senior security officer's uniform, but are obviously on their toes. The Colonel walks up to the opticon eye set next to the armoured portal in the weapons store.

'State your business,' a disembodied voice says from a speaker grill just above the opticon.

'Permission to enter?' asks the Colonel, in a near-perfect imitation of the burr of a Typhon accent.

'We've orders to let no one in,' says the guardsman from inside.

'I've got written confirmation,' replies the Colonel, waving a bunch of important-looking films that we scrounged from the data library. We wait for about half a minute, exchanging nonchalant shrugs with the two guardsmen as we wait for the other man's decision.

'Them orders – let's see them,' he says finally and there's a loud clank as a lock-bar drops away from the door and it swings open on powered hinges. The Colonel strides purposefully in and the door whines shut behind him.

Striden's almost hopping from foot to foot with nerves and I give him a stern glare, hoping he'll calm down before the guardsmen get suspicious. I feel a trickle of sweat running down my right side and have to fight my own unease, hoping it doesn't show.

'Taking his time, isn't he?' comments one of the guardsmen, glancing back over his shoulder at the heavily constructed door. I just murmur and nod in agreement, not trusting my linguistic ability to impersonate a Typhon. It was probably a smart move to leave Loron, Lorii and Gudmanz in the archive chamber. These guardsmen seem to be keyed up at the moment, and they're bound to have been told to be on the lookout for any pale-skinned strangers with a tech-priest. I suspect the Colonel's plan is the best one now; the chances of pulling off a fancy subterfuge at the last access tunnel have passed us by.

The awkward silence is broken by the portal hissing open again. The Colonel stands there with a compact stub gun in his right hand, a bulky silencer screwed on to the end of the barrel.

The talkative guardsman looks back and his eyes widen in surprise a moment before the first bullet smashes his head to a pulp, spraying blood and brains across the floor just to my right. The other guardsman turns quickly, but his lasgun is only half-raised when the next shot punches into his chest, hurling him back against the wall.

'Grab them and drag them inside,' orders the Colonel, taking a step out of the armoury. 'I have signalled the others in the archive room from inside, they will be here shortly. And find something to clear up that mess.'

'TIME TO GET SERIOUS,' Lorii says as we walk together between the high-stacked crates of power cells and ammunition.

'Let's just hope nobody else drops in for fresh supplies,' comments Loron from behind me.

'We want something with a bit more firepower than lasguns,' the Colonel tells us from up ahead, as he scans the rows of boxes and racks of guns. 'We need one-hit kills if we are going to challenge their numbers.'

We search around for a few more minutes before Gudmanz uncovers a shelf of fifteen bolters. Freshly cleaned, they gleam in the bright, white light of the armoury, in my eye as beautiful as they are deadly.

'Ammunition is in those bins overhead,' says Gudmanz, pointing to a row of black containers hung over the bolters. Lorii grabs one and pulls it down, letting it drop to the floor. Inside are dozens of bolter magazines, loaded and ready to go. She and Loron start transferring the ammo to the heavy work trolley pushed by Striden.

'I want something with a better rate of fire,' I mutter to myself, looking around for a more suitable weapon.

'And the Emperor's rewards are bountiful for those who labour in His name,' says Kronin with a smile, using a crowbar to lift the lid off a wooden crate, revealing rows of frag grenades within. He starts tossing them to Striden, who places them on the trolley next to the bolters.

'Is this what you would like?' Gudmanz asks, holding up a long rifle. It's finished in black enamel, oozing menace and lethality.

'Ooh, that looks mean,' I say appreciatively, walking closer. 'What is it?'

'Fractrix pattern assault laser,' he says with a smile, running a gnarled hand lovingly along its length. It's the first time he's looked happy since I met him. 'Five shots per second, twin power pack capable of fifteen seconds' continuous fire. Multiple target designation range-finder. I used to be overseer on one of the manufacturing lines,' he adds, glancing at me.

'Reliability?' I ask, knowing that there's always a catch, otherwise everyone would have them.

'Oh, it is very reliable,' he assures me. 'The only drawback is that the focus prism needs to be changed every one thousand shots, and that requires a tech-adept. Not practical for extended battle conditions, but perfect for our task.'

I take the gun from him and heft it to my shoulder, closing my left eye to look through the sight along its length. I can't see anything at all and give a confused glance towards the tech-priest.

'You must disengage the safety link before the optical array is powered up,' he tells me, pointing towards a fingernail-sized stud just above the trigger guard. I give it a push and the assault laser gives a little hum as the power cells warm up. Sighting again, I look back towards the others. In the small circle of the gunsight, each is surrounded by a thin light blue glow, outlining their silhouette.

'It can detect heat patterns as well,' Gudmanz tells me proudly. 'You might not be able to see the person, but you will be able to see their outline.'

I grin to myself, swinging the laser so that it is pointing at the Colonel. One squeeze of the trigger and a storm of las-bolts will tear him into little pieces. I ask myself why I shouldn't do it. Why shouldn't I pull the trigger? But I know the answer really. For a start, I'm beginning to realise that the Colonel wouldn't have done to us what he did, if he thought there was any alternative. He has his own reasons, and to him they justify any act, including killing three million people. I have an idea what it might be, but I'm not sure. Second, he's the only one who has the vaguest chance of getting us out of Coritanorum alive. He has the mysterious contact on the inside, and he's been studying this place longer than any of us, and probably knows more about it even than Gudmanz. I think he's spent the best part of the past three years planning this operation, and I'm sure that includes getting out again in one piece. He might not be planning on bringing us along, who knows, but if I stick close to him then I've got the best chance there is. I press the safety stud again and the small circle goes black.

'Flak jackets and helmets are along the next aisle,' the Colonel says, pointing over to the left. He turns and sees me with the gun pointing towards him. He calmly meets my gaze.

'It suits you,' he says and then turns away, completely unconcerned. He knew he wasn't in any danger. Bastard.

'Right,' I declare, slinging the assault laser over my shoulder by its strap, 'now I need some really good knives.'

'REMEMBER WE NEED one alive,' Gudmanz reminds us as we push the trolley of guns and ammo, concealed under a bundle of camouflage netting, towards the accessway. It must be almost midnight outside, though the glow tubes are shining just as brightly down here as ever. Everybody's sleeping, or at least that's what we hope. According to the schematic, the nearest plasma chamber is only around eight hundred metres from the access portal, so the plan is to hit the enemy hard and fast. We get the guards on the door, using a live one to bypass the eye-scanner, and then leg it as quick as possible, storming the plasma reactor room and then holding off the Typhons while Gudmanz does his thing. The tech-priest thinks it will take a couple of hours to deactivate all the wards on the plasma chambers, hence the gratuitous amount of ammunition on the trolley being pushed beside me by Striden. Six people fighting off an entire city? I fragging hope the Emperor is backing us on this one. Once that happens, we've got roughly a couple of hours to get clear.

We round the corner into the accessway and don't even need the order to open fire. I fire the assault laser from the hip, spraying dozens of red energy bolts into the Typhons by the gateway, pitching men off their feet, scouring burn marks along the walls. Loron and Lorii open up with their bolters, the explosive rounds detonating in a ripple of fiery blossoms, blowing fist-sized holes in the Typhons' chests and tearing off limbs. I see a guardsman's head blown apart by a direct hit from the Colonel's bolt pistol. One of them manages to return fire, the snap of his lasgun just about heard in breaks between the roar of the bolters. A las-bolt zips off the wall and catches Lorii across the shoulder, spinning her to the ground. Striden brings up his shotgun, the half-random blast shredding the remaining guardsman, scattering a mist of blood across the passageway. And then, as suddenly as it started, the fight is over. A few seconds of concentrated bloodshed and the job's done.

The Colonel dashes forward and starts picking his way through the mangled remains of the Typhons while we reload. Loron is bent over his twin sister, an anguished look on his face.

'Is she all right?' I ask, walking over.

'I'm fine,' Lorii replies, pushing herself to her feet, blood streaming down her left arm in a red swathe. Loron tears a strip from a dead guardsman's tunic as Lorii strips off her flak jacket and shirt. Leaving Loron to bandage her, I check on Striden and Kronin, who are at the main corridor end of the accessway, checking nobody is going to stumble upon us. I hear the Colonel give a satisfied grunt and turn to see him dragging one of the Typhons towards the eye-scanning reticule beside the gate. He pushes the man's face into it and a moment later the doors begin to slide open.

'We are in,' says the Colonel, placing his bolt pistol under the guardsman's chin and blowing his brains out, scattering bits of skull over the scanner and wall. We stand there for a second, staring at the strange scene of the Colonel cradling the headless corpse.

'Get moving!' he shouts, dropping the body with a thump, and we jump to it, Kronin and Striden grab the trolley and run forward, the Colonel and Gudmanz up front, me and the twins covering the back. When we're all through the gateway, I hit the lever that closes it, and as the doors grind back into place, I ram a grenade into the power cabling leading to the locking bar. As I run off, I hear the crump of the grenade detonating and glance back, noting with satisfaction the twisted mess of wires left by the explosion.

My attention is drawn to the front by the sound of the Colonel's bolt pistol and I hurry forward, assault laser ready. Some guardsmen are up ahead, just around a bend in the main tunnel, using the side corridors for cover. Las-bolts spit down the passage towards me, zinging off the walls and floor, leaving faint scorch marks. The Colonel's crouched down inside an opened door, poking out now and then to fire off a shot, the bolts tearing chunks of metal from the walls.

I leap forward, rolling across the floor as a ragged lasgun volley flares towards us, slamming through a doorway on the left of the passage. As I steady myself and come up to a crouch, I aim my gun at the nearest Typhon, about twenty metres down on the same side of the corridor. In the laser's sight, his head and shoulders are brought into sharp focus as he leans round the corner for another shot, and I squeeze the trigger gently. Half a dozen red bolts flash into his upper body, a couple of them punching straight through and dissipating further down the tunnel. Another fusillade of laser fire forces me to duck back into the room.

This is gonna take forever, I tell myself, realising that the longer we're pinned down here, the more troops are going to come pouring into the area.

'Grenades!' I bellow, pulling one from my belt. As I hurl it down the passageway, three more clatter along the floor next to it, thrown by the others. One brave guardsman dashes from cover to grab them and toss them back, but a shot from either Loron or Lorii punches through his leg, the impact of the bolt severing it at the knee. His screams echo down the passage for about a second before the grenades explode, flinging him into the air. Even as the blast dissipates, I'm charging down the corridor, assault laser at my shoulder, using the sight to pick off the Typhons through the smoke and haze.

I must have missed one down a sidetunnel, because as I'm pounding forward I feel something slam into the right side of my head, making my ears ring and my knees buckle. Turning, I see the Typhon, a middle-aged man, his uniform slightly too tight for him. I see his eyes narrow as he lines up his next shot, the muzzle of his lasgun pointing directly at my face. Something smashes into me, hurling me down the passageway, and the only thing that registers is the smell of Lorii on top of me. The las-bolt flashes above us as we roll across the metal floor. Sliding to a halt, Lorii's back on her feet in an instant, a laspistol in her hand. Her first shot is a bit low, the energy blast ripping into the guardsman's thigh, sending his next shot into the ceiling as he falls sideways. Her next is straight and true, punching into his plump face with a small fountain of blood and shattered teeth, hurling him backwards.

'You're either a hero or an idiot,' she says with a smile as she helps me to my feet. 'Lucky for you, I'm just as brave or stupid.'

In the stillness, I hear a man groaning, quickly silenced by a round from Striden's shotgun. I pull off my helmet and look at it, still a bit dazed from the hit. There's a charred gouge just where my right ear would be, almost burnt through. I poke at it with my finger and I'm shocked when my fingertip passes straight through. The las-bolt had been within the thickness of a piece of parchment from actually getting through! Thanking the Emperor for his protection, I stick my helmet back on and pick up the assault laser.

The roar of Loron's bolter echoes along the corridor from behind; more Typhons must be advancing on us. The Colonel comes dashing around the bend, virtually dragging Gudmanz with him, Kronin charging along beside him with the metal trolley, madly wobbling left and right as its wheels skitter in all directions at once.

'Get him to the plasma chamber,' the Colonel yells, pushing Gudmanz towards me and Lorii. Grabbing the aged tech-priest between us, we head off up the tunnel with Gudmanz. I can hear the shouts of the others and the ring of shots on the corridor walls and ceiling. The steady thump of Striden's shotgun punctuates the near-constant thundering of Loron's bolter and Schaeffer's bolt pistol, and I can see the flicker of intense muzzle flash throwing their hazy shadows against the wall.

Gudmanz is panting badly, barely able to stand up as we haul him by the arms along the passageway.

'How much further?' asks Lorii between gritted teeth.

'Just another... another two hundred metres perhaps,' gasps the tech-priest, face pale, eyes showing the pain wracking his rapidly ageing body.

Just then, a round object about the size of my fist bounces off the ceiling and drops to the floor just in front of us.

'Grenade!' hisses Lorii, dropping Gudmanz and leaping forward. With a powerful kick she sends the grenade back the way it came and there's a shout of alarm a moment later, followed swiftly by the explosion. I dump Gudmanz against the wall and ready the assault laser, even as Lorii throws herself prone and swings the bolter round from where it was hanging across her back.

'About a dozen of them,' she tells me before opening fire, spent cases cascading from the bolter's ejection vent and piling up next to her.

'Door to my left...' I hear Gudmanz wheezing from behind me.

'What?' I snap, firing blindly along the passageway as I look back at him.

'Door to my left... leads through... five bunkrooms,' he explains between ragged gasps for breath. 'Get you... behind them.'

'Keep them occupied!' I tell Lorii as I plunge through the door.

'Will do!' I hear her reply.

As Gudmanz said, I'm in one of a line of linked bunkrooms, each about a dozen metres long, three-tiered beds lining the left wall, kit lockers on my right. I can see into the next couple, but then the sharper curve of Coritanorum's innermost ring puts the others out of sight. I can't believe they wouldn't cover this approach and I drop down to a crouch. I have to keep the element of surprise as long as possible, and I dump the assault laser onto one of the bunks as I sneak past, drawing one of the six combat knives I've got strapped across my chest and to my thighs.

It feels good to have a knife in my hand, I'm a bladesman at heart, always have been. I don't mind admitting that I prefer the personal touch you get when you stab someone – shooting them from a distance seems a bit of an insult. Still, if some sump-sucker's shooting at me, I'll return the compliment as quick as I can, and I'm not going to risk my neck for the sake of the slightly greater satisfaction of sliding a blade between someone's ribs.

I duck back quickly when I catch a first glimpse of a guardsman up ahead. There's enough space for me under the bottom bed of the bunk tiers and I crawl under it. Pushing myself forward on my stomach, I can see the guardsman's boots, stepping back and forth as he keeps looking behind him to check that no one's got through the other way. I realise I'm holding my breath and pause for a moment to let it out. I don't have to be too quiet, I can hear the snap of lasfire and the cracks of the bolter rounds exploding from the tunnel, masking any noise I might accidentally make. I slide forward a few metres more, taking me just past the Typhon.

I wait again for a few seconds, trying to figure out the best way to take down the guardsman. Looking up, I see that the actual bed pallet isn't fixed to the frame, it's just laid on top of a couple of struts. I manage to roll onto my back, so that my feet are pointing towards the Typhon. With a grunt I push up with all my strength, flinging the mattress over and on top of him. There's a flash of light as his finger tightens on his lasgun trigger, sending an energy bolt searing into one of the lockers. Before he can recover, I leap on top of him, and I hear his breath rushing out as he's winded. Without even looking I slash and stab a dozen times under the bed pallet, feeling the knife cutting into flesh and scraping along bone. He stops struggling and a crimson pool begins to spread out around me, soaking into the tattered grey bedclothes.

Rolling back to my feet, I can see another guardsman, kneeling in a doorway in the next room, his attention fixed outside as he fires his lasgun down the main corridor. He doesn't notice me until the last moment, a startled cry spilling from his lips a moment before the knifepoint drives up into the soft part under his chin. I tug at the knife to get it free, but it's stuck in the top of his jaw and I let it go and pull another one from the bandoleer. It's then that I look up and see another Typhon just across the corridor, ten metres from me. He notices me too and as he brings his lasgun up to fire, I force myself back, rolling the dead guardsman on top of me. I lie there for a second or two as las-bolts thud into the corpse, feeling it rocking from the impacts. Teeth gritted and eyes screwed up from the closeness of the shots, I fumble with my free hand for the dead man's lasrifle. More energy bolts sear into the body and I feel one pluck the material of my trousers, scorching the hairs and skin of my left calf. My hand closes around the trigger guard of the discarded lasgun and I swing it towards the corridor, finger pumping on the trigger, blasting randomly for a good five seconds.

I wait a moment for more return fire, but none comes, and I risk a peek over the now-ragged body. The doorway where the guardsman was is empty, except for a foot poking around the frame from inside, a smear of blood on the gleaming tiles. Letting out my breath slowly, I lie there, waiting for my heart to stop its frenzied battering against my ribs.

Someone stands over me and they grab my shoulders, hauling me to my feet. It's Schaeffer, Gudmanz behind him leaning gratefully against the bunks, hand mopping sweat from his face, handing me the assault rifle with the other

'We do not have time for you to lie around, Kage,' says the Colonel, leaning out of the doorway with bolt pistol ready, checking the way ahead. 'We take the next turning to the left and at the end are the doors to the plasma chamber.'

Loron and Lorii come along the corridor cautiously, relaxing as soon as they see my ugly face.

'Wondered if you made it or not,' says Lorii, her eyes checking me over for signs of injury. I'm covered in blood and little scraps of charred flesh, but none of it's mine in any appreciable amount.

'Kronin, Striden,' says the Colonel as the two of them jog up through the bunk rooms pushing the trolley. Schaeffer grabs the trolley from Striden, pushing it out through the door. 'You two cover the main passageway until we gain access to the plasma chamber.'

As a group we hurry to the turning that leads to the reactor, guns ready but not needed. Kronin and the Navy lieutenant take position either side of the side tunnel, checking both approaches, while the rest of us dash for the huge armoured door at the far end.

'Any smart ideas how we get in?' Loron asks when we're stood in front of it. You can tell just by looking at it that the blast door is solidly built.

'Seems I've spent my whole life trying to get through fragging doors lately,' bitches Lorii, looking over the welded metal plates with a scowl.

'We have melta-bombs,' Gudmanz points out, pulling a cylindrical canister from the now much smaller heap of ammo belts and energy packs on the trolley. Twisting off the top, he up-ends the tube and ten discs, each about the size of your palm, clatter to the floor.

'How many do we need?' Schaeffer asks the tech-priest, picking one up and turning it over in his hand. It's four centimetres thick, split into two halves around its edge. On the top is a bright orange button, set into a small well.

'Do I look like a demolitions expert, Colonel Schaeffer?' Gudmanz rasps back, slumping to sit against the wall. 'Almost all of my memo-pads were removed, remember?' he adds with a sour look at the Colonel.

'Frag it, let's use the whole lot,' Lorii decides for us, grabbing a couple of the melta-bombs, at Gudmanz's prompting twisting the two halves in opposite directions to activate the magnetic clamp. We each grab a handful and start slapping them onto the door, putting most of them at the edges around the huge hinges.

'Better save some, just in case,' Loron suggests as I grab the fourth and last canister. I toss it back and look expectantly at the door.

'You need to activate the charges,' Gudmanz tells us with a heavy sigh, forcing himself to his feet, using the wall as a support. 'Press the red activator, it sets a five-second delay. Then clear away quickly, because although most of the melta-blast is directed towards the door, there is a slight backwash.'

'Kage and I will set the charges,' the Colonel says, thrusting the trolley away.

Just then there's the distinctive zing of a las-bolt against metal and Kronin gives a startled cry and pitches back from the end of the corridor, smoke rising from the scorch mark on his flak jacket, just above his heart.

'Hurry!' hisses Striden, swivelling on his haunches and firing his shotgun down the corridor. The Colonel and I glance at each other and then start stabbing at the fuse buttons. We've done just about half of them when the Colonel grabs my collar and hauls me backwards, sending us both diving to the floor. There's a wash of hot air over my back and a deafening clang as the armoured door crashes to the floor. Looking back, I see the doorway is now a ragged hole, a thin cloud of smoke hanging in the air, the walls spattered with droplets of cooling steel.

'Go!' barks the Colonel, jumping to his feet and pulling his bolt pistol free. He leaps back a moment later as a hail of las-bolts ping off the walls around us. I can hear Striden shouting something but can't make out the words over the boom of his shotgun. Loron comes running up to us, dragging the unconscious Kronin with him.

'How many behind us?' asks the Colonel, firing blind into the plasma chamber with his bolt pistol.

'Most of them, I think,' he tells us with a worried look. I check over my shoulder and see Lorii's taken up position where Kronin was, her pale face given a yellow tinge by the flare of her bolter as she fires along the main corridor.

I edge out from what's left of the bulkhead around the ruined doorway, and I can just about make out the dozen or so

Typhons stationed inside the reactor chamber, taking cover behind data terminals and coils of pipes which snake in every direction. The chamber's big, vaguely circular, or hexagonal maybe, it's hard to see the walls because of the clutter of machinery. A huge datascreen is set on to the wall at the far side, scrolling with numbers. I can't see any other doors at first glance. A fusillade of las-bolts screams towards me and I duck back quickly.

'We have to get inside,' Gudmanz wheezes.

'Suggestions welcome,' I snarl back, unslinging the assault laser and unleashing a storm of lasblasts towards a head poking around a buttress jutting from a wall to my right. Peering through the door again, I see someone walk into the chamber along a metal gantry hanging five metres or so off the floor. He's dressed in the worker coveralls that seem to be so common around here, and I can see that he's got two autopistols, one in each hand, more ammo clips thrust into his belt. I give a gasp of shock as he opens fire with the pistols, spraying bullets into the back of the Typhons, cutting down half of them in the first hail of fire. As they turn and look up at this new threat, I push myself forward firing wildly with the assault laser. I can hear the Colonel's bolt pistol thundering just behind me as he follows. Las-bolts ricochet off the metal mesh of the gantry and the stranger vaults over the rail, still firing with his free hand. Caught between the attack on two fronts, the guardsmen are dead in a matter of seconds.

'Everybody in here!' Schaeffer calls out, and I look down the corridor to see Striden and Lorii running back. A Typhon appears at the far end but is sent scurrying back by a salvo of bolts from Loron.

'Our mysterious accomplice, I presume,' Lorii says, inspecting the newcomer where he stands looking down the corridor, reloading the autopistols.

'Last Chancers,' the Colonel says, waving a hand towards the stranger, 'may I introduce the man we are currently fighting for: Inquisitor Oriel.'

'THEY SEEM TO be holding back,' calls Loron from the gaping hole of the doorway into the plasma chamber.

'Their officers are probably cursing the architects of Coritanorum at the moment,' says Inquisitor Oriel, pushing the autopistols into the belt of his coveralls. He is clean shaven, with a narrow face, and thin black hair. He exudes an aura of calm, tinged with a hint of menace. 'The whole inner circle is designed to be a final bastion of defence, which works in our favour now, not theirs. It's what makes this whole mission possible.'

I can see his point. The plasma chamber is octagonal, about twenty metres from wall to wall. There are a few free-standing display panels, still littered with dead Typhons, and power coils snaking from apertures in the walls to a central terminal in the wall opposite the entrance, shielded from view by a huge datascreen. The access way is four, maybe five metres wide, almost impossible to come down more than four abreast, and thirty metres long at least, a real killing zone.

'The Inquisition?' says Lorii, still dumbfounded. She's crouched next to Kronin, who's slouched against the wall, still out of it. He's barely alive, the lasblast caught him full in the chest.

'Makes sense,' I say. 'Who else would have the resources or authority to destroy a sector base?'

'It will not be long before they try another attack,' the Colonel tells us, calling us back to the matter in hand. 'Gudmanz, link in and start the overload. Revered inquisitor, how many ways into this chamber are there?'

'Just the main gate and the maintenance duct I came through,' he says, pointing to the gantry above our heads. 'That's why we can hold them off with just a handful of men.'

'What about the duct?' I ask, casting a cautious glance upwards.

'I left a little surprise just outside for anyone who tries to come in that way,' he reassures me with a grim smile.

'You've changed,' says the Colonel, glancing at the inquisitor, taking us all a bit aback. I'm surprised they've seen each other before, but then again I guess I shouldn't be. Between the inquisitor and the captain of the twins' penal battalion, I suspect the Colonel has been out and about a lot more than we realise.

'Mmm? Oh, the beard? I required a change of identity once the command staff learned who I was,' he tells us. 'It was the easiest way. That and a suitable alter-ego as a maintenance worker.'

'Something's happening,' calls Loron, drawing our attention to the corridor outside. I can see some movement at the far end, heads popping into sight to check what's going on.

'Mass attack?' Lorii asks, taking up a firing position next to the gateway, the bulky bolter held across her chest.

'There are no other options, it seems,' the Colonel agrees.

'Should we be building a barricade or something?' suggests Striden, thumbing more shells into the breech of his shotgun.

'One way in, one way out,' Lorii points out, jabbing a thumb back down the access corridor. 'When it's time to go, we'll need to get out fast.'

'I never even thought about getting out,' Striden admits, running a hand through his sweat-slicked hair. 'Getting in seemed ridiculous enough.'

'You don't even have to be here!' I snap at him. 'So quit complaining.'

The attack is heralded by a storm of fire along one side of the corridor, las-fire in a deadly hail that rips along the wall, impacts into the doorway and comes flaring into the plasma chamber. As we're pinned back by the covering fire, a squad of guardsmen charges up the other side of the accessway, bellowing some kind of warcry.

The Colonel and I toss a couple of frag grenades through the doorway and the warcry turns to shouts of panic. Bits of shrapnel scythe through the door as the blast fills the passage, and as the smoke clears, I look around the edge of the doorway and see the Typhons in a pile of twisted corpses, caught full by the blast as some of them tried to turn back and ran into the others behind them.

'Score one to the Last Chancers!' laughs Lorii, peeking above my shoulder for a look.

'How many do we need to win?' I ask her and she shrugs.

'Of the three and a half million people left in Coritanorum,' the inquisitor tells us from the other side of the doorway, 'seven hundred thousand are fully trained guardsmen. That's how many we need to score.'

'Seven fraggin' hundred thousand?' I spit. 'How the frag are we supposed to get out?'

'When the plasma reactors go to overload, getting out is going to be the matter on everyone's mind, Kage,' the Colonel answers me from beside Oriel. 'They will not be too keen to stand and fight when that happens.'

'Good point, well made,' agrees Loron. 'The only fighting we'll be doing is over seats on the shuttle!'

'Another attack is being launched by Imperial forces on the northern walls,' the inquisitor adds. 'They have two fronts to fight on.'

'What happens to our men when this place goes boom?' asks Loron.

Our banter is cut short by a succession of distinctive 'whump' noises, and five fist-sized shapes come bouncing into the plasma room.

'Fragging grenade launchers!' Lorii cries out, pushing me flat and then throwing herself across Kronin. The grenades explode, shrapnel clanging off the walls, a small piece imbedding itself in my left forearm. Another volley comes clattering in and I roll sideways, putting as much distance as I can between me and the entrance. More detonations boom in my ears and debris rings across the equipment around us.

'Are you trying to blow up the reactor?' Oriel bellows down the corridor.

There's a pause in the firing and the inquisitor looks at us and smiles.

'Well, they don't know that's what we're trying to do anyway,' he chuckles. 'They'll be wary of any heavy weapons fire from now on.'

IN THE NEXT half hour, they tried five more attacks. The bodies of more than a hundred men are piled up in the corridor now, each successive wave being slowed by the tangles of corpses to clamber across. A muffled explosion from above, just before the last attack, indicated someone trying to come in through the maintenance duct and running into the inquisitor's booby trap.

It's been quiet for the past fifteen minutes or so. Gudmanz is still plugged into the plasma reactor, face waxy and almost deathlike. He's sat there in a trance; I did wonder if he had died, but Lorii checked him and he's still breathing. Who knows what sort of private battle he's fighting with the other tech-priests inside the terminal network. We're running low on ammo, I've had to ditch the assault laser, which stopped working during the fourth assault. I must have used up my thousand shots. I've got one of the spare bolters now, a big lump of metal that weighs heavily in my hands, a complete contrast to the lightweight lasgun that I'm used to.

'I can't see what they can try next,' says Loron.

'Oh frag,' I mutter when I realise one of the options open to them.

'What now?' the Colonel demands, casting a venomous glance at me.

'Gas,' I say shortly. 'No damage to the reactor, but we'll be dead, or asleep and defenceless.'

'They can't use normal gas weapons,' Oriel informs us. 'The ventilation of each circle is sealed to prevent an agent being introduced from the outside, but it also means that any gas will be dispersed into the surrounding corridors. It's another of the defence features working against them.'

'I've heard of short-life viruses,' Striden points out. 'We had a few warheads on the Emperor's Benevolence. They're only deadly for a few seconds. A base the size of Coritanorum might have something like that.'

'Yes they did,' Inquisitor Oriel confirms with a grin. 'Unfortunately their stockpile seems to have been used up by someone.'

'The watchtower and the security room…' Lorii makes the conclusion. 'Very neat.'

'I thought so,' the inquisitor replies, scratching an ear.

Just then, someone shouts to us along the corridor.

'Surrender your weapons and you'll be dealt with fairly!' the anonymous voice calls out. 'Plead for the Emperor's forgiveness and your deaths will be swift and painless!'

'I bet…' mutters Loron in reply.

'You're the damned rebels!' Lorii shouts back. 'Ask for *our* forgiveness!'

'That'll stir them up a bit,' Oriel comments. 'Only the command staff are the real rebels.'

'So why's everyone fighting us?' I ask. 'If they're still loyal, they could overpower the commanders easily.'

'Why should they?' he retorts, shrugging lightly.

'Because it's what someone loyal to the Emperor would do,' I reply. It seems obvious to me.

'I don't get it,' Striden adds. 'I can see Kage's point of view.'

'Why do you think they are rebels?' asks Oriel, gazing around at us.

'Well, you, the Colonel, everyone says they are,' answers Loron, nodding towards the inquisitor and Schaeffer.

'My point, exactly,' agrees Oriel with a wry smile. 'You know they are rebels because you have been told they are rebels.'

'And the Typhons have been told that we are the traitors,' I add, realising what Oriel is saying. 'For all we know, they could be right, but we trust the Colonel. We don't decide who the enemy is; we just follow orders and kill who we've been told to kill–'

'And so do they,' finishes Oriel, glancing back down the access tunnel.

'So that's the reason why this rebellion at the sector command is so dangerous and must be dealt with,' Loron follows on. 'If they wanted to, the command staff could convince admirals and colonels across the sector that anyone they say is the enemy. The command staff could say that any force that moved against them was rebelling against the Emperor.'

'It is one of the reasons, yes,' confirms the Colonel.

Our thoughts on the perils of the chain of command are interrupted by more las-bolts flashing through the door.

'Some of them have sneaked up through the bodies,' the Colonel tells us after a look outside. 'More are moving forward.'

'Cunning bastards,' curses Lorii, kneeling beside me, bolter ready.

'Return fire!' orders the Colonel, levelling his bolt pistol through the door and firing off a couple of shots.

THE FIREFIGHT CONTINUED sporadically for the best part of another hour. There's no telling how many Typhons worked their way along the tunnel, skulking among the mounds of dead, almost perfectly camouflaged by the piles of uniformed corpses. I haven't fired a shot in quite a while. We're beginning to get seriously concerned about the ammunition supplies, and every bolt or las-shot has to count. The Typhons, on the other hand, are quite happy to blaze away at the first sign of one of us poking a head or gun into view.

I'm lying prone on the right hand side of the doorway, Lorii crouched over me. On the far side are the Colonel and Loron, while Oriel and Striden are sheltering behind a panel of controls and dials almost directly opposite the entrance. A shuddering gasp from Gudmanz attracts our attention and I look back to see him staggering away from his terminal at the further side of the chamber, the neural plug whipping back into his skull.

'Have you done it?' demands the Colonel.

'Do you hear any warning klaxons, Colonel Schaeffer?' he rasps back irritably. 'I've set up blocks and traps so that the overload process can only be rectified from this room, not from another terminal.'

'So how much longer?' I shout over to him.

'Not long now, but I will need some help,' he replies. The Colonel gives a nod to Striden, who rises from his hiding place, shotgun roaring. A moment after he's jumped clear the Typhons' return volley slams into the data panel, sending pieces of metal spinning in every direction. Gudmanz grabs Striden and pushes him out of sight behind the screen. My attention is snapped back to the corridor by the thump of booted feet.

'They're charging!' snaps Loron, his bolter exploding into life, the small flickers of the bolt propellant flaring into the tunnel. To my left I glimpse Oriel rolling out from behind the panel, autopistol in each hand, firing into the tunnel while he rolls. As his roll takes him to his feet, he drops the pistol in his left hand and sweeps the Colonel's power sword out of its scabbard. With a yell he leaps straight at the attacking Typhons, the blue glare of the power sword reflecting off the corridor walls.

Meeting the charge head on, the inquisitor drives the blade through the stomach of the first Typhon, a spin and a backhand slash opens up the throat of the next. The inquisitor ducks beneath a wild thrust of a bayonet, lopping off the Typhon's leg halfway up the thigh, arterial blood splashing across his coveralls. In a detached part of my brain I watch Oriel fighting, contrasting the fluid, dance-like quality of his movements to the precise, mechanical fighting style of the Colonel. The autopistol chatters in his right hand as he blasts another Typhon full in the face, the power sword sweeping up to parry a lasgun being wielded as a club, its glowing edge shearing the weapon in two. Oriel bellows something that I can't quite catch over the scream of dying men and the noise of the autopistol, his face contorted with rage.

I see a Typhon rising out of a mound of corpses behind Oriel, left arm missing below the elbow, his remaining hand clutching a bayonet. Without even thinking, I pull the trigger of the bolter and a moment later the guardsman's lower back explodes, his legs crumpling under him, his spine shattered. The Typhons turn and flee from the inquisitor's wrath, the slowest pitched to the floor in two halves as Oriel strikes out once more. Las-bolts flare from the far end, kicking the corpses into jerky life again. One seems to strike Oriel full in the chest and a blinding flash of light burns my eyes. As I blink to clear the purple spots, I see Oriel still there, diving for cover over a pile of dead Typhons.

'He has the Emperor's protection,' Lorii says in an awed whisper.

'Witchery!' cries Striden, eyes wide with horror.

'Or technology,' Loron adds, sounding just as scared.

'Conversion force field,' the Colonel tells us calmly as he clicks fresh bolter rounds into an empty magazine. We exchange bemused glances, none of us sure what he's talking about. Everything goes quiet again as Oriel crawls back to the door, and I can hear Gudmanz chanting a sonorous liturgy from behind me.

'And the fourth seal shall be raised, glory be to the Machine God,' he intones, voice echoing off the metal walls. 'And the departure of the fourth seal shall be heralded by the tone of the Machine God's joy. Now, if you please, Lieutenant Striden.'

There's a clang of something ringing against metal and a hiss from a panel to my left. From somewhere above us, a high-pitched wail blares out three times.

'How much longer?' the Colonel shouts as Oriel hands him back the power sword, the blade a dull grey now that the energy flow is switched off.

'Four of the seven seals have been lifted, Colonel Schaeffer,' Striden calls back. 'Not long now, I gather.'

'Here they come again, they're getting desperate!' Loron draws our attention back to the corridor. The narrow tunnel seems choked with Typhons pouring towards us, their faces masks of desperation and terror. I guess they've found out what we're doing, if they hadn't already guessed. They'll fight even harder now, battling to save their homes, friends and families. After all, like us, they've got nothing to lose. If they fail, they're just as dead.

I'd find the pointless slaughter sickening if it wasn't for the image of the pardon that lingers in the back of my head. That, and the piles of ash which is what the men and women running towards me really are. All because some commanders have decided to dare the Emperor's wrath and fight for their glory and not his. I don't see any of them down here throwing themselves headlong at a wall of firepower for their ideals.

This isn't combat, they stand no chance at all. Switching the bolter to semi-auto, I send a hail of tiny rockets exploding down the accessway, punching Typhons from their feet, gouging chunks in those already dead. The guardsmen fire madly back at us, more las-shots zinging off the walls than coming through the doorway. They keep coming, hurdling over the dead and the dying. They're all shouting, at us or themselves, I can't tell.

It's only when the bolter starts clicking that I register its magazine is empty, I feel that detached from what's going on. My body is working on its own, without any conscious effort from my brain. Lorii drops one of her magazines next to me and I pull the empty out and slam the new one home. The attack is faltering by the weight of fire concentrated into the corridor, the Typhons can't physically get any further forward.

I fire: an arm goes spinning into the ceiling. Another shot: a man is thrown backwards, his intestines pouring from the gaping hole in his gut. Another shot: half a man's head disappears in a cloud of blood. Another shot; a lasgun explodes under the impact. Another shot: a helmeted head snaps backwards. Another shot: a woman hurls herself sideways, clutching the stump of her left wrist, hair matted with the blood of her comrades. This isn't a battle, it's a firing range with living targets.

Most of the Typhons turn and run, and I fire into their fleeing backs, knocking them from their feet, each roar of the boltgun followed by a man or woman losing a life. Someone's shaking my shoulders, screaming something in my ear, but I can't hear over the whine of the siren. My brain filters the information slowly and I feel like I'm surfacing from a dream. Yes, there's a siren ringing around, its screeching tones echoing off the walls and floor.

'We've done it!' Lorii is shouting in my ear. 'They're running for it! We've done it!'

'Kronin's dead,' I hear Striden say, and everybody turns to look at him, leaning against the wall over Kronin.

'Dead?' Loron asks, clearly shocked. I'm surprised too, I hadn't spared a thought for the wounded madman while I was battling for my life. I feel a touch of sadness that he died alone and unnoticed. He was alone when he was still alive, it seems disrespectful that none of us saw him die. I offer a prayer for his departing, tortured soul, hoping it isn't too late.

'Internal bleeding probably,' Oriel proclaims, snapping me from my thoughts. 'Now it is time for me to depart as well.'

'WE HAVE NOT succeeded,' Gudmanz whispers heavily. We're just a short way from the nearest shuttle terminal, on our way to life and freedom, but a few Typhons have decided that they're going to take us with them, forcing us to take temporary cover in a terminal alcove along the main corridor. Oriel went in the opposite direction, who knows where he was headed. A few minutes ago the blaring alarms stopped, which was a great relief to my ears and nerves. I don't need any reminders that in a short while this whole city is going to be non-existent.

'What do you mean?' demands Schaeffer, grabbing the front of the tech-priest's robe.

'The warning siren should not stop sounding,' Gudmanz says, brushing away the Colonel's arm and pointing to the terminal. 'Let me go, and I will find out.'

Everyone is staring at the tech-priest as he deftly manipulates runes and dials on the terminal. His shoulders seem to sag even more and he turns to look at us, face a picture of despondency.

'I am sorry, I have failed,' he says, slumping to the floor. 'I failed to find a hidden failsafe. The reactors will not overload.'

'Oh frag,' I mutter, dropping to my knees.

'Is there nothing we can do?' the Colonel demands, visibly shaking with anger.

'The coolant failsafe is located not far from here. It may be possible to dismantle it,' Gudmanz replies, though obviously without much hope.

'Which way?' snarls Schaeffer, hauling the tech-priest to his feet.

'Back towards the plasma chamber, corridor to the left marked "energy distribution",' he tells us. 'I did not think it was important.'

'You fragging idiot!' Loron swears, grabbing Gudmanz and slamming his back into the wall. 'You useless old man!'

'Let's just get out of here!' I tell them. 'This is the only chance of getting out of this city alive.'

'Damn right,' agrees Lorii, staring at the Colonel.

'Enough of this!' snaps the Colonel, dragging Loron away from the tech-priest. 'We get to this failsafe and deactivate it. We must hurry before the Typhon guards and security realise they are in no danger. Otherwise, they will throw everything they have at us. The panic at the moment is the only thing in our favour.'

'The mission's failed,' I tell the Colonel, looking him squarely in the face. 'We have to get out of here.'

'The mission cannot fail,' the Colonel replies, pushing Loron away, staring straight back at me.

'Why not?' demands Lorii hotly stepping towards the Colonel. 'Because you say so?'

'Don't try to stop us,' warns Loron, raising the bolter in his hands so that it's pointed at the Colonel.

'You would not dare,' Schaeffer hisses at the white-skinned trooper, staring straight at him.

'We are leaving!' Loron replies emphatically, his eyes just as hard.

'Coritanorum must be destroyed!' Schaeffer exclaims, and for the first time ever I notice a hint, just a hint, of desperation in his voice. I push Loron's gun away slightly and turn back to the Colonel.

'Okay, tell us,' I say to him quietly, standing between the Colonel and the others, trying to calm things down. If some fool shoots the Colonel, by accident or on purpose, we'll never get out of here. 'Why? Why can't this mission fail?'

'We do not have time for explanations,' the Colonel says between gritted teeth. I lean closer, still meeting his icy gaze.

'You have to tell us,' I whisper in his ear, drawing his eyes to mine. He gives a sigh.

'If we fail, all Typhos Sector will be destroyed,' he tells us. He looks at our disbelieving expressions and continues. 'I do not know all of the details, only Inquisitor Oriel has those.' He pauses as we hear a door slam shut further up the corridor. The Typhons are doing a room by room search for us.

'In brief,' he says casting an eye at the door. 'The command staff of Coritanorum has fallen under an alien influence. A genestealer in fact.'

'A genestealer?' I say, confused. 'You mean, one of those tyranid bastards we fought on Ichar IV? They're just shock troops. Sure, they're deadly, fast and able to rip a man to pieces in a heartbeat, but there'd have to be an army of them to stand against seven hundred thousand guard. What's the problem?'

'As I said, I do not fully understand this,' the Colonel continues, talking quickly. 'They are not just efficient killers, they are infiltrators too. Genestealers have some way of controlling others, some kind of mesmerism I believe. It creates an element within the society it has infected that is sympathetic to it. They protect it, allow it to control others, building up a power base from within. This can lead to revolt, rebellion and other insurgencies, as it has here. More to the point, as the power of this influenced cult grows, it begins to send a sort of psychic beacon, so I am told, as an astropath might project a message across the warp. Tyranid hive fleets can detect this signal and follow it. Hive Fleet Dagon appears to have located Typhos Prime and is on its way here now.'

'This still doesn't add up,' butts in Lorii. 'This all still seems very extreme, especially if the tyranids are already on their way. If we were recapturing Coritanorum to restore it as a command and control base, I could understand it, but we're not. What difference does it make if it's lost to this genestealer infection or destroyed?'

'The loss of Coritanorum as an Imperial base would indeed be grievous,' the Colonel agrees, still speaking rapidly. 'But not as terrible as its secrets falling into the hands of the tyranids. The Navy is endeavouring to stop Hive Fleet Dagon, but we have to assume it will fail. When the hive fleet arrives here, the tyranids will assimilate all of the data from the base and its corrupted personnel, learning the innermost secrets about the Imperial forces in the sector. They will find out where Navy bases are, where worlds ready for raising Imperial Guard regiments can be found, our strategies and capabilities. Without Coritanorum, the fight will be deadly enough, but if the tyranids possess such information they will overrun the sector much more easily. In fact, it is impossible to believe how they could be resisted at all.'

'Five hundred billion people,' I breathe quietly. 'It's a fair trade, you think? The death of Coritanorum and its three and a half million buys a better chance for the other five hundred billion people living in the sector.'

'People can be replaced,' the Colonel says grimly, giving us each a stern look. 'Habitable planets can not. Worlds stripped by the tyranids can never be recovered or repopulated.'

Another door slams shut, nearer this time.

'Do you think your lives are worth that?' he says with sudden scorn. 'Is that worthy of your sacrifice? Was I wrong in giving gutterfilth like you the chance to make a difference? Are you really the worthless criminals everyone thinks you are?'

I exchange looks with the other Last Chancers, volumes spoken in that brief moment of eye contact. It's not about pardons, or even saving the sector. It's about doing our duty, doing what we swore to do when we joined the Imperial Guard. We took an oath to protect the Emperor, His Imperium and His servants. We may not have chosen to be Last Chancers, but we chose to put ourselves in danger, to be willing to sacrifice our lives in the course of our duty.

'Move out!' barks the Colonel, shouldering open the door and leaping into the corridor, bolt pistol blazing in his hand. We jump out after him and set off at a run, Typhon lasfire screaming around us. Gudmanz gives a yell and pitches forward, a ragged, charred hole in the back of his robe. Striden stops to pick up the tech-priest but I grab the lieutenant's arm and pull him forward.

'He's dead,' I tell the Navy officer when he struggles. 'And so is everything else on over fifty worlds unless we get to that failsafe.'

LUCKILY FOR US, the Typhons aren't expecting us to double-back, probably they assumed we would cut and run. Can't blame them, only their commanders understand what's at stake, if any of them really know. They're totally disorganised now: an unexpected attack from within, thrown into disarray by the alarms, scattered to the shuttle ports, assaulted from outside by the Imperial army. The Typhon officers must be tearing their hair out by now.

Gudmanz's information was accurate. We come across a sign to 'Energy Distribution' and the side-tunnel leads us into a chamber looking a lot like the plasma room, although quite a bit smaller, barely four metres across. It's filled with lots of pipes, tanks and cables, with dozens of gauges, their needles flickering, red lights spread across panels on every surface.

'What can we do without Gudmanz?' asks Striden, looking meaningfully at me. We all look at each other for inspiration.

'Oh great,' says Loron, hands flopping to his side dejectedly. 'We're all ready to do the right thing, and now because that decrepit tech-priest got himself killed, there's nothing we can do about it.'

'There must be something,' argues Striden, looking around the room.

'We're Last Chancers,' I say to them with a grin. 'If in doubt, shoot it!'

As I open fire on the snaking cables and pipes with the bolter, the others join in, firing at everything in sight, sparks cascading as equipment banks explode. We keep the attack up for a few seconds, a few wisps of smoke and steam hissing around us, but it doesn't seem to be having much effect, lots of our fire ricochets harmlessly off the reinforced conduits.

'Hey!' Lorii calls out, pulling something off her belt. It's the last cylinder of melta-bombs. 'These might come in useful!'

'You're beautiful,' I tell her as she hands them out. I decide to put mine on a pipe that passes up from the floor and out through the ceiling, wider than I could wrap my arms around. Pushing the triggers, I take a couple of steps back. The pipe begins to glow white and a second later explodes into a shower of vaporised metal and plastic. I hear similar detonations, thick oily smoke floods the room, panels explode with multi-coloured sparks and suddenly the air is filled with a deafening scream as the alarms start sounding again. Striden gives a delighted laugh and Loron is punching me on the shoulder, grinning like a fool.

'Time to go,' the Colonel orders, heading for the door.

Loron jogs out first, the rest of us following close behind. Just a short hike to the shuttle bays and we're clear. Loron glances back and smiles, but when he steps out into the main corridor his head explodes, splashing blood across Lorii who's right next to him.

She gives a strangled scream, the droplets of blood on her face so dark against her alabaster skin, her searing blue eyes looking like they'll pop out of their sockets. I grab her and pull her back as more las-bolts slam into the wall nearby, but she turns and claws at my face, her nails gouging a trail across my forehead. I grimly hold on to her as she fights to get free, but she brings her knee up with unbelievable strength and my groin explodes with pain, making me instinctively let go of her and collapse to the ground clutching myself. Striden makes a lunge for her but a right cross to the chin sends him flying back. Stooping to grab her brother's bolter, she plunges forward, firing both guns as she charges into the corridor.

'She's going the wrong way!' I cry out, seeing her racing left, away from the shuttle pad.

'She will buy us extra time,' the Colonel says coldly, turning right at the corridor. I can still hear the roar of the bolter to my left, but there's no sign of Lorii. I hesitate for a moment then push myself to my feet, about to go after her. Striden steps in front of me, and puts a hand against my chest.

'She doesn't want to live, Kage,' he says, face sombre. 'Getting yourself killed is not going to save her.'

I'm about to push him aside when I hear a high-pitched scream resounding along the corridor. I can hear the Colonel striding away behind me, his boots thudding on the metal floor. Striden steps away and walks past, hurrying after the Colonel. I stand there alone, straining my ears for the sound of another bolter shot. There's nothing. I realise with a start that I'm the only Last Chancer left. I feel empty, hollow. Alone in my soul as well as physically. Lorii's death seems to sum it all up. Ultimately pointless and futile. Why did I want this? Do I really think any of this will make a difference, a year from now, ten years, a century? There aren't any heroes these days, not like Macharius or Dolan, just countless millions of men and women dying lonely deaths, unnoticed by most, unremembered by history. I feel like falling to my knees and giving up just then. The will to live that has carried me through three years of hell just ebbs out of me. The bolter in my hand feels heavier than ever, weighted down with countless deaths.

I taste blood in my mouth and realise I've been biting my lip, biting so hard that it's bleeding. The taste brings me back to my senses. I'm still alive, and I owe it to them as much as to myself to survive, so that this is remembered, that whatever happens, this sacrifice and misery doesn't die with us. I turn on my heel gripping the bolter tight once more, filled with purpose again, and start jogging after Striden.

* * *

'IT'S DOWN HERE!' Striden argues, taking the turning to the left.

'Straight on,' counters the Colonel, pointing along the main corridor.

'I remember the map,' the Navy officer insists, walking on without looking back at us. Somewhere behind us I hear another emergency bulkhead slamming down. I guess it must be an automatic response, I can't imagine any of the Typhons hanging around long enough to close all the blast doors. Not that it'll do any good either, as far as I can tell. Another clang makes me look around and I see the last tunnel behind us to the right is sealed off now. The Colonel plunges after Striden and grabs him by his collar. A moment later and the bulkhead closes, a wall of metal sliding down from the corridor ceiling, cutting me off from the pair of them. I stand there dazed for a moment, not quite believing they've gone.

The sudden pounding of boots tears my attention back down the corridor and I watch seven guardsmen come running into view. None of them look in my direction as they sprint away from me. I guess the shuttles are that way, and run after them. The constant sound of the siren is making my ears ache, a shrill tone that cuts straight into your brain. I almost run head first into a pair of Typhons as they come barrelling out of a door to my left. I smash one of them, a young man with a long nose, across the jaw with the bolter. The other glances at me in confusion before I pull the trigger, the bolt tearing into his chest, the recoil almost wrenching off my arm. His round face stares at me horrified for a moment before he slumps back against the door. I grind the heel of my boot into the face of the first one, crushing his head against the floor with the sound of crunching bone.

The distraction means that I've lost the men I was chasing, and I pause for a moment, listening out for them. Walking along for a couple of minutes, I think I can catch the sound of their running from the next corridor to my left. Hurrying forward, I suddenly notice something moving out of the opposite tunnel. As I look over, my fingers go numb and the bolter clatters to the floor. Staring straight back at me is the genestealer. Just like the ones on Ichar IV. Its black eyes, set in its veined, wide dome of a skull, meet mine, and there's death in that gaze. It stalks quickly towards me on its long double-jointed legs, slightly hunched over. Its four upper limbs are held out for balance, one pair tipped with bony, dagger-like claws, the lower with more hand-like talons that slowly unclench as it approaches.

My eyes are drawn back to its alien gaze and I feel all the life leeching out of my body. They're like two pits of blackness and I feel as if I'm falling into them. I dimly note that it's standing right in front of me now. But that seems unimportant, all that really registers are those eyes, those pits of shadow.

It opens its long jaw, revealing a mass of razor-sharp teeth. So this is how I die, I dimly think to myself. It leans even closer and I notice its tongue extending out towards me, some kind of opening on the end widening. It's strangely beautiful, this killer. There's a sleekness about the deep blue plates of chitin over its sinewy purple flesh. There's a perfection of purpose in the claws and fangs which I can admire.

Heart of the Jungle.

The thought just pops into the back of my head, and it stirs something within me. It's like another voice, prompting me to remember feelings of alien influence. Memories of helplessness. Fighting for control of myself.

Ichar IV.

This time the memory is more vivid. Piles of bodies, torn apart by the same kind of creature in front of me now. Forests stripped to bare rock, even the dirt consumed by the tyranid swarms. A massive bio-titan strides across the ruins of a water recycling facility, crushing buildings underfoot, horrendous weapons unleashing sprays of bio-acid and hails of flesh-eating grubs.

Typhon Sector.

In an instant my brain multiplies the horrors of Ichar IV by fifty. This is what will happen.

I snap out of the hypnotic trance just as the genestealer's tongue brushes my throat.

'Frag you!' I snarl, acting on instinct alone, lashing out with my fist, the knuckles of my right hand crashing against its jaw in a perfect uppercut. Taken completely by surprise by the blow, the genestealer stumbles backwards, clawed feet skidding on the hard metal floor, scrabbling for purchase before it topples over. It stays down for just a moment, before springing to its feet, muscles tensing to lunge at me with the killing attack. I'm strangely calm.

The wall beside us explodes in a shower of metal and the genestealer turns and leaps away. More detonations ripple along the floor just behind it as it dashes for safety and then disappears with a flick of its tail through an air vent.

'Thanks Colonel,' I say without turning around.

'Not this time,' Inquisitor Oriel replies, walking past me, a smoking bolt pistol in his right hand. 'I stopped the abomination getting out of the city, but it eluded me yet again. I almost had it this time.'

I'm still dazed, and the inquisitor picks up my bolter and places it into my unfeeling hands.

'This will be as sure as I get,' Oriel is saying, more to himself than me, I think. 'I will not let it get away from me again. It dies in Coritanorum.'

I just nod, my body quivering with aftershock. A genestealer was two metres from me and I'm still alive. Still alive. Oriel has forgotten me, walking up the corridor towards the shattered vent muttering to himself.

The sound of nearby engines rumbling into life draws my attention back into the real world and I start stumbling towards the shuttle pad. About a hundred metres further down the corridor I hear the whine of jets to my right. Following the noise, I come across a huge set of double doors and stumble through them. Inside are twenty or so Typhons, fighting with each other as they try to scramble up an access ladder to one of the two shuttles still left in the hangar. Those at the top are trying to push the others back so they can open the hatch. The rest of the vast open space is filled with scattered barrels and crates, hastily tossed out of cargo holds to make room, by the looks of it. The air shimmers from the heat haze and smoke left by the departed shuttles. No one is paying me any attention whatsoever.

'That's my shuttle,' I say to myself, pulling the last of the frag grenades from my belt and tossing it to the top of the boarding steps. The explosion hurls men into the air, sending them tumbling down to the gridded metal flooring, some of them raining down in bloodied pieces. The bolter roars in my hand, shells punching into the survivors, pitching them over the handrails, tearing off body parts. None of them is armed and the execution takes a matter of seconds.

Racing up the steps, wounded men groaning as I step on them, I'm filled with fresh vigour. Only a few minutes from freedom now. Only a short journey to the rest of my life. I plunge through the hatchway and head into the cockpit. The shuttle pilot turns in his seat and shouts at me to get out. He gives a cry of alarm when I pull one of the knives from the sheaths across my chest, and flails madly for a moment, unable to fight properly within the confines of his gravity harness. His hands and arms are torn to ribbons by the blade as he tries to protect himself, a constant shriek coming from his throat. The shriek turns to a wet gurgling when I manage to find an opening and plunge the knife in.

Ditching the bolter and knife onto the floor, I sit down in the co-pilot's seat. I look over the controls and a doubt starts nagging at me. How the frag do you fly a shuttle? Well, I can work it out, it can't be worse than driving a Chimera, surely? If my freedom relies on working this out just enough to fly a few kilometres, I can do it. I owe myself that much. I start chuckling at the irony of it. It was stowing away on a shuttle that brought me to the Colonel and the Last Chancers in the first place, and now stealing one is going to get me out of it. Through the cockpit viewports, I see a handful of Typhons come running into the hangar, firing back through the entrance. It must be the Colonel down there, but that's his problem. There's another shuttle, he can get out on that. Those Typhons might decide to try to snatch this one off me, and I don't know if I can stop them. Nope, I'm damned sure I'm not waiting for the Colonel. He promised me my pardon and my freedom, and I'm going to get it.

A sudden realisation hits me like a sniper's bullet. The pardon's worth frag all without the Colonel's signature and seal on it. Just a piece of paper with meaningless words in High Gothic written on it. Oh, what the hell, I think. Everybody's going to be running around like headless sump spiders after all this. Nobody's going to notice me, one guardsman among a million. Maybe the Colonel will hunt me down if he gets out, but then maybe not. He might think I'm dead, or he might give me my pardon anyway. He doesn't know I'm sat here, deciding whether to help him. Would he blame me?

No he wouldn't, and that's the problem. Running out on him is what he'd expect me to do. That nasty thought, the one that's been bugging me ever since I got to this planet, rises again. Man or criminal? Worthwhile or worthless? I glance back outside, and I see one of the Typhons kneeling, a plasma gun held to his shoulder. The ball of energy roars out of sight and I make my decision.

Picking up the bolter and heading back to the ladder, I discover there's only four rounds left in the magazine, and I've got no more spares. Five guardsmen, four rounds. Why can't the Emperor cut me a fragging break and give me a full magazine? Cursing, I jump down the steps three at a time.

One of the Typhons catches sight of me as I dash across the open hangar, and I veer left, diving for the cover of some metal cases as las-bolts scream towards me. Four rounds, five guardsmen. Raising the bolter to my shoulder, I look over the top of the crates. A las-blast sears just past my left ear and I pull the trigger, seeing the fiery trail of the bolt as it speeds across the hangar in a split second, tearing through one Typhon's shoulder, spinning him to the decking. The next goes down to a shot to the head, but the third is only caught a glancing hit on the arm. The three survivors are looking rapidly between me and the entrance when one of them is pitched off his feet by a blast to his chest. I fire the last round as they turn on the Colonel, who's charging into the hangar, power sword gleaming. Striden follows him, bolt pistol held in both hands as he snaps off another shot, the Typhon thrown half a dozen metres as the bolt catches him high in the chest. The last one seems to give up the fight, shoulders drooping as the Colonel rams a metre of powered blade through his midriff.

I burst from cover and give a shout. Striden almost shoots me but pulls himself short just before firing.

'Kage?' says the Colonel, noticing me as I leg it across towards them. 'I thought it was Inquisitor Oriel helping us.'

'Never keep a good man down,' I tell him.

As he turns to look at me, I'm shocked to see his left arm stops just above the elbow, the end a charred mess. I've never seen the Colonel hurt in battle before. Not even the tiniest scratch, and now he's missing an arm. That scares me, and I'm not sure why. I guess I thought he was invincible. I think I'm more bothered by it than he is, as his icy gaze flicks around the chamber, checking for enemies. He doesn't seem to have noticed he's got an arm missing. A devil in a man's body, I once called Schaeffer. I'm reminded of that fact looking at him, standing there with one arm, as alert and poised as ever.

'Plasma blast,' he explains, following my gaze.

We clamber hurriedly up the boarding ladder of the nearest shuttle. I'm about to get in after the other two when I hear a shout from behind. Turning, I see Inquisitor Oriel racing across the hangar towards us.

'She's all ready to go,' Striden calls out from inside.

Oriel bounds up the steps but I step into his path as he ducks to get into the shuttle.

'What is the meaning of this, lieutenant?' he demands, straightening up.

'How did a genestealer get here, months or years of travel from the nearest hive fleet?' I ask him, all the pieces beginning to fall into place in my head.

'I am an agent of the Emperor's Holy Orders of the Inquisition,' he snarls at me. 'I could kill you for this obstruction.'

'You didn't answer my question,' I tell him, folding my arms. I'm right, and this man has a lot to answer for.

'Stand aside!' he bellows, making a lunge for me. I side-step and smash my knee into his stomach, forcing him to his knees. He looks up at me, aghast, surprised I've got the guts to strike him. Lucky he wasn't expecting it; I don't think I could've laid a finger on him otherwise.

'You said you couldn't let it get away from you again,' I say to him as he kneels there wheezing. 'You let it escape didn't you? Frag, you might have brought it here, for all I know.'

'You don't understand,' he gasps, forcing himself to his feet. 'It was unfortunate, that is all.'

He makes a grab at the holster hanging from his belt, but finds it empty.

'Looking for this?' I ask, holding up the bolt pistol which I grabbed when I kneed him in the guts. 'Four thousand dead Last Chancers. Unfortunate. Three and a half million dead Typhons. Unfortunate. A million guardsmen from across the sector. Unfortunate. Risking fifty worlds. *Unfortunate?*'

'You could never understand,' he snaps, stepping back a pace. 'To defeat the tyranids, we must study them. There's more than a few million people at stake here. More than fifty worlds. The whole of the Imperium of mankind could be wiped out by these beasts. They must be stopped at any cost. Any cost.'

'I guess this is pretty unfortunate too', I add, ramming the grip of the pistol into his chin, tumbling him down the steps. I step backwards through the hatch and pull it shut, cycling the lock wheel.

'Let's go!' I call out to Striden. As I strap myself in next to the Colonel, the engines flare into life, lifting us off the ground. I'm slammed back into the bench as Striden hits the thrusters onto full, the shuttle speeding from the dock like a bullet from a gun. We pass through a short tunnel, jarring against the wall occasionally under Striden's inexpert piloting, before screaming into the bright daylight, blinding after the glowstrips of the past few days. I look back and see Coritanorum stretched beneath me, built into the mountains almost fifty kilometres across.

A ball of orange begins to spread out behind us, a raging maelstrom of energy surrounded by flickering arcs of electricity. Two others erupt just after, forming a triangle until their blasts merge. The immense plasma ball expands rapidly, hurling stone and metal into the sky before incinerating it. For a moment I think I see a black fleck racing before the plasma storm, but it might be my imagination. Then again, there was another shuttle in the bay. Mountains topple under the blast and all I can think of is the pile of ash that'll be left. A pile of ash worth three and a half million lives because someone made a mistake. My thoughts are drawn back to my own survival as I see a howling gale hurling rock and dust towards us.

'Faster!' I bellow to Striden as the shockwave crashes through the air. The ground's being ripped up by the invisible force, rock splintering into fragments, the high walls exploding into millions of shards. With a final convulsive spasm the plasma engulfs everything. The light sears my eyes, the boom of the explosion reaches my ears just as the shuttle is lifted up bodily by the shockwave, hurled towards the clouds. The hull rattles deafeningly from debris impacts, the metal shrieking under the torment of the unnatural storm, bouncing us up and down in our seats. I hear Striden laughing in his high-pitched way from up front, but I'm more concerned with my heaving guts as we're spun and pitched and rolled around by the blast.

As it passes, and the passage begins to smooth, I hear this strange noise and turn to look at the Colonel.

He's laughing, a deep chuckle. He's sat there, one arm ending in a ragged stump, dishevelled and covered in the blood and guts of others, and he's laughing. He looks at me, his ice eyes glinting.

'How does it feel to be a hero, Kage?' he asks.

EPILOGUE

THE COLONEL WAVES away the orderly fussing over his arm with an irritated gesture. I stand there impatiently, waiting to get my hands on the pardon. We're back in the commissariat relay post where we were told about our final mission. The door behind me creaks open and Schaeffer's personal scribe, Clericus Amadiel, walks in, the hem of his brown robes flowing across the floor. There's someone else with him, a young man, his face tattooed with the skull and cog of the Adeptus Mechanicus. Amadiel has the bundle of pardons in his arms, while the tech-adept is carrying some piece of bizarre equipment that looks like a cross between a laspistol and a spider.

'Here are the documents, Colonel,' Amadiel says slowly, placing them one at a time on the bare wooden desk in front of Schaeffer.

I restrain myself, wanting to grab the whole bunch and find mine. The Colonel, deliberately making his point, signs the pardons of the others – Franx, Kronin, Lorii, Loron and Gudmanz. Pardons for dead people, keeping the alive waiting. He works slowly and methodically, the clericus holding the parchments for him while he signs them with his good arm. Amadiel passes him a lighted red candle, and with the same infuriating slowness, dribbles a blob of wax onto the parchments, which the Colonel then seals with a stamp produced from the scribe's sleeve. Eventually, perhaps a lifetime later, the Colonel pulls mine forward.

'There are a number of conditions attached to the continuing application of this pardon, Kage,' he tells me sternly, finally looking up at me.

'Yes?' I ask, suspicious of what the Colonel might say next. I didn't think he was the type of person who would try to wriggle out of something. He has some honour, that much I'm sure.

'First, you are to discuss no details of the Last Chancers' activities in Coritanorum with anyone unless specifically ordered by myself or a member of his Holy Emperor's Inquisitorial Orders,' he says gravely, counting the point off with a raised finger.

'Forget this ever happened, right sir?' I confirm.

'That is correct,' he replies with a nod. 'We were never here, a malfunction in Coritanorum's reactors caused the citadel's destruction. An Act of the Emperor.'

'Understood,' I assure him. I'd been expecting something like this ever since the shuttle landed and we were bundled into another one of those black-painted commissariat armoured cars.

'Second,' he says raising another finger, 'you are on parole. The pardon is revoked if ever you transgress any Imperial Law or, should you remain with the Imperial Guard, any article of the Imperial Guard Code and Laws of Conduct,' he says, as if reading it out from a script inside his head.

'I'll keep my nose clean, sir,' I tell him with a sincere nod.

'I doubt that,' he says suddenly with a lopsided smirk, mentally throwing me off balance. That was almost a joke! 'Just make sure you do not get caught doing anything too serious.'

'Don't fret, Colonel,' I tell him with feeling. 'As much as I've enjoyed your company, I never want to see your face again.'

'Those are the conditions,' he concludes, scribbling his signature on the scroll and whacking down the seal. With a casual gesture, he offers it to me. I reach out cautiously, still half-suspecting him to pull it away at the last moment, laughing cruelly.

I'm afraid to say that I snatch it from his grasp, eagerly reading the words: *freedom… pardoned of all crimes.* Freedom!

'What will you do now, Kage?' the Colonel asks, leaning back in the rickety wooden chair, making the back creak under the weight.

'Stay in the Guard, sir,' I tell him instantly. I'd been thinking about it on the bumpy half-hour shuttle run. More to take my mind off Striden's poor flying than anything else. We had to ditch eventually, when another storm broke. He raises a questioning eyebrow and I explain. 'I joined the Imperial Guard to fight for the Emperor. I swore an oath to defend His realms. I aim to keep that oath.'

'Very well,' the Colonel says with an approving nod, 'your final rank of lieutenant will be transferred to whatever regiment you end up joining. There are quite a few here to choose from. But I recommend you stay away from the Mordians.'

'I will,' I say emphatically. 'I kinda like the uniforms of the Trobaran Rangers, so perhaps I'll see if they take me.'

'Notify Clericus Amadiel as soon as you have made your choice. He will ensure any necessary paperwork is in order,' the Colonel says, nodding in the scribe's direction. Amadiel looks at me with his fixed, blank expression.

'There is one other thing,' the Colonel adds as I'm about to turn to the door. He beckons the tech-adept forward with a finger.

'I can remove your penal legion tattoo,' the adept says, raising the peculiar gadget as if in explanation.

I roll up my sleeve and look at my shoulder, barely making out the skull and crossed swords emblem. Above the badge you can just make out '13th Penal Legion', and underneath I know is written '14-3889: Kage, N.', though you can't see it now past the white scar tissue.

'I'll keep it,' I announce, letting my shirt sleeve drop down again.

'Keep it?' stutters Amadiel, unable to stop himself.

'To remember,' I add, and the Colonel nods in understanding. The memory of four thousand dead is etched into my brain. It makes a strange kind of sense that it's tattooed into my skin as well.

We don't exchange another word as I salute, turn on my heel and march out, hand gripping the pardon so tightly my knuckles are going white. Outside the bunker, the two provosts click their heels to attention as I walk between them, and I studiously ignore them. A day ago, they would have shot me given the slightest chance or reason.

As I pick my way across the shellhole-pocked mud, I glance back and see the Colonel emerge. A sudden whine of engines and a downblast of air heralds the arrival of some kind of stratocraft – long, sleek, jet-black, no insignia at all. A door hisses open in the side and three men jump out, swathed in dark red cloaks that flap madly in the downwash of the craft's engines, and the Colonel nods in greeting. The four of them climb back in again and with a whoosh it accelerates back into the clouds

again in less than ten seconds. That's the last I'll see of him, he's
probably already planning the first suicide mission for the next
bunch of poor bastards to be called the Last Chancers.

THE EMPTY BOTTLE smashes as I casually drop it to the floor, the
shards of pottery mixing with the glass and ceramic of the four
other bottles that proceeded it. I'm drunk. Very drunk. I hadn't
had a drink in three years and the first glass went straight to my
head. The second went to my legs, and the rest has gone, well,
Emperor knows where! That's how it's been for the past two
months, every night in the officers' mess, crawling back to my
bunk when they throw me out.

   I'm out on Glacis Formundus, back on garrison duty again,
with the Trobarans and Typhons for company. I still don't
really know anyone, I've spent every night here drinking my
pay away, trying to forget the past three years, but it isn't easy.
Parades and drills are so dull, my mind wanders back. To
Deliverance, to Promixima Finalis, to False Hope and all the
other places I fought and my comrades died in their hundreds.
I swill the Typhon wine around the silver goblet for a while,
pretending I can smell its delicate bouquet through the smoke
of the ragweed cigar jammed into the corner of my mouth.
Gazing up at the thousands of candles hanging from the dozen
vast chandeliers that light the marble hall with their flickering
glow, I wonder if there's a candle there for each dead Last
Chancer.

   The mess seems filled with Typhons today, giving me surly
looks like they know something, but they can't, I'm sure of
that. We won a great victory at Coritanorum, we won the war
and preparations have begun to receive Hive Fleet Dagon,
which is why we're stuck out here for the moment. A great victory, but nobody else seems like celebrating. Everybody in the
mess is sombre. I don't know what they've got to be so
unhappy about, having to eat fine meat, dining on fresh veg-
etables, drinking, whoring, gambling and wasting their lives
instead of fighting. I guess that's why I haven't fitted in, because
I've begun to miss combat. Shouting orders at a bunch of uniformed trolls as they march up and down the parade ground is
no substitute for crawling about in the mud and blood, kill or
be killed situations that bring you to life. Miserable bastards,
don't they know we've just won a war?

Everyone else's grim mood has brought me further down. I think about the other Last Chancers. The dead ones. The ones who got their pardon too late. Three thousand nine hundred and ninety-nine of them. All dead. Except me. I start to wonder why I'm alive and they're not. What makes me special? Was I just lucky? Have I been set aside from harm by the Emperor? I'm tempted to think the latter, which is why I joined up again, to pay him back for watching over me these past three years. Emperor, I wish these Typhons would cheer up, the miserable fraggers.

'What did you say?' a man demands from over towards the bar, three metres to my right. He's decked out in blue and white, the Typhon colours, gold braiding hangs across his left breast, a cupboard full of medals adorning the right. A colonel I reckon. I must have spoken out loud.

'Wha?' I mumble back, unable to recall what I was thinking, trying to drag my brain out of the drink-fuelled murk.

'You called me a miserable fragger,' he accuses, stepping through the haze of ragweed smoke to stand on the other side of the small round table. I sit back, letting my elbows slide off the table and peer back at him.

'We've just saved the fraggin' sector, and everyone's moping around like their sister's died,' I say as two more Typhons, both majors or captains by the uniforms, step up behind him.

'I had to leave my wife and go to some bastard slime pit in the middle of nowhere,' the one on the left stabs a finger at me, some froth from his ale still stuck to his huge, drooping moustaches. 'What's to be happy about?'

'Welcome to the fraggin' Imperial Guard,' I say, shrugging my shoulders and knocking back the last glass of wine.

I try to get up but the first one, a bald, middle-aged man, thrusts me back onto the bench with a gnarled hand on my shoulder. As I thud back into place, one of them pulls my pardon from where it's been jolted out of one of the chest pockets on my jacket. I always keep it there, a good luck talisman. The stub of the cigar drops into my lap and I brush it to the floor.

'What's this? Penal legion scum!' he hisses, looking at what's written on the parchment.

'Not any more. I'm a proper officer now,' I tell them, still half-baked with the wine. 'Look, I'm sitting around on my fat arse doing nothing, shouting at the troopers and trying to jump a lass from the local town, I must be an officer.'

'You should've been hanged!' Big Moustache adds, looking over his comrade's shoulder. 'You're a disgrace to the Imperial Guard.'

'You'd all be dead if it wasn't for us,' I mumble back. 'Should thank me, ungrateful bastards.'

'You think so?' the third one demands, his piggy nose thrust into my face. 'You're nothing! You're scum!'

'You should all be killed!' Baldy declares, face a bright red now.

'We were!' I snarl back, sickened by their attitude. 'They were fraggin' heroes. You part-time soldiers don't even deserve to lick their boots!'

'You traitorous filth,' Pig Nose bellows, pulling an ornate sword from its scabbard and waving it at me. Something inside me snaps, looking at these prissy, pompous, spoilt, officer-class weevil-brained snobs. A feeling I haven't felt since Coritanorum surges through me, a feeling of energy and vitality, of being alive, infusing me with strength and power.

'I'm a man, a soldier!' I scream back at them, hauling myself to my feet. 'They were all soldiers, real men and women! Not scum!'

Pig Nose makes a clumsy swipe with the sword, but he's too close and I easily grab his wrist. I trap the basket hilt in my left hand and twist, wrenching it easily from his grasp, as easy as taking sweetmeats from a babe.

'You want it rough?' I shriek, slamming the hilt into his pig nose, causing blood to cascade over the white breast of his tunic. They begin to back away. I hear murmurs from around the room. 'You're Guard, can't you fight me? What did you get those medals for? Polishing? Shouting? Fight me, damn you!'

I take another step forward, lashing out with the hilt into Big Moustache's stomach, doubling him over. They stumble away again, eyes darting around looking for the trooper that's going to fight for them.

'No one else to fight this battle,' I snarl. 'You'll have to get bloody and dirty now.'

There's a clamour all around as people scramble for the doors. Chairs and tables are overturned as people back off from the madman screaming and waving a sword around. This is the closest half of them have ever been to a fight. The alcohol mixes with my anger to fuel me with blood lust, a red mist descends in front of my eyes and I keep seeing little piles of ashes, faceless strangers clawing at me from my dreams, men cut down and blown apart. My head whirls with it and I feel dizzy. It's like four thousand voices are crying out for blood in my head, four thousand men and women crying to be remembered, asking for vengeance.

'This is for Franx!' I shout, plunging the sword into Pig Nose's guts. The others try to grab me, but I lunge back at them, slashing and hacking with the sword.

'For Poal! Poliwicz! Gudmanz! Gappo! Kyle! Aliss! Densel! Harlon! Loron! Jorett! Mallory! Donalson! Fredricks! Broker! Roiseland! Slavini! Kronin! Linskrug!' The litany of names spills from my lips as I carve the three arrogant Typhons to pieces, hacking into their inert bodies, blood splashing across the light blue carpet to create a purple puddle. With each stroke, I picture a death. All the ones I saw die, they're stored up there in my head and it seems like they want to rush out. 'For fraggin' all of 'em! For Lorii!' I finish, leaving the sabre jutting from the chest of Pig Nose.

People are shouting and grabbing at me, someone's throwing up to my right, the coward, but I push them away, remembering at the last second to turn back and snatch the pardon from Baldy's dead fingers. I stumble out of the door and start running off into the streets, the rain cascading off my bloodied hands as I stuff the pardon back into my pocket.

I WAKE WITH a banging in my head loud enough to be all the forges on Mars. My throat feels as if several small mammals have nested in it for a year and my limbs feel weak. With hazy recollection the events of the night before come back to me. I can feel the Typhons' dried blood caked on my hands. I really should try to control my temper. My next instinct is to check that I have my pardon. I fumble in my pocket and my heart leaps into my throat when I find it empty.

Just then I hear a tearing noise and force my eyes open. Someone's stood over me where I'm collapsed against an alley wall. The sun reflects off a window behind him, so he's hidden in shadow. Squinting into the light, all I can see are two pin-pricks of glittering blue. Two pieces of flashing ice. He drops something and I see my pardon, torn in two, fluttering to the wet ground. He pulls a bolt pistol from his belt and points it at my face.

The first thing that pops into my head is, 'What the hell is he doing here?'

The second is, 'How in all that's holy did he get his arm back?'

'I knew you would come back to me, Kage,' the Colonel purrs savagely. 'You are one of mine. You always will be. I can kill you now, or I can give you one more Last Chance.'

Oh frag.

ABOUT THE AUTHOR

Gav Thorpe works for Games Workshop in his capacity as Warhammer Loremaster (whatever that is). Something to do with making stuff up and designing games, apparently. He has written an armful of short stories for *Inferno!* magazine, and people constantly nag him for more Last Chancers stuff. You may be worried to known that when he is thinking really hard he has a tendency to talk to the mechanical hamster with which he shares a flat.

More Warhammer 40,000 from the Black Library

FIRST & ONLY
A Gaunt's Ghosts novel
by Dan Abnett

'THE TANITH ARE strong fighters, general, so I have heard.' The scar tissue of his cheek pinched and twitched slightly, as it often did when he was tense. 'Gaunt is said to be a resourceful leader.'

'You know him?' The general looked up, questioningly.

'I know *of* him, sir. In the main by reputation.'

GAUNT GOT TO his feet, wet with blood and Chaos pus. His Ghosts were moving up the ramp to secure the position. Above them, at the top of the elevator shaft, were over a million Shriven, secure in their bunker batteries. Gaunt's expeditionary force was inside, right at the heart of the enemy stronghold. Commissar Ibram Gaunt smiled.

IT IS THE nightmare future of Warhammer 40,000, and mankind teeters on the brink of extinction. The galaxy-spanning Imperium is riven with dangers, and in the Chaos-infested Sabbat system, Imperial Commissar Gaunt must lead his men through as much in-fighting amongst rival regiments as against the forces of Chaos. FIRST AND ONLY is an epic saga of planetary conquest, grand ambition, treachery and honour.

More Warhammer 40,000 from the Black Library

GHOSTMAKER
A Gaunt's Ghosts novel
by Dan Abnett

THEY WERE A good two hours into the dark, black-trunked forests, tracks churning the filthy ooze and the roar of their engines resonating from the sickly canopy of leaves above, when Colonel Ortiz saw death.

It wore red, and stood in the trees to the right of the track, in plain sight, unmoving, watching his column of Basilisks as they passed along the trackway. It was the lack of movement that chilled Ortiz.

Almost twice a man's height, frighteningly broad, armour the colour of rusty blood, crested by recurve brass antlers. The face was a graven death's head. Daemon. Chaos Warrior. *World Eater!*

IN THE NIGHTMARE *future of Warhammer 40,000, mankind teeters on the brink of extinction. The Imperial Guard are humanity's first line of defence against the remorseless assaults of the enemy. For the men of the Tanith First-and-Only and their fearless commander, Commissar Ibram Gaunt, it is a war in which they must be prepared to lay down, not just their bodies, but their very souls.*

More Warhammer 40,000 from the Black Library

NECROPOLIS
A Gaunt's Ghosts novel
by Dan Abnett

GAUNT WAS SHAKING, and breathing hard. He'd lost his cap somewhere, his jacket was torn and he was splattered with blood. Something flickered behind him and he wheeled, his blade flashing as it made contact. A tall, black figure lurched backwards. It was thin but powerful, and much taller than him, dressed in glossy black armour and a hooded cape. The visage under the hood was feral and non-human, like the snarling skull of a great wolfhound with the skin scraped off. It clutched a sabre bladed power sword in its gloved hands. The cold blue energies of his own powersword clashed against the sparking, blood red fires of the Darkwatcher's weapon.

ON THE SHATTERED world of Verghast, Gaunt and his Ghosts find themselves embroiled within an ancient and deadly civil war as a mighty hive-city is besieged by an unrelenting foe. When treachery from within brings the city's defences crashing down, rivalry and corruption threaten to bring the Tanith Ghosts to the brink of defeat. Imperial Commissar Ibram Gaunt must find new allies and new Ghosts if he is to save Vervunhive from the deadliest threat of all – the dread legions of Chaos.

More Warhammer 40,000 from the Black Library

SPACE WOLF
A Space Wolf novel
by William King

RAGNAR LEAPT UP from his hiding place, bolt pistol spitting death. The nightgangers could not help but notice where he was, and with a mighty roar of frenzied rage they raced towards him. Ragnar answered their war cry with a wolfish howl of his own, and was reassured to hear it echoed back from the throats of the surrounding Blood Claws. He pulled the trigger again and again as the frenzied mass of mutants approached, sending bolter shell after bolter shell rocketing into his targets. Ragnar laughed aloud, feeling the full battle rage come upon him. The beast roared within his soul, demanding to be unleashed.

IN THE GRIM future of Warhammer 40,000, the Space Marines of the Adeptus Astartes are humanity's last hope. On the planet Fenris, young Ragnar is chosen to be inducted into the noble yet savage Space Wolves Chapter. But with his ancient primal instincts unleashed by the implanting of the sacred Canis Helix, Ragnar must learn to control the beast within and fight for the greater good of the wolf pack.

More Warhammer 40,000 from the Black Library

RAGNAR'S CLAW
A Space Wolf novel
by William King

ONE OF THE enemy officers, wearing the peaked cap and greatcoat of a lieutenant, dared to stick his head above the parapet. Without breaking stride, Ragnar raised his bolt pistol and put a shell through the man's head. It exploded like a melon hit with a sledgehammer. Shouts of confusion echoed from behind the wall of sandbags, then a few heretics, braver and more experienced than the rest, stuck their heads up in order to take a shot at their attackers. Another mistake: a wave of withering fire from the Space Marines behind Ragnar scythed through them, sending their corpses tumbling back amongst their comrades.

FROM THE DEATHWORLD of Fenris come the Space Wolves, the most savage of the Emperor's Space Marines. Ragnar's Claw explores the bloody beginnings of Space Wolf Ragnar's first mission as a young Blood Claw warrior. From the jungle hell of Galt to the polluted cities of Hive World Venam, Ragnar's mission takes him on an epic trek across the galaxy to face the very heart of evil itself.

More Warhammer 40,000 from the Black Library

INTO THE MAELSTROM
An anthology of Warhammer 40,000 stories, edited by Marc Gascoigne & Andy Jones

'THE CHAOS ARMY had travelled from every continent, every shattered city, every ruined sector of Illium to gather on this patch of desert that had once been the control centre of the Imperial garrison. The sand beneath their feet had been scorched, melted and fused by a final, futile act of suicidal defiance: the detonation of the garrison's remaining nuclear stockpile.' – **Hell in a Bottle** by *Simon Jowett*

'HOARSE SCREAMS and the screech of tortured hot metal filled the air. Massive laser blasts were punching into the spaceship. They superheated the air that men breathed, set fire to everything that could burn and sent fireballs exploding through the crowded passageways.' – **Children of the Emperor** by *Barrington J. Bayley*

IN THE GRIM and gothic nightmare future of Warhammer 40,000, mankind teeters on the brink of extinction. INTO THE MAELSTROM is a storming collection of a dozen action-packed science fiction short stories set in this dark and brooding universe.

More Warhammer 40,000 from the Black Library

STATUS: DEADZONE

An anthology of Necromunda stories, edited by Marc Gascoigne & Andy Jones

'KNIFE-EDGE LIZ closed on Terrak Ran'Lo. The old man was moving for cover, crouching behind a side-table. She fell upon him, dragging him to the ground. His breath was wine-rancid, his eyes glazed with age. He looked at the woman, her face sprayed with the blood of the inquisitor, and his eyes span.

"A message from the Underhive," Liz spat and pulled the trigger.' – **Rat in the Walls** by *Alex Hammond*

'OUTSIDE THE Last Gasp Saloon, Nathan Creed examined the scrap of parchment. If the map was genuine, Toxic Sump's dome was built directly on top of another, much older settlement. Who knew what ancient treasures lay buried beneath the ash? Creed took the cheroot from his mouth and spat into the dust. The prospector had known. Now he was dead.' – **Bad Spirits** by *Jonathan Green*

ON THE SAVAGE factory world of Necromunda, renegade gangs struggle for survival in the shattered tunnels and domes beneath the teeming hive-cities. STATUS: DEADZONE is an awesome anthology of dark science fiction short stories from the devastated urban hell of Necromunda.

Warhammer fantasy from the Black Library

TROLLSLAYER
A Gotrek & Felix novel
by William King

HIGH ON THE HILL the scorched walled castle stood, a stone spider clutching the hilltop with blasted stone feet. Before the gaping maw of its broken gate hanged men dangled on gibbets, flies caught in its single-strand web.

'Time for some bloodletting,' Gotrek said. He ran his left hand through the massive red crest of hair that rose above his shaven tattooed skull. His nose chain tinkled gently, a strange counterpoint to his mad rumbling laughter.

'I am a slayer, manling. Born to die in battle. Fear has no place in my life.'

TROLLSLAYER IS THE opening salvo in the death saga of Gotrek Gurnisson, as retold by his travelling companion, Felix Jaeger. Set in the darkly gothic world of Warhammer, Trollslayer is an episodic novel featuring some of the most extraordinary adventures of this deadly pair of heroes. Monsters, daemons, sorcerers, mutants, orcs, beastmen and worse are to be found as Gotrek strives to achieve a noble death in battle. Felix, of course, only has to survive to tell the tale.

Warhammer fantasy from the Black Library

SKAVENSLAYER
A Gotrek & Felix novel
by William King

'BEWARE! SKAVEN!' Felix shouted and saw them all reach for their weapons. In moments, swords glittered in the half-light of the burning city. From inside the tavern a number of armoured figures spilled out into the gloom. Felix was relieved to see the massive squat figure of Gotrek among them. There was something enormously reassuring about the immense axe clutched in the dwarf's hands.

'I see you found our scuttling little friends, manling,' Gotrek said, running his thumb along the blade of his axe until a bright red bead of blood appeared.

'Yes,' Felix gasped, struggling to get his breath back before the combat began.

'Good. Let's get killing then!'

SET IN THE MIGHTY city of Nuln, Gotrek and Felix are back in SKAVENSLAYER, the second novel in this epic saga. Seeking to undermine the very fabric of the Empire with their arcane warp-sorcery, the skaven, twisted Chaos rat-men, are at large in the reeking sewers beneath the ancient city. Led by Grey Seer Thanquol, the servants of the Horned Rat are determined to overthrow this bastion of humanity. Against such forces, what possible threat can just two hard-bitten adventurers pose?

Warhammer fantasy from the Black Library

DAEMONSLAYER
A Gotrek & Felix novel
by William King

THE ROAR WAS so loud and so terrifying that Felix almost dropped his blade. He looked up and fought the urge to soil his britches. The most frightening thing he had ever seen had entered the hall and behind it he could see the leering heads of beastmen.

As he gazed on the creature in wonder and terror, Felix thought: this is the incarnate nightmare which has bedevilled my people since time began.

'Just remember,' Gotrek said from beside him, 'the daemon is mine!'

FRESH FROM THEIR adventures battling the foul servants of the rat-god in Nuln, Gotrek and Felix are now ready to join an expedition northwards in search of the long-lost dwarf hall of Karag Dum. Setting forth for the hideous Realms of Chaos in an experimental dwarf airship, Gotrek and Felix are sworn to succeed or die in the attempt. But greater and more sinister energies are coming into play, as a daemonic power is awoken to fulfil its ancient, deadly promise.

Warhammer fantasy from the Black Library

DRAGONSLAYER
A Gotrek & Felix novel
by William King

THE DRAGON opened its vast mouth. All the fires of hell burned within its jaws. Insanely, Felix thought the creature looked almost as if it were smiling. Some strange impulse compelled him to throw himself between Gotrek and the creature just as it breathed. He fought back the desire to scream as a wall of flame hurtled towards him.

DRAGONSLAYER is the fourth epic instalment in the death-seeking saga of Gotrek and Felix. After the daring exploits revealed in Daemonslayer, the fearless duo find themselves pursued by the insidious and ruthless skaven-lord, Grey Seer Thanquol. Dragonslayer sees the fearless Troll Slayer and his sworn companion back aboard an arcane dwarf airship in a search for a golden hoard – and its deadly guardian.

IN THE GRIM DARKNESS
OF THE FAR FUTURE,
THERE IS ONLY WAR...

You can recreate the ferocious battles of the Imperial Guard and the Space Marines with WARHAMMER 40,000, Games Workshop's world famous game of a dark and gothic war-torn future. The galaxy-spanning Imperium of Man is riven with dangers: aliens such as the ravaging orks and the enigmatic eldar gather their forces to crush humanity – and in the warp, malevolent powers arm for war!

To find out more about Warhammer 40,000, as well as Games Workshop's whole range of exciting fantasy and science fiction games and miniatures, just call our specialist Trolls on the following numbers:

In the UK: 0115-91 40 000

In the US: 1-800-GAME

or look us up online at:

www.games-workshop.com